AND ALL THE KING'S MEN

AND ALL THE KING'S MEN

Gordon Stevens

KNIGHT

Chapmans Publishers Ltd
141–143 Drury Lane
London WC2B 5TB

BRITISH LIBRARY CATALOGUING IN PUBLICATION DATA

Stevens, Gordon, 1945–
 And all the king's men.
 I. Title
 823.914[F]

ISBN 1-84429-078-6

First published by Chapmans 1990

Photoset by Rowland Phototypesetting Ltd
Bury St Edmunds, Suffolk

Printed in Great Britain

This edition published 2004 by
Knight, an imprint of
The Caxton Publishing Group

For A.J.

For Albert Guérisse,
also known as Pat O'Leary,

And for the men and women
of the British Resistance
and the Special Operations Executive
who helped me with this book and upon
whose real lives it is based.

PROLOGUE

ONE DAY, I knew, I would go there, one day I would stand beside the grave and remember as I had promised. Yet even now that I know the truth I can think of no reason for being at that place at that time on that day.

The afternoon was cold, late November, the rain cutting from the east and the last of the afternoon light fading fast. The church stood alone, set back on the slightest of bends on the left of the road, the graveyard around it swept with leaves and the hawthorn hedge in front thin and bare. The wood of the lych gate was old and green with moss, and the path that led from it was ragged and neglected. Thirty yards on was another gate, smaller and now overgrown. There was no door in the front of the church facing the road, only the stained-glass windows, the light from the church illuminating the brilliance of their colours and piercing the gloom, the path disappearing to the rear. From inside came the words of a hymn, the Twenty-third Psalm to the tune of Crimond. A funeral, I knew, yet no hearse, no one in the graveyard, no sexton or grave-diggers.

The grave was in the small triangle of ground at the rear, the trees hanging over it and sheltering it from the river behind, the land rising beyond. Beside it were three others, the headstones identical and the white marble standing out in the falling light. Two were family graves, the first open to receive the last human remains of the soul they were laying to rest that afternoon, the sides cut with a military precision and running wet. I knelt in front of the fourth and wiped away the water from the headstone with my hand, saw the name. The rain trickled down my back and my trousers and shoes were heavy with mud. Sorry it's taken so long, I thought, but you knew I would come.

The last verse of the anthem drifted from the church and settled in the trees.

And in God's house, for evermore,
My dwelling place shall be.

In the church a woman began the requiem, the voice and the words unknown yet familiar. On the hill behind the river, in the darkness of the afternoon or of another time, I saw the men, the guns in their hands and their bodies soaked with fear, running not for themselves but for the man whose life they had been entrusted to protect. On the road at the front I heard the lorries halting and the soldiers jumping down. In the corner of the churchyard nearest the village I saw the boy pushing through the gate and coming to the place where I now knelt. In the church the woman came to the two lines with which the poem began but which the poet had repeated. I leant forward and wiped the water from the marble again, looked at the inscription beneath the name, the same two lines carved into each of the headstones.

In the porch at the rear of the church the door opened and the coffin was carried out, the woman behind it, the priest on her right and the son on her left. Even in the dark I knew it was the son, now nearly sixty, knew the man they were laying to rest beside his mother that November afternoon was his father. I wondered who the woman was and why she had come. Behind them came the mourners, only a handful and all in their seventies and eighties. I left the grave and stood beneath the trees against the river.

They came to the place and stopped, the mourners watching as the bearers lowered the coffin into the ground. Why here? I looked from them to the grave nearest the river close where a bridge had once crossed it. Why in a small churchyard in Kent? Why not where you were born or where you died? And why with the man they were laying to rest in the wet and the cold?

The rain was harder, colder. The pall bearers moved back and the priest shuffled forward and stood looking down, his lips moving in the rites of death. From the tower of the church behind him came the sound of bells. The priest's head came up and his shoulders and back

8

straightened, then the bells fell silent again as they had fallen silent for those long and terrible months. The minute seemed to last forever, the water running down the faces of the mourners, the church and the trees remembering with them, the river still and silent.

Not a prayer, I understood, not the last rites of human mortality, but the lines of the poem by Keats which the woman had read in requiem, the words on the white marble of the gravestones.

Shed no tear – O, shed no tear!
The flower will bloom another year.

The priest stood back and the woman stepped forward to take his place. As she did so, I saw her face and knew I must be wrong; in the wet and dark of that Kent churchyard it seemed to me that the woman standing at the graves beneath the trees by the river was the Queen of England.

BOOK ONE

Recruitment

November 1939 – April 1940

1

NOVEMBER 1939, BERLIN. Somewhere, Drake knew, the eyes were waiting for him: at the station, at the hotel, at the meeting with the contact that evening. No option, he also knew, no way he could cover himself, even establish his back door out. The train shuddered as it crossed the points into the city and the rain ran in streams across the window. Around him the other passengers rose and shook the creases from their clothes. To his left the elderly couple with whom he had shared a schnapps smiled their goodbyes to him; he stood up and helped them with their case. The eyes, he thought again. Somewhere, everywhere. There was a hiss of steam and the *Reichsexpress* pulled into Anhalter Bahnhof. He opened the door, stepped down and knew the eyes had seen him.

Sicherheitsdienst, the assumption was automatic: Department Amt IVE, counterintelligence, probably Gestapo as well.

Do nothing to make yourself conspicuous, he told himself, especially at the ticket barrier, at the point where they are waiting for you. To his right the elderly couple were embracing a son and daughter-in-law, hugging a grandchild they had not seen for two years; the young believing that the future was theirs, he thought, some already betraying their own parents to the men who were scouring the platform for him.

The eight o'clock S-bahn from Alexanderplatz to Lehrter Bahnhof, Menzies had said, the contact would be on the train, third carriage from the front.

Don't look at the eyes, don't let them know you're the one they're looking for; he saw the movement as the other eyes picked him up. Part of the game, he reminded himself, let you know they had seen you, watch how you reacted. He hunched his shoulders to conceal his height and the squareness of his stance and called for a porter to take his case.

'*Wo wohnen Sie?*' 'Where are you staying?'

'*Der Adlon.*' Everybody stayed at the Adlon close to the Brandenburger Gate. Three sets of eyes following him, another two at the barrier, more beyond.

'*Brauchen Sie ein Taxi?*'

They stepped through the barrier.

'Taxi, yes.'

The eyes peeled off him and looked for another.

The foyer of the hotel was busy. He checked in, using the American identity under which he was travelling, then went to the room on the fourth floor, the bell-boy arriving with his case almost immediately. He tipped the man, locked the door, went to the bathroom, stripped, turned on the shower and stood beneath it, working through the arrangements for the evening and reflecting on the fact that the contact had insisted the man he meet be an Englishman, and the irony that Menzies had chosen him.

Charles Anthony Drake was forty-one years old, the second son of an established and landed English family. The first-born had been raised to inherit both the estate and the financial and political responsibilities which accompanied the position; those born after him had been steered into the Foreign Office and the professions. Drake, however, more than the others, had been affected by two aspects of his lineage. The first was that his mother was a Scot, the eldest daughter of a clansman; because of this he had spent most of his youth on the west coast of Scotland rather than the family home in England, considering himself closer to his mother's parentage than his father's. The second was his propensity to a clandestine attitude to life, encouraged and developed by his days with the family gillie on the Scottish moors. On a Tuesday morning in the spring of 1917 Drake had left his Cambridge college and enlisted in the war to end wars. In 1918 he had seen service in Archangel in support of the White Russian campaign against the Bolsheviks in what would become known as guerilla warfare, and in 1920 had tasted his first experience of counterinsurgency in Ireland. In 1924 he had enrolled at the University of Heidelberg, from where was born his fluency in German and his entry into the wilderness of mirrors, though his family wealth enabled him to maintain an independence which was of value both to him and his country. From 1928 he had alternated as poacher/gamekeeper in a variety of guises and an assortment of situations. When war had been declared two months before, in September 1939, he was still unmarried.

When he had finished showering, Drake towelled himself dry, changed into a fresh set of clothes and examined the room.

The bed was not yet folded back. He noted the precise point on the pattern of the pillow where the sheet crossed it, and the exact measurement of the bed cover from the floor, then went to the escritoire in the corner of the room next to the windows. The hotel stationery was in a leather binder in the top drawer on the right. He readjusted the headed notepaper slightly so that the lower curve of the emblem on the second sheet touched the upper rim of the emblem on the third, then laid his clothes in the large wardrobe along the wall opposite the window and placed the single suitcase at the bottom of the wardrobe, noting its position and that of the Leica camera inside it.

Eight o'clock each Tuesday evening for the three weeks following the initial message, Menzies had said; two were already gone, the last tonight.

It was six hours to the meeting. Drake left the hotel, making a point of informing the receptionist that he would be out all afternoon, went to the Café Kadinski on Unter den Linden and ordered coffee and cognac, choosing a seat from which he could observe the street. When he had finished he walked to the Tiergarten, remembering the Passport Control Office in the consulate there which had served as a front for British Intelligence, and took a cab to the *S-bahn* at Alexanderplatz. Already it was almost dark.

The station was busy, the ticket hall on the ground floor was packed with civilians and soldiers. He bought a ticket then made his way up the steps to the area above. The bar was in the centre, between platforms three and four; he asked for a beer and positioned himself in the corner. Five hours before he would wait again, he thought, before he would wonder who was waiting for him.

Contact codenamed A 54, Menzies had said, senior officer in the Abwehr, the Espionage, Counterespionage and Sabotage service of the German High Command with access not only to the Party, of which he was a member, but to the Oberkommando der Wehrmacht, the Armed Forces High Command itself. Part of the network recruited by Moravec, head of Czech Military Intelligence.

The train swung into the station; Drake waited till the doors were shutting, then jumped on, checking that it was not possible to pass between the carriages and looking at the maze of streets below the railway line.

The contact between Friedrichstrasse and Lehrter Bahnhof, Menzies had said, third seat on the left, third carriage from the front.

It had been A 54 who had warned Moravec of the German invasion of Czechoslovakia, given the British time to get him and some of his people out. Now Moravec had contacted London again, said that A 54 had passed a message to him, that he had something important for them, but that he would only give it to an Englishman.

The train pulled out of Friedrichstrasse, swinging above the houses and factories, the river and the burnt and blackened shell of the Reichstag to the left.

Why me? Drake had asked.

'Because SIS in Germany and most of Europe has been rolled up, the Z Circuits are in danger, and you have remained independent of both.'

'What's he offering?'

'We think an avenue into the German opposition to Hitler.'

The station at Lehrter Bahnhof was crowded. For the next twenty minutes he examined the area, the exits and the streets leading from them, then returned to the platform. By the time he returned to the hotel it was ten minutes to six. He took a schnapps in the lounge, allowing his return to be noted, then went upstairs. He had been out of his room for two minutes under four and a half hours, more than sufficient time for it to be searched if he had been followed or his presence noted. The papers in the escritoire were as he had left them, the bedclothes undisturbed and the case, and the camera in it in the positions he had left them. No point in their disturbing the room anyway, no reason at all when all they had to do was wait for him on the train that evening. At ten minutes to seven Drake left the hotel, took a cab to the Kempinski, entering by one door and leaving by another. Then he bought a copy of the *Berliner Tageblatt* and took a second cab to Alexanderplatz. It had begun to rain again, the water

16

lying in pools in the gutters. He checked the side streets round the station, confirmed that there were neither more nor fewer people or vehicles than he would have considered normal, and went inside.

It was eleven minutes to eight. The trains to Lehrter Bahnhof ran every half-hour at this time of the evening. He bought a ticket and walked up the stairs to the platform, looking for the eyes yet knowing they would wait till he had made contact. Five minutes to eight, still no eyes. Third seat on the left, fourth if it was taken, third carriage from the front. Eight o'clock. The train drew into the station. Third carriage, nobody in the third seat on the left, only three people in the carriage at all. He stepped on and sat in the fourth seat on the right. One couple, middle-aged, well-off, one man by himself, also middle-aged, also well-off. Either of the men in the carriage, he thought, only one of them carrying a newspaper.

The train pulled into Friedrichstrasse. No eyes on the platform, he noted. Behind him the couple rose and left, the doors shut and the train pulled out. He moved to the left, third seat from the front, and waited. The man who had been by himself walked down the carriage and sat facing him. His hair was silver grey and immaculate, and the suit beneath the overcoat equally well-cut.

'*Garnichts in der Zeitung heute.*' The accent was *Hochdeutsch*, the High German of the traditional Prussian ruling class. 'Not much in the papers today.'

'*Ja, nicht viel.*' The code was simple. 'No, not much news.' He waited for the trap to close on him.

'*Sind Sie mit der Zeitung fertig? Möchten Sie tauschen?*' The duelling scars ran the length of the man's right cheek, the two lines almost parallel. 'If you're finished with your paper perhaps you'd like to swap?'

'*Natürlich.*' He was searching the face for the first blink of betrayal, detecting something else. 'Of course.'

The envelope was thick and folded inside. 'Same arrangement tomorrow night.' The words took him by surprise. Not what he expected – one meeting then out. 'Any questions, ask then.' The train pulled into Lehrter Bahnhof. Without looking back the contact left the compartment and stepped onto the platform.

By the time Drake returned to the Adlon it was ten-thirty. He checked the room, hung the coat in the bathroom, and placed his shoes by the radiator to dry. Two months since the declaration of war against Hitler, he thought, yet in London they were still referring to the lack of hostilities as the Bore War, in England the politicians were still talking of peace and the generals were hardly preparing for war. He returned to the bedroom and opened the envelope. Across the top of the first fourteen of the twenty-three sheets of closely-typed foolscap folded tightly inside were the words *Armeegruppe B, Der Chef des Stabes* and the signature at the end of the last sheet was that of von Rundstedt. Contained on them was part of the battle order, including division and battalion strength, for the German seizure of Norway. The other nine sheets carried the name of the Armed Forces Supreme Command, and was entitled 'Directive Six: Operation Yellow.' The second paragraph on the first page was a summary of the exercise: 'An offensive action on the Northern flank of the Western Front crossing the area of Luxembourg, Belgium, Holland and France'.

It was time to leave Berlin, the city was no place to be with the documents he had been given that evening, yet the contact had wanted another meeting, suggested there would be more. He thought about the contact, why the man had insisted on a British connection when none of the documents, although referring to the war against Britain in general, were specific to it. He was back on the train, seeing the look in the man's eyes. Not betrayal, he realized. Fear.

AN HOUR BEFORE the meeting, Drake removed the Mercedes 500K from behind the Kempinski and repositioned it by the river opposite the Reichstag, then made his way to the *S-bahn* station at Alexanderplatz, bought himself a ticket, and went upstairs. The first two men appeared at five minutes to eight, two minutes later another three men came up the stairs and stood talking at the top. At the end of the platform the Lehrter Bahnhof train came into the station. First carriage, no contact, two possible eyes. Drake wondered when they would take him, if he would make it to the back-up car. Second carriage, no contact, one more possible eye. Third carriage, third seat empty, the contact sitting where he had sat the night before. The door opened, he stepped in and the train pulled away. On the platform the two groups converged, then one stayed in place while the second ran for the exit.

The contact was waiting for him. There were two questions London would ask him about the documents from the night before, Drake knew.

'When will you go into Norway?'

'Still undecided, probably April, depending on the weather.'

He was forgetting about the eyes, wondering why the man was risking so much. 'And Holland, Belgium and France?'

'Immediately after.'

Something else, he knew, the secret for which the contact had summoned him to Berlin. The train stopped at Friedrichstrasse then pulled away; the contact reached inside his coat and handed him an envelope.

'You know you're under surveillance?'

The contact nodded, watching him.

Drake opened the envelope and scanned the sheets of paper crammed inside, sensing that the contact needed to see that the Englishman understood their significance, to know that it had all been worthwhile. In the top right corner of each page were the initials T 14 after the number of the house on Tiergartenstrasse. Down the left margin was a list of names, the Jews predominant and the addresses opposite.

'Die Sonderfahndungsliste.' The contact glanced once down the carriage behind Drake. 'The Gestapo arrest list.'

The train passed the point where he had positioned the car. Drake saw the other names, the other addresses.

Baker-Noel, Philip J. 43 South Laton Place, London SW1.
Simpson, I. L. Unilever House, Blackfriars.
Tynan, Anna H. 15 Grosvenor Crescent, London.

The train was approaching the river, beginning to cross it. More pages, more names and addresses. He looked up, not understanding, seeing again the look in the man's eyes.

'Die Sonderfahndungsliste für England.'

Drake was still confused, unbelieving – refusing to believe.

'Operation Sea Lion. The invasion of England.'

THE RAIN WAS turning to sleet, Josef Straube turned the car into the yard at the rear of the house and slipped on the handbrake. In the first-floor window he saw Schellenberg looking down at him, then the figure disappeared and he switched off the engine and hurried inside.

Straube had been with Schellenberg since 1936, two years after the former law student had come to the attention of Reinhard Heydrich and his superior Himmler during the bloodletting of the Brown Shirts by the SS. When Himmler had strengthened his position, Heydrich, as his chief lieutenant, had moved with him, heading the *Sicherheitsdienst*, the SD, when it had been recognized as the sole intelligence and counterintelligence agency of the Nazi Party. At the same time Schellenberg had been rewarded for his faithfulness. When Heydrich had created the RSHA, the Main Security Office, and united under his personal control the entire repressive machinery of Party and State, one of his first appointments had been that of Walter Schellenberg as head of Amt IVE, counterintelligence within the Fatherland. And Schellenberg's first appointment in turn had been that of Josef Straube. The building from which the system operated was known simply by the name of the Berlin street on which it was situated, the Prinzalbrechtstrasse.

'Did they buy it?' The room, like the rest of the building which had been taken over for the operation, was barely furnished – a metal desk, two chairs and telephone – there had been no time to worry about refinements.

'I think so.' Straube hung his overcoat on the hook on the back of the door and felt in the jacket pocket for his cigarettes.

'But you think the English accepted the story about a link into the opposition to the Führer?'

Straube held the cigarette like the policeman he was, cupped in the palm of his hand so that it could not be seen. 'Probably.'

Schellenberg took two glasses and a bottle from the desk drawer and poured them each a schnapps. Straube was, like himself, always careful, always covering his back. It was why Schellenberg had recruited him in the first place. 'I hope so.'

Straube accepted the drink. 'When will you tell Berlin?' Will you tell Berlin at all, he meant; even then, who in Berlin will you tell? The *Brigadeführer* was always two steps ahead, always seeing the game that was forever being played around them.

'When you have delivered.'

THE CAFÉ BACHUS was fifty yards away, the car parked in the precise position they had decided outside so that the light by the door shone on the road immediately behind it and the steps leading to it. At the table by the window of the café Straube poured himself a coffee; opposite him the silver-haired man with the military bearing and the smart suit glanced outside then back at the table. The evening was dark and the street outside deserted. Schellenberg wondered if the English really had fallen for it – a general, links with the opposition to the Führer, the initial contact through a double agent, then the meeting in The Hague with the representative of the British Z Circuit and the local SIS head of station. The suggestion that the general wished to meet them but could not risk rousing suspicion by excessive travel, then the agreement for the meeting in the Café Bachus fifty yards the Dutch side of the German border crossing at Venlo. Always the chance that they were walking into a British trap rather than the British into theirs, Schellenberg thought.

At the top of the road, to his right, Straube saw the headlights, the vehicle moving slowly. The British had been nervous about coming so close to the border right from the beginning.

'Lean forward so they can see you,' he told the man opposite him.

The car passed by the café, the driver looking up and seeing Straube and the distinguished-looking man who shared his table. Everything arranged, Straube ran through the plan for the last time: the English car would park behind his, his own carefully positioned so there was no alternative. The man whom the English thought was a general would remain at the table, Straube greeting the English as they stepped from the car – a straightforward handshake if all was well and Schellenberg could spring the trap. The capture and interrogation of the men in the car vital for the background document on British Intelligence which would accompany the Gestapo arrest list for England.

The car came past again and stopped behind Straube's. Too close to it, Schellenberg's driver muttered, no room to pull forward, just as they had calculated. In the window of the café Schellenberg saw Straube leave the table and walk outside. The driver of the English car switched off the engine and opened his door. Straube reached forward and shook the man's hand, the signal clear.

'Go.'

The three Mercedes crashed through the flimsy wooden barrier of the border crossing, their headlamps full on and the men on the running boards clinging on. The passenger in the English car looked up. The first assault car was already into Holland and blocking it in, the men bundling the two occupants into separate vehicles. Straube was already running for his own car. He started the engine, pulling away as the man who had played the role of general ran from the café and tumbled in beside him. Less than thirty seconds after the English car had stopped the assault teams were back in Germany with their prize.

At fourteen minutes past nine Schellenberg made the call to the Prinzalbrechtstrasse. *Obergruppenführer* Heydrich, as he had expected, was not in his office. Schellenberg requested that he be contacted and informed immediately that the Venlo operation had been concluded and that the *Obergruppenführer* might care to conduct the first interrogation personally in the morning. Heydrich, he knew, would enjoy passing the information immediately to *Reichsführer-SS* Himmler, who would equally enjoy informing the Führer himself.

There was a knock at the door, Schellenberg put his hand over the mouthpiece and shouted for whoever it was to come in. Straube entered and informed him that the convoy was ready to leave for Berlin. Schellenberg thanked him then purely as an afterthought, requested Heydrich's office to return him to the switchboard and the operator there to connect him to his own office. The duty officer answered immediately. Without announcing himself, Schellenberg requested information on the three surveillance operations he knew were being conducted in Berlin that night.

The first two cases were dealt with summarily. Only when the duty officer detailed the third did Schellenberg begin to take notice. Prussian, *Abwehr*, he remembered the case notes and the thinnest of evidence on which he had already decreed the man's guilt.

'*S-bahn* trip last night, repeating the pattern established over the past two weeks, another tonight. We think he made contact with someone, but we weren't close enough to be sure.'

The *Abwehr*, Schellenberg was aware, was always competing with the SD for the attention of the Führer. He began to see how he could make a second use of the two British agents he had seized that night – the protection their arrest would afford him if the attempt to gain an advantage over the *Abwehr* went wrong.

'Pick him up.'

2

THE CROSS-CHANNEL ferry berthed at Dover at five minutes to ten on the Sunday morning, its departure from the Continent having been delayed because of the late arrival of a member of the Dutch royal family en route to London. Drake allowed the other passengers to clear the ship before him, then passed through the police control, left the dock and collected the Bentley Tourer from the rear of the hotel where he had left it eight days before.

The road from Dover was quiet, he swung out of the town onto the top of the Downs overlooking the cliffs and picked up the A2 towards London. That night he would see Menzies and pass him the information, by the following morning it would be in the hands of the politicians and the decision makers.

The air was cold and crisp, the road winding in front of him, ahead and to the right rose the tower of the cathedral at Canterbury. Before him Drake saw a road sign, the side road dropping off the main carriageway and disappearing into the countryside to his left. Abruptly, without quite knowing why, he pulled the Bentley into the side, got out, leaving the door open and the engine running, and stood looking down the road and across the fields and woods which flanked it. From the direction of the village to which the side road led he heard the bells of a church. There was something about the place, something about the church and the road where he now stood. If Hitler really was going to invade, this was the way he would come.

He returned to the car and continued the drive to London.

THE FARM WAS sheltered in the hollow at the top of the hill, the track running in front of it to the road half a mile to the right and the other farm higher up, to the left. The barns and outhouses were neat and well kept, the ground in front rising slightly then dropping across the field to the river at the bottom, the small wooden footbridge across it leading through a line of trees to the church on the other side. The couple who left the farm were dressed in their Sunday best, the husband was in his mid-thirties, six feet tall, his face brown and lean with the seasons, his wife three years younger, slim and tall, her brown hair loose and her looks handsome despite the years of hard work. The morning was ringing with the sound of the bells and the clamour of the rooks, and the smell of the dinner in the range drifted from the kitchen. The door shut and their son ran to them.

'Which way, Dad? Road or field?'

There would be too many days when the winter would dictate that they took the long way by road, Jack Masters thought. At five that morning, when he had left the farmhouse to feed the cattle, it had been hard and cold, the first frost gripping the ground.

'Field.'

'Good.'

They turned left, up the track toward the other farm where Ted and Sarah and their children lived, Boy Jack already striding ahead of them. Just like his grandfather, Jack looked at the way his son pushed his hands in his pockets. Just like his father, Fran watched the boy, even though he was still only nine, the image of her husband.

The church was crowded, they took their seats and looked round the congregation, thirty adults, another twenty children. Ted and Sarah, of course, Stan Bradley, who ran the King's Arms and whom they all knew was not averse to a little poaching on the side; Harry Downton, who owned the grocer's store in the village and who sang louder than most but who still made a profit on the items he supplied for the church functions; Mrs Dempster, who was in charge of the post office and the small telephone exchange at the rear and whom the children called Quizzie Lizzie because she knew everybody and everything; Ned the postman, who called everyone 'dearie'.

'Hymn number twenty-nine. "Fight the Good Fight."'

It seemed such a long time since she and Jack had sat in the kitchen and listened to the Prime Minister telling the nation that he had informed Herr Hitler that Britain demanded the withdrawal of

German troops from Poland, Fran thought. Since the Sunday, only two mornings later, when the vicar had told them that the Prime Minister had just spoken on the wireless and that from eleven o'clock that morning the country was at war with Germany. Only eight weeks, yet in that time they had waited fearfully for the sky to be filled with German bombers, then almost forgotten the war when nothing had happened.

The winter sun shone through the stained-glass windows, the colours sparkling across the floor of the church, the pulpit on the right and the varnish on the panelling on the walls behind it warm and brown and peeling slightly. The hymn ended and the reading began. 'Suffer little children to come unto me.' The Reverend Brian Markham was tall and deceptively built, slightly older than Fran and Jack. He had been at Ardley nine years, just long enough to christen Boy Jack. When the reading was finished he closed the Bible and smiled. 'The sermon this morning is short.'

They all chuckled, sometimes the vicar was very funny. Especially, as Harry Downton frequently suggested with a nod of the head and a sly tipple of the hand to the mouth, when the bottle for visitors which Mrs Markham kept on the sideboard of the sitting-room at the vicarage was a little emptier than it had started the morning.

The sermon ended. 'Church announcements. Christmas choir practice begins on Tuesday, Mrs Markham will be pleased to see whoever can attend. Guy Fawkes is next Sunday, so we will be holding the bonfire on Saturday. The ladies' committee are providing the food and the men, I gather, might be providing something else.' They laughed as they always laughed. He came to the final announcement and they understood why he had chosen the reading.

'As we all know, the government has decided that, because of the danger of bombing, the children of London and other major cities are being evacuated to the country. We shall be expecting those children assigned to us in the next few days.'

Fran remembered the evening she and Jack had gone to the cinema in Canterbury, the Pathe Gazette news pictures of the trainloads of children, the labels with their names round their necks and their gas masks in white cardboard boxes.

The vicar looked round them again. 'I'm sure we will take them into our homes with love and affection.'

Fran knew what Harry Downton was going to say and felt for his wife. 'Especially if they bring their big sisters.'

It was no more than a whisper, yet it seemed to echo between the walls. The Reverend Brian Markham smiled as if he had not heard. 'The last hymn this morning is the Twenty-third Psalm, to the tune of Crimond.'

They rose to sing. The poor little things, Fran thought, the poor parents in London and the other cities having to send their children away as they waited for the bombing. At least they looked well clothed and happy on the news film and in the newspapers. At least they would be safe in Kent.

THE BELL HARRY Tower of the cathedral reached into the winter sky; below it the workmen were perched on the scaffolding, removing some of the stained-glass windows and nailing boards over the others. The streets around the cathedral walls were crowded and the shops were busy.

Jack and Ted parked at the rear of the Corn Exchange and went for a cup of tea, then loaded the plough points and chicken feed onto the pick-up and began the five-mile drive home. The Austin Seven had begun its life as a saloon; three years ago they had pooled their savings and bought it between them, then sawn off the back of the bodywork and converted it themselves.

The day was dry and the sky a bright but thin blue, there was no danger of rain to spoil the evening. Funny place Kent, Jack thought as he always did when he drove across the Downs, especially this part. Heart of the English countryside, yet from the point where he turned off the A2 towards the village he could see the English Channel and smell the salt of the sea.

When he reached the farm the sandwiches that Fran had made for the evening were stacked on the table. Boy Jack helped them hurry through the rest of the farm work, the dark already closing in and the air colder. At seven they made their way to the village.

For the past two weeks the pile of wood in the centre of the green had been growing steadily. That morning the effigy had been hauled on top and fastened into place with a rope. When they arrived the vicar was leading the children in a singsong while their mothers spread the food on a long trestle table, next to it another laden with drinks from the King's Arms. At half-past seven Jack, as captain of the cricket club, stepped forward and lit the fire, the anticipation gleaming on the faces of the children.

'Hope we don't get any German bombers.' The vicar glanced up at the sky.

'Hope we don't get the constabulary.' Stan Bradley, the publican, reminded him of the blackout regulations.

Slowly the straw began to crackle and the flames took hold, spreading into the wood and creeping towards the figure at the top, the fire suddenly searing hot.

'Good time, dearie?' The postman stopped by Fran and smiled at the excitement.

'Great time, Ned.'

The flames reached the effigy, devouring the clothes and consuming the face and rope which held the figure in place. Slowly it began to topple, and the children cheered. Then the head came loose and the entire body disintegrated in a burst of red and blue.

When the flames had died to a smouldering heap of ashes the women came round with the food, Fran and Sarah helping, Jack, Ted and the other members of the cricket team following them with the drinks, and Stan Bradley breaking open the cask of beer at one end of the table. After they had finished serving the children Fran stood on the edge of the crowd and watched.

'Penny for them.'

She had not even noticed Jack by her side. 'Nothing,' she tried to shrug it off. 'Something silly, that's all.'

He put his arm around her. 'Me too, love.'

THE FOLLOWING MONDAY morning Quizzie Lizzie in the post office began informing anyone who passed that the evacuees were due that day. When Jack and Ted went to check, the area in front of the railway station at Canterbury East was filled with the first children from London. Most of them were well dressed, each with the white cardboard box for his or her gas mask, a small case, and a discreet label round the neck giving the child's name. Just like the pictures on the Pathe Gazette or in the newspapers, Jack thought, even though most of them were looking round silently, not laughing as the reports had said. The best dressed ones, he noticed, were whisked away in cars, the others walking to their new homes.

That afternoon he and Fran drove to the village and joined the growing crowd outside the schoolroom, Boy Jack coming out to stand beside them. Some of the people they knew, others not, Ardley being used as a distribution point for the cluster of villages in the area. At four, when there was still no sign of the coach, they returned to the farm and fed the animals, leaving Boy Jack in the village. It was gone five when he ran into the barn and told his father that the refugees had arrived. Jack washed and changed, then the three of them drove back. As they arrived the colonel and his wife, from the big house at the edge of the village, left the schoolroom with two girls, their coats and cases bright and new and their hair well groomed. They were followed by the butcher and his wife, the evacuee with them also well dressed. Behind Fran and Jack, Ned the postman and his wife joined the queue.

The late afternoon was dark, no light spilling round them because of the blackout regulations. The only thing Jack noticed as they moved closer to the door was that as the evening drew in the children being taken to their new homes were not quite as well dressed as those who had left earlier, and none of them as smart and clean as those he had seen in Canterbury that morning.

'Scrag end.' Ned saw what he was thinking.

'Looks a bit like it.'

The children now were poor, their clothes homemade and badly fitting and their cases as battered as the expressions on their faces. After another ten minutes Fran and Jack were almost at the door. The queue of people was moving more slowly, even though there were fewer of them, the children now being taken away poorer and ever more badly dressed. When Jack, Fran and Boy Jack finally stepped into the schoolroom itself the movement of people in front of the officials' desks at the top of the room had stopped. What they really wanted were two sisters, she heard someone saying; they were really after two brothers, another voice. The dark-suited official with the paperwork in front of him and the expensively-dressed woman with the twin set and pearls seated beside him were nodding in understanding and agreement. Despite the stove the room was cold, the draught cutting through as the door opened and shut.

Fran stood on tiptoe and looked to the far wall where the evacuees had been placed. Sitting on the wooden bench, white with tiredness and incomprehension, were a boy and a girl. Even though she guessed the boy was her son's age he seemed so small and thin, his hair like a scarecrow's, and the glasses he wore were so thick that she could not understand how he could see through them. His jacket was too small and his boots too big. On his lap, instead of a case, he held a small bundle wrapped in newspaper and tied with string. The label round his neck was large with a name scrawled across it. Beside him the girl's dress was thin and the dirty coat she wore was two sizes too small.

'Last of the litter,' Ned muttered quietly.

In front of them a couple shook their heads and turned away, another couple following them out, those remaining unsure what to do and the woman at the front beginning to close her folder.

'Bugger this.' There was silence as everyone heard Jack's voice. For one moment Fran saw the look of horror on her son's face then the realization of what his father was about to do. The whole world on the move, Jack thought, the high and the mighty and the low and the innocent, somebody always ready to look after the first but few caring about the second. He pushed his way to the front.

'Masters, Hope Farm. Who do you want me to take?'

You couldn't manage both of them? He saw the expression in the official's eyes.

'The boy will be a help on the farm.' Ned had elbowed his way to Jack's side. 'We'll have the girl.'

'Ernest Simmons.' The official began the paperwork and the hall emptied.

'You know what they say about the runt of the litter?' The postman winked at Fran.

'What's that, Ned?'

'Best of all.' He signed the form and pushed it back at the official.

Fran crossed the floor and smiled at the boy. 'Hello Ernie, I'm Auntie Fran.' She reached down to take his bundle; instinctively he pulled back, holding the package as if it was the only thing in the world which he possessed.

'Hello, missus.'

DRAKE WAS INFORMED at eleven and arrived in Portsmouth by mid-afternoon. He spent half an hour walking round the docks, then drove to the headland to the north, the Isle of Wight in front and slightly to the right already disappearing in the grey. Only once did he leave the position, to collect the hip flask he had left in the Bentley. As it grew dark he pulled the collar of his overcoat up, jammed his hands in his pockets, and waited.

The *Kelly* came out of the night like the ghost she would soon become, the smoke billowing from her funnel and the phosphorescence streaming in her wake. A signal lamp flashed a morse message and Drake turned, looking for the acknowledgement from the watchers on the defences of the docks to his right. Mountbatten at the helm, he knew, Randolph Churchill, the son of the First Sea Lord, Winston, in attendance.

The destroyer passed between the sea forts protecting the passage to His Majesty's dockyard, Portsmouth, and a tug pulled the barrier shut.

Drake turned down the grassy slope at the rear of the embankment and drove back to the dockyard. The arrival, he had been informed in London, was secret, yet already a crowd had gathered. Where the Duke of Windsor would step again onto English soil a red carpet had been laid, the guard of honour already drawn up, a line of policemen commanded by an inspector near the head of the carpet and a Marines band already in position to their left.

Slowly and carefully Mountbatten edged the vessel close to the dockside, the tide pulling against her, the figure at the bow standing alone, the dark blue naval overcoat wrapped round him, a white scarf round his neck, and his hands tucked deep into the pockets. Even in the half-light those on shore could see the silver in his hair and imagine the expression on his face.

Forty-five years since the Duke of Windsor had been born, twenty-eight since his father had made him Prince of Wales.

The engines were full astern and the wheel hard over, the first lines thrown ashore and the destroyer pulled fast against the granite and oak of the dockside.

Nearly four years since the old king had died and the man in the bow of the destroyer had been proclaimed Edward VIII.

The gangplank was pulled into place and the engines of the *Kelly* faded into the sound of the wind from Europe. The crowd on the dockside waited, the officials and officers present suddenly unsure what to do.

'Squad 'shun!'

It was the police inspector who broke the silence, crashing his men to attention, his own back stiff with pride, the men of the guard of honour and the bandsmen of the Marines following suit. Slowly Windsor woke from his apparent trance and turned his head, withdrew his right hand from the warmth of his greatcoat, the smile which had endeared him to the nation coming to his face, and began to wave. In the dock area behind the band the crowd began to cheer, quietly at first, then louder.

Nine years since he had met the American divorcee, Mrs Simpson, almost three since he had abdicated and plunged the nation into crisis.

At the edge of the gangplank the Marines colonel raised his baton. On the bow of the *Kelly* the Duke waited, his back straightening.

Two and a half years since Windsor and Mrs Simpson had married.

The baton fell and the music lifted from the band, carrying over the water and drifting into the darkness. The first chords of the national anthem.

Two years since Edward and Mrs Simpson had been entertained by Hitler at Berchtesgaden, since they had smiled and talked with him, shaken his hand in public for all the world to see.

At the door to the bridge, the Duchess emerged and stood looking at her husband. In the light at the side of the quay, Drake saw, the men were erect, their faces on the Duke. One face in particular, one man above all other men – the police inspector who had broken the silence when the *Kelly* had arrived, the man with the courage to be the first to call his men to attention.

> *God save our gracious King,*
> *Long live our noble King,*
> *God save the King.*

The anthem ended and the band began 'Greensleeves'. On the deck of the *Kelly* Windsor waved one last time then returned along the deck to where his wife was waiting and walked down the gangplank and along the red carpet, past the guard of honour, to the car waiting at the end. When the royal party had departed, the crowd began to drift away, but only when the last of them had gone did the police inspector allow his men to stand down from attention.

DRAKE'S MEETING THE following evening was neither at the War Office, which he occasionally visited, nor at the house in Queen Anne's Gate with its connecting passage to the offices of British Intelligence in Broadway Buildings, nor even at any of the other addresses in central London which his profession might have suggested. Instead he went to his club.

Menzies arrived precisely on time. They took whisky in the lounge, each with a dash of soda, then went through to the dining-room.

'The Duke will see the King by Sunday.' As head of SIS Menzies was always well-informed. 'He will ask for equal treatment for Mrs Simpson, in line with other spouses of members of the royal family, and will be refused. He will be back in France within two weeks.'

'And then?'

'They'll find a job for him in France; he'll be back and forth across the Channel, I expect, but nothing will change.'

'And the material from Berlin?'

There was a tone bordering on disgust in the way Menzies replied. 'The politicians are still trying to make up their minds about it.' He played the drink around the glass. 'And what did the band do when Windsor came in last night?'

There was not the slightest hint of frivolity in the question, both men all too aware how the answer might be interpreted elsewhere.

'They played "God Save The King."'

THE NEWS OF the Duke's return was on the wireless, Jack and Fran had finished the evening's work and were sitting in the kitchen, the boys asleep upstairs.

'What does it all mean, Jack?' The abdication crisis was still fresh in their minds, the sides people had taken, Winston Churchill standing up for the Duke until the last moment, then the reports that Edward had finally gone and his younger brother George was King. 'Why is he coming back?'

Her husband shook his head. 'No idea, love.'

It was two weeks since the evacuee had arrived. On the first morning, when the boys had left for school, Ernie had been wearing the clothes in which they had first seen him, what Fran had assumed were his others still wrapped in newspaper in the corner of the drawer she had allocated him in the room he now shared with Boy Jack. She had waited until the third day to suggest he change them so that she could wash the first set. When he finally agreed to open the package the clothes were even smaller and more ill-fitting than the others. That evening she had washed both sets and made sure that the larger ones were dried and ironed overnight for him to wear to school the following day.

Each morning until then, and each evening when they returned from school, the evacuee had remained in the bedroom while Boy Jack helped his father with the farmwork. The following morning, however, with his clothes looking and smelling clean and slightly smarter, he stood in the corner of the barn watching. His shoes were leaking and his feet were wet. In the evening Fran had sat him on a chair in the kitchen and helped him put on a pair of woollen stockings and boots which Boy Jack had outgrown, then watched as he ran across the yard and took his place in the corner of the cowshed as her husband did the milking.

The next day she had collected an assortment of clothes which Boy Jack had also outgrown, washed and ironed them again, even though she had put them away clean, so that they also smelt fresh, and placed them in Ernie's drawer. On the second morning after that the evacuee had worn one of Boy Jack's shirts, on the fourth morning another pair of trousers and a coat which fitted him. It had been on the fifth morning, as Jack was feeding the cows and waiting for Boy Jack to bring him the rest of the hay, that he heard the sound in the yard and looked outside.

The evacuee was dragging a large bale across the ground. He was too small to lift it, so that the hay was dragging in the mud, and the rain was running down his face. Rather than help, Jack had returned to the cows and waited. After two minutes the boy had stumbled into the shed with the bale and dumped it in the corner with the others.

'Thanks, Ernie.'

The boy's face had beamed with delight.

'All right, mister.'

3

SCHELLENBERG SAT AT the desk as if the man in the basement did not exist and fingered through the pages of the various reports in front of him: an update on the interrogation of the Englishmen seized at Venlo, the details of the operations his men would conduct that night and the personal histories of the men, women and children who would disappear forever, the report he would personally present to *Reichsführer-SS* Himmler that afternoon.

Sometimes, experience had taught him, an individual became hardened to pain. Not oblivious – no one could be oblivious to the torment which was inflicted in the basement of the Prinzalbrecht-strasse – but more able to endure it. Sometimes therefore, he had also learned, it was the waiting which broke a man.

'This is what he will say this afternoon.'

On the paper was written the confession of the man being tortured. He closed the file and began to leave. 'I have an appointment at three. When I return we'll see how he dances.'

The engine of the Mercedes was running. Schellenberg stood patiently while the driver held the door open for Heydrich then joined the *Obergruppenführer* in the rear seat. The car slid out of the Prinzalbrechtstrasse and turned into the Tiergarten. Four blocks later they passed the building which until the previous September had housed the British Embassy and Consulate, and the Passport Control Office that had served as a front for the British Secret Intelligence Service. The knowledge never failed to amuse Schellenberg, the historic whim which had determined that the location should be

34

mere minutes from the forbidding building from which he now worked.

'The man you are holding.' Heydrich offered Schellenberg a cigarette from the silver case and withdrew one for himself. 'The *Abwehr* are making noises. What can I report he has told you?'

'That he has admitted his part in the opposition to the Führer and named others.' There was no hesitation in the answer.

'Including those who will be useful to us?'

'Of course.'

'And what if I am asked for clarification?'

'He will dance tonight. I was thinking you might wish to make the Führer a gift.'

Heydrich drew deeply on the cigarette. 'I think that might be a good idea.'

The car stopped in front of the building, which served as headquarters for the *Reichsführer-SS* and they hurried past the guards on the steps outside and into the foyer. The halls were long and marbled, their footsteps echoed as they strode up the sweep of stairs and into the complex of rooms on the second floor. When they were told to enter the room Himmler was seated at his desk. Behind him, draped by swastikas, hung an oil painting of the Führer at Nuremberg, other paintings and photographs on the remaining walls.

The last occasion on which Himmler and Schellenberg had met had been the ceremony at which the Führer had personally congratulated the men who had taken part in the Venlo operation. After it the Berlin newspapers had carried photographs of the two men seized and reported links between British Intelligence and a plot to either overthrow or assassinate Hitler. Only when the *Reichsführer-SS* gestured that he should sit, however, did Schellenberg open his briefcase, withdraw the three copies of the report he had been instructed to prepare, and hand the first to Himmler and the second to Heydrich.

'Your instruction, *Herr Reichsführer*, was to prepare contingency plans on certain aspects of the British system both before and after the invasion of England.'

The project was not within his normal sphere of responsibility – he was Amt IVE, counterintelligence. It did, however, augur well for his continued rise within the Party as well as allowing him a taste of the power which could be his in the future. It was also, he was aware,

35

an indication both of the warring between the various factions within the Nazi Party and a demonstration of his loyalty and allegiance to the Himmler-Heydrich grouping.

'Specifically, the importance of the King to the English people, his probable conduct in the case of invasion, and the necessity of replacing him should we feel he would not co-operate with us.'

He deliberately excluded any suggestion that the Führer had not totally committed himself to Operation Sea Lion.

'The monarch is important both to the country's constitution and the national psychology of its people.' His words and the manner in which he delivered them were designed to show the logic of the legal profession in which he had been trained and in which he had already served the Party in a number of posts. 'Note, however, that I use the word "monarchy" rather than "monarch".' His argument was similarly chosen to give his superiors what they wanted, and what they in their turn knew the Führer would wish to hear. 'The allegiance is to the position rather than to the person occupying it. There is ample precedent of the nation accepting a new ruler, whether that person comes from overseas or assumes the throne through unexpected circumstance.'

They understood the reference as he intended they should and sensed where he was leading them.

'It is probable that George and his family will leave England as soon as the invasion starts. It is unlikely that, after the completion of the war, he would either return or that we would wish to have him. In any case, George is not accepted by the vast majority of the English as their right and lawful King.'

'The Duke of Windsor –' Himmler fully appreciated Schellenberg's line of reasoning – 'where is he now?'

'Paris. Since his return from England he has been serving with the British Military Mission at French General Headquarters.'

'So what do you suggest?' Himmler knew how Hitler would remember the meeting at Berchtesgaden, the Führer and the Duke of Windsor shaking hands, Mrs Simpson behind them.

'There are two points at which the Duke might be useful. Before invasion, by using his influence to bring about conciliation between Germany and England, or after, when his brother has fled and he would be seen as the monarch who answered his people's call when they needed him.'

'But?' The *Reichsführer-SS* sensed the caveat which Schellenberg was about to introduce.

'But it is possible either that Windsor might refuse, or that others might also approach him.'

Ribbentrop, Himmler was already calculating, the former Ambassador to London now Foreign Minister, was probably already sending his emissaries to make the first contact in France. 'So what is it that you propose?' He began to understand why Heydrich placed such faith in his subordinate.

Schellenberg edged his chair closer to the desk. 'I would call it a back-up, *Herr Reichsführer*.'

Ally himself with Ribbentrop in case the scheme succeeded, Himmler understood immediately, but maintain a distance and arrange an alternative in case it failed.

'Who?' The more Himmler thought about it the more he became convinced that the Foreign Minister had already made the first move.

'There are two possibilities. The first is this man.' Schellenberg indicated a photograph in an appendix to the report. 'Aged seventy-three, a retired banker living in Hamburg. He has been a member of the Party since 1938 but his line to the English throne is long and not particularly direct, and he himself may be much too old.'

He drew their attention to a second photograph. 'Wilhelm Johan Sebastian Richter. Aged forty-eight, an engineer in Munich. A distant but direct descendant of Queen Victoria.'

'Good.' Himmler lifted a telephone, ordered an attendant to bring them schnapps, then swung back. 'And how would the English react if it was Windsor?'

On Schellenberg's right Heydrich moved in his chair and spoke for the first time. 'What did the English do when the Duke returned to Portsmouth?'

'They played "God Save The King."'

BY THE TIME Schellenberg returned to the Prinzalbrechtstrasse it was ten minutes past five. He went to his office, confirmed that the teams who would make the arrests that night were on stand-by, then descended to the basement. Josef Straube was waiting for him.

'Is the film unit ready?'

'Everything is prepared.'

'Let's see how the bastard dances then.'

A long drop and the neck was broken immediately, a short drop and the execution was by asphyxiation, slow and agonizing, the legs kicking in a waltz of death.

They went through to the room. The meat hook was screwed into a beam in the ceiling, the noose had been already drawn in the piano wire and the 35-mm movie camera and sound equipment were ready.

'Begin filming.'

The camera was pointed at the door and the prisoner led in. The man was naked and his hands were tied behind his back. Quickly, brutally, they stood him beneath the beam, placed the noose round his neck, and tightened it. Then they lifted him by his arms, hung the piano wire onto the meat hook, and stood back. Slowly, as if to music, the body began to turn, the feet a mere twelve inches from the floor, the fear and pain already twitching across the man's face and the legs already beginning to kick.

Twenty minutes, Schellenberg estimated, half an hour if he was lucky. The Führer would prefer that. It was unfortunate that the prisoner had not admitted anything, named others. And there was always the possibility that he had not been involved in the conspiracy against the Führer, that perhaps the contact with the unknown person on the *S-bahn* train had been about something else.

THE RECEPTION GIVEN by the American Ambassador in the palace at Potsdam was due to begin at eight-thirty, but not until quarter to nine was Schellenberg collected by a driver and driven there. The large reception area was festooned with decorations, almost as if Christmas had come early, the three hundred or so people present spilling into adjoining suites. At the top of the room an orchestra was playing. Schellenberg smiled at someone who appeared to recognize him and accepted a glass of champagne from a waiter.

Though the American Embassy had long been a focal point in the political and social life of Berlin itself and Germany as a whole, its importance had been magnified by America's decision to remain neutral following the outbreak of war in the September.

Schellenberg drained the glass and took another.

In the side streets in the Lichterfelde and Neukolln quarters of the

*city as well as in Potsdam itself the men checked names and addresses,
and the first cars began to converge.*

At the far end of the room the orchestra broke into light jazz and
the guests laughed and clapped; to his right the American Ambassador
was talking to a German in his mid-forties, tall and distinguished.
Schellenberg remembered seeing him at an official function and tried
to recall his name. As he watched the Ambassador called to another
guest. American, Schellenberg noted the details of the second man
without even thinking, late fifties, same height as the other man but
bigger build, the muscle beginning to slacken.

'Mr Donovan, may I introduce you to Doktor Fuchs.' Wealthy,
the details of the first came back into Schellenberg's mind, senior
member of the Party, afforded honorary SS rank when he had joined.
'Herr Fuchs, meet William Donovan, visiting us from America.' The
two men shook hands. To his left Schellenberg picked up the faintest
trace of a political discussion and drifted towards it.

*On Walter-Linse-Strasse and Karwendelstrasse, in the Lichterfelde
quarter of the city, the lorries were driven into position.*

The Ambassador's glass was empty. He called a waiter and asked
for two more champagnes and an orange juice. 'Mr Donovan was
Deputy US Attorney General during Prohibition,' he half explained.
Fuchs turned enquiringly to Donovan.

'Alcohol was illegal.' The American wondered why he felt forced
to explain when the German clearly understood. 'It was my job to
enforce the law. The habit stuck.' There was a trace of Irish in his
accent. 'Totally against human nature but there it is.'

'Many things are totally against human nature, Mr Donovan, but
why Deputy Attorney General?' The smile was as arrogant as the
way in which the question was delivered, the English impeccable.
'Are you a lawyer or a politician?'

'Both.' The Ambassador answered on Donovan's behalf.

William J. Donovan was fifty-six years old, five feet ten inches tall
and built like the American footballer he had once been. The son of
an Irish railroad worker, he had won a scholarship to Law School at
Columbia where he played quarterback for the Columbian Lions and
where a fellow student had been Franklin Delano Roosevelt, who
would become President. After Columbia Donovan had practised law
as an associate in his home town of Buffalo, then founded his own
firm.

'Democrat or Republican?'

At the outbreak of the 1914–18 war he had helped organize Catholic relief programmes in Europe, by the end of the war he was his country's most decorated soldier. In 1918 he had married the only daughter of one of Buffalo's wealthiest families, resumed his law practice and been drawn into politics.

'Republican.' Donovan understood why he had taken an instant dislike to the man and decided to end the conversation as quickly as he could. 'And yourself?'

'In Germany there is only one party worth bothering about.'

'And you are a member of it.' There was an edge to Donovan's voice.

'Of course.'

The waiter returned with two glasses of champagne and one of orange. Fuchs took the glass from the tray without even thanking the man.

'If you will excuse me.' The Ambassador confirmed that the First Secretary would return Donovan to his hotel pending his early departure in the morning, and moved on. On the left side of the room Schellenberg decided the conversation was innocent and drifted away.

In Neukolln the first teams closed in on the three houses by the Koernerpark.

'And what are you doing in Germany, Mr Donovan?'

'Business.' Donovan kept his reply short. 'My firm represents a number of large corporations and banking institutions who have interests not only in Germany but also in the countries against whom you are at war. I am assessing the situation for them.'

'In view of the neutrality which your President Roosevelt has followed?' The delivery was almost rude.

'What sort of doctor are you, Herr Fuchs?' Donovan ignored the question.

'I am a scientist.'

'And where do you work?' He began to regret extending the meeting.

'Industry.' The reply was noncommittal.

'And how is German industry at the moment?'

In the house on Weser-strasse the woman kissed the child good-night and returned to her husband in the sitting-room of the apartment on the first floor.

'German industry, like the Fatherland itself, is fine.'

'I thought there were a number of problems.'

'What sort of problems?' The smile on Fuchs' face was almost one of condescension.

'The Jewish problem, for example.'

Fuchs laughed. 'Don't worry, Mr Donovan, I wouldn't expect the Jewish problem to be with us much longer.' The smile had not left his eyes. 'If I were a betting man I would imagine that the Führer already has the matter in hand.'

At the end of the room the orchestra was playing Bach.

At the end of Weser-strasse the Scharführer *checked the number of the house in which the next suspects lived.*

'I also understood there were labour shortages in certain areas.'

In the adjoining room Schellenberg tired of the conversation he was having and drifted again into the main reception.

'In that case, you can't have heard of the DEST.' The expression, both in Fuchs' voice and on his face, was of total superiority. 'If you haven't, then you must allow me to show you how efficient it is.'

It was almost, Donovan thought, as if Fuchs had sought to engineer the opening. 'I leave tomorrow morning.'

Schellenberg accepted another champagne and passed by them. Something about the man, Donovan thought, watching him as he crossed the room. '*Sicherheitsdienst.*' Fuchs' eyes were blue and hard. 'Section Amt IVE, counterintelligence within the Fatherland. Responsible for the Venlo snatch.' The incident at the border had attracted international attention.

Donovan began to ask how he knew, then stopped himself. The arrogance of the man, he thought, the pathological need to demonstrate his knowledge of and contacts in an organization of which he must have known the American disapproved.

'Sometimes, Mr Donovan, there are certain things an individual should make it his business to know.'

A confrontation – Donovan thought back over the conversation, yet everything with a double meaning, if he wished to see it that way and was prepared to take the chance. All the information he would have volunteered about himself had he been Fuchs, all the questions he would have put had he been testing the American.

'Tell me about the DEST.'

'The *Deutsche Erd und Steinwerke GmbH* is a private company

41

formed by the SS last year which provides labour at certain establishments that the SS owns.' To an observer the tone of the conversation would not appear to have changed. 'The principle it established in doing this is already being applied to key industries where labour is short.'

'And what is that principle?'

'If you really don't know then you must allow me to show you.'

It was the second time Fuchs had issued the invitation. At Donovan's side the First Secretary informed him that his car was ready.

In Weser-strasse the men left their cars and closed on the houses on their list. In the sitting-room of the first-floor apartment the woman heard the sudden banging on the other side of the street, crossed the room and peered through the side of the curtains.

'I'll be back after Christmas.'

'Good.'

Thank God it is not me and my husband they are coming for, she thought. Thank God it is not my child.

The two men turned from each other as if the conversation had been merely social and as if the invitation had neither been made nor accepted, Fuchs engaging immediately in another conversation and Donovan making his farewell to the Ambassador.

In the centre of the main reception Schellenberg checked his watch and wondered about the night's operations.

In the car at the top of Weser-strasse the *Scharführer* confirmed the names as the men, women and children were loaded into the lorries. In the sitting-room of the apartment the woman hesitated then turned back and looked again through the side of the curtains.

'They're coming.' It was a scream, a whisper, she was not sure. On the street below men in long coats were moving quickly across the pavement and assembling at the door of the house, looking up. 'They're coming for us.'

Her husband crossed the room to the window and looked outside without moving the curtain.

'Quick. The child.' No sense in running now, they both knew. They should have fled the country when they had the chance but did not believe what was happening, could not believe it would happen to them. No good now whatever they did or wherever they tried to go.

'Out the back.'

Try anyway, don't give in. Don't give up without a fight. Whatever you do don't go passively into the system which they describe as legal but from which there is no return. In the bedroom the woman lifted the child from the bed and wrapped him in a dressing-gown. In the kitchen at the rear the husband opened the window, climbed out, hung by his hands and dropped the twenty feet to the ground below.

In the street at the front of the house the assault team forced open the door and began running up the stairs to the apartment on the first floor.

Three blocks away, Donovan saw the people being pushed into the lorries and asked the First Secretary what was happening. The man shrugged his shoulders, either through lack of knowledge or indifference, and thought about how quickly he could return to the reception.

The child was still asleep in her arms. The woman ran to the window and looked down. Such a long way – she did not know whether she could do it. There were three apartments on the first floor; the men outside were confused, began checking the numbers. The woman leaned out as far as she could and dropped the child. In the dark her husband could hardly see the bundle as it came towards him, then felt the first force of it and caught his child tight and safe. The woman dropped, her ankle turning under as she landed. She ignored the pain, picked herself up and hobbled after her husband. He turned, saw she was injured even though she tried to disguise the fact and slowed for her. They came out of the alley and turned into Potsdamer Strasse.

There was no reply from the apartment. The men knocked again, their fists drumming on the door. Two minutes they had waited, almost two and a half – plenty of time for the bastards inside to wake if they were asleep, more than enough time for them to answer. The *Scharführer* nodded and the men smashed through the door. The lights in the apartment were on and the rooms were empty. One man checked the sitting-room to the right while another ran to the bedrooms, a third to the kitchen. The window was open and the curtain was fluttering in the night air.

'Potsdamer Strasse. They can't have got far.'

He should make it back at the reception by ten-thirty, the First Secretary was thinking, as long as his passenger didn't invite him into the hotel for a drink and to talk about the good old days. They slowed for the junction with Weser-strasse. More lorries. Donovan glanced to his right as they stopped at the junction – more people being rounded up. Thirty yards down the road he saw the men run from the house and towards the cars, shouting at the drivers to start the engines. The First Secretary accelerated away down Potsdamer Strasse.

The figures were a hundred yards ahead of them, running as fast as they could, Donovan saw, yet already slowing, one limping badly and the second holding something, trying to help the first. Eighty yards. The men in Weser-strasse would have reached the cars, the thought and connection were automatic, would be turning into Potsdamer Strasse after them. The figures were fifty yards ahead. A man and a woman, he saw, the woman limping. *If I were a betting man*, he remembered Fuchs' words, *I would imagine that the Führer already has the matter in hand*. They were level with the couple, the man glancing across at them, still running. A child, Donovan realized what the man was carrying. They were five yards past, ten, almost fifteen.

'Stop!'

The driver braked automatically. Even before the car stopped Donovan had opened the back door.

'Get in.'

They did not understand what was happening, but did as they were told. Donovan saw the fear in their eyes as he pushed them inside, then shut the door on them and the car pulled away.

Less than a minute later the first of the black Mercedes overtook them, then a second, engines screaming. The child in the man's arms began to cry. A mile on the father tapped Donovan on the shoulder and said that they were near where he should leave them. Close to the station at Lichterfelde-West the man indicated that they should stop. They got out and stood on the pavement, aware they had to move quickly but unsure what to say.

'Good luck,' Donovan said.

They moved away, the child still in the father's arms and the mother hobbling by his side.

'It may be out of order, Mr Donovan,' it was the first time the First Secretary had spoken, 'but I feel it my duty as an officer of the United States government to remind you of the neutrality of our country in this affair.' In the shadows the couple turned once, the man raised his hand in thanks, then the gloom closed round them. 'None of this is of any concern to us whatsoever.'

Only when the couple had disappeared and the street around them was empty did Donovan turn back to the driver. When he spoke his voice was quiet, the faintest reminder in it of the young man whose grandfather had crossed the Atlantic from Ireland.

'Like hell it's not.'

THE PORK WAS sizzling in the oven of the range, Fran turned it and checked the potatoes. Ted had killed the pig three days before, jointing it and salting the meat in the room behind his kitchen. It had already been dark two hours, the wind rattled against the door and she could hear the rain on the windows. Jack left his boots in the scullery and came into the kitchen; the water had run down inside his coat and his hands were red with cold. Fran put the pork and potatoes onto the serving plate, made the gravy and called the boys for supper.

'Need some help later, Dad?' Boy Jack watched as his father carved the meat and his mother laid it on the plates with the vegetables and poured the steaming gravy over them. 'Ernie and I will help, won't we?'

'Yeah.' The evacuee picked nervously at the meal.

'You all right?' Fran looked across the table.

'Yes thanks, missus.'

'You're sure?' It was unlike Ernie not to eat his share. In the past weeks the boy had grown taller and begun to fill out. Each morning now he was up helping Jack and Boy Jack, each evening he could hardly be dragged away from the animals and whatever work was needed.

'Sure, missus.'

By the time the others had finished Ernie's meal was untouched. When the three went outside again the rain was even harder. There were twenty bales to carry from the barn to the cowshed and the rain was driving across the yard. By the time they had finished the boys were exhausted and went straight to bed. Within ten minutes Boy Jack was almost asleep, the only thing which prevented him, even when he pulled the clothes over his head, was the sobbing from the far corner of the room.

'What's wrong?'

45

'Nothing.'

'Must be something.' He heard Ernie trying to stop the tears.

'My hands are hurting.'

Downstairs, Boy Jack could hear, his parents had put the wireless on. 'Why are you *really* crying?'

There was a long silence.

'I'm hungry.'

'Why didn't you eat your supper?'

'I couldn't.'

'Why not?'

'I'm not allowed to.'

Don't be silly, Boy Jack wanted to say, nobody stopped you. Mum even asked if you were feeling all right. '*Why* not?'

'Because I'm a Jew.' The voice was half hidden beneath the bed clothes.

'What's that?' At the door of the bedroom Boy Jack saw his mother, her hand shielding the light of the oil lamp.

'What's wrong, Ernie?'

There was no reply, only the snuffling sound as the child tried to control his sobbing.

'He's hungry.' On the landing behind his mother Boy Jack saw his father and knew the question they were going to ask. 'He wasn't allowed to eat supper.'

'Why not?' Fran came into the room and sat on the evacuee's bed. 'Nobody stopped him.' The boy pulled farther down the bed.

Fran reached across and moved Ernie's glasses away from the edge of the dressing-table, then pulled the clothes back so she could see his face.

'It was pork.' It was as if he was afraid to tell her. 'I'm Jewish.'

Gently she sat him up and wiped his face with the corner of the sheet. 'Why didn't you say anything?'

He was still sniffing, his nose running. 'I thought you would send me away.' Jack reached down, lifted him out of bed and wrapped a blanket round him.

'Come on, Ernie, there's some bread and cheese downstairs. Let's have supper.'

'Thank you.'

It was the first time he had not called them 'Mister' or 'Missus'.

46

TEN DAYS AFTER his departure from Berlin, William Donovan returned to the United States. On the third day after his return he journeyed to Washington for the session of Congress at which President Roosevelt spelt out the twin themes of American neutrality and the need for the country to defend itself.

That evening Roosevelt entertained in his office in the White House the Hungarian-born vice president of the Lehman Corporation, Alexander Sachs, who had played a key role in Roosevelt's New Deal programme and was now a close and respected confidant. In his briefcase Sachs carried a report from an exiled European scientist, Leo Szilard, on the work upon which he and others were engaged and a letter of recommendation from the physicist and Nobel Prize winner, Albert Einstein. The immediate outcome of the meeting was the formation of the so-called Uranium Committee under the chairmanship of Bureau of Standards director Dr Lyman J. Briggs, which would atrophy for the next ten months but which would result in the project called Manhattan and the revolution called Little Boy.

IT WAS THE week before Christmas.

Drake crossed St James's Park and headed towards Birdcage Walk. It was already dark; he avoided a couple walking the other way who had not seen him, turned into Queen Anne's Gate and entered number twenty-one. The light inside was almost overpowering. He cleared the security check, followed the connecting passage to the offices on Broadway and turned up the stairs.

Four-thirty on a Friday afternoon – the telephone call from Menzies requesting a meeting just half an hour before.

The Head of Intelligence was waiting for him, the curtains were pulled as usual and the coals glowed in the grate. They sat by the fire and a secretary brought them tea. Too early for whisky, Drake supposed.

'The Berlin material.' Menzies settled back in the Chesterfield. 'I have finally received reactions to it from the armed services and the Prime Minister's office.

'The Norway plans and Directive Six.' Menzies chose his words carefully. 'The War Office thanks us for our troubles but thinks the plans are provisional, even theoretical, though they would, of course, appreciate any more information, preferably including the precise timings of various stages of the attack. The politicians have not even said thank you.'

He stirred his tea.

'The reaction to the Gestapo arrest list has been similar. The military maintains that Hitler has neither the power to conquer Europe nor the ability to cross the Channel. They also point out, of course, that they would have no trouble stopping him if he did. The politicians' attitude is that although we are at war, an accommodation with Hitler is not only possible and desirable, but that that feeling is shared by the other side. The arrest list is therefore not only invalid, they even doubt whether it is genuine.'

'Which means they don't believe in Sea Lion either.'

'So it would seem.'

Drake remembered the eyes of the man on the train and wondered why he had been summoned.

'What are you doing tomorrow?' asked Menzies.

It did not matter that he had intended to travel back to Scotland for Christmas and Hogmanay. 'Nothing.'

'Good. Breakfast at Chartwell. Six-thirty.'

The house and grounds in Kent had been bought by Winston Churchill in 1922. Why Churchill, Drake wondered. What was the old fox playing at? 'I thought that Winston closed Chartwell when he moved to the Admiralty.'

It was the second time Winston Churchill had held the posts at the Admiralty, the first during the 1914–18 war, before the catastrophe at Gallipoli had forced his resignation. In the wilderness years of the thirties Churchill had been the lone voice crying out against Hitler, now he was First Lord of the Admiralty in the War Cabinet of Neville Chamberlain.

There was the trace of a smile on Menzies' face. 'He did.'

'So why have we been invited?'

'I think it best that he tells you himself.'

'And who else will be there?'

'Wait and see.'

THE SNOW GLEAMED in the black of early morning. Drake crossed the Weald of Kent, drove through the village of Westerham, its inhabitants still asleep, and up the hill to the south. He turned in the gate in the long brick wall and stopped on the gravel drive.

48

Menzies' car was already parked outside the door. As Drake drew up, Menzies came out of the house to greet him. Behind him, another car stopped, the driver getting out and opening the rear passenger door.

'General Ironside.' Menzies introduced the Head of Home Command. 'Charles Drake.' They hurried to the warm inside and followed Menzies down the stairs to the breakfast room. 'The Old Man's waiting.'

From the outside the house gave every appearance of being empty: the windows had been boarded and the gate had been closed again as soon as the other car had entered. Inside, most of the valuables had been removed and the furniture and items which remained had been draped in dust covers. At the bottom of the stairs they turned right, through the small hall and into the dining-room. At the far end, where the full-length windows overlooking the gardens and ponds were curtained and boarded, was a large circular table.

Churchill had already begun breakfast. His plate was piled with scrambled eggs and bacon, and a cigar smouldered in the ashtray on the table. Now he rose to greet them, pulling the dressing-gown tight around him, welcoming Ironside, Menzies clearly having spent some time with him already, then turned his attention to Drake.

'Good to have you on board.' The hand shake was firm and the suggestion undeniable. 'Help yourself to breakfast.'

Drake wondered how many other conspiracies had been born in this room in this way, how many others welcomed into the fold. Six-thirty in the morning: the First Lord of the Admiralty, the Head of British Intelligence, the Head of Home Command. And himself. He served himself scrambled egg and sat down.

'The Gestapo arrest list.' Churchill came immediately to the point. 'How genuine is it?'

'The man who gave it me believed it was genuine. So do I.'

'Then why is it that many of my esteemed colleagues in the War Cabinet prefer not to share your opinion?'

'Possibly because they do not yet believe that war with Germany is inevitable.'

'And what do *you* suggest?' It was almost a growl.

'That we should assume it is.' Drake wiped his mouth and placed the napkin on the table. 'We should assume not only that Hitler possesses the will to conquer Europe, but that the Allies lack the strength to stop him.'

'And what does that mean we should do?' The voice was still a growl.

'It means that we should prepare now for invasion.'

There was a silence round the table. Ridiculous – the country at war yet not at war, the government still not totally convinced that the situation could not be redeemed.

'How?'

'How would you yourself suggest?'

Churchill rose from the table, selected a fresh cigar from the box on the sideboard and lit it. 'I have been briefed on your background, Mr Drake. I know some of the places you have been and a little of what you were doing there. You now work in MI(R); the brief of that department, and I quote, "is to investigate every possibility of attacking potential enemies by means other than conventional military forces."'

'So what are you suggesting?'

'The application of that brief to this country.'

Neither Menzies nor Ironside had the office to implement such an action, Drake knew, nor Churchill the responsibility within Cabinet to approve it – the War Cabinet that had not merely rejected the Gestapo arrest list but had even refuted the assumption on which it was based. Winston Churchill breaking again with the establishment wisdom and instructing him to act upon it.

'I'll begin immediately.'

When they left an hour later the first sun was shining on the white of the snow. Their drivers had been waiting three hours, though they had not spent the entire time in the cars. It had been Ironside's driver, however, who had talked their way into the kitchen and secured them bacon and eggs, and tea and toast, and Ironside's driver who had returned to the car first to make sure it was warmed. As the three men stepped out of the house and shook hands, Churchill waving goodbye, she opened the rear door and took the general's briefcase.

The woman was in her early twenties, Drake noticed as he crossed to his car, slim and attractive even in the ATS uniform, her hair pinned up under her cap.

'Home, Mary, fast as you can.' It pleased Ironside, though he would not have admitted it, that it was his driver who looked the smartest and his driver who sped away from the driveway first.

'Good breakfast, Mary?'

'Yes, thank you, sir.'

'Hope you got in first.'

'Of course.'

The sky was heavy with more snow. They descended the hill and entered Westerham. 'Good meeting, sir?'

It was as far as she would take the conversation unless he himself wished to pursue it farther, and was one of the reasons, after checking her record, that he had chosen her from the pool of drivers available to him and his staff. 'Fine, thank you.'

Mary Atkinson was twenty-two years old. In 1938 she had joined the FANYs, the First Aid Nursing Yeomanry; in 1939, shortly before the outbreak of war, she had been transferred to the ATS and trained as a driver, though she would always consider her parent body to be the FANYs, a point she had made forcefully to Ironside when he had questioned her on the subject, and which had been another reason for his selection of her.

There had been two others. The first, which he deemed unimportant but pleasant, was her looks, and the second, which he considered vital, was that she was discreet to the point of not even discussing with her fellow drivers the various locations and meetings to which she took him.

'Any plans for Christmas?' He opened the briefcase and withdrew a file.

'Going home for a few days, plus a couple of parties. And you, sir?'

'Family affair.' He was looking forward to it.

They left Westerham and turned for London.

BOY JACK WOKE at six, Ernie two minutes later. Fran heard them as they felt along the beds, then the rustle as they found what they were looking for and the excited chatter as they lay back and tried to sleep. At half-past six Boy Jack pushed the door open and stood at the foot of their bed, the evacuee behind him.

The night before, as a special treat, they had been allowed to stay up until ten. At one in the morning, as Jack and Fran waited to slip the presents onto the beds and put up the decorations in the room, they had still been awake. At three they had finally gone to sleep.

'Mum, can we open the presents?'

'Do you know what time it is?'

51

'Nearly seven o'clock.'

There was a silence.

'Mum?'

'What now?'

'Happy Christmas.'

'All right,' she conceded, 'come on.'

He climbed into the bed and wriggled between them, his feet cold where he had waited outside their room. On the landing the evacuee waited.

'Come on, Ernie.' Jack rolled over and saw the figure in the doorway. 'There's room for you too.'

The boy scampered into the room and found himself a space on the bed.

'Happy Christmas, Uncle Jack.'

There were four presents in each bag, as well as fruit and nuts. Ernest's parents had sent his presents through the post, plus one for Boy Jack. In addition to making a present for his son, Jack had made one for the evacuee.

All summer, when the water in the river behind the church was warm and the other boys played with their boats, Boy Jack had talked of what he wanted for Christmas, now he began tearing at the paper and looking excitedly at his father and mother.

Each night Jack had worked on them in the kitchen when he had come in from the farm and the boys had gone to bed, until the curves of the hulls were perfect and the paintwork smooth and white.

Boy Jack held the yacht up for them all to see. 'Great, Dad. Absolutely smashing.'

'Thanks, Uncle Jack, Auntie Fran.' Ernie gave them both a hug.

When they had finished the farm work and the chicken was cooking in the range, they walked to the church. The snow in the fields between the hill and the river was eighteen inches deep, but the inside of the church was warm with the atmosphere Fran always enjoyed at this time of year, the children telling their friends about their presents, and the vicar beaming from the pulpit as he invited them to sing the next carol. When the service was over they stood outside, talking and watching the children build a snowman in the triangle of ground beneath the trees by the river.

'Come on,' Fran took the initiative, 'or we'll never have dinner.'

'See you this afternoon.'

It was a Christmas custom, tea with Ted and Sarah, an exchange of presents for the children, Boxing Day tea at Fran and Jack's.

'Four o'clock.'

The smell of the Christmas dinner in the oven of the range was almost overpowering, the chicken juicy and tender, its skin crisp and brown, the roast potatoes sizzling round it. By the time they had eaten, Boy Jack and Ernie managing two helpings of pudding, there was barely time to clear the table before the King's speech.

Jack switched on the wireless in the corner of the room and they heard the voice of the announcer.

'There now follows a Christmas message from His Majesty King George.'

Not the real King, the confusion was deep in both their minds, not Edward, who had been born to be King, who had raised the nation's spirit. George, his younger brother, who had never been meant to be King, who had a lovely wife and two beautiful girls, but who never smiled as if he meant it.

'A new year is at hand. We cannot tell what it will bring. If it brings peace, how thankful we shall all be. If it brings struggle we shall remain undaunted.'

The King's voice was hesitant and undramatic, the slightest stutter in it.

'In the meantime I feel that we may all find a message of encouragement in the lines which I would like to say to you.'

They weren't really at war, Fran thought. Of course they were at war, but as yet there hadn't been any fighting. Not like the stories of the 1914–18 war which her father had told her, the young men marching off to Europe with their guns and their songs. Of course there had been fighting, she reminded herself, but there hadn't been the bombing and the parachute landings they had all feared.

'I said to the man who stood at the Gate of the Year, "Give me a light that I may tread safely into the unknown."'

Fran pulled herself out of her thoughts and listened to the wireless. The voice was suddenly different, stronger, more fluent.

'And he replied, "Go out into the darkness, and put your hand into the Hand of God. That shall be to you better than light, and safer than a known way."'

The speech ended and the national anthem began. Without saying a word Jack rose from the table, went to the scullery, pulled on his coat and boots, and stepped outside. When Fran looked ten minutes later he was standing by the oak at the top of the field, hands in pockets, staring across the fields and river to the church below. She put on an overcoat and went to him.

'What is it, love?' She slipped her hand through his arm.

'I was wondering whether I should join up.'

'You've already asked – Ted as well. Farming's a reserved occupation, they won't have you.'

'So what do I tell Boy Jack when he asks?' What do I tell myself, she knew he really meant.

'Come on,' she tried to shake him out of it. 'It probably won't come to that. Chamberlain will sort something out.'

They walked back to the farm, collected the presents for Ted and Sarah's family and set off across the track at the top of the field. The light was gone from the day. Funny times, thought Fran, and wondered how they would look back on them, if Chamberlain really would sort it out.

The boys were running ahead of them. Just like his grandfather, Jack remembered he had thought of his son, just like himself, the way he ran, the way he behaved – not merely *like* him, almost as if he *was* him.

In front of them the boys disappeared into the darkness.

In seven days' time, Jack thought, it will be 1940.

THE WINTER SUN was shining over the ponds in front of the house. It was half-way through January, already the new year had come and gone. Churchill lit his second cigar of the morning and invited Drake to lead the discussion. It would be the last meeting at Chartwell. When the spring came even the ponds would be concealed from the air, though Churchill would keep open one of the small cottages in the grounds for his occasional personal use.

'The basic assumption', Drake began, 'is that even if Britain was invaded, it would continue the war against Hitler. The organization would be divided into three distinct sections.'

Outside there was still hope of peace, still the deceptive void of the Phoney War. Yet he was already planning for the unthinkable that would follow defeat.

'The first would be the actual fighting units. Their function, in the event of invasion and the enemy obtaining a foothold, would be to slow down his advance. For this reason the initial units would be based on a line five to ten miles inland round the south and east coastlines, expanded later.' He anticipated Ironside's intervention and moved to circumvent it. 'Some would assume that the enemy could not be held at its landing points and that the army would be retreating. This assumption is invalid.' His voice was emphatic. 'What it does assume is that if the enemy did succeed in establishing a beachhead and the army, for reasons outside its own control, could not hold it at that point, then the army might consider an orderly withdrawal to a GHQ line of its choice which CIGS would decide was the crucial line of battle.'

Churchill's silence invited him to continue.

'The second section would be Intelligence, the gathering of information on enemy troop movements and strengths.' He glanced at Ironside. 'Vital for the type of decision you might face.'

The general nodded his agreement.

'The third section would be Communications, the link between the Intelligence system and GHQ.' There would be refinements in the future, he anticipated, possibly a radio system for the fighting units. But at present there was neither time nor resources for anything else.

'Each system would be totally separate. Intelligence and Communications would obviously know of each other, though neither would know the personnel involved or details of where they were based or how they operated. Neither of them would know of the fighting units, and the fighting units would not know of their existence. Nor would one fighting unit know details of any other.'

It all seemed so straightforward, yet only when Drake looked round the table was he aware of the implications of what he was proposing: an organization so secret that only a handful of people would know of its existence, against a background which precluded the Prime Minister from being amongst those who knew.

For one long terrible moment he hesitated. Then Churchill sat back in his chair, drew on the cigar, and resolved the doubt.

'And who will you recruit?'

Until now they had used the conditional, the word *would*; until now they had merely been discussing the theoretical possibility of such an organization in Britain. Now Churchill had used the word *will* for the first time.

'In the initial fighting units farmers, gamekeepers, poachers, people who know the land. Cell leaders first, let them select their own people from their own kind.

'In the Intelligence system, people whose jobs mean they can travel locally without suspicion – doctors, midwives, postmen and the like.

'In Communications, women, the ATS and the FANYs; the army will be too hard-pressed for us to recruit men from its ranks.'

Churchill left the table and walked to the windows.

'A name?' Ironside asked. It was the first time anyone other than the First Sea Lord or Drake had spoken. 'It will need to be run-of-the-mill, as if it were an off-shoot of a regular formation.'

'Auxiliary Units.'

'Operational code names will also have to be innocuous.'

'Local names to coincide with the local area. Fruit and vegetables in the country, industrial names in the towns, so they can be slipped into conversations without rousing suspicion.'

At the end of the room Winston Churchill was staring across the countryside, as if envisaging the moment when such an organization might be called upon to act and trying to comprehend what it would mean.

'I assume, Mr Drake, that you have already begun to put your plans into operation?'

'Yes.'

'And when, may I ask, will we know the details of them?'

Churchill was still staring out the window.

'Never, sir.' All eyes except Churchill's were suddenly on Drake. 'If the organization you have asked me to create is to succeed, even to survive, it must be so secret that not even you must know its details.'

The silence seemed to last for ever. Slowly Churchill turned from the window and looked at him.

'Splendid.'

Mary Atkinson saw the door of the house open and the four men leave, The Old Man shaking hands with each and watching as they walked to their cars.

Whatever they were planning, she suddenly thought, however important it was, it was all based on the single unspoken assumption that when it was necessary Churchill himself would be Prime Minister.

4

WALTER SCHELLENBERG'S FLIGHT to Munich left Berlin's Tempelhof airfield at ten. He spent the time reading the file his office had prepared on the man named Wilhelm Richter, a precis of which had been forwarded to *Reichsführer-SS* Himmler following their discussion on the British monarchy, and working through the minutest detail of the roadblock that would end Richter's evening. When he arrived at the Vier Jahreszeiten, Schellenberg confirmed the dining arrangements personally with the manager, then took lunch. At two-thirty he briefed the team responsible for the events which would unfold, apparently haphazardly, in exactly eight and a half hours' time.

The vehicle he had specified was large and black. At four-thirty he left the hotel and was driven to the corner overlooking the house. Outside was parked a small off-white family saloon. As Schellenberg's car turned into the street the saloon pulled away and the car he had selected took its place.

Persuasion, Walter Schellenberg had long learned, was seldom achieved by a single element – more often by a combination of factors from the complexities of flattery, greed or sexual lust to the simple desire to abide by straightforward bureaucratic rules. The one element against which all others worked best, however, was that which he exercised to perfection, that of fear. The only thing Wilhelm Richter would notice when he returned home in half an hour, would be the unmistakable black Mercedes of the *Sicherheitsdienst*.

Schellenberg left the car, went up the steps and rang the doorbell. It was answered by a maid.

'Good afternoon. My name is Schellenberg. Is Herr Richter in?'

'I'm sorry, Herr Richter is not home from work.' She had not yet seen the Mercedes or the man sitting at the wheel with the long overcoat and the trilby. 'Perhaps you could come back.'

He reached into the inside pocket of his coat and held the badge in front of her. 'I assume Herr Richter will be home at five-thirty as usual. Perhaps I could wait for him.'

The maid saw the car behind him. He stepped inside. 'Frau Richter and the children are still on vacation?'

'Yes.' She wondered how he knew, then realized that he knew everything.

Wilhelm Johan Sebastian Richter left his office, took his customary glass of Pils with a schnapps chaser at the usual bar, and drove home. The afternoon was grey, matching his mood, the rain beginning to fall. His wife and children had been on holiday for two weeks now. He disliked their being away, but what he objected to more was that they were with his wife's parents, fully aware how they despised him because he had neither the wealth nor the influence that his ancestry suggested.

He turned into the street and saw the Mercedes. It had stopped raining, started again; he switched on the windscreen wipers, turned them off then on again, tried to work out what the car was doing and why they had come for him. A mistake, he tried to convince himself, nothing to do with him at all. He parked behind the car, walked up the steps, feeling for the keys, and glanced back. Slowly and deliberately the driver turned his head and stared at him then looked back at the road. No mistake, Richter knew. He stepped into the room, shouted for the maid and saw the stranger.

'My dear Herr Richter.' Schellenberg's voice was friendly, amplifying the confusion. 'I really am so sorry to intrude like this.'

Richter did not know how to react or what to say.

'My name is Walter Schellenberg. I'm from Berlin.'

Richter muttered the first thing which came into his head. 'Just passing through Munich?'

'No. I came to see you.' The reply was devastating, the pause which followed it deliberate. 'As Frau Richter and the children are away, I wonder if you might join me for dinner?' There was no explanation and no option. 'Shall we say the Vier Jahreszeiten at seven-thirty?'

'Of course.' Richter's disorientation was total.

'In that case I'll arrange a car.'

'I have one.' Richter heard the panic in his voice and felt the turning in his bowels.

'Oh no, my dear chap, I couldn't put you to so much trouble. Besides, the hotel is so terribly good at that sort of thing.'

It was only when Schellenberg had gone that Wilhelm Richter realized his visitor still had not told him why he had come.

SCHELLENBERG WAS WAITING in the cocktail bar when Richter arrived, the champagne already on ice. He rose and shook his hand.

'My dear Richter, so glad you could make it.' He gestured to the waiter to open the bottle. 'I do apologize for bursting in on you like that this afternoon, but I wasn't sure about catching you.'

The man knew everything, Richter was still thinking: where he lived, what time he would be home, even the fact that his wife and children were away.

'Good God!' It was as if Schellenberg had just realized. 'I still haven't told you why I'm here.'

'No.' Richter's bowels had not stopped moving.

Schellenberg waited until their glasses were filled then leant forward. 'It's hardly a military secret that there may come a time when, despite our best intentions at peace, we have to push west. I have been assigned the task of analysing where problems in logistics might occur.' He saw the first relief seep into Richter's body. 'You were involved in this type of thing in fourteen-eighteen. It seems to me, therefore, that you are the obvious person to tell me where those sort of problems occurred last time.'

'Of course. Yes, of course.' It did not occur to Richter to question why the *Sicherheitsdienst* should be involved in logistical planning.

The manager approached them, waited until they turned to him, and offered them the menu. Schellenberg thanked him. 'I believe you know my guest.'

'Of course.' The manager had never met Richter. 'May I say what a pleasure it is to have you in our hotel, Herr Richter.'

For the first time since he had seen the Mercedes outside his house Richter began to relax. 'My pleasure. How good it is to see you again.'

Schellenberg glanced through the menu then looked up at the

manager. 'Perhaps we could ask what you would recommend.'

'If I may say so, the oysters are particularly fine tonight and the venison really is rather good.'

'In that case, perhaps we might leave the wines to you as well.' There was the slightest hint of camaraderie in the way Schellenberg glanced at Richter.

The quarry relaxed a little more. 'I think that would be an excellent idea.'

The manager bowed and left, and Schellenberg resumed their conversation.

'The trouble is that while there is a great deal to be learned from the past, most people are too hidebound or prejudiced to recognize the value of it.'

Wilhelm Richter remembered the attitude of his wife's family. 'I agree.'

If only it could always be so simple, Schellenberg thought.

After ten minutes the manager informed them that their table was ready. When they followed him through to the restaurant, Richter noted with satisfaction that they had not only been afforded the best table but that the personal attention they were so clearly receiving was drawing looks both from guests and staff.

He also found it satisfying, when they discussed Schellenberg's project, how much he remembered, how much he actually knew about the subject – how much, as the evening progressed, his ideas of twenty years before matched those of Schellenberg today. It seemed totally natural, therefore, that he began to enjoy the conversation, especially when it changed from a discussion of military logistics to a more general discussion of values and the position of an individual within society: how an individual might be outstanding, have much to contribute, yet not be recognized; even worse, be treated in a manner in which formal manners were a shell of lies covering a slurry of spite and envy.

As the evening drew to a close it was Richter, or so it seemed to him in hindsight, who suggested that the meeting had been so valuable that it should be repeated.

'There is only one problem –' Schellenberg indicated to the waiter that his guest should have first choice of cigars – 'I'm afraid it might mean you nipping up to Berlin once in a while.'

It was already arranged, from the office Richter would occupy, to the documents he would be given with the 'Top Secret' stamp across the top and the signature of the Führer at the bottom, even to the texture and colour of the underwear which the upper-class whores who would be available to Richter in Salon Kitty would or would not wear according to his proclivities.

'I think I could manage a couple of days in Berlin.' Richter selected a cigar and rolled it affectedly between his fingers. At the side of the table the waiter poured them another brandy. In the side streets the cars began to assemble. 'Yes, I think a couple of visits to Berlin would be quite in order.' Richter sat back and indicated to the waiter that his should be a double. At the junction of Karl-Theodore-Strasse and Belgradstrasse the teams checked their radios and eased their vehicles into position.

At ten minutes to eleven, when they rose from the table and walked to the foyer, Schellenberg insisted that his driver take Richter home, Richter pretending to protest then accepting, allowing Schellenberg to escort him to the vehicle. The Mercedes was large and comfortable. Schellenberg's driver held the rear door open for Richter, Schellenberg shook hands and told him how much he had enjoyed the evening, then welcomed Richter's response when he suggested they would be in touch with each other soon.

It was five minutes to eleven. At the corner of Rechte Wiese and Kleine Wiesen Platz and in the side streets behind, the teams moved to stand-by.

The SD driver drove quickly, overtaking swiftly and confidently. The first car edged in front of them, Richter, half asleep on the back seat, not noticing, and the other cars closed around them.

It was eleven o'clock exactly, they reached the junction of Karl-Theodore-Strasse and Belgradstrasse.

Richter felt the sudden braking and jerked out of his stupor. He leaned forward and saw the headlamps, the vehicles slewed across the road in front of them, blocking their way, the men in the long leather coats pulling open the doors of the car in front and dragging the driver and passengers out. The fear returned, total, terrible. His bowels were churning and the brandy turned acid in his throat. He remembered the rumours about the camp at Dachau, on the outskirts of the city, and felt the sudden wet in his trousers. The men in the long coats were coming forward, surrounding the Mercedes, guns on him. I'm a colleague of Herr Schellenberg's – his mind was racing –

you can check with him at the hotel, get him to confirm that everything is all right. They were around the car, he could see their faces through the rain.

Without even looking at them the driver wound down his window, reached inside the pocket of his jacket with his left hand, right still on the steering wheel, withdrew a small leather holder and raised it to the window, holding it open with two fingers so they could see his identification. The reaction was immediate, the men standing back and snapping to attention, the cars in front of them pulling out of their path, tyres screaming. The driver eased his foot off the clutch and accelerated through.

For the first time in his life Wilhelm Richter experienced the almost sexual thrill of absolute power.

5

WILLIAM DONOVAN LEFT New York on 28 January and arrived in Germany on 14 February, Konrad Fuchs having requested that the lawyer grant him three days in the middle of the frenetic commercial schedule imposed upon him by his Wall Street clients: two days to travel to and from the village of Adelboden, outside Munich, where Fuchs' family retreat was situated, and the day between to visit the place Fuchs wished to show him but which he declined to name.

By the time Donovan's train reached Munich it was already dark, the snow lying in the streets and upon the roofs opposite the station. The connecting train to Adelboden was scheduled to leave in half an hour. Donovan took a schnapps and coffee, and wondered again why Fuchs had invited him, why he had agreed to come.

The Adelboden train was less grand than the express from Berlin, but left on time, the lights of the city soon behind and the darkness of winter immediately closing in so that Donovan could see nothing of the countryside through which they were travelling. Two hours later, having stopped at a number of other towns and villages, each seemingly smaller than the one before, the train pulled into Adelboden. The platform was deserted except for one man, and the name of the village was on a wooden board. Donovan was the only person to step down from the train.

'Herr Donovan?'

The man took his case and escorted him through the small wooden office, where an official checked his ticket, to a Mercedes parked outside. The engine was running and the car was warm.

63

Twenty minutes later the headlights picked up the open gates at the bottom of a drive, the driver swung through and they stopped at the foot of the steps into the house.

Konrad Fuchs was waiting for him in the hall.

'Mr Donovan, I'm so glad you made it.'

A manservant took Donovan's case from the driver and carried it upstairs.

'A quick drink to warm you while Franz runs you a bath, then dinner.'

The room in which they ate was oak panelled, a log fire roared at one end and the walls were lined with the heads of animals, the Prussian austerity broken only by an occasional family photograph of Fuchs, his wife and their two children.

'The house was originally a hunting lodge.' Fuchs noted Donovan's interest. 'It has been in my family for a hundred and fifty years.' He laughed. 'The story goes that my great-grandfather won it gambling. I use it both for family holidays and as a retreat.'

'Why have you asked me here?' Donovan closed the pleasantries.

'Tomorrow I will show you something, then you will better understand what I have to tell you.'

For the next hour they discussed general matters, each man delving gently into the other's background, Donovan replying guardedly to Fuchs' questions about his career as a lawyer and politician, and Fuchs describing briefly his job as a scientist. At ten Fuchs suggested that because of their early start in the morning his guest might wish to retire.

Donovan woke at seven, bathed, dressed and went downstairs for breakfast. The log fire was still blazing but the room felt cold. Fuchs was seated at the head of the table, a cup of coffee in front of him. In place of the casual suit which he had worn the evening before he was now dressed in the black uniform of an honorary colonel of the SS, the jackboots polished and glistening. Apart from the formal courtesies they breakfasted without speaking, Fuchs' unexpected appearance intruding upon whatever relationship they had formed, and Donovan querying his judgement in agreeing to the meeting.

When they left the hunting lodge the day was breaking, the snow silent round them. Both men sat in the back of the Mercedes but still did not speak. They had been travelling for eighty minutes when Fuchs ordered the driver to stop and stepped out of the car. The road was deserted and the air was cold, his breath forming clouds. He went to the boot, took out the greatcoat and cap and put them on, and requested Donovan to put on his overcoat and a trilby he gave him.

'Whatever happens, stay close by me and say nothing.'

Donovan did as Fuchs instructed, then both men returned to the car and the driver pulled away. The sky was clear blue and the snow lay on the trees, the icicles hanging like ear-rings from the branches. It occurred to Donovan that he had never seen such a beautiful morning. Through the naked trunks and stems on the left he saw the barbed wire.

'Remember, say absolutely nothing.'

They came past the end of the trees and he saw the double layer of the perimeter fence, the dog run between the two lines of wire and the watchtowers every thirty yards. Military establishment – the thought was automatic. He wondered why Fuchs was bringing him here. In front he saw the gatepost. The machine guns on the watchtowers faced in, he suddenly realized. The driver stopped at the gateway. Fuchs straightened his cap, stepped out of the car and strode forward in the same arrogant manner in which he had conducted himself at the Embassy reception, his hands clenched behind his back and his shoulders straight.

The bastard – Donovan watched as Fuchs waited in front of the wooden and wire gate with the offices on either side and the guards clustered around it – he really damn well loves it. The officer in charge left the gatehouse, saw the black of Fuchs' uniform and the insignia of his rank, and snapped into the Party salute, Fuchs doing likewise.

On the archway above the gate Donovan saw the words and tried to translate them: *Arbeit Macht Frei* – Work Makes Free.

Fuchs spun on his heels, returned to the car and the gate was pulled open. Only when they were inside could Donovan appreciate the organization of the establishment to which Fuchs' SS status had gained them entry. The camp, he estimated, was six hundred yards long and three hundred yards wide. Inside the perimeter fence, and running its entire length, was a strip of grass some fifteen feet wide, then a roadway. In the centre, placed in grids down and along the camp and each identical, were rows of huts, more roadways between them. What he assumed to be the administrative block was along the top of the camp on his right. Above the cluster of trees in the bottom left corner rose a tall chimney.

No soldiers except for those on sentry duty, Donovan thought, no tanks or training equipment. Fuchs instructed the driver to turn left down the first road between the huts and Donovan saw the men. They were like skeletons, their heads shaven, and their eyes large and white. Even from inside the car Donovan could see that the coats and trousers they wore gave no protection at all from the cold, and they shuffled as if they had lost all hope. At the corner of one block a line of men were climbing into the backs of the convoy of waiting lorries. As he watched, one of the guards began whipping a man who had fallen in the snow. From another block he saw two prisoners pushing a handcart with a pile of bodies and limbs tangled on it. In the clear blue sky above the chimney Donovan saw a thin line of yellow smoke.

'Right at the junction, right again, then right at the top to the gate.'

The bastard, Donovan thought again, so many men – hundreds, thousands of them – yet the bastard hasn't even noticed them or been affected by their condition.

The driver straightened the car and slowed for the gates; the guns and watchtowers facing in, Donovan remembered, beginning to realize. The barrier in front of them was still closed, Fuchs wound down his window and waved his gloves at the gate officer. The barrier opened and they drove out. A mile down the road Fuchs ordered the driver to stop, stepped out of the car, and removed the greatcoat and cap.

'Where have we just been?' Donovan stood beside him and tried to come to terms with what he had just seen.

'Dachau.' Fuchs folded the coat and placed it in the boot.

The morning was even more beautiful than before but Donovan no longer noticed. 'I'm sorry.' He was unsure how to say it. 'I misjudged you totally.'

Fuchs closed the boot and looked at him. 'I hope that most people continue to do so.'

THE LOG FIRE was roaring at the end of the room. Both men had bathed and changed. Fuchs poured them each a drink and sat down.

'What is Dachau?' Donovan accepted the glass.

'Dachau is a camp for the political opponents of the Führer. It was built in 1933, as soon as the Party came to power. It is also a model for the future.'

'And what is the DEST?'

'When the *Deutsche Erd und Steinwerke, GmbH*, the German Clay and Brickworks Company, was formed, one of its first commercial transactions was the purchase of brickworks and stone quarries in Germany. As Hitler has expanded outside the Fatherland, so has the DEST.'

'And will do so in each of the countries which Germany takes over?'

'Precisely.' He stood up, looking at the fire.

Donovan waited.

'There are two distinct problems: the first is that the state has a large number of political prisoners and the second is that its industry is suffering from a shortage of labour. The obvious solution, to use the prisoners as labour, is not necessarily satisfactory because what the state would really like is to see them dead. It was the DEST which came up with the solution.' He warmed his hands against the fire. 'You want to kill a man but you also want him to work for you; if you kill him he cannot, yet at the same time you want him dead.' He shook his head in disbelief. 'The solution is both evil and brilliant.' He looked at Donovan. 'There is a formula, written or unwritten I do not know. You give a man enough food to work on, but not enough to live on. Eventually he dies, but before that he has worked for you.'

Donovan could not believe it. 'And this is happening?'

'In small ways. The system will expand in the future.'

'What is it called?'

'We are a logical race. You concentrate people in camps to achieve this, so you call such places concentration camps.'

'Death camps?'

Fuchs shook his head. 'No, that would not be logical. Death camps are where you would send people simply to exterminate them, without wishing to get work out of them.'

'And what is Dachau?' He remembered the faces of the men.

'At the moment Dachau is still for political prisoners, the process is only just getting under way. In the end camps like it will be built where a labour shortage exists. Quarries, armaments, it really doesn't matter.'

'For example?'

'The brick factories run by the DEST at Neuengamme and Sachsenhausen, or the synthetic rubber factory near Auschwitz.'

Donovan fell silent again. 'So why are you telling me this?' he asked at last.

'Because you are an American who has access to the President. Your government knows about Dachau and where it will lead, the British also, but nobody is prepared to stand against what is already happening or to recognize its consequence. In the end, when the war is over and if Germany loses, then you will blame us for what happened, but you will be equally responsible for allowing it.'

Donovan rose and walked down the room. 'I will speak to President Roosevelt.' They both knew what he was saying: *I will speak to the President, but in the end there is nothing he can do except wage war on Hitler, and the American people and its Congress have determined a course of neutrality.* He remembered what else Fuchs had said, about a solution to what in Berlin Donovan had taunted him with as the Jewish problem, remembered the man and woman running for their lives in the street, and how the diplomat had rebuked him.

'If there's anything else I can do.' He knew how it sounded, saw again the lorries at the top of the street and the child the man was carrying. American neutrality, the man from the Embassy had insisted, none of our business. He turned away in shame.

6

THE RESTAURANT WAS quiet, the table in the corner farthest from the
window. It was six-thirty in the evening, they would leave before
most other people arrived. Drake waited until the waiter had taken
their order.

'You've thought about what I asked?'

'A great deal.'

The guest was one of several Drake had entertained, the identity
of each known only to himself, none of those he was meeting knowing
even the smallest detail of the others and some not even assuming
there would be others.

'And you have made a decision?'

'Yes.'

It was three weeks since the first approach, two since the meeting
at which Drake had outlined his plans and detailed the role of the
other person in them.

'It's not just me. If that was the case the answer would be different,
but I have a family.'

The waiter brought their first course.

'I understand.'

At eight-thirty that evening Drake left London and drove west,
staying overnight in Oxford and continuing his drive the following
morning. Shortly after ten he reached the village of Highworth,
almost lost in the folds of the Cotswolds, and parked in front of the
post office.

The village streets were empty and cold. Outside the Saracen's

Head a man was pulling sacks of coal from a lorry, his body bent double and the leather draped over his back black with dust. In the square where the market had been held on the first day Drake had come to Highworth there was only one old man, a dog curled at his feet.

The entrance to the post office was through a narrow passage, the name of the post mistress in neat white lettering on the sign above the door. Its bow window, the white paint peeling, protruded onto the pavement, and the church tower was just visible above the row of shops opposite.

Drake glanced through the window and went inside, the ceiling so low that instinctively he ducked. At the counter a young woman was buying a stamp and talking to the post mistress. Only when the customer had gone did he turn to the counter.

'Very soon now, Mrs Stranks.'

The post mistress was in her late fifties with white-grey hair, a gentle smile on her face, the hardness not showing in her eyes. She had seen his car the moment he had stopped outside but had given no indication to the customer that she knew him.

'I'll be waiting for them.'

He returned to the car, drove out of the village and headed north. At the foot of the next hill he crossed the stone bridge over the river and began to climb into the village of Coleshill, the church on the left. At the top he turned right, through the large wrought-iron gates, and almost immediately swung left, the stable block on his right, and followed the sweep of the drive until it stopped in front of the house.

Coleshill House had been built by Inigo Jones as a Palladian manor. Now the gold dome with which he had topped his creation had been wrapped in blankets, whether from the threat of the enemy or of the men he would soon send there Drake was unsure.

The army captain who met him was in combat gear.

'How's it going?' Drake knew that his entry into the grounds had been monitored.

'Almost ready. Self defence and weapons training, sabotage and demolition.' They walked up the steps and into the dining-room in the section of the house they occupied. 'The assumption is that they'll be operating mainly at night, so we'll train them for that, either during the night or during the day wearing goggles. That way they can practise and we can see where they're making mistakes.'

Drake nodded.

'The railway yards at Swindon are only ten miles away, useful for teaching them how a railway line is put together.'

'And taken to pieces?'

The captain grinned.

After lunch they inspected the outbuildings and woods, then Drake drove to Hannington Hall, five miles west of Highworth. He stayed until shortly after five, then began the drive to Haverhill, close to the east coast, stopping overnight in Cambridge. He spent the following night in Essex, confirming the arrangements at the farm, then turned south.

The man he planned to see, like all those he would visit in the following days, did not know he was coming. When Drake called at the house, shortly after midday, the man's wife informed him that her husband was out but that he would be back at four. Drake thanked her and went to the pub in the middle of the village. When it closed he left the car outside and spent the next ninety minutes examining the village and the roads leading to and from it, the green opposite, the cricket pitch to the rear and the church half a mile away, the trees and river behind it.

THE SHOPPING BAG was piled with groceries. Fran watched as Harry Downton added up the prices he had marked in pencil on the back of the paper bag, trying to match his speed.

'Jack busy again, I suppose?'

'Jack's always busy.' She knew he was trying to confuse her.

'That'll be seven and ninepence.' He was always quicker than she was.

She handed him the ration book, and found three half-crowns and a threepenny piece to pay him.

'Thank you, Mrs Masters.' There was almost a smile of triumph on his face. 'See you next time.'

Ted and Sarah were waiting in the pick-up, looking tired. Ted had not shaved that morning and Sarah's eyes were red. They saw her coming and opened the passenger door, Sarah squeezing closer to Ted so that Fran could sit in the cab with them.

'Stan Bradley's in the money again, I see.' Ted's delivery was dry and sardonic. Outside the King's Arms was a sports car, its green bodywork splashed with mud.

Fran remembered what Jack had said about Stan's poaching. 'Not much good for ferrets, though.'

The lunch she had left Jack was still in the range, the plate still clean on the table. He worked too hard, she often told him, up at six, sometimes not even stopping to eat, particularly at this time of year when he was not only trying to finish the jobs that had accumulated through the winter but was up half the night with the lambing. It was the same with Ted and Sarah, the same with all of them. She took off her coat, unpacked the shopping, and began to make supper.

Boy Jack and Ernie came in an hour and a half later, Jack a full hour after that, tired and cold. He pulled off his boots, left them in the scullery and came into the kitchen in his stockinged feet.

'How's it going?' Fran took the supper from the oven and called the boys.

'Could be worse.' He washed his hands and sat down. 'Last night's lambs are all fine. Cows went through the hedge over by Ted's – had to spend half the morning getting them back.'

'So what are you doing tomorrow?' She spooned the potatoes onto the plates.

'I was going to Canterbury, but I'll have to mend the fence now.' She ladled the gravy over the meat and sat down.

'Stan Bradley's in the money. Either that or he's got rich relatives.'

'Why, what's Stan done now?'

She told him about the car parked outside the pub.

'All right for taking us to cricket,' Jack laughed. 'Better than sitting in the back of the pick-up. What sort was it?'

'Bentley Red Label open-bodied tourer. Bodywork by Park Ward. British racing green. Has to be pre-1931 because they dropped the red background on the car badge after the company was taken over by Rolls-Royce that year.'

They looked at Boy Jack in amazement.

'Ernie told me,' he admitted, the face of the boy at his side grinning in triumph. 'Passed it on the way home from school.'

EVEN AFTER THE sun crept over the hill the morning remained cold. Fran made her way across the fields to the point in the top pasture where she knew Jack would be working. As she approached she could see him crouched over the hedge, laying the branches, the old mack held in place by a length of baler twine round his waist. He heard her coming and looked up.

'Brought you some sandwiches and soup, knew you wouldn't make it back to the farm.'

'Thanks, love.'

He finished the section and rubbed his hands together. 'Chilly when you're not moving much.'

Fran handed him the thermos of soup, and the sandwiches wrapped in paper.

'Don't you stay, love, you'll get cold. I'll see you later.'

'All right. Don't work too late.'

He watched as she cut back across the top of the fields, then climbed through the hedge, sat facing across the slope and waited.

'Jack Masters?'

He did not move. 'Wondered if you were coming this way, saw you down at the bottom.'

There was no way he could have been observed, Drake knew.

Jack turned his head and looked at the stranger. 'Rooks. You unsettled them.'

Not enough to make them move, Drake knew, not even enough to make them change their call. He sat down.

A city man, thought Jack, yet not a city man. A man who was used to moving in the country, used to watching and waiting. Not a gamekeeper, more like a poacher. He wondered why the man had come and how he knew his name.

'That Fran? Boy Jack at school? How's Ernie settling in?' Drake reached into his pocket and handed the farmer an identification card.

Jack examined the card and handed it back. Defence Regulation 51B, he assumed, the army wanting to commandeer land. Compensation afterwards, but no good to him now when he needed the acreage. Not land, he suddenly thought, not a desk officer looking for sites for guns, then remembered what Fran and the boys had said about the car in the village.

'What do you think about the war, Jack?'

'I'm not sure.' He remembered the changing moods, the fear and despair when the Prime Minister had declared war in September, then the strange peace of the Phoney War. 'I don't think anyone is.'

'What do you think might happen this year?'

'I don't think even the government knows what might happen.'

The wedges of cheese in the sandwiches were as thick as the bread. He took one and passed the others to Drake.

'What if I said that Hitler has plans to invade Norway next month?' He took a mouthful of sandwich. 'That he intends to invade Holland, Belgium and France after?'

Jack knew the stranger expected him to ask how he knew, instead he poured a cup of soup from the flask and screwed the top back on. 'I don't think he does have those sort of plans.' He offered the cup to the other man. 'At least, I don't think the politicians and generals think he has.'

'What if I said that by next June, July at the latest, Hitler could be on the other side of the Channel? That by the autumn he might have invaded England?' The farmer was careful, just as Drake had been warned he would be.

I'd say that the politicians don't believe you, Jack thought. I'd say they still hoped they could talk their way into peace. I wonder who you really are and what you want. 'What about the British Expeditionary Force?' he asked instead. 'What about the other armies, the French and the Maginot Line?'

'But suppose the British and their allies couldn't hold Hitler? Suppose the Germans came through the Maginot Line where it was weakest, even round it?'

'So what do you want?'

'I'm recruiting.'

'For what?'

The soup was finished. Drake pulled a brandy flask from his pocket, undid the top and passed it to Jack.

'It might not be necessary,' he began. 'It might be that the politicians come to an agreement with Hitler. It might be that even if they don't, Hitler can be defeated before he reaches the Channel. It could also be that even if Hitler does invade, the army can hold him wherever and however he lands.'

But, thought Jack Masters.

'But if Hitler does get this far and the conventional forces can't hold him, or need help to do so, then it would be too late. We must start planning now.'

'So what are you recruiting for?'

'The British Resistance.'

Jack sat back and looked across the fields.

'What does it involve?'

'A network of small units, highly trained and well equipped. In the event of invasion and the army failing to hold the Germans on the coast, you wait till the enemy is over the top of you then come up. Try to delay them, destroy as many supplies and as much equipment as you could, sabotage petrol and munitions dumps, airfields, give the army time to regroup, to fight back.'

'Sounds a bit dangerous to me.'

'If invasion took place and you were called upon to act, your life expectancy would be four days, a week at the most.'

'What would I tell my wife?'

'Up to you.'

'Other people?'

'Nobody else must know anything.'

Jack broke the last sandwich in two, gave half to his visitor and began to eat the other. 'You're asking a lot.'

'I've asked a lot more of others.'

'How do I know you are who you say you are?' He wondered why he was inclined to believe the man. 'Anyone could have an ID card.'

Drake gave him the number of his office in London and told him to check.

'Not good enough, it could be any number, anyone could answer.'

'The Admiralty. Get the number yourself. Extension five three nine. Ask for *him*. If there's a query give the name Cromwell and say it's reference Sea Lion.'

When Jack returned to the farmhouse Fran was in the yard feeding the chickens.

'Cup of tea, love?'

'No, thanks. Just remembered something in Canterbury. Anything I can get you?'

Yesterday evening, she remembered, he had said he could not go.

'No, thanks.'

The tin in which they kept the loose money was in the kitchen dresser. He took a handful of coins, left the house, walked up to Ted and Sarah's and collected the pick-up.

The city was busier than he had expected, the soldiers from the barracks mixing with the locals. He parked by the station, went to the telephone boxes and dialled the operator.

'Good afternoon, can you give me the number for the Admiralty in London please?'

The operator told him the number. He inserted the money, dialled, heard the ringing tone and the connection and pressed button A.

'Admiralty. Can I help you?'

'Five three nine.'

There was a change in the woman's tone. 'Putting you through, sir.' He waited as she made the connection then heard the extension ringing.

'Private Office.' The voice was upper class and officious. He wondered whether he had the wrong extension.

'Is he there?' He wondered who *he* was.

'He's in conference. Who wants him?'

'Cromwell. Reference Sea Lion.'

For the second time Jack heard the change in tone. 'Hold please, I'll check.' There was the slightest delay. 'Putting you through now.'

'Yes.'

He recognized the voice immediately. 'Thank you,' he said and put the phone down.

The sun was setting over the Downs. He turned off the road and switched off the engine. In the distance he could see the Channel, could imagine Fran and Boy Jack and Ernie in the kitchen. 'Great, Dad,' Boy Jack had said as he held the yacht up on Christmas Day. 'Really smashing.' He started the car, pulled back onto the road, and tried to work out how and what he would tell Fran.

IRONSIDE LEFT THE conference with Churchill and hurried to his car, aware that he was already late for his meeting that evening and still intrigued by the anonymous telephone call the First Lord of the Admiralty had received.

'Aldershot, Mary. Fast as you can.'

There was a military convoy in Whitehall – there seemed to be military convoys everywhere. She turned south of the river and was in Aldershot by six-forty. The sergeant was waiting for her.

'CO wants to see you, Atkinson. You can clean the car later.'

Mary cursed, thinking of the party to which she had been invited that evening, and went inside. The commanding officer's room was on the first floor. She knocked on the door, straightened her skirt, heard the order to enter, went in and stood to attention.

The commanding officer looked up. 'How long have you been with us, Atkinson?'

Mary wondered what the meeting was about. 'Six months, ma'am.'

'And you were with the FANYs before that?'

'Yes, ma'am.'

The colonel looked again at the paper in front of her. 'You've been asked to volunteer.' The woman's manner was brisk and to the point. At any other time, in any other year, Mary might have asked for what she had been asked to volunteer, who had suggested her. 'Interview in Harrods lounge, ten-thirty tomorrow morning. The sergeant has your travel warrant.'

THE KITCHEN WAS warm. Fran sat looking at the fire in the range and thinking about Jack. Ever since he had returned from Canterbury he had been almost lost in his thoughts. She wondered what it was that could preoccupy him so much and why he did not share it with her.

'I've been thinking, I think you should learn to drive.'

She looked at him in surprise. 'I already do. I can drive the tractor round the farm, even drive the pick-up a little.'

'I mean learn to drive properly, drive the pick-up on the road, go into Canterbury by yourself.'

'Whatever makes you say that?' What is it, Jack Masters? What is it you cannot tell me?

'In case something happens to me.'

'Why, what's going to happen to you?'

He still had not resolved in his mind how much he should tell Fran. 'In case I ever broke a leg, or if you fancied taking everyone to the sea one day.'

'Or in case you wanted help with the cricket club.'

'Not quite.' He realized how preposterous it sounded.

'I think it's a good idea.'

He pulled himself up from the chair. 'Time to check the lambs.'

The night was cold. One ewe was about to lamb, the feet already protruding. He knelt by the animal and eased the lamb out, standing back as the mother separated the membrane and began licking the newcomer, the lamb already trying to stand, already searching for the milk.

The ewe in the corner was distressed. Jack took off his coat, lathered soap over his arms and felt inside, the ewe too distraught to object. 'Twins, all caught up.'

Fran knelt beside him and held the feet as he tried to free the tangle of limbs and bodies.

'All right, pull a bit.'

He eased the legs together and she began to pull.

'It's coming.'

The head was beginning to show.

'Gently now, not too hard.' He was talking to himself as much as to her.

The first lamb slid out, the second following immediately.

'Damn!'

The second lamb was not breathing. Fran cleared the mucus from its mouth and nose while Jack checked that the first was well.

'Come on.'

She was already running across the yard and into the kitchen, holding the door for Jack as he carried the lamb in, and opening the lower oven of the range. Jack placed the lamb inside and stood up, leaving the door open. The sweat was pouring from him but his arms and hands were frozen.

'I had a visitor today.'

She put on the kettle. 'I know.' She saw the way he glanced at her. 'I didn't know you had a visitor, but I knew there was something.'

They sat at the table, willing the lamb to live and warming their hands round the mugs of tea.

'It's about the war.' He hardly knew how to begin. 'It's unlikely, but it seems there's a chance that by the summer Hitler will have conquered Holland, Belgium and France and will be at the Channel.'

Everybody still expected peace – if not peace then a quick and sudden victory. They had talked about it together and with Ted and Sarah, had assumed that if the Phoney War ended and the proper war began it would be fought in the trenches of France like the 1914–18 war.

'If he gets to the Channel, there's a possibility he'll invade.' He saw the incredulity on her face. 'In case there's an invasion they're organizing a Resistance.'

Of course they *had* thought about invasion, but only in the fear and panic of the previous September.

'Who's *they*?' she asked. 'The cricket club?' They both realized how laughable the conversation sounded.

Jack knew it was best to tell her from the beginning. 'This afternoon, after you brought the soup and sandwiches, I had a visitor.'

'The big car in the village?'

'He was recruiting.' He was unsure why he did not answer her directly.

'Why did he come to you?'

'No idea.' He knelt by the range and checked the lamb, then returned to the table. 'The idea is that if the enemy lands and the army can't hold him, then the Resistance will try to delay his advance, attack his supply lines, fuel and ammunition dumps, that sort of thing, to give the army time to reorganize and fight back farther up.'

Fran could still hardly believe what he was saying. Hitler would never get anywhere near the coast, the army would beat him in Europe, thrash him even before he left Germany. 'Who's *they*?' she asked again.

'The man who came works at the War Office. He showed me an identity card. Even though what he said seemed to make sense, I couldn't really believe it. It all sounded so ridiculous. Why has he come to me, I kept on thinking. What am I supposed to do? Here I am, working away, minding my own business, when suddenly someone I don't know comes up, tells me stuff that should be secret, and asks me to join some resistance movement in case Hitler conquers Europe and there's an invasion.'

She smiled at the way he told it. 'So what did you do?'

'I said anybody could have an identity card and he told me to phone the Admiralty in London.'

'Why?'

'So I could check that what he was telling me was the truth.'

'That's why you went to Canterbury?'

'Didn't want Quizzie Lizzie to listen in.' They both chuckled.

'And who did he tell you to speak to?'

'He didn't. He told me to find the number myself and gave me an extension to ask for. When they answered I was to give them a couple of words and just ask for *him*.'

'And who did you speak to?'

He thought again how absurd it sounded and wondered if even his wife would believe him.

'Winston Churchill.'

The lamb crawled out of the range and stood on the kitchen floor, bleating for milk. They pulled on their coats and Jack carried it back to the ewe, Fran going in front with the tilly lamp.

'Why weren't you going to tell me?'

After the warmth in the kitchen, the wind in the yard seemed even colder. They huddled together against the bales and watched the lamb suckling.

'Because they might torture you or Boy Jack for what you knew.'

In fifty years' time, she thought, nobody would believe that a husband and wife could have this conversation in a farm in Kent.

'But they would torture us anyway.'

THE LONDON TRAIN was crowded, but Mary found a seat and settled down. Opposite her a man in a bowler hat and city suit perched his *Daily Telegraph* on his gas mask box and turned to the crossword page. Twice during the evening before she had warded off questions about why she had been told to report to the CO, and when someone had asked her what she was doing the following day she had invented a story about the War Office without being quite sure why. In front of her the businessman solved the first clue and fiddled in his coat pocket for a pen. In fifty years, the thought made her giggle slightly, nobody would understand the spirit of a time in which a young woman was going to meet someone she did not know, for whatever reason she did not know, having been volunteered by someone whom again she did not know, except that it was all clearly secret and rather fun.

Waterloo was busy. She took the underground to Knightsbridge and arrived at Harrods fifty minutes before her appointment. There were sandbags at the entrances to the tube station and the doors of the store, and the windows were taped. She made her way to the lounge, sat in the corner and ordered tea.

On two occasions a young woman arrived, spoke to the head waiter and was directed to an ATS officer in the far corner who wore the insignia of a major on her uniform and tartan of the Clan MacDonald instead of a uniform skirt. At a quarter past ten Mary left the lounge and went to the powder room. When she returned the ATS officer was alone. Mary waited until ten-thirty then approached the woman.

'Miss Atkinson? Please sit down.' The major called for a fresh pot of tea. 'Thank you so much for coming, especially at such short notice.'

It was all too friendly, Mary thought instinctively.

'How long have you been with the FANYs now? Almost two years, isn't it?'

She waited for the trap. 'Since April 1938.'

A waiter brought the tea. 'Don't worry,' the ATS major smiled at him as he unloaded the tray, then at Mary. 'I expect we can manage, can't we?'

Mary smiled back.

'Milk and sugar?'

'Milk, thank you. No sugar.'

The officer poured a cup and passed it to her.

'You didn't have any trouble finding your way in the snow when you took General Ironside to Chartwell, then?'

It was not even part of the conversation, merely an interlude while the tea was being poured.

'I take a lot of people to a lot of places.'

The expression on the major's face barely changed. 'Toast and marmalade, perhaps?'

'Toast and marmalade would be very nice, thank you.'

JACK FINISHED REPAIRING the hedge and walked back to the track at the top of the field. Drake was waiting for him, though there was no sign of the Bentley.

'Getting warmer.'

He began to load the spare poles into the back of the pick-up. 'Especially when you're working.'

'You made the phone call then.'

'Yesterday afternoon.'

'But not from the village.'

'Canterbury. No point people here knowing my business.'

'And what did you tell your wife?'

'The truth.'

Drake had known he would.

Jack threw the last of the poles into the pick-up. 'So where do we go from here?'

'The village post office, Highworth, on the Swindon to Faringdon Road, four-thirty Thursday week. I'll get you some extra petrol coupons. You'll be free by the Sunday afternoon.'

THE PARTIES SEEMED as endless as they had been round Christmas and the New Year. The previous evening had not ended until two and Mary seemed to have spent the entire time dancing. She reported for duty at seven; at eight she had finished cleaning the general's car and was going for a cup of tea in the mess when she was told to report to the Warrant Officer. The woman was waiting in her office.

'Special Duties,' she said. 'Friday. Train to Marks Tey, in Essex, change onto the Cambridge line and get off at Haverhill. There'll be a car waiting for you outside the Rose and Crown.'

She handed Mary an envelope.

'Travel warrants. Make sure you catch the ten-twenty from Liverpool Street.'

She did not say, nor was she in a position to know, what Special Duties were, and Mary did not ask.

JACK LEFT HOME at ten in the morning; all the previous night he had worried about what he should say to Fran, yet in the end he merely said goodbye.

The post office was on the right side of the High Street as he drove down it. He arrived ten minutes before four-thirty, parked outside and entered the door in the alleyway on the right, noting the name of the post mistress, Mrs M. A. Stranks, on the sign above it.

Except for the white-haired elderly woman, the shop was empty. For one moment Jack thought he had come to the wrong place then saw that the woman was looking at him.

'Can I help you?'

He realized that he had not worked out what he would say, only thought that he had been told to report to the post office.

'I was told to come here.'

'If you would wait a moment.'

She disappeared through the door at the rear and dialled a number on the telephone clipped to the wall.

'There's a parcel for you.'

Without waiting for a reply she returned to the room. 'You came by car, could you leave it behind the church, then come back.'

She hadn't missed a thing, Jack thought. He did as she asked; when he returned to the post office an army lorry with a covered back was parked outside. The only identification it carried was a red and white plate on its front wing bearing the number 490.

THE TRAIN FROM LIVERPOOL Street took two hours and seemed to stop at every station. By the time she reached Marks Tey Mary was hungry and tired. She checked on the time, ran into the village, bought a cake and was back at the station five minutes before her connection.

The Cambridge train pulled into Haverhill at one-thirty-five. She left the station and walked to the Rose and Crown pub on the far side of the road. In the car park at the side was an army car with the number 490 on a white and red formation plaque on its wing. The engine was running and the rear offside door was open.

The driver said nothing. She got in, saying nothing herself, and the driver pulled away. For the next twenty minutes they drove through a maze of narrow lanes. Only when she was totally lost did they enter a large farmhouse set back from an isolated lane on the outskirts of a village. The driver stopped the car and escorted her inside, still not speaking.

How she longed for a cup of tea.

The officer who took charge of her was from the Royal Corps of Signals. 'This way.' Tea at last, Mary thought.

The room was empty except for a desk and chair. There were no windows. On the desk were a microphone and a red light. The officer told her to sit down and gave her a sheet of paper.

'When the light comes on, read this aloud.'

He went out and shut the door behind him. She tried to read the message on the paper and watch the light at the same time, but could not help thinking about how thirsty she was. Her throat and mouth were dry and the room felt as if it was closing in on her. The light came on and she began to read.

The passage took two minutes. When she finished the officer came back into the room with a cup of tea.

'Drink this, then the driver will run you to the station.'

THE DOOR WAS in the corner of the building, the barbed wire and the sentries he had negotiated behind him. Jack slid his fingers across the door until they made contact with the handle, the smoked glass of the goggles making it difficult for him to see, and wondered what awaited him in the room itself. There had been two initial training sessions at Coleshill, then more at the house in Kent called The Garth, on the edge of King's Wood outside Bilting. He checked around and behind him, turned the handle, and went in.

When the exercise was completed, he went into the part of the house used as a billet, collected his bag, and returned to where he had left the pick-up.

Drake was waiting for him. 'Time to start recruiting, Jack,' he said simply.

GENERAL IRONSIDE'S BRIEFING with the War Cabinet's committee on defences in the South of England finished at five. He stayed a further fifteen minutes, comparing notes with the other service chiefs present, then was driven back to GHQ Home Forces. Even in early evening the parade ground was busy; Mary stopped the car, opened his door and saluted.

Good girl, he thought, never let the side down, especially when it mattered. ''Bye, Mary,' he said for the last time.

She washed the car, filled it with petrol, and went inside. The travel warrant and instructions were waiting for her.

THE FIRST BUDS were opening on the oak at the top of the field. The air was warmer and the days longer, the light was already lasting until well into the evening, and the Downs were showing the first tinges of fresh green. Jack left the house and walked to the farm at the top of the track. Ted and Sarah had just finished supper.

'Fancy a pint?'

The two men left the house and walked across the fields towards the road bridge to the south of the village.

'Boy Jack sailed that yacht of his yet?'

'Last week. Went like a dream.'

'Good boy, that Ernie.'

'He's coming on.'

They crossed the bridge and turned towards the village.

'Called in to see you last Sunday. Fran said you were away.' It was almost as if Ted understood what he was going to say.

'Had to go somewhere.'

'Seem to have been away a lot recently.' They were walking together as they had done since boyhood, hands in pockets and side by side. 'We've known each other a long time, Jack. What's up?'

THE NIGHT WAS dark. He had been waiting behind the hedge since twelve, now it was almost four. For the three previous nights he had also waited: for Stan Bradley to leave the pub and do his poaching. For three nights Stan had locked up and gone to bed. Only on the fourth had he slipped out of the back door, the ferrets jumping in his sack, and disappeared into the black. In the silence Jack heard the gentlest of rustling and saw the shape two yards away.

'Hello, Stan. Good night's work?'

The man turned, suddenly dangerous, then realized who it was. 'Christ, Jack, you made me jump! Almost gave me a heart attack.' He thought he knew why the farmer was waiting for him. 'Not on your land, Jack, or Ted's.'

'I know.'

'So what the hell are you doing here at this time of night?'

THE ROLLER WAS heavy, the men grunting as they pulled it up and down the cricket pitch. It was two nights before the first practice and ten days before the opening friendly of the new season. In the corner of the field the boys were holding a game, a strange mix of East End and Kent accents, Ted coaching them.

Four in a patrol, Drake had told Jack: himself, now Ted and Stan. Still one other . . .

Behind the stumps Boy Jack took a return ball and whipped off the bails.

'Just like his old man,' somebody joked. 'Have to watch out for your place soon, Jack.'

There were plenty of men he could ask, plenty of men in the village who would say yes, but not many he could trust – not trust in the way most people would mean it. Most of the men, all of the men, in the village would stand in the streets and fight the Germans face to face – be prepared to die in the attempt. Trust in another way, trust to face not just the pressure of the training sessions at Coleshill House and The Garth but the pressure of keeping things to himself, of not being able to tell anyone.

The practice finished, the boys turned for home and the men drifted towards the King's Arms.

Ned would have done it, he thought, Ned would have been just the man, but the postman was too old, couldn't run fast enough, not even on the cricket pitch. And sometimes recently he had wondered whether Ned had something going just as Ted had suspected of himself.

'Cheers.' He raised his glass and heard in his mind the words of the King's speech on Christmas Day: *I said to the man who stood at the Gate of the Year, 'Give me a light that I may tread safely into the unknown.' And he replied, 'Go out into the darkness, and put your hand into the Hand of God. That shall be to you better than light, and safer than a known way.'* 'Sorry, lads.' He downed his drink and stood up. 'Something I've just remembered.'

The Reverend Brian Markham was eating his supper when Jack reached the vicarage.

'How's the cricket pitch shaping up? Sorry I couldn't make it. Had to go over to Bridge, poor old Mrs Frampton is in a bad way.'

For ten minutes, while the vicar finished his meal, they talked about the cricket club and the coming season, then the vicar led Jack into the sitting-room, asked his wife not to disturb them, and closed the door.

'Something on your mind, Jack?'

He was suddenly unsure what to say, knew that he was wrong, that he should not have come. 'It's about the war, about what we might be asked to do.'

The Reverend Brian Markham nodded his understanding. 'About standing up and being counted, perhaps?'

'Something like that.'

'But you're in a reserved occupation, which means that you will not be called upon.'

'Nor will you.'

'Stan Bradley's in the money,' Fran had joked the evening before the meeting with the stranger in the field. 'Either that or he's got rich relatives.'

86

'It was you he came to see, wasn't it?'

The smile on the vicar's face was not that which beamed down upon his congregation each Sunday morning and evening. 'He was at Cambridge with my older brother. Got to know him quite well. I was the one who recommended you to him.'

THE BUS RIDE from Swindon to Highworth took fifty minutes. Mary got off outside the market place and walked back up the High Street to the post office, noting the details above the door. The post mistress asked her name and disappeared into the back of the shop. The covered truck that arrived fifteen minutes later carried the identification number 490. The driver left Highworth and turned west. Twenty minutes later the truck stopped at a granite manor-house on the top of the hill just before the cluster of houses which formed the village of Hannington. Mary was escorted inside and given the single sheet of paper which would silence her for the rest of her life. Only when she had signed it was she informed of the existence of that part of the organization into which she had been accepted as a volunteer.

THE MEETING WAS like many of the meetings which Drake had had recently, the restaurant was quiet and the table was in the corner away from the window. Even the conversation was a replica of what had gone before.

'You've thought about what I asked?'

'I promised that I would.'

'And what have you decided?'

The infrastructure of each of the three sections of the Auxiliary Units was in place, those initially recruited had received at least some training and were recruiting others where necessary. Drake had briefed Churchill in general on the development of the project, withholding particulars as he had warned. There was one part of the British Resistance, however, about which he had told no one, not even The Old Man himself.

'You're asking a great deal.'

It was four weeks since the first approach, three since the meeting at which Drake had detailed his plans and the role of the other person in them.

'I'm asking for everything.'

'But not only if invasion takes place. You're also asking for everything before.'

'I am aware of that.'

Of the thirty-six people he had approached twenty-nine had said they would consider the request; of those, only thirteen had agreed to continue when they had been told what was involved. And of those thirteen, perhaps two, three at most, would come through when it mattered.

'No option is there really.' It was a statement rather than a question.

'It depends on what you think.'

His guest laughed. 'As I said, no option.'

'Thank you.'

'I suppose you've already decided on a code name.' It was only half a joke.

Two questions London would ask him about the documents the contact had given him Drake had thought the second time he had met the man on the Berlin S-bahn.

'When will you go into Norway?'

'Still undecided, probably April.'

'And Holland, Belgium and France?'

'Immediately after.'

'I thought the code name should be Prospero.'

AT SEVEN THE following morning Drake was woken by the ringing of the telephone. He rolled out of bed, crossed to the lounge and picked up the handset.

'Drake?'

He recognized Churchill's voice immediately.

'We're just getting word. Hitler's invaded Norway.'

It was Tuesday, 9 April 1940.

BOOK TWO

Invasion
April 1940 – September 1940

1

THE CLOUD WAS small and insignificant. Boy Jack and Ernie saw it when they went to help Jack feed the animals – hardly a cloud, just the slightest smudge of grey against the clear blue of the morning sky somewhere to the north-east. It was Saturday morning, the morning they enjoyed the most, no school and a cricket match in the afternoon. Fran watched them through the kitchen window. Sometimes it seemed as if Ernie had always been on the farm, yet it was only five months. She remembered the day in November when he had come, now it was almost the end of May and they were nearly through spring. Not just Ernie growing up so fast, but everything else happening so quickly.

The first reports in the newspapers of victory in Norway, then the sudden and unexpected defeat, the emergency debate in Parliament and the call for the Prime Minister, Chamberlain, to go. The worry, if she had but known it, over what would happen to the Resistance if Churchill went with him.

Fran poured the tea and called the three of them into breakfast.

'Bit of cloud in the sky,' Boy Jack informed her.

'Hope it isn't going to rain,' Ernie added.

The evening match at Wootton, she thought, the policeman running onto the pitch with the news that Hitler had just invaded Holland and Belgium. The wireless broadcast by Chamberlain the same evening stating that he had resigned as Prime Minister and that Churchill had taken his place.

The match was due to begin at two-thirty. After lunch they all washed and changed, then walked with Ted and Sarah and their boys to the village.

'Cloud's still there.' Sometimes the conversation between Boy Jack and Ernie was like the discussions between the old men who sat in the sun on the bench outside the King's Arms. 'Not moved much though.'

The endless convoys of troops pouring through Kent to join the British Expeditionary Force, the soldiers young and laughing, waving and singing as they headed for the Channel.

As soon as play began, the wives set up the tables in the pavilion and laid the tea. The last Barham wicket fell and the men came off and sat round the table, Fran, Sarah and the other women pouring the tea and the boys clustered round the door and hoping for leftovers.

'The lads are doing well.' Harry Downton stretched across the table for a second slice of cake, ignoring the anxious looks of the boys gathered at the door and the sandwiches still on his plate. 'Read all about it in the papers.' He called for another cup of tea. 'Soon be over, you mark my words.'

The continued reports of British success against Hitler's blitzkrieg, then the wireless broadcast calling for Home Defence Volunteers. The first parade of the Ardley detachment, the men armed with broomsticks and drilled by the retired colonel, Harry Downton wearing an armband on which he had asked his wife to sew three stripes.

The tea ended and the match began again. It was almost unreal, Fran thought, the Phoney War over and now the real war in Europe, yet in England they were still playing cricket. She folded the tablecloth and tried to dispel the turning in the pit of her stomach whenever she thought about Jack.

When they returned to the farm that evening, the cloud was still in the sky; the next day it was slightly bigger, by the following morning it had grown. At midday on Monday, when Fran and Sarah went shopping in the village, they could hear the first sounds, the thud of the artillery and the faint but constant background noise of battle on the wind.

'Funny goings on at the coast,' Quizzie Lizzie at the post office informed them. 'They're commandeering all the pleasure boats there, fishing boats as well, anything that can put to sea. Nobody knows why, something about the navy can't get in close enough to the beaches.'

By the time they reached the farm Jack and Ted were back from Canterbury. 'Same stories in town,' Ted told them. 'The *Medway Queen* sailed this morning, four o'clock, all the shrimp boats from Gravesend as well, the cockle boats, the lifeboats, anything that can float.'

'Why?' asked Fran. 'Where are they going?'

'Something about the Expeditionary Force. Somewhere in France. Never heard of it before, place called Dunkirk.'

The evening was light. After the boys had gone to bed the two couples stood on the top of the hill and looked towards Europe, the sky to the east now thick with grey and the sounds of battle louder and closer.

The following morning, when Jack went to milk the cows, the pall of smoke hung above the Channel like a shroud. At two o'clock Ted came to the farm and told them that they should go to the main road. When Fran asked him why he said simply that they must see for themselves.

The lines of lorries crawling inland seemed unending. Some of the soldiers were almost naked, many clutched blankets round the remnants of their uniforms; the faces were fixed and shell-shocked, and their bodies exhausted with fatigue and despair, the eyes staring at the villagers clustered by the roadside. Hardly any of them, Jack noted, carried guns. Yet more soldiers were being taken from the coast by rail, Fran only half-heard Ted telling her, houses and barns near the main junctions were being converted into makeshift feeding stations.

'What is it, Jack?'

THE MOOD IN the war room was grim. Churchill waited while the brigadier read the latest report, his shoulders hunched and his face set.

'The evacuation of the British Expeditionary Force from Dunkirk began on 27 May and ended at four o'clock this morning. In the past eight days 345,000 men have been taken off. The last men came in from the front line at midnight.'

'How much equipment and arms did we manage to bring out?'

'Hardly any.'

'What about the French?'

'We evacuated a hundred thousand.'

'And how many did we leave on the beach?'

The brigadier looked down. 'Thirty thousand,' he said quietly.

CHURCHILL'S LAST MEETING of the day was at nine. Menzies arrived for it early, using the rear garden entrance to Downing Street. Exactly on time Churchill swept into the room, offered him a drink and then came to the point.

'Friends in Washington.' For many months now he had written regularly to President Roosevelt, sometimes informing him of the change of situation in Britain or encouraging Roosevelt's efforts to raise awareness of the growing threat in Europe. Often, and increasingly so in past weeks, he had sought to counter the advice he knew the President was receiving from the American Embassy in London and which Ambassador Kennedy was himself not inclined to gloss over in his discussions, both formal and informal, with British officials.

He put down his glass and passed Menzies a copy of a letter Kennedy had written to him stating the American's belief that Britain was ill-prepared for war and had shown little commitment to supporting its allies in Europe.

'I assume he says the same to Roosevelt, only stronger. He has already made public his feelings that the British Expeditionary Force was inadequate; the fact that it was forced to leave most of its weaponry on the beaches of Dunkirk will only strengthen his position. He will also choose to forget the fact that we evacuated one hundred thousand French troops and emphasize the fact that we left behind thirty thousand.'

'And this is the message which Washington is receiving from London?'

'Yes,' replied Churchill.

'But I thought that the military attaché was more inclined to support us and therefore provided a balance against Kennedy.'

'He was. He has since been replaced.' He brought them back to the reason for the meeting. 'Stephenson is on his way to New York to head the Securities Exchange Commission. His boat arrives the day after tomorrow.' The organization had recently been established to serve as the official front for British Intelligence in North America as well as a liaison point between the two countries. 'Who can he reasonably approach to represent our interests to Roosevelt?'

'Donovan.' There was no hesitation.

'Why?'

'To begin with, he and Roosevelt were at law school together and have maintained that contact even though Donovan is a Republican and Roosevelt a Democrat.'

Churchill refilled their glasses and waited.

'Donovan first came to Europe in 1914 to supervise the delivery of relief supplies to the German-occupied territories as part of a Catholic relief programme. Most of his war record after that is well known.' Even in Downing Street Menzies was reluctant to disclose an intelligence source. 'What is not known is that during this period Donovan was recruited as a courier in our White Lady network and worked for SIS until America entered the war.'

Churchill's surprise was genuine; Menzies wondered again how far he should go, even with the Prime Minister.

'Four years ago, at a time when intelligence from North Africa was particularly thin, he obtained permission from Mussolini to visit Ethiopia. His reports were of the greatest value.'

'But?'

'But although William Donovan is a friend of this country, he is first and foremost an American.'

THE SLAB OF iron was balanced precariously between the trees; they crouched round it while Brian Markham packed the gun cotton into position, inserted the detonator and snapped off the top, then ran for cover. Already the four had split naturally into two pairs: Jack and Ted, and Stan Bradley the publican and Brian Markham the vicar. It had not seemed strange to any of them that whilst they continued to address the vicar formally in the village, they slipped naturally into calling him Brian during the training sessions at The Garth.

There was a loud crack and the iron rose twenty feet in the air and dropped down again.

'Better than last time.' The instructor's humour was dry. The previous week Brian Markham had attached too much explosive and the iron had flown into the sky making them run for cover.

The exercise finished and they went to the kitchen.

'Operating base.' Jack led the discussion as Ted made a pot of tea. 'We need to decide on where we put our OB.'

Each of the Auxiliary Units had received the instruction and the specifications which accompanied it. The OB would be totally secret yet quickly and easily accessible; it would be entered by a concealed door with special mechanisms so that the entrance could not be accidentally opened; it would be large enough for the men to live in and to store the supplies and equipment they hoped they would sometime receive; they should be able to approach it either without being seen or without rousing suspicion or interest, and the concealed entrance should be so positioned that it could be entered without leaving footprints or other clues to its existence. It should be able to be constructed without rousing suspicion, and as most OBs would be underground, there should be a way of disposing of soil or chalk, again without arousing interest.

After twenty minutes they had reduced their options to two sites: one in the woods to the west of the village and the other beneath a ruined building to the south.

'There is a third, of course.' They looked at Brian Markham in surprise. 'Or at least there might be.'

'Where?'

'The church.' The vicar poured them each another mug of tea. 'Apparently there was once a crypt under the church, with a door to it in the side wall. Nobody used it, and when the pulpit was rebuilt they covered the door with panelling and forgot about it.'

'How do you know? I've never heard about it. Even my dad never mentioned it.'

It was almost time to start training again.

'When I first came I found a key which didn't fit anything. One day, when I was in Canterbury, I bumped into Mr Brown and asked him about it.' They all remembered the white-haired vicar who had served the parish for as long as anyone could remember. 'He said that he had been told the story by the vicar before him.'

They left the kitchen and returned to the demolition area.

When they met at the church the following evening the countryside was quiet and the birds sang in the trees between the churchyard and the river at the back. The upper walls were white and the lower covered in varnished panelling: the pulpit was against the side wall on the right as they looked towards the altar; the steps to it were wooden, with a handrail next to the wall. The wood was polished and seemed to shine uniformly with the wear of ages, but the lower section, when they examined it more closely, appeared slightly less old than the upper.

Brian tapped the panelling on the wall adjacent to the pulpit then eased his hand through the carved wood stays connecting the handrail to the stairs and tapped again; there was no difference in sound.

'Doesn't mean a thing,' Ted pointed out. 'All the panelling is laid off the wall anyway.'

They placed a carpet from the vestry on the stone floor so they would not mark anything and began to dismantle the stairs, trying to keep the lower section together and disconnecting the handrail from it. After ninety minutes they lifted the lower section away and removed the stays from below the handrail so that the panelling behind was exposed.

Fulcrum system, Jack was already thinking, the stairs and panel swinging out together when the entry point was opened but concealing it when it was shut. If they managed to find the door without taking the whole pulpit to pieces, he thought, *if* there was a crypt in the first place.

The panelling on the wall was in three-foot widths, the joins covered by wooden strips simply but finely carved. Gently, taking care not to mark any of the wood, Brian eased off the strips on either side of the panelling behind the stairs and laid them to one side. Then he slid a chisel behind the right edge of the panelling, pulled it off the wall slightly so that the heads of the nails were sticking out, and removed them.

JE, Jack noted the initials of the craftsman whose work they were now dismantling and wondered what his name was.

The vicar slid the chisel back under the right-hand edge of the panel and began to ease it slowly away from the wall. At first it seemed stuck, then began to give. Behind it they saw the stone and felt the disappointment.

'Keep going,' Jack told him.

The last of the sun was shining through the stained-glass windows of the west wall. The Twenty-third Psalm, Jack thought without knowing why, the last two lines:

And in God's house, for evermore,
My dwelling place shall be.

The vicar pulled the panel away and they saw the hole behind.

THE WOOD WAS empty.

Mary left the control station at nine, dropped down the hill, keeping to the trees, and turned into the village. The morning was sunny and warm. Already half-way through June, she thought, everything beginning to move quicker now, gathering speed. In the sky above the Channel, Max and Sandy and the other boys would be protecting the convoys the navy was insisting on pushing through the narrow straits between Dover and Calais. Each morning she worried about them, each evening when she managed to get off duty and went to the Black Swan she looked to see who was missing. Each night, when she could, she sat in the corner with them and the WAAF girls who manned the strange assortment of outposts springing up along the coast, and laughed and joked as if none of them had a care in the world.

Mrs Potter had her breakfast on the table – eggs from the chickens she kept in the back garden, sometimes bacon from the butcher's when the old lady managed to persuade him.

'Morning, Mrs P.'

'Morning, dear.' Mrs Potter was white-haired and frail looking. Her husband had died in the mud of the Somme when she had been thirty-three. 'Didn't overdo it last night, I hope?'

Mary had been billeted in the cottage five weeks. During that time Mrs Potter had never asked Mary what she did and Mary had never told her.

'You should know me by now, Mrs P., I never overdo it.'

There were six shifts a week, from eleven in the morning till nine the following morning, two hours between shifts to return to the billet, have a decent breakfast, wash some clothes, and return to the control station. Five girls to the bigger stations, three to those the size of the one at Wootton, two on duty at any one time and the third trying to sleep in the bunk at the back of the room. The information would come in, should invasion actually take place, from the intelligence network created round the country. Even when they rehearsed it, perhaps especially when they rehearsed it, Mary could not believe it was for real.

The control station itself, codenamed Cricket, was based in an inconspicuous green corrugated-iron shed, one door and no windows, in the woods above the village. The zero station, to which they would transfer in the case of invasion, was underground and entered by a concealed trap door a hundred yards away, close enough to reach if invasion came and the enemy closed in on them, far enough away to give them a chance of not being discovered until their work was done. The telephone and radio links in the control station were duplicated in the zero station, incoming from the agents in the field, outgoing to headquarters at Hannington Hall, the radio sets high frequency low power, broadcasting on sixty and eighty megacycles.

Mary washed her dishes, did her washing, wrung the clothes as dry as she could, then hung them on the line in the back garden. After Dunkirk, especially now the Luftwaffe was appearing in the skies, she wondered whether it would *really* happen. She said goodbye to Mrs Potter and returned to the control station.

THE MEETING BETWEEN the new Head of British Intelligence in America, Stephenson, and the Wall Street lawyer, Donovan, took place in the St Regis Hotel, New York, the morning after Stephenson arrived. It lasted three hours. Four days later the American President, Franklin Delano Roosevelt, entertained Donovan at the White House. The meeting took place in the Oval Office at six in the evening, Roosevelt having already worked an eleven-hour day and Donovan having travelled from New York.

Amongst the documents on the President's desk was the draft of a speech he would make the following day to the Pan American Scientific Congress already meeting in Washington. Those parts of the speech already finalized dealt with the German sweep across Europe and its political consequence; those on which work still remained concerned the role of the scientist, not only in the past but the future. Attached to the last sheet, though Roosevelt would not refer to them in the speech he would make, were three documents. The first was the report which the scientist Szilard had presented to the President ten months before; the second was the letter of support from the Nobel Prize winner Albert Einstein which had accompanied it, and the third was the latest recommendation from the Uranium Committee which Roosevelt had instigated as a result of that meeting.

For the first ten minutes they discussed the report which Donovan had submitted following his discussions with Konrad Fuchs in the hunting lodge at Adelboden, Roosevelt expressing his appreciation, even his sympathy, but pointing out the political realities of America's neutrality. In some ways, Donovan thought, it was a repetition of the conversation he had had with Fuchs after their visit to Dachau. Then Roosevelt turned the conversation to the purpose of the meeting.

'I have heard again from Winston Churchill.'

'And what's Winston saying now?'

A copy of the message was on the President's desk. 'He's asking for guns, ships, anything.' For the past three years Roosevelt had warned of Hitler in Germany and Mussolini in Italy. Now Hitler controlled Europe and Mussolini had joined him. 'The country is naked.'

He passed the telegram over the desk. Donovan read it without comment and handed it back. 'What about Kennedy?'

The President handed him a file from the drawer on the right of the desk. 'Ambassador Kennedy continues to be critical. The summary is on page nine.'

The report from the United States Embassy in London was a fuller version of the letter the Ambassador had sent to Churchill. During the two and a half months of the campaigns in Norway, Holland, Belgium and France, it said, Britain had been less than committed and badly led, and its withdrawal from France in particular was to be regretted. The British decision to abandon large numbers of French at Dunkirk was to be condemned. It was the Ambassador's firm belief that Britain had neither the heart nor the capability of pursuing the war against Hitler. Should compromise between London and Berlin not be achieved, Britain would lose the war and America should not support her.

Donovan closed the report and returned it. 'What does the Cabinet say?'

'The Cabinet is undecided as to whether Britain and Germany will come to an agreement or continue to wage war. In the latter case there is the possibility that Hitler will invade. The question of who will win is an open one.'

The President's secretary brought them coffee. Roosevelt waited until the woman had left the room, then came to the point of the meeting. 'Churchill has invited me to send an observer to London.'

Roosevelt looked tired, Donovan thought, the lines dark under his eyes. Whoever took America into the war would be charged with the deaths of many thousands of its young men. Yet whoever kept America out would be responsible for the consequences.

'You know my beliefs, Mr President, but you also know I will tell you the truth.'

It was, he thought, as if Roosevelt had not yet made up his mind whether or not to accept Churchill's offer. The white telephone on the desk against the window rang. Roosevelt rose, walked to the desk, picked it up and listened for fifty seconds, then replaced the receiver and returned to the chair. At ten that morning local time, Roosevelt had been informed, France had signed an armistice with Germany.

'When would you be free to go?'

'Immediately, Mr President.'

'I would appreciate that immensely.'

THE FOLLOWING AFTERNOON the President addressed the Pan American Scientific Congress. He spoke of the German challenge, of how technology had shortened the distances of the modern world and removed what he referred to as the mystic immunity which Americans had once felt from European war, of the role of the scientist and his creations.

'You who are scientists may have been told that you are in part responsible for the débâcle of today . . . but I assure you that it is not the scientists of the world who are responsible.'

Even as he looked round the auditorium he thought of the recommendation from Szilard and the letter from Einstein. When he had first read them and ordered action be taken upon them war had just been declared between Britain and Germany and he had been preoccupied with the position of the United States in that conflict. Now Germany had swept through Western Europe and Britain faced possible defeat. Each had marked a turning point, yet the decision he would one day face on the Szilard document would be the greatest crossroads of all.

'What has come about has been caused solely by those who would use, and are using, the progress that you have made along lines of peace in an entirely different cause.'

Three days later, the decision based in part on fears of reports emanating from the Kaiser Wilhelm Institutes in Germany and in part upon the work of the British scientists reporting to the MAUD committee in London, the President authorized that the responsibilities of the Uranium Committee be subsumed under the newly-formed National Defence Research Council.

WALTER SCHELLENBERG'S MEETING with *Reichsführer-SS* Himmler was late in the afternoon. Reinhard Heydrich was already present.

'The Duke of Windsor. Where is he now?'

'Spain.' Schellenberg assumed that a full account was necessary. 'On May the 28th, at his own request, Windsor was attached to the Armée des Alpes on the Italian frontier. On June the 19th, after our successful sweep toward Paris, he and the Duchess left France and crossed into Spain. They arrived in Madrid on June the 23rd and are staying at the Ritz.'

'And who is handling the matter there?'

The *matter* was that which they had discussed in the same room before Christmas: the possibility of a future role, both in the internal politics of Britain and its external relationship with Germany, for the former King.

'Herr Ribbentrop's people. I understand that Ambassador Stohrer has already established contact with the Duke through a number of Spanish emissaries; the most important are Don Ramón Serrano Suñer, General Franco's brother-in-law and the Spanish Interior Minister and Don Miguel Primo de Rivera, the Civil Governor of Madrid and son of the old Falangist dictator, who was Windsor's guide when he toured the country in 1927. Windsor apparently thinks highly of him. Kriminalkommissar Winzer, of the Gestapo, is in charge of relations between the German and Spanish police.'

Sometimes, though he would not admit it publicly, he wondered how much Hitler's concern with the Duke of Windsor was delaying a decision on Operation Sea Lion, the invasion of England.

'But you are ready if Ribbentrop's diplomats fail?' Himmler was anxious, conspiring.

'Of course.'

DRAKE RECEIVED THE summons at three and arrived in Downing Street at ten minutes to five. He was shown to the war room and given a cup of tea. On the walls were a variety of maps, some of England, others of Europe. For five minutes he stood looking at the largest of the European maps and seeing the spread of the German armies from the English Channel in the west to the border with Russia in the east. There was a commotion behind him and Churchill came into the room and closed the door.

'Your people, how are they placed?'

'Most of the units have been recruited, none is armed.'

Churchill grunted. 'If I bought you a month, two at the most, would it help?'

Two months would almost take them to September. 'Anything would help.'

Churchill had not even sat down.

'In the next few weeks you should be aware of one thing. There will be speculation of deals with Hitler, secret negotiations. Speeches will be made, here and elsewhere, which will be open to various interpretations. There will be many people who believe what they think they hear, even more who want to believe it. You and your people should not be among them. It will merely be a buying of time.'

'What about the Duke of Windsor?'

Churchill's reply was oblique.

'Precisely.'

OFFICIALLY AT LEAST, Schellenberg should not have been in possession of the telegram. When Heydrich's clerk telephoned and asked if he could attend an urgent meeting in the *Obergruppenführer*'s office in ten minutes, he knew it was something to do with its contents.

Ten days before, after a little over a week in Madrid, the Windsors had left Spain for Portugal and were now staying at the summer villa of a prominent banker, Ricardo Espírito Santo Silva, close to the fashionable fishing town of Cascais and the coastal resort of Estoril, seventeen miles west of Lisbon. The move, presumed to be at the instigation of British Intelligence, had left Ribbentrop's plans for a diplomatic approach floundering and freed the Führer to concentrate on the British invasion plans. Two days ago, however, the BBC in London had announced that Windsor had been offered the governorship of the Bahamas. Twenty-four hours later the German Minister in Lisbon, Hoynigen-Huene, had despatched to Berlin the telegram, a copy of which was in Schellenberg's file on the Duke. It stated that Windsor considered that the reason for the appointment was to keep him away from England, that he intended delaying his departure to the Bahamas in the hope of an early change in his fortune, and that he described himself as a firm supporter of a peaceful compromise with Germany. Predictably, the Hoynigen-Huene telegram had caused great excitement at the castle at Fuschl, near Hitler's retreat at Berchtesgaden, which Ribbentrop had appropriated and where he was now staying.

In all the machinations surrounding the travels of the Duke and Duchess to Portugal, it had not escaped Schellenberg's attention, nor his sense of humour, that the villa in which they were now staying took its name from a cliff on the coastline on which it was situated: The Boca do Inferno, The Mouth of Hell.

The *Obergruppenführer* was alone; he gestured to Schellenberg to sit and offered him a cigarette. 'You know of the latest information from Lisbon?'

Schellenberg confirmed that he had a copy of the telegram.

'In that case you will be interested in the reply.'

He leaned forward and passed Schellenberg a copy of a second telegram. It was from Foreign Minister Ribbentrop and addressed to the German Ambassador in Madrid, and was marked *Top Secret. Special Confidential Handling.* The Duke of Windsor was to be lured into returning to Spain. He would be kept there, and approached by intermediaries with a German message following up his position reported in the Lisbon telegram. In order to ensure the co-operation of the Spanish authorities the telegram also reported that the British Secret Service planned to assassinate Windsor.

Sometimes, Schellenberg thought, the Foreign Minister's fantasies exceeded even the Führer's.

'How will this affect Sea Lion?'

'It won't. The Führer will announce his decision in three days' time.'

DRAKE WAS OBSERVING a training session at The Garth when he received the message. By the time he reported to Downing Street it was early evening. The Old Man was showing the tiredness of his years, he thought and suddenly knew why he had been summoned.

'This morning in Berlin Hitler announced Directive Sixteen, the invasion of England.'

THE PLANES MOVED across the sky like the gnats which hung over the river, drawing away from each other then closing again. Boy Jack and Ernie watched fascinated.

'Dogfight.'

They had picked up the word from the newspaper and wireless reports. Not *any* dogfight, however, the first they had actually seen. In the sky to the south the planes were still circling and diving. Most of the dogfights had been over the Channel, they knew, the Spitfires and Hurricanes from Manston and Hawkinge protecting the convoys, plus the occasional battle above the docks and ports along the coast. Now the battle in the sky was creeping inland over Kent. In front of them a plane spiralled out of control towards the ground, a trail of smoke from its fuselage.

'Not one of ours.' There was a confidence in Ernie's voice.

'Messerschmitt,' Boy Jack agreed.

'Home Guard will soon be out.' The Home Defence Volunteers had just been renamed the Home Guard, as Harry Downton never tired of telling anyone at the cricket matches.

'Why isn't your dad in the Home Guard?'

In a week it would be the end of July and they would be on holiday, could spend as much time as they wanted on the farm or sailing the yachts in the river behind the church.

'Too busy on the farm. Besides, Harry Downton is good enough to protect the whole village.'

They laughed and ran down the hill to school.

THE CONTROL STATION was silent.

'Time you were away, Mary.' Beatie made a pot of tea and called to Liz.

The arrangement was informal; the official schedule allowed for one day off each week, but when the station was quiet and they knew that no visits were planned the three took it in turns to have extra evenings off.

'Where are you going tonight?'

It was the first of two rules they had imposed upon themselves, both for security and to protect the arrangement, that the other two should know where the third was going. The second rule was that they should return to the control station by midnight.

'Black Swan as usual.'

At eight-fifteen Mary left the wood and began the cycle ride to the pub. The evening was pleasant and the moon was full. The two MGs were amongst the gaggle of cars parked outside. From inside came the sound of a piano. She hid the bike behind a hedge fifty yards away, straightened her uniform and hair, and went in. The bar was crowded with RAF crews and WAAFs, the fighter pilots always the noisiest.

The base at Manston was part of Fighter Command's 11 Group, covering the South of England, 10 to the west and 12 north, 13 covering Scotland. Each group was divided into sectors, each with a sector station. Though it lay within the Hornchurch sector, however, Manston was a forward station for Biggin Hill. Sometimes the pilots and their planes were stationed there and sometimes they were pulled back to Biggin itself.

In the far corner, by the window where they always sat, she saw Max and Sandy and the rest of the gang. Mary bought herself a half of bitter and pushed her way through to them.

'Here she comes, the lady of the night.'

Max was already drunk. Whenever she saw them in the evenings nowadays he and Sandy seemed to be drunk. He rose, kissed her on the cheek and offered her his chair, then grabbed another from the next table. She smiled at the others and sat down.

'What do you mean, the lady of the night?' It was the only person there she did not know.

'She comes from the dark, she vanishes into the dark.'

She made a face at him. 'When the war's over, Max, you should go on the stage.' There was a roar of approval from Sandy. 'I work funny hours,' she explained to the newcomer.

'What do you do?' He was slightly older than she was, about twenty-four Mary guessed, dark hair and a laughing face. On his uniform he wore the ribbon of the DFC.

'I'm a driver.'

'Where?'

He was seated next to a WAAF from one of the radar stations which provided information on enemy movements on which the fighters were scrambled and directed to intercept their targets.

'Up the road.' It was not the first time she had used the story.

'Mary, may I introduce Johnny Watson, just joined us. Johnny Watson, may I introduce Mary.' Max gathered the glasses together and a semblance of order returned to the table. At the piano someone began to play a Vera Lynn song.

'How was it today?' It was bad form to ask, she knew, but sometimes they wanted to talk about it anyway.

'You go up, you come down.' Sandy pulled the ear of the golden Labrador sitting on the floor beneath the table. 'Today wasn't so bad, actually. We got up first, they weren't expecting us.' He laughed. 'First time at least.'

Max was shouting for help with the drinks and one of the WAAFs went to assist.

'How many times?'

'Four.'

She glanced across the table and saw that the newcomer was looking at her. 'Still protecting the convoys over the Channel?'

Sandy shook his head. 'Not any more. The navy's stopped trying to get ships through during the day.' At his feet the dog was lapping at a beer. 'Besides, the enemy's changing tactics, pushing more stuff inland.'

'Getting ready for the big one?'

He laughed it off as they always did. 'Probably.'

Max weaved through the crowd, four pint glasses in each hand, and crashed them onto the table in triumph. 'We're off to a dance later. Then Sandy knows a little place where they're having a party.'

'Sorry, Max, not tonight.' Mary remembered the midnight rule.

When the round was finished they left in the swirl of chaos and noise which Max and Sandy always seemed to generate around them, the Labrador coming suddenly to life and following them.

'Will you be here tomorrow?' The newcomer had delayed slightly as the others left.

Nice eyes, she thought, the eyes which went with the job but lovely eyes nevertheless. 'I'm not sure.' The following night was Liz's evening off, she wanted to explain.

'Try.'

'All right.'

THE CHECK CALL was at one. At twelve-thirty Mary left the control station and walked along the path towards the edge of the woods. A hundred yards along it she stopped by the stump of a pine tree jutting from the ground two feet from the right of the track, checked that she was not being observed, then reached down and twisted the single branch which protruded from the stump. A section of ground three feet square swung back. She stepped from the path without touching the ground between it and the hole, and climbed down the fifteen-feet drop into the zero station. When she was at the bottom she lit the tilly lamp and operated the mechanism which closed the trap door above her.

The room at the bottom of the drop was eight feet square and carved into the chalk. Along one wall ran a table on which were placed the radio and telephone systems, one set for incoming messages from the agents in the field and the second for onward transmission to Hannington Hall. Against the table were two chairs for the women on duty and on the end wall was a bunk bed on which the third would rest. The remainder of the limited space was taken up by a supply of food and emergency rations. In the rear wall, concealed behind a steel bookshelf, was the tunnel to what they jokingly called the back door. At the end of the tunnel was a concealed and secure exit to a point behind the bushes six feet from the road which skirted the wood.

The instruction for the use of the back door, like that for the regulation issue .38 Webley they shared between them, was clear and unambiguous. They should continue receiving and transmitting until the enemy had discovered them and was beating its way through the concealed trap door above them. Only then could they decide between the bolt hole and the pistol.

Mary had crawled along the tunnel once, been terrified by the tightness around her, could not imagine what it would be like pulling herself along it with the German tanks outside and the storm troopers breaking through the door above. After that she had worked it out for herself, purchased the bicycle and put it in the shed at the bottom of Mrs Potter's garden, told the others what she intended to do.

It was one o'clock. She connected the telephone link and began to speak.

'Cricket check call. Repeat. Cricket check call.'

'Thank you, zero Cricket. Clear now, please.'

JACK LEFT THE house shortly before eight; it was unusual for him to go out on a Sunday night, Fran thought, except for the weekends when she had seen the extra petrol rations he had somehow acquired. The boys were playing outside. She turned on the wireless, made herself a cup of tea, and sat at the kitchen table. What is happening, she asked herself. Does everyone else experience the same dread when their husbands go out?

It was time for the news. The music on the wireless stopped and she heard the voice of the announcer.

'Her Majesty, Queen Elizabeth.'

A mistake, she knew. It had to be the King, the Queen never made speeches on the wireless. Invasion, she thought. That was why Jack had gone out tonight, that was why the King was speaking on the wireless.

'War has at all times called for the fortitude of women. We, no less than men, have real and vital work to do.'

Not the King. She felt the relief and turned up the volume.

'I know that you would wish me to voice our deep and abiding sympathy with those on whom the first cruel and shattering blows have fallen, the women of Poland.'

The voice was concerned but clear and confident.

'We have all a part to play, and I know that you will not fail in yours.'

Fran wondered what her role was and turned off the set.

WHEN MARY LEFT the control station that evening the clouds were already gathering. By the time she reached the Black Swan they had filled the sky. The two MGs were not amongst the cars outside. She realized she did not know which was Johnny's, even if he had a car, and hurried inside. As she entered the bar he stood up to greet her.

'What would you like?'

The bar was less busy than on a Saturday night though no less boisterous. 'Where's the gang?' There was concern in the question.

'London. Max has found a new night club.'

'Half of bitter, please.'

No involvement, she warned herself, stay part of their game, or how they tried to forget their game, especially the nights when one of them did not appear.

'Cheers.'

The storm broke and they heard the sound of the rain, hard and merciless, crashing against the window.

'You're very fond of Max and Sandy.'

'They're good fun, you should have gone with them tonight.'

He shrugged it off. 'Prefer to be here.'

They were both uncomfortable.

'You said you were a driver. Cars?'

'That's right.'

'Where?'

'I drive a general.' Don't ask me any more, her eyes were telling him, I'm not supposed to talk about it, not even supposed to say I'm his driver. He understood and looked to see if she wanted another drink. The rain outside was even harder.

'Christ!' He pushed his chair back and began to run.

'What's wrong?'

He was half-way to the door. 'The bloody sun roof's down.'

'I'll help.'

By the time they had unrolled the roof from behind the seats and clipped it into place around the windscreen and along the sides of the car they were both drenched to the skin.

'What the hell are you laughing at?'

'You.'

She was standing in a puddle, her hair was flat and she could feel the water trickling down her back.

'You should see yourself, Johnny Watson.'

The rain was running down his face and into his eyes. She lifted her hand and wiped it away. At least the storm would prevent the Luftwaffe flying in the morning.

WHEN THE LORRY arrived the rain was still pouring from the sky and the ground by the bridge to the north of the village where they had waited since just before eight was turning to mud. If the bloody delivery had been on time, Jack thought, if the driver hadn't got lost, he could have been dry and at home in bed now. They unloaded the boxes and carried them along the foot of the field at the bottom of the hill, over the bridge and into the church.

There were two locking mechanisms to the steps which concealed the secret door to the crypt: the first secured the outside of the steps and the second the panel itself. Both could be operated from inside or outside the operating base.

Brian unlocked the stairs, then the mechanism which controlled the entrance itself, and the panel and steps swung on a pivot to reveal the opening. Ted lit a tilly lamp then he and Jack climbed into the crypt and Stan and Brian passed the boxes down.

The OB was fifteen feet long and eight feet wide. Ventilation came through a small hole in the wall to the outside which they had made and concealed. They had cleaned the crypt and brought in camp beds and jerry cans which The Garth had supplied.

There were four boxes. Each should contain the weapons and explosives which they had been trained to use, though one had been suspiciously light. The first box was half full of tins of bully beef, the second the same. The third was empty and the fourth contained two packs of gun cotton, three detonators, four knives, a Thompson sub-machine-gun and a limited amount of ammunition.

For a full minute they stood staring before anyone spoke.

'Bloody hell.' It was Stan who broke the silence. He picked up a can of beef. 'What do they expect us to do, throw these at the bloody enemy?'

THE SUMMONS FROM the Foreign Office gave Schellenberg no option. Herr Ribbentrop requested his presence that afternoon. Nothing could be discussed on the telephone, the matter was too important. It was something to do with the Duke of Windsor, Schellenberg knew, something Ribbentrop was planning after the Hoynigen-Huene telegram from Lisbon and the Foreign Minister's secret reply to it. Before he left the Prinzalbrechtstrasse he had spoken on the telephone to a number of contacts in the Foreign Ministry and reported to Heydrich, both verbally and in writing.

Ribbentrop spent no more than two minutes on pleasantries before coming to the point. According to emissaries the Duke of Windsor saw a role for himself in the future relationship between Germany and Britain and would, to this end, shortly return to Spain where it was considered he would be safer. Protection for the Duke from the British Secret Service was needed, both in Portugal at the moment and when he and his wife crossed the border. The Foreign Minister understood that Schellenberg had good contacts in Lisbon and

Madrid and had suggested to the Führer that he should therefore direct such security.

He was like a fly in one of the webs which he himself weaved, Schellenberg was aware. If the project succeeded his role in it would be diminished but if it failed he was already being set up to take the blame.

'And Windsor has agreed?'

'He has not opposed the idea.' Ribbentrop's answer was meant to convince but did not. The Foreign Minister lifted the telephone, indicated that Schellenberg should listen on the second ear piece and asked to be connected to the Führer. When Hitler's peculiar hollow voice came on the line Ribbentrop reported that the plans for Windsor were advanced and that Schellenberg would fly to Madrid by special plane in the morning.

At least, Schellenberg thought, he had already set up the alternative; at least the descendant of Queen Victoria was standing by.

The following morning Schellenberg left Berlin-Staaken, stopping over at Bourges, and arrived in Madrid in the evening. He checked into the hotel where a room had been reserved for him, using the civilian cover of Government Counsellor, then left and made his way to the safe house where he would, in fact, spend the night. At eight he dined with Ambassador Stohrer.

The Windsors were still at Estoril, and emissaries were in regular contact. Since Schellenberg's meeting with Ribbentrop, however, there had been two developments. The first was that the details of the Duke's return to Spain had been finalized: he and the Duchess would attend a hunting party close to the border, where they would 'accidentally' meet some old friends, including the first emissary, Don Miguel Primo de Rivera, and be invited by the Conde de Montarco to join him at his castle at Ciudad Rodrigo, twenty-five miles across the border into Spain. The second was that, officially at least, the Duke and Duchess would leave Lisbon for the Bahamas by boat on 1 August, in seven days' time.

'But the Duke is still in agreement?' Already, Schellenberg noted, the crucial details were different.

'The Duke has not rejected the plan.' The Ambassador's response echoed the Foreign Minister.

'But he has been informed of it?'

'It has been decided, at this stage, that it is better that he not be informed of the full details.'

The Boca do Inferno, Schellenberg remembered. The Mouth of Hell. When he left the Ambassador, he spent an hour with the Gestapo representative in Madrid, discussing the case and being given his contacts in the Portuguese Secret Police. The following morning, after telegramming Ribbentrop and confirming with the Prinzalbrecht-strasse that the team responsible for the cross-border snatch at Venlo the previous autumn were on their way, Schellenberg flew to Lisbon.

Despite Portugal's neutrality the capital was already a hot-bed of espionage and intrigue. Two years before he himself had used the city as a base for an intelligence operation in French West Africa. His first meeting, therefore, after his formal appointment with Minister Hoynigen-Huene, was with a Japanese agent of the Gestapo who had helped set up that scheme and his second was with the Gestapo contact, codenamed C, a senior officer in the Portuguese Secret Police.

That evening he telegrammed Berlin, via the Embassy in Madrid, that he was in possession of a plan of the villa at Boca do Inferno as well as full details of the servants and guards. By the following afternoon he reported that an agent had been installed in the Duke's house and that what he termed a protective service against the British Secret Service would be operational by the following morning.

The following evening Schellenberg was informed of the arrival in Lisbon of a British delegation to Windsor led by an old friend and advisor of the Duke, Sir Walter Monckton. That night having done all he could to satisfy Berlin that his plans were in place, Schellenberg sat in a bar less than four hundred yards from the villa where Windsor was entertaining his latest guests and considered how he would extricate himself from Ribbentrop's web if the whole structure collapsed around him.

WILLIAM DONOVAN'S AUDIENCE with King George VI was at ten. He was collected from Claridges forty minutes before by an official car arranged by Downing Street, driven to Buckingham Palace and conducted to the study overlooking Constitution Hill. The King was sitting behind a large desk set against a bow window. To his right as Donovan entered was a framed family photograph of his wife and two daughters, the cabinet boxes stacked to one side. Churchill was already present, staring out of another window closer to the door.

'Your Majesty.' Donovan bowed as the King rose and came round the table to greet him.

'Mr Donovan, thank you for coming. A great deal has happened since we met.'

The lawyer had wondered whether the King would remember. 'After the address to Congress in your visit in 1938, sir. I recall it well.'

'The White House reception. Your wife Ruth was with you.' George indicated the chairs round the fireplace opposite his desk and they moved across the room. 'Mr Churchill has been telling me a little of your visit here.'

For the past seven days William Donovan had been subjected to what British Intelligence considered necessary to persuade him that the country warranted his support. He had visited the code breakers at Bletchley and the fighter bases to the south of London, as well as the chain of sector stations and radar installations which would control them. He had been briefed by Lord Beaverbrook on the increase in war production and been shown the Spitfire factories at Southampton as well as the plans, in the case of invasion, to remove such facilities to the North.

'It's been most interesting, sir.'

Coffee was served. For the next thirty minutes they talked of the war in general, George stating what he called his absolute belief in the need to maintain the special link between their two peoples whilst admitting that the general mood in America was for neutrality.

'You must be faithful to your country, Mr Donovan. You cannot return to Washington and tell President Roosevelt that he should support us if you do not genuinely believe that yourself. You must never lie to your country or yourself.' The King leaned forward. 'But we need you, Mr Donovan, we need whatever help your great country can give us against the danger which now threatens us all.'

'But what happens, Your Majesty, if that threat becomes real? What will you do if England is invaded?'

'England will fight back.'

'No, Your Majesty. What will *you* do?'

George looked at him. 'Whatever is necessary.'

Donovan considered the response. 'A number of other families who consider themselves in special danger if invasion took place have sent their children to America. Some politicians who are sympathetic to your cause consider that if you also were to send your daughters it might create more support for you in America.' It was a subject he had been briefed to raise, even though his instincts rebelled against it. There was the slightest noise behind him, he turned in his chair and saw the Queen standing in the doorway. He had not heard her enter and wondered how long she had been there. Opposite him the King smiled. Donovan stood and bowed, unsure what she would do or say.

'My daughters will not leave me, Mr Donovan. I will not leave my husband, and my husband will not leave his people.'

'Thank you, ma'am.'

When the audience ended, Churchill and Donovan left together.

'What about Windsor?' Donovan asked the question he could not put to the King. 'According to our Embassies in Madrid and Lisbon the Duke is extremely vulnerable; we have regular reports that he is having frequent meetings with representatives of the German government.'

'Probably,' agreed Churchill.

'So why do you not simply insist on his leaving Europe?' He knew it was a question Roosevelt would ask.

Churchill turned to look at him. 'You know how lacking we are in everything; you have visited our aircraft factories and seen how hard they are working.' He felt in his pocket for the cigar case. 'How many days has Hitler delayed over invasion because of his preoccupation with the Windsors?'

'Ten, probably fifteen.' Donovan saw and began to smile.

'And how many Spitfires and Hurricanes can Beaverbrook build for me in a day?'

He selected a cigar and stuck it in his mouth.

THE DAYS WERE already shorter and the light in the kitchen faded earlier each evening. Fran pulled the curtains tight, lit the oil lamp and served supper. At half-past eight Jack left in the pick-up, telling her only that he would be back by five.

'Where's Dad going this evening?' Boy Jack asked as she cleared the kitchen.

'Canterbury. He has to see some people there.'

'Is Uncle Ted going with him?'

'I expect so.'

The evening was warm. She left the house and sat on the stones at the top of the fields, trying to forget the knife edge in her stomach. Each day now there seemed to be more dogfights in the sky, each day there seemed to be more German planes. Please God may the weather turn bad. Please God may there be storms until winter, even though we would lose the harvest. Please God may the invasion never come.

Please God may she never lose Jack.

She heard Ernie's footsteps behind her.

'Nice here, isn't it, Auntie Fran?'

'It's lovely.'

In the past year he had grown so much, almost as tall and as strong as Boy Jack. When the war was over and Ernie went back to the East End of London, they would miss him, Boy Jack especially, Jack as well, as if they had lost a part of the family.

'Thank you for having me.'

'Don't be silly.'

THE MOON WAS the thinnest sliver of a crescent, lost occasionally behind the clouds; even so the evening had not been properly dark until ten and they had waited on the ridge above the camp until past midnight before Jack decided they should move.

The perimeter fence was fifty yards away. Inside it was a clear space of some fifteen yards, then the beginnings of the roadways round the camp, beyond that the headquarters building which was their target for the night. The sentries were spaced at intervals inside the barbed-wire fence, occasionally walking along the perimeter either to whisper to the next man or to share a cigarette.

They slid down the slope and closed on the fence.

They had done this sort of exercise so often, had been trained by the instructors from the Lovat Scouts how to steal past a man without even rousing the slightest suspicion, but that was all it had been in the past, an exercise. Now the order had come from The Garth that they should escalate the level at which they practised, should infiltrate the British army camps clustered round the south coast. Except the camps would not be warned and if they were spotted the sentries, armed and on alert for the first German invasion troops, would shoot them on sight.

The guard on the left was twenty-five yards away, the man on the right slightly less. Jack cut through the wire, bent it back and slid through. No prisoners, they had agreed; if a guard spotted them but they managed to reach him before he shot them they would not waste time telling him they were British. There was the sound of a plane in the sky. He saw the guards glancing up and moved across the open ground inside the fence, the others close behind him. Brian at the rear pulled the wire back into place so the hole would not be spotted before they had exfiltrated. The plane droned on. They paused momentarily at the edge of the road, then moved noiselessly to the corner of the building.

Easy.

Stan slid a knife between the two halves of the window, eased back the lock, and they moved inside. The offices were empty. On a clerk's desk in the second room on the right they found a sheet of regimental notepaper, stamped it with a rubber stamp to provide evidence of the operation, and left the building, pausing only as a staff car came past the window, its lights doused according to the blackout regulations.

Too easy.

The sentries were still in position along the perimeter. Jack crossed the roadway, slid quietly along the grass to the fence, found the hole, pulled it open and moved through, waiting to the side while Ted and Stan followed, each man motionless until the one in front had crossed safely. In the grass ten yards away he sensed the moment when Brian moved forward, then heard the sentry turn and ask the man to his right for a light.

Pull out now, he reacted logically. You're right where they'll meet. Just enough time to make it up the slope, even if they saw you. The guards were turning, coming closer together. Twenty yards, fifteen. No way he could run, he knew, no way he could leave Brian on the inside. Ten yards, down to five. *Still*, he could hear the voice of the instructor: *If you lie absolutely still no one will see you, even if they're close enough to pee on you.* The guard on his right walked past, within two feet of the fence, three feet from Jack, stopped five yards past and pulled out a packet of cigarettes. Jack heard the match strike and smelt the tobacco in the air. Face down, he told himself, don't let them see even the whites of your eyes. The men were silhouetted against the sky, holding the cigarettes so that the burning could not be seen. Three German spies caught on the coast this afternoon, one was saying, already sent to London for interrogation. Rumours of twenty Germans landing just north of Deal. The man turned away from his companion, stepped toward Jack and laid his rifle against the fence. *Absolutely bloody still*, the voice reminded him. He heard the grunts as the man struggled with the buttons of his trousers, then the stream of urine splashed through the wire twelve inches to his left. When he had finished the sentry buttoned up his trousers, picked up his rifle and walked away. Twenty seconds later Brian came through the hole. Only when they were clear of the area did he ask Ted and Stan why the hell they were smirking.

'Nothing, Jack. Just thought you were going to ask him if he wanted you to hold it so he could have a smoke at the same time.'

By the time he returned to the farm it was five in the morning. Fran heard him as he put the kettle on the range and went downstairs. He was looking exhausted, as if whatever he had gone through since she had last seen him had been mental as well as physical. She made him breakfast then dressed and went outside to feed the animals. Upstairs the boys got out of bed. When the four of them had finished the animals, they sat down for breakfast proper round the table in the kitchen. Then Jack and the boys returned to the fields and Fran fetched Sarah in the pick-up and drove into Canterbury.

The workmen were at the junction where the turning to Ardley cut off the main A2 road from Dover to Canterbury and London. She stopped the pick-up and watched as they removed the road sign and threw it onto a pile of others in the back of their lorry. The foreman saw the way she was looking at what his men were doing.

'Official orders. Can't let the Germans know where they are, can we?'

As long as Ernie was with them, she thought, as long as the government didn't take the evacuees away, they were safe. When she went to the village later that day even the sign bearing its name had been removed.

WILLIAM DONOVAN ROSE early and took breakfast in his room. The driver of the army staff car that collected him was Scottish, spoke only when asked a question, and even then his replies were monosyllabic and conveyed no information whatsoever.

The drive took two and a half hours, Donovan's bewilderment and growing impatience at not knowing where he was going increased by the total and sudden lack either of road signs or place names. At five minutes past ten they left what he did not know was the A20 at Ashford and turned north-east. Some six miles later, abruptly and without warning, the driver slewed the car off the main road and up a rough track into the woods on the side of the hill. Two hundred yards up the track, on the right, was a collection of rough outhouses. Opposite them the track went through an open gate, paths leading from it into the woods. The driver drove through the gate and stopped the car.

The house to the left seemed to be a huddle of roofs, red-tiled and angled; a captain in battle dress came out of the house and greeted him.

'Welcome to The Garth. Some coffee, perhaps?'

Donovan noted that the man did not introduce himself. 'That's just what I need.'

'We've got thirty minutes.' The captain led him inside. 'He's expecting us at eleven.'

Donovan still had no idea where he was or why he had come.

At twenty-five minutes to the hour they left The Garth, the captain riding in the front passenger seat and Donovan in the rear. At the bottom of the track the driver turned right, then almost immediately right again, through the woods, the road degenerating into a series of winding and narrow lanes. Without warning, the car stopped at a gate into a field at the foot of a line of hills. Leaning against it was a man wearing farmer's clothes; his jacket was tied in place by string and there was dried mud on his boots. In the sky above them a dogfight began. Donovan stepped out, and the car drove off.

'So you're Wild Bill Donovan.' The man turned his attention away from the planes and stared at him. 'My old dad told me about you. The Fighting Irish, wasn't it? Apparently he bumped into some of your blokes after Landres-et-St Georges.'

'I'd like to meet him.' Donovan meant it.

'Died from the gassing two years ago.' The man looked at Donovan's shoes, climbed the gate and set off up the field, keeping to the edge. Donovan looked once down the road where the car had disappeared, climbed after him, and followed him across the field, through the woods at the top, into some more fields, then into another copse. Even when he was walking through the woods, Donovan suddenly realized, the man moved without making even the slightest sound.

Without warning he found himself in a field on the top of the Downs. The field was bare, a hundred yards from side to side and almost two hundred yards long, sloping gently to the south. In the centre, and commanding the road below and the flatlands beyond, was a wooden sheep trough, eight feet long and two feet wide, rabbit holes scattered in the ground below it. He followed the man across the field and sat with him on the rough wood. Above him the planes were still circling, one beginning to fall, the black trailing behind it.

'If Hitler invades, this is one of the ways he'll come.' Even though the man's speech was slow Donovan could hardly understand the Kentish burr. The guide pointed to the flatlands below: some three hundred yards away was a main road, and beyond that a railway line, the rails sparkling in the sun. 'Got to, you see. Most direct route from the coast to London. Good roads and railways.' There was a faint chuckle. 'If there're any left.'

He glanced at the planes then turned his attention to the terrain again. 'Our job is to stop him. Well, not stop him quite, more like slow him down.'

Donovan knew the slowness was a cover for an animal cunning.

'The plan is that when Hitler invades we go underground, come up and have a go at his belly when he's on top of us. Destroy supplies and communications, sever road and rail links vital to the enemy advance. Give the boys the chance to recover, fight back.' The words were a mix of army jargon and local dialect. 'That's the idea, anyway.'

'Who are you? Not army?'

'No.' The man took a pair of field glasses from his jacket pocket and focused them on the railway line. 'Auxiliary Units.'

'Auxiliary to what?'

'Auxiliary to nothing. We're Resistance.'

Donovan began to understand. 'What are your chances?'

'What were your chances at Landres-et-St Georges? Wounded yourself, weren't you? Kept fighting till it was over.'

It was the battle for which Donovan had been awarded the Congressional Medal of Honour.

'Something like that.'

The farmer took the binoculars from his neck and passed them over. 'Want a look?'

Donovan raised them to his eyes and scanned the area below. 'Look at what?'

There was no reply; he turned and realized he was alone in the middle of the field.

Goddam stupid, he thought.

He stood up and examined the trough, then looked around the field itself, the hedges too far away for the man to reach in the two or three seconds when Donovan's attention had been diverted. A hiding place, he knew, to do with the trough, the seemingly innocent apertures in the slope in front not rabbit holes but observation points commanding the strategic area below.

Not so stupid after all.

He bent down and examined the trough more closely, searching for the counterpoint which would open it but seeing nothing.

'Want to come down, then?'

The voice came from the point in the trough which he had just inspected.

'You're damned right I want to come down.'

MARY LEFT THE control station and cycled to the Black Swan. Johnny's car was parked between Max's and Sandy's. That day, more times than she cared to admit to herself, she had stepped outside the control station and looked at the dogfights above Kent. The pub was crowded, the gang in the corner which they seemed to have made their own. Some old faces missing, some new ones. She fussed over the dog, bought herself a half and went to the corner.

'Rolls-Royce safely hidden?' Sandy had seen her hide the bike once and told everyone about it.

'With you lot around it needs to be.'

A pilot from another group began to play the piano.

'Just saying to Johnny that the two of you should come to this new place in London.' Max had settled his arm round a WAAF from one of the radar stations. 'Really good fun there.'

She glanced at Johnny. 'Give me some notice and I'll arrange my day off.'

'Excellent.' Max turned his attention to the WAAF.

'Hair's looking better tonight.' Johnny slid his arm round her waist.

'I just hope you've left the hood up.'

'Come on, Johnny.' Sandy collected the glasses. 'Can't carry them all myself.'

Mary watched them pushing their way to the bar and saw the way Max was looking at her. You're bad for him, Mary. He's beginning to care and the one thing you can't afford in this terrible bloody business is to care. About anything, but particularly about whether you live or die. If you make it through one day you just get pissed that evening and hope to Christ you make it through the next. He disentangled himself from the WAAF and leant across.

'Good luck.' He kissed her on the cheek and turned back to the others.

When she and Johnny left at ten the rest were still drinking. They drove to Manston and parked off the road which ran along the side of the airfield.

'It's getting worse, isn't it?' Even in the dark the base seemed isolated and exposed. 'When will we know?'

'Whether Hitler really is going to invade?'

She nodded.

'When he changes his air tactics.'

'What do you mean?'

'Hitler will only invade if he has total air superiority. For us to prevent that three things are vital.' His voice was crisp, it was as if he were giving a briefing. 'First, our radar must continue to give us advance notice that the enemy is taking off in France so that we can scramble early and get above them as they cross the Channel. Secondly, our sector controls must be able to direct where our planes go. Thirdly, the stations themselves must be maintained intact so that our planes can take off and, equally importantly, land again.'

The Spitfires and Hurricanes on the other side of the perimeter fence were at their dispersal points. In less than nine hours, they would be on readiness, probably already in the air.

'So once he starts attacking the radar and the airfields we know that invasion is on the way?'

Johnny nodded.

'But what about the planes? Beaverbrook is building more every day now.'

'It's not the planes he's after.' She wished she had not asked. Don't tell me, Johnny. Don't admit it even to yourself. 'It's the pilots he's after. We're the ones in short supply now, the ones we can't get enough of.'

The night was still. They sat without talking.

'What do you do, Mary? What do you *really* do?'

She shook her head. 'I'm a driver.'

He put his arm around her. 'It's not the fear of dying, you see.' It was as if he understood what she wanted to ask him, as if, just for once, he needed to break through the shell he and Max and the others had built around themselves. 'That's why I carry a gun in the cockpit. It's the fear of being trapped in the cockpit and burned alive.'

THE MORNING WAS warm, the gentlest of breezes lifting off the Atlantic. When Schellenberg confirmed with Berlin that the Venlo team was in position, he was informed that the Conde de Montarco, who would welcome Windsor to his castle at Ciudad Rodrigo after the Duke had been tempted into Spain from his hunting party near the border, was still in Madrid. In the middle of the afternoon he was requested to attend an urgent meeting at the German legation in Lisbon.

The message, from Ambassador Stohrer via Minister Hoynigen-Huene, was simple: Ribbentrop's envoys to Windsor had failed. The Duke had declined the invitation to the hunting party and, under pressure from the British, would leave Lisbon for the Bahamas as scheduled in two days' time.

Thank God it was Ribbentrop's people. He felt the relief surge through him and tried to disguise it. Thank God he had cleared himself with Berlin. He knew how Heydrich would enjoy the situation and how Himmler would exploit the Foreign Minister's failure.

An hour later he was recalled and handed a telegram from Ribbentrop. The bastard! For the second time that day he disguised his reactions. The Foreign Minister was still trying it on, still tangling him in his web. The message read simply: 'The Führer orders that an abduction is to be organized at once.'

He drove to the villa at Estoril, decided what he would do, returned to Lisbon and telegrammed Berlin informing Ribbentrop of the measures he had set in motion, the various tactics he had already instigated to frighten the Duke and Duchess into believing that their lives were in danger from the British, the plans to delay the departure of their boat, and the movements of the Venlo team in preparation for the kidnapping.

That evening, unaccompanied and without informing anyone,

Schellenberg made his way to a café in the Alfama area of the old city. The Gestapo contact codenamed C was waiting for him.

If the kidnap plan failed, he knew, then he would take the blame; yet if it succeeded and Windsor was successfully moved to Spain he would also lose, since there would be no way after such an action that the Duke would agree to co-operate. He called for another bottle and refilled the glass of the man opposite him.

'Tomorrow I have been ordered to take the Duke of Windsor across the Spanish frontier by force.' His voice was relaxed and his message clear.

The secret police chief raised his glass. 'You must know that I cannot help you in this. You also know that in order to protect myself I have to act on the information you have just given me.'

'Of course.'

THE FOLLOWING MORNING the security screen round the villa at Boca do Inferno had been doubled. Schellenberg informed Berlin that because of this an abduction attempt seemed improbable but that he was preparing an alternative course of action. The following morning, Thursday, 1 August, he telegrammed to Ribbentrop a seven-point plan aimed at preventing the Duke and Duchess from leaving that afternoon and requesting guidance. That evening before Berlin had had a chance to reply he watched with relief as the American vessel carrying the former King to the Bahamas moved slowly down the Tagus and into the blue waters of the Atlantic.

WILLIAM DONOVAN'S FINAL meeting with Winston Churchill was attended by the Foreign Secretary, the heads of the three services, Sir Stuart Menzies, General Ironside and a select handful of advisors. The conference began at nine-thirty in the morning. For ninety minutes Donovan received a final briefing from, and in turn cross-examined, the heads of the army, navy and air force. Finally he asked the single question for which President Roosevelt had sent him to England.

'If Hitler *does* invade, how will you hold him?'

'We will hold him *before* invasion. He will not invade unless he has guaranteed and total air superiority to protect his forces from the Royal Navy when he crosses the Channel.'

'And what is the role of the Royal Navy if invasion takes place?'

'It depends on whether Hitler has achieved that air superiority.'

'If he has?'

'Then the Royal Navy would be severely restricted in what it could do and would almost certainly suffer massive casualties. In that event it is possible the navy would be withdrawn to save it for a later day.'

Donovan understood the frankness of the statement.

'Given the enemy's numerical superiority, both in machines and pilots, how close is he to an *actual* superiority in the air?' The question was directed at Air Chief Marshal Dowding, Commander-in-Chief Fighter Command.

'At present the situation is balanced.'

'But?'

'Yesterday Goering ordered Eagle Day – the elimination of the RAF from the skies over England.'

'And how would he achieve that?'

The Prime Minister indicated that Dowding should continue. The explanation took a little under ten minutes and was a fuller account of that which Johnny Watson had told Mary at Manston.

When Dowding had finished Donovan thanked him and turned to the Prime Minister. 'What is the latest intelligence on the preparation of an invasion fleet?'

Churchill nodded to an air commodore, the man reached into his briefcase, took out three series of black and white aerial reconnaissance photographs and passed them across the table.

'Canals and other waterways leading to the coast, taken two weeks ago.' The thin stretches of silver were empty. He gave Donovan the second set. 'Same locations last week.' There was little difference. He passed the final set across the table. 'These were taken yesterday.' The canals were beginning to fill with barges, the wharves and quays around them, as well as the countryside beyond, packed with trucks and equipment.

Donovan studied them closely then handed them back and looked at Churchill. 'I assume, Prime Minister, that there is a code for invasion.'

'Yes.' The voice was gruff, almost hostile.

'And may I ask what it is?'

'Cromwell.'

THE ROAD FROM Canterbury was busy with lorries. Everywhere Jack and Ted looked there were soldiers. Just like the lads going out to Norway and Holland and France, Jack thought. Not so many guns though, and then only small stuff, none of the heavy artillery they would need if the Germans really came.

The day was bright and the sun was beginning to rise over the cathedral yet even in its warmth Jack could not shake off the chill of waiting that hung over the city.

Ernie's case, an old one given to him by Fran, was by the door of the scullery, a belt strapped round it where the lock had broken. From the kitchen Jack heard the sound of the boy sobbing. Fran and Boy Jack were sitting at the table on either side of Ernie.

'Two o'clock at the school.' His son looked at him. 'We heard just after you left.'

First they had taken away the sign posts, now the evacuees. 'Come on.' He put his arms round the boys. 'Let's look at the calves before you go. They'll miss you.'

'You'll look after them while I'm away?'

'Course we will.'

The coach was by the village green, the other families standing in a group, watching as the children mixed together for the last time. The evacuation from the coastal area of children who had already been evacuated to them the year before was compulsory; evacuation of local children was the personal decision of the families concerned. At the door of the bus a teacher was ticking the names off against a list. Only two were local.

'Simmons, Ernest.' The teacher ran a pencil down the list and ticked off the name. 'Case in the luggage hold. We'll be leaving in twenty minutes.'

Jack watched as Ernie and Boy Jack bundled his case into the space at the rear of the coach. Ernie turned, a question in his eyes: If I have to go, why doesn't Boy Jack have to come with me? If Boy Jack can stay, then why can't I?

He knelt by the boy and put his arm round his shoulders. 'We all know why you're being moved, that it'll be safer where you're going. But we all wish you could stay with us.'

'You'll be here when I come back, won't you, Uncle Jack?'

'Of course we will.'

'That's not what I meant. You'll *all* be here.'

'Yes, we'll all be here.'

The teacher called for them to board the coach.

'Bye, Auntie Fran. Bye, Uncle Jack.' He kissed them both.

Boy Jack walked with him to the steps.

'Bye, Jack.'

'Bye, Ernie.'

Remember us, Fran thought, remember my husband above all. Remember the man who taught you how to milk a cow and how to mend a fence. Remember him for you may never see him again.

The boy began to climb aboard.

'Ernie.' The evacuee looked at the farmer. We're proud of you, Jack wanted to say, we're proud of how you've grown up and how you've become part of our family. 'Make sure you're back in time to milk those cows.'

The boy tried to smile and sat down. The coach pulled away, the children waving, and the locals waving back.

Even after it had disappeared no one moved. This is it – Fran could sense the mood – if you really *are* coming then let's be having you.

THE LIGHTS OPPOSITE the White House were beginning to glow in the dusk. It was almost the end of August, another summer coming to an end and another fall beginning. Roosevelt turned back into the room and sat down again at the desk. The President seemed more tired than at their last meeting, Donovan thought, the eyes sunk deeper and the walking stick never far from his grasp.

'You are aware that Ambassador Kennedy has not wavered in his opposition to siding with the British?'

'The Ambassador and I exchanged views whilst I was in London.'

His report to the President had made clear that whilst parts of his visit to England had been deliberately manipulated, its recommendation took full cognizance of that fact.

'You are also aware that the majority of Americans still believe we should remain neutral?'

'I am.' The Kennedy faction was in the ascendancy, Donovan had always understood. Now for the first time he began to fear that they had won. There was a knock on the door and the President's secretary reminded him that he was due to leave for a dinner engagement in ten minutes.

'Joseph Kennedy's opposition to US involvement is economic – that we will put a great deal in and get little out.' The President was thinking aloud. 'The opposition of others is political: they do not want us embroiled if the side we support turns out to be the loser. Both arguments are correct. The American people are also right in not wanting their sons killed in what they see as someone else's war.'

'What about Lease-Lend?' It was something which had been suggested and scrutinized: the lending of US war material, in the first instance destroyers, in return for the leasing by Britain to the United States of bases in geographic areas controlled by the British which America considered strategic to its own defence but to which the British had always denied them access. 'That way we could be of help without committing a single American life, as well as getting something in return.'

Plus, Roosevelt anticipated Donovan's proposal, a direct sale of other arms, based on the fact that the British could pay because they had already transferred their financial reserves to Canada and South Africa.

'As you know, not even the President has power to transfer weapons of war. Only Congress has that power, and even if it chose to exercise it the process would be long and public.'

Kennedy's people had been at the President, Donovan knew, as well as at his advisors.

'As you also know,' Roosevelt continued, 'the June amendment to the Navy Appropriations Bill specifies that no war equipment may be transferred to a foreign government without certification by either the Army Chief of Staff or the Chief of Naval Operations that it is not wanted for the defence of the United States. This afternoon Admiral Stark testified to Congress that the destroyers the British want are still of value to us. He did not make the statement in order to thwart any help this country might wish to give the British, but the effect of what he said is the same. I'm genuinely sorry, Bill.'

The lawyer nodded. *When the war is over and if Germany loses,* he could hear Fuchs' voice after the visit to Dachau, *then you will blame us for what happened, but you will be equally responsible for allowing it. Auxiliary to nothing,* the man had said as he sat on the sheep trough on the hillside in Kent, *we're Resistance. None of our business,* he could hear the voice of the Embassy official in Berlin, *the United States is neutral.*

'Thank you, Mr President.'

The drive from La Guardia to Downtown New York was quick, most of the traffic travelling in the opposite direction. Friday afternoon, and the city was wrapping up for the weekend. By the time he reached the offices a number of staff had already left. For ten minutes he briefed those remaining on what happened at the White House, then sat with them drinking coffee and trying to shake himself clear of the black clouds gathering over him, the conversation gradually turning to what the members of his staff were doing that weekend.

'What about you, Jim? Planning anything special?'

James Withrow had been with the firm six years, but was already considered one of its brightest and most able lawyers. 'My son's birthday; we always go away fishing for it.'

Donovan cursed himself for forgetting. 'I'm sorry, Jim, I should have remembered. You'd better go, and thanks for staying.'

At eight he left the offices and was driven to the duplex on Beekman Place. His wife, Ruth, was away and the rooms felt empty; wherever he turned he heard the voices of Konrad Fuchs and the nameless man on the hillside in England. On Saturday, he cancelled a theatre engagement in the evening, but agreed reluctantly to honour a luncheon the next day. On Sunday morning he spent an hour walking, then wrote a letter to Fuchs, which he tore up and burned immediately he had finished it. Then he was driven to the lunch, leaving the address and telephone number where he could be contacted.

As the meal was drawing to a close, Donovan was informed that he was wanted on the telephone. He excused himself and followed the waiter to the adjoining room.

'Mr Donovan, it's Jim Withrow.'

He recognized the voice anyway. 'Jim, I thought you were away fishing with your son.'

'Something came up.'

It must have been important to prevent the man from fulfilling his birthday promise to his son.

'Mr Donovan, I think you should contact the President.'

Roosevelt's schedule was already filled and Donovan had only just persuaded the President's private secretary to allow him a few moments before the President left for an official dinner. For four minutes Donovan summed up the points they had discussed less than eighty hours before, the various ways in which American war materials might be made available to Britain and the legal restraints which prevented them.

At two minutes to seven there was a knock on the door and the President's secretary reminded him that he was due to leave. Roosevelt thanked him and wondered again why Donovan had requested the meeting.

'But what, Mr President, if there was a precedent?'

'What precisely?'

Donovan opened the briefcase at the side of his chair, withdrew a folder, extracted two copies of a legal document from the folder, passed one to Roosevelt and read a precis from the other.

Between the years 1804–15 the United States found itself engaged in naval warfare with a number of North African states, the so-called Barbary Wars. During that time certain emergency powers were conferred upon Presidents Jefferson and Madison.

The legislation, like the war itself, had long been forgotten.

These powers have not been repealed. It is the considered opinion of my office that such powers are still on statute and could therefore be used in the present situation.

'How much did it cost to dig that little surprise up, Bill?' There was the beginning of a smile in the corners of Roosevelt's mouth.

'More than you can imagine, Mr President.'

The secretary returned to inform him that he was now running late. He nodded and slumped back in his chair. 'How much do they *really* need us, Bill?'

'A lot.'

'And how much time is left?'

'The invasion fleet is almost ready.'

Roosevelt turned in his chair, staring again across the White House lawn then swung back to his desk and lifted the telephone.

'My engagement this evening: send my apologies and notify them that I will be late. Inform Downing Street that I would like to speak to Mr Churchill in thirty minutes' time and get me Ambassador Kennedy in London.' He replaced the receiver. 'What made you so sure, Bill? What did Churchill and his cronies say that so convinced you?'

'Not Churchill, Mr President.' One day he would tell him; he suspected that he would understand.

THE CONTROL STATION was dark, no light penetrating the door, only the soft glow of the tilly lamp in the corner. The bunk was hard and narrow, and the blankets rough. Outside, Mary's body clock told her, it was getting light.

Dawn readiness. They had slept in the dispersal hut in case of a surprise attack: by five the machines had been warmed up and the oxygen, sights and ammunition tested.

The stove in the corner of the crew room was glowing gently. He lay back in the armchair and stretched his legs. Almost time for breakfast, he was thinking, bacon and eggs and a nice cup of tea. The telephone on the desk in the corner rang. Even before Max put it down they were running, the klaxon on the airfield already sounding and the first engines starting up.

'Hello, Tennis leader. Patrol Canterbury, Angels twenty.'

'Roger, Short Jack.'

Short Jack was the call sign for Biggin Control.

They were climbing fast, already above the thin strand of cloud. Sun in the east he was thinking, have to get height to get the advantage this morning. Five thousand feet, ten, fifteen. The eight planes around him seemed motionless against the sky, below him the curve of the horizon began to change.

'Tennis leader. Vector one-twenty — bandits at fifteen thousand feet heading west — over.'

'Hello, Short Jack. Listening, out.'

Twenty thousand feet. Remember the Hun in the sun.

'Hello, Jaunty squadron. Patrol base, Angels eighteen.'

Another patrol up, unusual for this time of day, must be building up.

He saw them.

'Hello, Short Jack, Tennis leader calling. Tally ho, Tally ho. Heinkels with 109s. Ahead and below. Hello, Tennis squadron, B flight take the bombers, A flight take the fighters with me. Line astern — go.'

They were banking, diving, the black dots suddenly larger, taking shape. Twenty, he was counting, more, probably forty, fifty. Horizon turning in front of him. Christ that was only the start of the top fighter layer, more following, the bombers beneath. Going for the airfields, he realized. Still not been spotted, still in with a chance.

Remember the rules. Even now he told himself. Don't follow a plane down after killing it. Straighten up only when about to attack. Never fly a straight course for more than two seconds.

They've seen you, turning for you. In amongst them, everything so fast. Bandit in half-roll. Kick rudder left, turn gun button to fire. Five-second burst. Bandit through sights, tracer from all eight guns thudding home. Check mirror. Nothing onto you. First flame from bandit, check mirror again. Another bandit, already in trouble. Gun button again.

'Tennis Blue Two to Blue One. Break, break, break. Bandit on you.' Dive and twist before even confirming the enemy on your tail. 'Still behind you, Blue One, port.' Still twisting, trying to see where he was. 'Still there, Blue One, still on you.' The first holes in the starboard wing, see them subconsciously, slide starboard and climb. 'Still there, Blue One. Can't get to him.' Turning, diving, almost black out with G force. Too early in the morning for it, too nice a day to get chopped. Bank right. Where the hell was the bastard? 'Still on you, Blue One.' Engine screaming. More power, for Christ's sake sort it out. First last image in mirror, nothing except the dark of the shape and the red white of the machine guns, then the sudden smell as the glycol spurted into the cockpit, and the first fire.

Unbuckle seat belt. Not much time, still just enough. The bloody heat. Cockpit hood, pull open. The flames coming at him, reaching him. Hood stuck, trying to open it, horizon, ground, everything in front of him spinning. Still time to open the bloody hood. The flames engulfing him.

The hands were helping her. She was screaming, still trying to pull away the cockpit cover, unable to move it. Hearing the voices. She looked up and saw Liz and Beatie bending over her.

'It's all right, Mary, you were only dreaming.'

THE BREAKFAST WAS on the table, the cloth clean and white and the tea in one of Mrs Potter's best china cups. The old lady looked at Mary as she tried to eat. 'Something wrong, dear?'

Mary smiled. 'Something silly, that's all.'

Mrs Potter took away the plate. 'Don't you worry, love, I'll keep it warm for later.'

'Thank you.' She watched as the woman went into the kitchen. 'Back in a moment, Mrs P.'

The telephone kiosk was outside the post office. She knew she should not, but went in and dialled the number.

'Crew room, please.'

The extension was answered immediately. She knew what the men would be thinking, could see them already reaching for their Mae Wests.

'I'm sorry. Is Johnny there?'

There was a silence. Then, 'Who wants him?'

She recognized Max's voice. 'Mary.'

There was a silence again. 'Sorry, Mary, Johnny's missing.'

She began to ask how, when, and heard the klaxon.

'Have to go, Mary. Scramble.'

THE CONTROL STATION was quiet and cold. Mary sat on the edge of the bunk.

'Max only said he was missing. Why don't you phone again?' Liz had made her tea and was sitting beside her.

'I can't, there must always be two of us here.'

She was still shaking.

'I can manage. Nothing's going to happen today.'

It was midday, the day outside bright and sunny. Whenever she looked outside the planes were tumbling in the sky. 'I *can't*. They'll think it's another scramble.'

THE FIRST PURPLE of the evening crept into the trees round the control station. Mary knew she could not delay the confirmation any longer. 'Cover for me, will you?'

'Course.'

She left the woods and dropped into the village. The streets were empty and quiet. She dialled the number of the air station and asked for the crew extension. Nobody there, she thought, nobody on stand-by at this time of the evening.

The phone rang only once before it was answered. 'Crew room.'

She recognized the voice and knew he had waited for her. 'Max, it's Mary.' She did not know what else to say.

'He's all right, Mary. Ditched in the Channel. He was picked up half an hour ago.'

She felt herself beginning to cry, hardly able to speak.

'He's really all right, isn't he, Max? You're not just saying it?'

'He's fine.'

Something else, she knew, waited for him to tell her.

'Sandy bought it over Ardley this morning.'

BOY JACK WAS early. Normally he stayed in the village as late as he could playing, or went home with Ted and Sarah's boys. Fran finished the animals and saw the way he was walking, feet dragging and head down. She went back to the house and began to make the supper.

'Where's Dad?'

She wondered what was troubling him. 'Canterbury. He'll be back later.'

'They called me a whitey.' He did not look up from the table.

'Who?'

'Dick and Les, some of the other boys from the village.' He could not bear to look at her. 'They said Dad was a whitey.'

'What's a whitey?'

'White feather job. They said that Dad's a coward, that he's not in the proper army or joined the Home Guard like everybody else. They said that when Jerry comes they hope we'll all be killed.' He was sniffing, trying to stop the tears.

Fran walked round the table and knelt beside him, her arm around him. Please help me, she thought, please may there come a day when I can tell my son the truth about his father.

'Dad has his reasons. He's worked it all out. He knows what he's doing.'

'So he's not a coward.'

The depth of loyalty in his eyes frightened her.

'No. Your father is a very brave man.'

'I knew he was.'

THE LAST MATCH of August was at Petham. There were only two more before the end of the season, both Saturday matches; the light in the evenings had gone too much. Ardley won the toss and elected to bat. A strange place England in the summer of 1940, Fran thought as she watched Jack and Ted walk to the wicket: the country at war, the dogfights in the skies above them even now and the battle between the two villages as bitter as the conflict between nations, yet they still clapped the other side's heroes onto the field.

After the match ended, Jack and Boy Jack tended the animals while Fran made supper. When she went to fetch them the countryside seemed settled, at peace. It was almost as if the land itself had accepted what was inevitable.

THE PRIME MINISTER returned to Downing Street having spent the day inspecting the coastal defences and attending a Chief of Staffs meeting in the war room. He retired shortly after midnight and was working again by six. At six-thirty the telephone rang.

'Yes.' Churchill was always gruff before breakfast.

'It's begun.' Dowding was matter of fact. 'Three waves approaching the coast now. Manston, Hawkinge and Biggin Hill have scrambled; Hornchurch and Tangmere are on readiness.'

'How many?' The voice was still stern, unshakeable.

'We calculate two hundred and fifty bombers in each, fighter escort above and below them.' There was a pause. 'Radar reports more taking off behind.'

2

_____

THE MORNING WAS sunny. As Fran and Jack left the farm, Boy Jack
ahead of them, they could see the clouds of smoke rising from the
coast and the waves of planes overhead. The church was full. When
the service was finished the Reverend Brian Markham closed the Bible
and came to the announcements.

'The government has decreed that until further notice the church
bells will only be rung as a warning in the event of invasion.' He
looked round the congregation and smiled. 'Thanksgiving is on
Sunday, October the 6th. The harvest supper will be held the Friday
before.'

They all knew what he was saying – that there would be no invasion
– and thanked him for it even though it was probably untrue.

WHENEVER MARY LEFT the control station the air seemed layered by
planes. Even inside she could hear the sound of the bombing. The
evening, when it came, was calm and peaceful. By the time she left
the woods the sounds of the birds had replaced that of the explosions.
Monday evening, thirty-six hours after the first waves of bombers
had appeared over the coast and the boys were holding out. She
turned the corner to the pub and saw Max's MG, Johnny's just
behind it, and felt the relief.

The room was crowded; she could not remember it so full for some
time. At the bar itself a flight lieutenant was already drunk, those
around him almost so. Max was pushing his way through, he saw

her and waved, then pointed to the far corner. Johnny was sitting at the table overlooking the garden, the blackout curtains drawn across the view.

'Hello, love.' His voice was quieter than usual and he looked white and drawn. She kissed him and sat down.

'What's happening? Why are so many people in tonight?'

'Today was a bad one.'

'How bad?'

Max came back with the drinks. In the other corner someone had started to play 'The White Cliffs of Dover' on the piano, people joining in and singing.

'We lost a quarter of the squadron.'

'What about reinforcements from the other groups?'

'They're holding them in case the attacks on the South are just a cover and the invasion is planned against the east coast.'

On the table next to them some of the girls from the radar stations were laughing.

'Where's Joan?' she suddenly asked. 'Where's Ruth?'

'They're bombing the radar stations as well.' Johnny pushed his glass towards Max. 'Your round again, isn't it?' Max bowed affectedly to Mary and left the table.

'Marry me.'

She thought he was joking then saw he was serious. 'Saturday's my day off.'

'Saturday's a long way off.'

'What else then?'

'Tonight.'

'I'm supposed to be on duty.'

'I know.'

He had never asked her again what she did.

'I've booked us a room.'

'Why?'

'In case Saturday doesn't come.'

For forty minutes on the Tuesday morning the skies had been quiet. Fran walked past the church and into the village. The post office was busy, Quizzie Lizzie supplying those who wished to hear with the gossip and rumours from the coast.

'Isn't it going well?' She pulled a copy of the morning's paper from beneath the counter and showed it to Fran: '100 GERMANS SHOT DOWN. THE RAF HAVE A BRILLIANT DAY.'

The night had been quiet, the noise beginning slowly, a distant hum turning into a rumble, then suddenly overhead, deafening and unending. The walls of the farmhouse began to shake and the plaster was falling from the ceiling of the bedroom. From the north came the boom of the anti-aircraft guns. They pulled on their coats and went outside. The sky to the north-east was alight, the huge orange-red glow spreading even as they watched, the sound deafening.

'They're bombing Canterbury.'

The following morning, as soon as they had dealt with the animals, Jack and Ted drove into the city. The south-east corner of the centre, bordered by the lower half of Burgate, Lower Chantry, St George's Place, Watling Street and St Margaret's Street had been destroyed. Some areas were still burning, the fire brigade trying to extinguish the flames, men and women helping, others simply standing and looking, dazed and unbelieving. Inside the wall part of the cloisters, the Library and the Deanery had been razed; in the centre of the rubble, reaching unharmed into the sky, stood the cathedral, saved by the fire-spotters who throughout the raid had maintained their positions on its roof and thrown off the firebombs as they landed.

They walked down what remained of St George's Street and into The Parade, the line of damage stopping suddenly. Off St Margaret's Street, on the edge of the destruction itself, was a small grocer's shop, its walls buckled and the shop barely intact. The woman who ran it was sweeping the glass and masonry from the shelves. On a child's blackboard on what remained of the front window she had chalked a notice: 'We never close.' There was a commotion behind them and they turned. Striding through the rubble, dressed in the uniform of the Royal Navy, the Queen at his side and the bodyguards of the Coats Mission close behind him, was the King.

'Morning, Mrs Best.' The King glanced at the name above the door. 'Still open for business I see.'

The cheering began from the back of the crowd and grew as loud as the night's bombing.

That evening Fran and Jack heard the bombers overhead and prayed that Canterbury would not again suffer; that night the first bombs were unloaded onto the dockland of the East End of London, the fires that they started serving merely as beacons for the massive raid which followed. The damage to housing in the area and the loss of human life was severe. The following morning George VI and Queen Elizabeth visited the area.

The same day Drake began the first of the meetings with those whose identities and roles were known only to himself. At seven on that Thursday evening he came to the appointment with the agent to whom he had given the code name Prospero. The meeting took place in a house which Drake considered secure and lasted an hour.

In the months ahead, there were two things about the conversation that night which refused to leave him. The first was unimportant: it was that the meeting with Prospero was the last he would have with any of those he had recruited before invasion. The second was his decision, queried by Prospero but insisted upon by himself, that for security reasons communication between them after invasion should be one way, Prospero to himself, and that they should never risk a communication from Drake to the agent.

That night the town of Maidstone, forty miles inland and occupying a strategic position close to the River Medway, mid-way between Dover and London, was bombed. The following morning the King and Queen, attended as always by their bodyguards from the Coats Mission, visited the scene.

MARY HAD MANAGED to speak to Johnny on the telephone the night before, but not been able to see him, had wondered about him all day as she listened to the sound of the bombers and the fighters to the south. She turned out of the woods and onto the side road towards the Black Swan. He'll be all right, she told herself. They only get one go at you and Johnny survived his the day he ditched in the Channel.

Saturday's a long way off, Johnny had said. Not so long now. She was pedalling harder than normal, could feel the anxiety rising again in her throat. Tomorrow. She had made sure she could get the day off; Liz and Beatie had altered the schedule so she could be away the night. She rounded the bend by the Black Swan. Not many cars. The panic gripped her. Hardly any at all. Not Johnny's MG. She dropped the bike and ran.

Stupid bloody fool, she thought, probably wrote it off like she was always teasing him he would. Or broken down. Max had given him a lift. She opened the door and went in.

Not so many as the other night, the realization shocked her. Not many at all. Nobody speaking.

Max was in the corner, his arm was in a sling, and the table in front of him was piled with glasses.

'Where's Johnny?' It was almost a scream.

'Hospital.'

She began to feel the relief then remembered the nightmare.

'He was caught over Dover. Royal Observer Corps say he was the only one left but he still went in.'

'Where? Which hospital?'

'Managed to bail out, they got to him almost immediately.'

'How bad?'

He could not answer.

'Which hospital?' she asked again.

'He won't want you to see him, Mary.'

In the far corner someone had begun to play the piano. Not tonight – she was getting up, going to stop them – not with Johnny lying with his body in cinders. Max laid his hand on her arm and shook his head. Don't stop them. Don't stop those who won't be here tomorrow.

She realized again how empty the bar was.

'We couldn't make it, Mary. In the end we couldn't pull it off.' She put her hand through his good arm and allowed him to talk. 'Too many of them, you see. Just kept on coming. We're taking off and landing in fields, roads, anything. Those who are left. Tomorrow and it'll be all over.' He shook his head. 'The girls as well. They had to stay in place, you see, keep reading the radar plots so Control could tell us where the enemy was coming from even though the bombs were falling on them.'

'Reinforcements from the other groups?'

'Gone as well.'

'What about you?'

'Crash-landed.' He sounded guilty for being alive. 'Mid-afternoon. By the time I got back it was finished for the day.'

'What's wrong with the arm?'

'Broken bloody collar bone.'

'So you're grounded?'

He laughed. 'Nobody else, is there?'

'But you're not flying tomorrow?'

He ignored her question and joined in the singing.

THE PATTERNS IN the sky were different. On other days they had been bold, brilliant, as the fighters weaved and dived, trying to close on the bombers, trying to shake the escorts off their tails. This morning, after the first extended raid at seven, there were no such patterns, as if there was nothing left, the bombers simply droning in, the cover above them, then dumping their loads and wheeling in a giant circle back to France.

Fran finished the farm work and began to make the sandwiches for the afternoon. It was almost like a ritual, she thought, a tradition which could not be broken. In the corner of the kitchen Jack's cricket bag was ready. She heard the next wave of bombers and buttered the bread.

THE HOSPITAL IN Ramsgate was on the western edge of the town. Mary leant her bike against the pillar by the front doors and went inside. The hall was clean and smelt of antiseptic. On the left, seated at a reception desk, was a nurse in a starched white uniform.

'Good morning. I've come to see Flight Lieutenant Watson.'

'It's a little difficult.'

'Why?'

The nurse hesitated. 'I'll get the doctor.'

On either side of the hall was a wooden bench, the only other furniture a jardinière of flowers. Mary had waited ten minutes when a middle-aged, grey-haired man in a white coat appeared.

'Good morning. I'm Doctor Jennings. I understand you were asking about Flight Lieutenant Watson.'

Mary stood up. 'Yes. I'd like to see him.'

'You understand his condition?' He looked tired, as if he had not slept.

'I know that he was shot down yesterday and badly burned.'

'Perhaps I should see if he's well enough.'

'Perhaps you shouldn't.'

He saw her determination. 'You're sure?'

'Yes, I'm sure.'

He nodded. 'Give me two minutes.'

She sat fidgeting until he returned.

'We're moving him soon, probably East Grinstead.'

They passed along a series of corridors and into a ward facing south, the curtains drawn across the windows.

'He's on regular injections of morphia, so he might sometimes be in a semi-stupor.'

The men in the beds were lying still, in the half-gloom she could not see their features. They stopped at the foot of the third bed on the right.

'Hello, Johnny, it's me.'

The right side of his face was lightly bandaged, the dressing extending down his right side and over his hand; his arm was propped in front of him and his body hung loosely on straps just clear of the bed. The bandages, Mary did not know, were not normal; in the short period while she waited in the corridor the doctor had ordered them to be applied to save her distress. Beneath them Johnny had been sprayed with tannic acid to form a hard cement to protect the skin from the air and encourage it to heal, and his eye had been coated with a thick layer of gentian violet.

Why you, Johnny, she thought. Why you, my dear precious Johnny? She bent over him and kissed him. 'Said I'd keep today for you, didn't I?'

The doctor brought her a chair. 'Ten minutes, then he will have had enough.'

'Thank you.'

She sat on his left, not knowing what to do or say. The doctor smiled and left. She knew she must not cry. Carefully, so as not to hurt him, she reached forward and held his hand between hers. There was the slightest movement of his head as he tried to look at her.

'Don't move, darling, no need to say anything.'

On the palm of her hand she felt the slightest pressure of his fingers as he tried to thank her. You'll be all right soon, she knew she should tell him, it's not much really. She looked at his face and knew it was a lie, that even if he lived he would always be like this.

The doctor was standing over her again. I think that's enough for now, she knew he was going to say.

'I'd like to stay for a while if you don't mind.'

'I'll get you a cup of tea.'

THE MATCH BEGAN at two-thirty. At ten minutes to three, with the
score at twenty runs for no wicket, Ted declared the Ardley innings
closed and the tea was served. As the men sat down Ted asked for
silence.

'Gentlemen, with your permission I would like to ask the ladies
and the families to join us.'

There were no objections.

The tea ended and the Barham innings began. When the score
stood at nineteen for no wicket, the facing batsman swept the ball to
the leg side. A certain two runs, all that was needed to win. After one
run, with the scores level, the batsmen stopped running and walked
back to the pavilion.

THE LIGHT FROM outside was almost gone. Mary saw the doctor
standing at the end of the ward and knew it was time to leave. Will
you be back tomorrow? She understood what Johnny was trying to
ask her.

'I don't know, Johnny.' Her words were almost a whisper. 'I don't
know if I *will* be back.'

She sensed the hurt in him and felt the strength seep from his
fingers. All right when I was well, she knew he was thinking, but not
now she had seen him, knew what he would be like for the rest of
his life. The doctor saw the change and came towards them.

She bent closer to him. A secret, they had told her, instilled into
her, a responsibility she should share with no one.

'You were right. I'm not a driver.'

The pressure came back into his fingers. Take care, Mary, he willed
her to understand, whatever you are, whatever you do.

The doctor was standing beside her.

'Where are his possessions?' she asked. 'He had a ring.'

'It's with everything else.' He opened the cupboard at the side of
the bed and handed her a small tin box. 'I'll wait for you outside.'

Inside the box were a watch, a wallet and a signet ring. On the
white of the pillow Johnny moved his head so that he was looking

at her. Mary removed the ring her grandmother had given her from her finger and placed it gently in his palm then took the signet ring from the box and slid it onto the ring finger of her left hand.

'Love you, Johnny. Always will.'

THE ANIMALS HAD been fed and shut away for the night. As Jack, Fran and Boy Jack sat down to supper, the vicar appeared at the door. He was panting, as if he had run up the hill.

'Quick word, Jack.'

The two men went outside.

'Lorry from The Garth arrived ten minutes ago. I told them to come back after dark. Loaded with ammunition, guns, explosives, everything we've been waiting for.'

'About bloody time,' said Jack Masters.

THE WAR CABINET met at seven-thirty. The air defences in the South of England no longer existed, they were informed. Reconnaissance photographs showed the first of the German invasion fleets leaving harbour. Shortly before eight the Prime Minister asked the committee's indulgence and spoke on the telephone with the King. The conversation over, he left the war room and walked the thirty yards to the signals sections. For the slightest moment, as he stood beside the operator, there was a hesitation. Then the moment was gone and the voice was firm.

It was seven minutes past eight on the evening of Saturday, 7 September 1940.

'Transmit Cromwell.'

3

HIGH TIDE AT Dover was at three, with two hours of slack water on either side. The night was quiet, no planes overhead on their way to bomb the cities. They lay in bed and waited. At one-thirty Fran heard the first explosion and saw the first flash in the sky; Jack was already out of bed and pulling on his clothes. 'I'll be back by morning. Don't leave the farm.' There was another flash in the sky, and another. At the bottom of the field they could hear the bells of the church ringing. Boy Jack came into the room. 'The invasion?' His voice was calm. Fran nodded. They dressed and went to the kitchen. She took the shotgun from the wall of the kitchen, loaded it, and placed it on the table, then made them a mug of tea.

The direct telephone connection to and from Hannington Hall rang at five minutes past three. Mary picked it up, Beatie looking at her and Liz already awake on the bunk. 'Enemy reported landing at Dover. Transfer to zero station. Repeat. Enemy reported landing at Dover. Transfer to zero station.' She had thought it would never come yet always knew it would. 'Cricket received. Repeat Cricket received.' Wish I was with you to look after you, Johnny. 'Thank you, Cricket. Good luck.' They collected the code books, checked that nothing that could be considered a security risk had been left, and walked the hundred yards to the entrance to the zero station.

Brian and Stan were already in the vault under the pulpit, Ted arrived thirty seconds after Jack. They checked the weapons and explosives then went to the village, Jack and Ted arriving together and Brian and Stan separately. The square between the schoolroom and the King's Arms was crowded, most people not knowing what

145

to do. Already the Home Guard had erected their barricades. By the time Jack returned to the farm it was getting lighter; Fran and Boy Jack were in the kitchen listening to the wireless.

'Any news?' he asked.

'The BBC say that Dover has been invaded, but that the enemy is failing to establish a foothold and that it will be over by tonight.' They both recognized the propaganda for what it was. 'And with you?'

'Ted and Sarah are fine. The village is quiet, Harry Downton is protecting the square.'

'I wonder where Ernie is,' the boy said.

At ten they left the farm and walked to the village. The square was still full, while Fran and Boy Jack talked to Sarah, Jack went to the back door of the King's Arms. There was still no news, nor did they expect there to be. The situation on the coast, according to the latest BBC report, had been contained.

THAT EVENING THE War Cabinet was informed that although beach-heads had been established from Margate, twenty miles east of Dover, to Dungeness, twenty-five miles west, and substantial numbers of troops and tanks had been landed, the army was holding its position.

THE ZERO STATION was quiet. For twenty-four hours now they had sat and waited. At ten that morning Mary positioned her bicycle in the shrubs by the bolt hole from the zero station and changed into civilian clothes. At least she did not know which code represented the area in which the hospital where Johnny was being treated was situated. At least she would not know when it had been overrun. The thought had been with her all night.

AT EIGHT-THIRTY that evening the War Cabinet was informed that, according to intelligence coming from the coast, the German beach-head had been consolidated and, preceded by parachute troops on key targets, the first tanks and infantry had begun to push inland. Due to lack of equipment the army was already experiencing difficulty holding the line. It was also informed that despite the strongest of recommendations, the King and Queen had refused to leave

Buckingham Palace or to send their daughters to a place of safety.

The following morning King George, accompanied by his wife and family, inspected the anti-aircraft batteries which had sought to protect the East End of London from the bombings of the previous week, the appearance of the monarch calming the flood of rumours sweeping the city. Ten hours later the King attended the meeting of the Cabinet in the war rooms below Downing Street; it was an evening which would scar him for the rest of his life.

The enemy, he and the Cabinet were informed, could no longer be contained on the coast, and a break-out was considered imminent. The army therefore intended an orderly withdrawal to a GHQ line, running east–west across the country with its apex at Maidstone, forty miles from the coast. The British Resistance would seek to delay the enemy's advance to enable the army to achieve its tactical objective. In the event of the GHQ line not holding, the army had already made plans for a series of defensive positions at successive points north, the last and most crucial being along the line of the Cheviots, north of Carlisle and running east–west on the border with Scotland, few roads or passes over the mountains and the coastal belts on either side narrow and therefore easier to defend. When he questioned the reference to the British Resistance, as well as the source of the intelligence coming from the enemy positions, the King was informed that the plans had been in place for some time.

THE RING OF the telephone broke the silence. Five-thirty in the morning. Mary knew what it was and reached for the handset.

'Cricket, this is Hedgehog. Tanks. Will identify them later.'

Liz was already encoding. The telephone rang again, the radio crackling as well.

'Blackberry, tanks. Approximately twenty.'

'Tulip. German tanks in village. Parachutists to north.'

This is it, Johnny. Hope you're all right.

'Strawberry, fifteen tanks with infantry follow-up.'

Beatie was off the bunk and transmitting while Liz continued the encoding.

'Orchard to Cricket.'

'Lace to Cricket.'

'Apple to Cricket.'

THE SOUND OF the battle from the south was sudden and intense. Jack hoped he had not left it too late. 'Ted and I will see to Fran and Sarah and the kids.' He knew that Brian and Stan would wish to make their own final arrangements. 'We'll meet you in the church.' The square was busy, the Home Guard reorganizing the barricades, one in the centre and the other on the edge of the village to the south, the grocer wearing his sergeant's stripes and watched by a cluster of boys.

'I see Harry's making his usual sacrifice.' Ted's voice was humourless; the grocer had put himself in command of the barricade in the square. 'Farthest from the enemy and closest to his shop.'

Fran and Boy Jack were waiting. Ted left Jack at the farm and drove up the track to collect Sarah and the children.

'It's time to go.'

They had already agreed on what they would do: Fran and Boy Jack would go to Fran's mother in Bearsted Green, near Maidstone, taking Sarah and her children with them, partly because it would be safer in Maidstone, mainly in case the Germans tried to track down the families of the Resistance.

'We're ready.'

They had not made specific plans after that, only that Jack would contact Fran when it was safe.

The smoke to the south was blacker, denser, the sounds of the guns drawing closer. The break-out from the coast, Boy Jack asked. Army can't hold them any more, Jack explained. What we've all been waiting for. They both looked round, hearing the shells.

'Don't let anything distract you,' he told Fran. 'Just make sure you get through.'

The pick-up came back down the track. He looked again at his son. 'Mum's got a lot of things to think about today. You're the oldest of the boys, so you're in charge.'

Boy Jack nodded. 'Good luck, Dad.' It was as if he knew.

Jack put his arm round the boy. 'Thanks.'

'We'll see you soon, won't we?'

He helped him into the back of the pick-up. 'Course you will.'

Fran and Sarah checked the petrol, refilling the tank from the jerry cans in the barn, while Ted and Jack packed bales of straw round the children to give them whatever protection they could. Then Fran and Sarah climbed in the front.

'Cheerio, son.' He kissed Boy Jack.

'Bye, Dad. See you at Gran's.'

Fran started the engine.

'Bye, love.' So many things to say.

'Bye, Jack.' Nothing at all left to say.

She released the handbrake and he watched the pick-up trundle down the hill. Right at the bottom. He did not realize he had not stopped waving to them. Then left at the top towards Canterbury. So much work before the winter, Fran thought, so many things to do before next spring. She waved for the last time and turned the corner out of sight.

'Come on, Jack. It's time to go.' Ted stood beside him. When they reached the church Stan and Brian were waiting.

In the sky behind them Fran could see smoke rising in billows, yet the lanes around them seemed just as they always were in early autumn, the first leaves tinged brown but none falling from the trees, as if neither the war nor the invasion existed. They came to the A2.

'Oh my God.' She was not sure whether the voice was hers or Sarah's.

The line of refugees fleeing the battle zone was unending, the men and women looking dazed, the children stumbling. Some were in cars and vans, an occasional lorry, the backs packed high with furniture and cases, even chickens. Others were on horses, in wagons, yet more pushing handcarts or prams. To the right, walking so slowly that she was hardly moving, was a young woman with three children, the youngest a babe in arms. Fran watched mesmerized and thought of the indecency that people in vans and lorries were saving their furniture when others like the woman could barely walk. She knew Sarah was thinking the same thing and stopped.

'Throw off the bales,' she told the boys.

The woman with the children saw what they were doing and tried to hurry, afraid she would miss her place in the back of the pick-up, others already stopping and looking. Sarah lifted the infant from her arms, waited till the woman was in the back and had pulled her other children up, then handed the child back to her. The woman was too shocked even to thank them. Others were climbing on – an old man and woman, the husband trying to help his wife up, another family – until there were fifteen people in the back, leaning on the roof of the cab and hanging over the edge. A plane screamed overhead. The people in the back and on the road saw the RAF roundels of the Spitfire and began to cheer. Smoke was pouring from the body and one wing was on fire. Three hundred yards on the plane dipped right and crashed to the ground, the ammunition exploding into the sky. The refugees were suddenly quiet.

Near Thanington where the A2 continued north to London and the A28 cut west towards Ashford, a group of armoured personnel carriers had stopped where the sign posts had been removed, the men in them dog-tired and barely able to keep awake, having driven nonstop from the east coast. Fran knew they were lost. She turned left.

Normally, she calculated, it would take them ninety minutes to reach Bearsted Green; today they would be lucky to be there by mid-afternoon, even early evening. She looked through the back window, tapped on the glass and saw the boys smile at her that everything was fine.

Most of the refugees had headed straight on, guided either by instinct or merely following those ahead. The road to Ashford, therefore, was relatively free of traffic. Between Chartham and Chilham, at the junction where she intended to turn north along the A252 to Charing, the road was blocked by a column of tanks, so she continued towards Ashford. Two hundred yards up the track they now passed was a place called The Garth. The trees cleared from the lane and she saw the fields and sky ahead, heard again the sound of the battle to the south. They came to the main A20, the other major road from the coast, and saw the fresh line of refugees, the same expressions on their faces and the same mix of bewilderment and panic in their eyes, vehicles trying to overtake, a man and woman pushing a pram loaded with an armchair, the woman leading a goat. Parents and children were everywhere, the tanks thundering towards the coast and the soldiers waving to the refugees to let them through. To the south and the north more planes dropped their bomb loads and sent the smoke and debris into the sky.

They turned right and headed towards Maidstone. The water temperature, Fran suddenly remembered, and looked at the dashboard; the needle was on the red. She thought she heard a thumping in the engine and wondered whether it had been there all the time.

'Got to stop.' She pulled off the road, half the pick-up still sticking out, and lifted the bonnet. A cloud of steam rose up, almost scalding her. 'The radiator's dry,' she told the people in the back. 'Have to get some more water and fill it up.' They were already climbing down and walking away. She took one of the petrol cans from the back, used as much as would fill the tank and emptied the rest by the side of the road. 'There's a farmhouse over there,' she told Sarah. 'Get some water.' Boy Jack was looking at her. 'We'll have to wait until the radiator's cold or we'll split it.' The boy nodded his agreement.

The woman and the three children were still crouched in the back, the mother still holding the baby close to her. She was young, Fran thought, no more than her early twenties, and realized suddenly that she was pregnant, four, five months, perhaps. Boy Jack climbed into the back again, made a mattress from the straw on the floor and eased her onto it. Then he began to tell the children a story.

The radiator was cool. They poured in the water and moved off, more people climbing on. It was gone three in the afternoon. No tanks or other vehicles were moving south any more, Fran suddenly realized, no more planes in the sky. Perhaps it had been decided that they should be left in peace, that even the enemy had decreed that they should reach her mother's.

The refugees spread across the road made it difficult for them to travel at anything more than a crawl. Twice more she stopped when the needle of the temperature gauge crept across the red. It was after four-thirty, almost five, three more hours before dusk. The first tanks passed again, forcing the refugees into the hedge, the grit and stones flying from their tracks, the trucks following, then more tanks. The ones she had seen earlier, she thought. Not going south to the battle, but north, away from it.

Work it out, Jack would have told her; see what's happening, what you have to do. Whatever it is, no matter how long it takes you, just get through. It was two miles to the junction at Charing, fifteen from there to Bearsted Green on the main road, twenty if she took the back roads.

'I'm turning off at Charing,' she told Sarah. 'It's longer but there'll be fewer hold-ups.'

More tanks were passing them, all going north. They came to the turning.

'We're going another way. You can come with us or you can make your own way,' Sarah leant out the window and told the people in the back. They turned off the A20 into the side road.

The men had shotguns.

There were three of them, hidden behind the corner two hundred yards from the main road, women and children behind them, their own truck lop-sided on the verge, its axle broken.

'Out.'

Fran pulled on the handbrake and stepped down, the others climbing from the back, nobody protesting or saying anything, the men still holding the shotguns on them. The women loaded their own children and furniture into the rear of the pick-up. One man climbed into the driving seat, the others on the running boards, the shotguns still in their hands, and drove back down the road. At the junction they stopped, then turned right towards Maidstone.

Slowly, still without speaking, the group which remained divided into two, the majority returning back towards the A20, Sarah and the boys following Fran and Boy Jack the other way. The pregnant woman and her children stood lost and frightened in the middle, not knowing where to go or what to do, the child in her arms beginning to cry. Fifteen miles by the main road, twenty the other way; they would probably be walking all night. The other refugees were almost out of sight, the woman still looking at them.

Not their responsibility, she told herself. In any case, the woman and her children would slow them down, make it more difficult. Their responsibility in the first place – if they hadn't stopped and helped her on board she wouldn't be here now. Not their responsibility at all, the woman would have been lost with her children anyway. Their responsibility no matter which way you looked at it. She walked back down the lane and lifted the babe from the mother's arms.

'Come with us,' Boy Jack told the woman. 'My mum knows what she's doing.'

They had been walking ninety minutes when she heard the bombs. Eight hundred yards to their left the Stukas dropped out of the sky, scattering the refugees into the fields and destroying the tanks and lorries, the screaming of their wings and engines adding to the fear and the panic. More followed, the onslaught not stopping, wave following wave, strafing the main road. Clearing the way for the German advance on the apex of the British GHQ Line at Maidstone.

They picked up the children and walked on.

THE CRYPT WAS quiet. Explosive charges wedged tightly together and worn in canvas sleeve like a belt, hand grenades, Smith & Wesson revolvers and knives on the belts, Thompson sub-machine-guns loaded, clip-on not circular mags, spare mags also loaded. There was no point leaving the bunker unprepared, the enemy parachutists might already be landing around them.

At the gate in the corner of the graveyard they split, Jack and Ted taking the targets to the east and south, Stan and Brian those to the west and north, beginning with the farthest then working back. The regular army would be taking care of the lines and bridges closer to the coast, but they had decided to double up in their area in case units of the enemy leapfrogged ahead. Two miles from the church Jack and Ted picked up the railway line, found the points and knelt by the track, Ted standing guard while Jack crouched by the fishplate connecting the rails. Charge wired into place, he worked automatically, detonator into slow-burning fuse then into charge, procedure repeated at adjacent rail tie-in. Light fuse, warn Ted and run for cover.

'APPLE TO CRICKET.'

After the first hectic hours the messages had become more regular and contained more information.

'Come in Apple.'

'Five tanks, approximately two hundred troops.'

To her left Beatie encoded the message.

'Thank you, Apple.'

Liz passed them each a mug of tea.

'Pigeon to Cricket.'

Mary recognized the man's voice immediately.

'Come in, Pigeon.'

In the exercises he had been the one they waited for, the one who always seemed able to cheer them up when they were feeling tired. 'Constant flow of tanks, mainly SS Panzer Division, on main road, all heading north.' He was also, they all sensed, the most accurate. 'Nineteen personnel carriers in village, another twelve already passed through also heading north.'

Beatie was already transmitting.

'Reports of petrol bowsers to north, not confirmed personally.'

She wanted to talk to him, ask what was going on.

'Message ends.'

'Thank you, Pigeon.'
'Take care, dearie, speak to you soon.'

THE VAULT WAS dark, they had extinguished the tilly lamp to save paraffin. Jack lay on the bunk and tried to concentrate on the targets, the approaches they had analysed and the ways they assumed the enemy would try to defend them. Please God may Fran have stayed off the main roads, he prayed, please may she and Sarah and the boys have got to Bearsted Green. He looked at his watch again; it was four in the morning.

WHEN THEY CAME through Leeds village the night was still dark; by six, when the first dawn began to break, they had barely covered another half a mile. It was another hour before they crept into the outskirts of Bearsted Green and picked their way through the tanks parked on the green.

Fran's mother had waited all night, sitting in the kitchen and staring at the door she knew her daughter would come through. Gently, carefully, she took the babe from the stranger's arms, sat the pregnant woman in a chair and eased off her shoes, bathing the blood off the blisters and sores which covered her feet then laying her in her own bed, her children beside her. In the front room Fran and Sarah tucked the others in the makeshift beds they had made for them and watched as they fell asleep.

When the house was quiet Fran sat with her mother and told her of the events of the past hours, drinking tea and falling into an occasional sleep, listening to the reports of the terrible events on the main road, of how the refugees had been bombed and strafed by the Germans, some even run over by their side as the tanks and artillery returned in the chaos and confusion to the north.

It was only when she was wrapped in blankets on the sofa, the last waves of sleep overtaking her, that Fran realized something else that had happened on the journey from the farm. They had been standing in the lane, the men with the shotguns taking the pick-up, the refugees turning away and the woman with the child in her arms in the middle, not knowing what to do. Fran and Boy Jack had gone back, Fran taking the child, and Boy Jack holding the hands of the other children.

'All right, Jack?' she had asked him.

'All right,' he had replied.

Not Boy Jack any more, she thought, the sleep overtaking her. The son had taken his father's place.

IT WAS TWENTY-FOUR hours since they had gone underground. They left the church and made their way to the west of the village. There was little they could do in daylight, so they would use the hours to identify and plan their targets. The grey-green vehicles of the Gross Deutschland infantry regiment were parked outside the King's Arms and a convoy from the Second Panzer Division on the cricket field. There was no sound of fighting. Both sides resting, Jack thought, probably preparing for a major battle. They pulled back and swept in a three-mile radius around Ardley; at four o'clock they returned to the bunker, prepared the explosives they would use that night and tried to eat. At six they left the church for the first of the night's targets, none of them close to the village, the fear of reprisals always a prime consideration.

The first purple of dusk was rising in the woods to the east.

There would be three main targets that night, Jack had decided: two infantry convoys to the north and west, and what seemed to be a supply group, also to the west, the bombs at each set to detonate at the same time.

'PIGEON TO CRICKET.' Eighteen contacts had reported to them during exercises, sixteen had come through since invasion and the German break-out from the coast. 'Come in Pigeon.' The previous evening twelve had still been in contact, that morning ten. 'Fifteen tanks, three personnel carriers, approximately two hundred troops.' By midday the ten had been reduced to seven. 'Message ends.' Now there were three. 'Thank you, Pigeon.' One of them was the man who called them *dearie*.

FRAN WOKE EARLY in the afternoon, Sarah and the boys a little later. The pregnant woman and her children came down at three. Even in the house they remained together; the only person to whom the children would speak, other than their mother, was Boy Jack. Gradually, however, they and their mother emerged from the fatigue and shock which gripped them and began to talk.

The woman's name was Helen, her husband was a docker at Dover who had been killed in the fierce fighting that took place round the port. She and the children had been part of the flood of refugees who had poured from the coast in the first hours of the invasion.

For supper that night they ate some of the smoked bacon which Jack and Fran had brought during the summer. Before they went to bed, Fran made sure their clothes were ready and a bag of food packed. Her mother understood and said nothing.

THE CAMOUFLAGE NETS were pulled over the lorries and the guards around them were no more than ten yards apart, so that it seemed impossible to get through. They left the cover of the trees, split into two pairs, and moved forward as they had done so often in practice, Ted close by Jack to his right, Brian and Stan to the left.

If you're in trouble stay perfectly still and no one will see you, the instructor had told them.

The guard was eight yards away, facing out, towards them, the first of the vehicles immediately behind him, the guard to his right smoking a cigarette. Seven yards. The sentry turned to his left. Six, not much space between the guards, probably enough. The guard was saying something to the man on his left, the one on the right crossing their line of path to listen, closing on them. Four yards. Just like the training, Jack thought. Three. Not at all like the training. Two yards, one. The man was looking straight at him, reaching down and undoing his trousers. Still, absolutely bloody still. The hot liquid splashed on him. Just like the training after all. The guard turned to his right, buttoned up his trousers, and asked the other man for a light.

The trucks were laagered together. Jack and Ted leapfrogged from vehicle to vehicle, covering each other, pressing the plastic explosive as close as they could to the fuel tank and caking it with mud, then inserting the time pencils into the detonators and the detonators into the charges. Thank God they had planned it, organized themselves, packed the timers in separate units according to their duration. Thank God they could do it with their eyes closed. He broke the glass phial of the timer and the acid began to eat into the copper wire inside.

They were almost finished. At the side of the truck someone lit a cigarette. Jack was so close he heard the match strike. He checked his watch, slipped under the front wheels and made for the next truck.

By the time they reached their third target it was five and they had almost exhausted the explosives and detonators they had carried with them. One more hour of safe darkness then the grey would seep into the black and the guards would be able to see them.

There were fewer lorries than in the other convoys, eight in all, closer together. They divided the remaining explosives and crept forward, the sentries not seeing them, and began to attach the charges. Suddenly, abruptly, the camp came awake, an officer shouting orders, the men climbing out of their sleeping bags and the guards suddenly alert.

'Christ,' Ted whispered, 'they're moving out.'

There was a smell of coffee in the air and the sound of an engine starting, someone calling the sentries. The guards moved back to the fires knowing the place was safe, that no one would attack it now everyone was awake, that it was too early for an attack from the air. They attached the remaining charges and slipped out, stopping twice. By the time they reached the rendezvous Brian and Stan were already there. All around them the convoys were pulling away and heading north.

THE FIRST BARRAGE struck Bearsted Green at six.

Fran felt the shudder as the shells came in, was already out of bed, dressing, calling Boy Jack. Why were they bombing Bearsted Green? Her mind was confused, racing. Upstairs Sarah was telling the boys not to be afraid. Helen's baby was crying in the next room. A second barrage descended on the village, a third to the north as the gunners found their range.

'Get dressed, fast as you can.' She pulled on her skirt.

'Out the back,' her mother was saying. 'We've got an air-raid shelter in the garden.' Helen was running down the stairs, the baby in her arms. 'Out the back door,' Fran's mother was telling them again, guiding Helen and Sarah, Fran and Boy Jack knowing the way. In the sky above them they could hear the screeching as the shells came in again and the crying and screaming of the people from the houses on either side. Not Bearsted Green she realized, pushing the children down the tunnel and into the shelter – the bridges over the river. In the woods around the village the artillery returned fire.

At least we'll be safe here, she looked round the shelter and tried to smile, at least they won't get us here. The baby was crying, Helen was trying to calm her, terrified herself. 'Don't worry,' Fran tried to comfort her. 'It'll be all right. We'll soon be safe.' Opposite her Boy Jack winked and smiled. The earth trickled down the back of her neck and she looked up. The thin sheet of tin that formed the roof was giving way, bending beneath the shock of the shells, the earth suddenly sliding onto them.

'Maidstone.' She knew that in Maidstone they would be safe, that the Germans would not wish to be held up by trying to take the bridge in the centre of the town. 'We've got to get to Maidstone.'

The roof was buckling even more, the earth cascading in and the sounds of the shelling all around them. They hurried to get out, the women pushing the children, Helen helping one of Sarah's boys.

'The food.' Fran's mother began to run up the path. 'I'll just get the food you packed.'

'*No!*' Fran heard herself screaming.

A shell struck the house.

She could see her mother again, running, going through the door, still running up the path. She herself was running, ignoring the shelling. The house collapsed in front of her, the ridge of the roof breaking and the walls caving in. The barrage was falling around them, German shells, English, she did not know, did not care. She was pulling at the rubble, screaming to her mother, tearing at the stone and wood, gashing her hands and ripping her fingernails. The shells were still falling.

'Come on, Fran.' The voice was quiet, yet even in the chaos of the shelling she could hear it. 'Come on now. You can't do any good. You have to leave her.' Helen took Fran's hand and helped her up. 'It's time to go.'

THE CHURCH WAS quiet. At ten, having eaten and rested, they moved back into the countryside, taking with them their remaining explosives and heading east. From the north came the sound of a major battle. Fifteen minutes after midday they were in position overlooking the main A2. The traffic along it was heavy, all heading north. Thirty miles away they could hear the sounds of the artillery exchanges. For the next hour they scouted the road, three miles to the south, then to the north. A mile before the crossroads to Ashford where Fran had turned west the *Wehrmacht* had opened the fields and were using them as a refuelling dump, a number of bowsers already in position. The target was right. Jack could imagine the damage if they not only blew up the dump but if they also attached explosives to a convoy and timed them to detonate when the vehicles were back on the road. But the timing was wrong. By tonight, when it was safe to approach, the battle in the north might be finished, but to try anything before then would be suicide.

The convoy pulled out and another arrived. He took the binoculars from his pack, examined the terrain around the petrol dump, the field behind it rising to woods at the top.

'The battle to the north is probably the most important of the campaign.' The others had anticipated what he was going to say. 'We can reduce the risks to ourselves by waiting till dark, or we can go now whilst we stand a chance of helping.' They were looking at him. 'By tonight it could be over. By tonight we might have won or lost.'

There was no need for further discussion.

'Ted and I will deal with transport that's about to leave, use time fuses. We'll take most of the explosives, aim to create as much confusion as possible on the road when the trucks go up. You shouldn't need much for the petrol bowsers.' There was no guarantee that a straightforward explosion would not only release the fuel but also ignite it, but the chain effect of even a single stick in the right place might still be devastating.

'The way out.' The only way they might survive was if they understood precisely what each man would do inside, and exactly how the four of them would get out.

He indicated a truck behind the largest bowser which seemed to be used for administration.

'We rendezvous there to exfiltrate. There's a ditch just behind it. We follow the ditch to the corner of the field, then pick up the hedge back up the slope to the woods.' He passed them the binoculars so they could see the detail. 'We go in from the same start point, keep the hedge between us and the target, cut through the hedge into the ditch at the bottom.'

He looked at them. 'Any questions?'

There were none.

THE RAT WAS at the door. They all heard it, scuffling, persistent, gnawing at the creepers and soil which concealed the entrance.

'Pigeon to Cricket.' It was the first call for five hours, the only person still transmitting to them.

'Come in Pigeon.'

They knew what was happening above them, could imagine the villages had been overrun, wondered where the tanks and troops were now. 'Village clearing. All tanks gone north.'

The rat had gone away. 'One personnel carrier thirty troops remaining.' Mary began encoding. Johnny, will I ever see you again? 'Message ends.'

The rat had come back. 'Thank you, Pigeon.' No one registered the warning. 'Bye, dearie.' It was the first time he had not told them he would speak to them again. 'Bye, Pigeon.'

The sound of the shots was deafening, crashing round the concrete of the zero station, one of them screaming, the bullets splintering the trap door. Liz was already stretching across her, reaching for the Webley, more shots echoing from above them and the bullets ricocheting round the walls.

Mary began pulling the shelf away from the entrance to the bolt hole. 'I'm trying the back.' The door at the top of the metal steps was beginning to give way. Beatie was standing mesmerized, unsure what to do. Mary slapped the woman's face hard. 'Come *on*.'

They heard the first German voices. Beatie was reacting, helping her move the shelving, Liz still standing gun in hand. There was another burst of firing. Mary pulled herself into the tunnel, Beatie beside her. Liz froze on the floor, her whole body trembling.

Everyone for herself, that was what they had agreed, no time to look after the others. Not Liz, though, not Liz who had changed time off with her the night she had met Johnny, who had comforted her when she had returned from the hospital. The shouts from the top were deafening. She pushed back, into the room, slapped Liz as she had slapped Beatie.

'Come on, Liz, while you can.' She heard the trap door being opened, slapped Liz again, realized the woman was too afraid, would never move. The gun was pointing at the bottom of the ladder. More shouts from above. She brushed past Beatie into the tunnel.

'Come on.'

Every instinct told her to run. She waited while Beatie pulled the shelving back into place and concealed the bolt hole. Sorry, Liz, sorry to leave you. She was at the end, feeling the door to the rear, fingers searching for the release mechanism. For Christ's sake nobody outside. The door opened and the sunlight came in. Behind her in the zero station she heard the distinct sound of the Webley, then the explosion of a hand grenade and the single awful scream.

The bicycle was where she had left it. She straightened and dusted the earth and chalk from her knees and clothes. Forty yards to the left a German truck was slewed across the road to form a roadblock, the soldiers looking towards the top of the zero station, the road to the right apparently clear. One way and you stand a chance, she told herself.

'Good luck, Mary.' Beatie turned right and began to hurry down the road.

'You too.' She looked again at the roadblock and picked the bicycle from its hiding place.

IT WAS GOING to be tight, they all knew. In the parking area on the far side of the admin truck a convoy was pulling in, the drivers climbing down from the cabs, some relieving themselves against the sides of their vehicles. 'Now.' They left the ditch and rolled the five yards to the truck.

The bowsers were tight against it, the vehicles to the right almost nose to tail. Hardly any explosives left, but Jack consoled himself with the damage they would cause with what they had. One bowser each, he indicated to Brian and Stan, one truck each for himself and Ted. The blood was thumping in his ears, the adrenaline pumping through him, every cell alert, seeing and hearing everything.

'Go.'

He moved right, no legs behind the admin truck, two yards perhaps three to the first of the waiting trucks. Just stand up and do it – safer than trying to hide, might be able to bluff it. He breathed in and rolled to the truck, Ted behind him. All right so far. He took the plastic explosive from the bag, pressed it into place, connected the timer and detonator, and activated the fuse. Brian and Stan were already waiting under the admin truck.

Ted crawled back from the second vehicle. Still no legs, Jack checked, nobody having a pee. He rolled across the space to the truck, scarcely believing their luck, and felt Ted roll into place beside him. No one in the dead area to the rear. He crossed the five yards, dropped into the ditch and turned to cover the others as they slid in behind him.

Stay here, he almost decided. Remain in the ditch till nightfall. Nobody will come, nobody will see you. Somebody bound to come.

Too close to the explosions anyway. He moved back along the ditch and through the hole they had cut in the foot of the hedge. On the A2 another convoy closed on the petrol depot, the drivers yawning with fatigue and the machine gunners in their positions on the cab tops thinking of ten minutes' relaxation and a mug of coffee.

Brian came through the hole and they began to edge up the side of the field. On the top of the cabs the machine gunners saw the bowsers and slid their weapons on to safety. Sixty yards to the safety of the woods. We might make it, Jack thought. We might just make it. He had done his job, done what the man in the field had asked so many months before – nothing more he could do. The lead truck turned off the highway and bumped into the area. Fifty yards to the wood. Almost there. Forty. The gunner saw them and shouted a warning, swung the Spandau. Jack heard and turned, saw the first flash then the sound of the machine gun, the guards from the dump running, opening fire. He was firing back, crouching, running backwards still firing, Stan and Brian just in front, Ted just behind. He ran out of ammunition and changed the magazine, barely stopping, the slope steeper than when they had come down, Stan and Brian still ahead, Ted lagging. Come on, Ted, for Christ's sake come on. The guards were running across the field, the machine gun raking the field, range wrong, arcing back at them – range still wrong, too low to get them. Stan and Brian were almost at the woods, Ted still behind. Twenty yards to go, out of ammunition again, no time for a mag change, just get there. The gunner arcing slightly higher. Run, Ted, for God's sake run.

Ted was stumbling, falling, the bullets taking him down, arms in air, the realization on his face. Jack turned back and grabbed his coat, began pulling him towards the woods. Behind him Brian and Stan left the woods, Brian firing, grabbing Ted's weapon, Stan helping Jack. The guards were slowing slightly, taking the cover of the hedge. Brian paused, changed mags, then began firing again. They reached the woods. Brian came in, changed mags again.

'Help me, Jack.' The colour was already gone from Ted's face.

'Don't be bloody stupid.'

He laid Ted in the hollow in the ground and undid his coat. Not Ted whom he had grown up with, he thought, not Ted who was Boy Jack's godfather, who had asked him to be godfather to his own first son.

'Legs are hurting, Jack.'

The shirt and chest were in shreds, the abdomen was pouring blood and the legs were broken and smashed, one hanging at a right angle from the knee down.

'No problem. I'll carry you, Brian and Stan will cover us.'

Not Ted who opened the batting with him, not Ted and Sarah with whom they shared everything.

The fire from below was increasing, more coming from the right. 'Thirty seconds, Jack.' It was the vicar. 'Your decision.'

'Help me, Jack.' Ted could barely speak. 'No comeback on Sarah and the boys.' Brian and Stan were returning fire. 'Please help me.'

Jack held the man in his arms and shook his head. 'I can't, Ted. Not to you.'

'Please, Jack.' The lips were barely moving, the words hardly audible. 'Sarah and the boys.'

'Almost here,' Stan warned.

The blood was frothing at Ted's mouth and his breathing was so shallow that Jack could barely hear it.

'All right, Ted.'

He lowered Ted to the ground, face up, and began, hands and fingers moving quickly and effectively.

'Everything done, Ted. No comeback on Sarah and the boys.'

'Thanks, Jack.'

THE FARM WAS empty, the evening was dark and the new moon barely showing. Below, in the direction of the village, Jack could see the fire burning in the square and imagine the lorries grouped round it, the tanks outside them, the battle to the north long over.

There was no reason for Fran and Boy Jack to be back, every reason for them not to be, yet somehow he had expected them to be there. He crossed the yard and checked the barn again. When he was finished he walked up the track, confirmed that the other farm was also locked and empty, then crossed the river behind the church and returned to the vicarage.

Brian Markham was waiting for him in the kitchen. He was wearing the shining black shirt of his church and the collar round his neck was white and gleaming.

'Anything?

Jack shook his head and tried to eat.

'But that was what you agreed, Jack – that Fran should stay away until you told her it was safe, that if you didn't get in touch with her she should only come back after a reasonable time had passed.'

Jack knew the vicar was right and tried to fight off the blackness. 'Bearsted Green,' he agreed. 'They'll still be at Fran's mother's.'

THE SILENCE HUNG on the morning like a shroud. Jack left before the countryside should have been awake. Even so, there were people walking, more lost than he was, some moving south and others north, men and women with children, old and young, some children by themselves. An hour later he passed the refuelling station and looked up to the woods, saying a quiet prayer for Ted.

At Thanington, where the A28 branched off the A2, the roadside was littered with debris, the remains of a horse still strapped in the cart it had been pulling and the flies buzzing over it. The road to Ashford, however, was relatively untouched, raising his spirits. It was only when he came to the A20 that the destruction began again. The damage was everywhere, the further he walked the more total and seemingly arbitrary it became, the occasional body and the remains of cars and bikes, prams and wagons, cases of clothes and personal possessions. Close to a child's pram, upturned in the ditch, was a teddy bear.

In the afternoon he passed through Westwell, then Charing. The destruction here was different. The road was clear, the *Wehrmacht* vehicles moving freely along it, the debris and shattered remnants of anything else pushed aside as they had prepared for their onslaught on Maidstone, the ditches piled high with broken vehicles and carts.

No bodies. He felt the relief.

He turned the corner and saw the pick-up.

It was half in the ditch, the holes where the machine guns had riddled it crisscrossing the back where the boys had been and the cabin where Fran and Sarah had sat, and the blood thick and congealed. To the north and south, as far as he could see, were more vehicles similarly destroyed, a tank and some lorries, cars and vans, the stinking remnants of another shire. But no bodies at all. He stood looking at the pick-up, not believing it, hoping that Fran had not been driving, that somehow they had been saved. No bodies: they're bound to be all right.

In the field to the right a farmer was filling the last earth back into a large hole with his tractor, two German infantrymen looking on, the rifles hanging from their shoulders, both men smoking. Jack crossed the road and saw what the man was doing. Fran and Boy Jack? Sarah and the boys? The man looked at him and stopped the motor. 'Too many to do anything else,' he said. They stood, not talking, Jack staring at the mass grave. 'Sorry.' Jack thanked him and moved on.

Not Fran and Boy Jack. Not Sarah and the boys. He tried to persuade himself they were waiting for him with Fran's mother.

Bearsted Green no longer existed, the buildings mere rubble, the pub at the edge of the green hardly identifiable and the church in ruins. He stood looking at where Fran's mother had once lived, hardly hearing the woman who came up to him.

'Dead,' she told him, not knowing how to put it more kindly. 'Inside when the house was hit.'

'Women and children?' The hope refused to leave him.

'Sorry, love.'

THE EVENING WAS dark and the winter was closing in. The farms at the top of the hill were as bleak and empty as they had been eight days before. In that time Jack had scoured the range of routes which Fran and Boy Jack might have taken and returned to Bearsted Green twice. He left the farm once more and went to the vicarage. Brian and Stan were in the kitchen. The vicar rose from the table and switched on the wireless. At nine o'clock exactly they heard the voice of Winston Churchill.

'I speak to you in sorrow, but not in defeat. In spite of the titanic efforts of the armed forces and the people of this great land, London has been forced to surrender and the forces of Adolf Hitler are in possession of large parts of the country, from Cornwall to Scotland.'

The voice changed slightly.

'The army and the people fought magnificently, from the coast of Kent to the rocks of the Cheviots. It is only because of their sacrifice that Herr Hitler has been unable to achieve his dream of total occupation of this great land of ours.

'The South may be occupied, but Scotland remains free, His Majesty and the royal family are safe and the Dominions have sworn their support for whatever we may do.'

There was an unfamiliar sadness about the speech as if the fire had been quenched.

'For the interim, however, and in order that our people in the occupied territories should not suffer beyond whatever is necessary, I have instructed the administration to liaise with the German forces of occupation, and have ordered the civil structure of the country, including police and local government, to assist in that liaison in so far as it relates to civilian and not political or military matters.'

The gravel crept back into the voice.

'There will be hardship and there will be suffering. There will be committed the most unspeakable atrocities. But when the history of this great nation is recorded let it be said that *this* was its finest hour.'

There was a silence. From the wireless came the voice of the announcer. 'His Majesty, King George VI.'

'Today we pass into the Darkness.'

Why Fran? Why Boy Jack?

'The night will be long, but the dawn will come as come it must.'

For a moment the King paused and they all heard the familiar hesitation in his voice.

'When I spoke to you all on Christmas Day, I read to you a poem. This evening I would like to read to you another, and hope that you take heart in it as I take heart in it.'

He began the poem by Keats.

All in vain, Jack thought – Fran and Boy Jack, Ted. Probably Ernie as well.

The King came to the lines with which the verse had begun and which the poet had repeated.

> *Shed no tear – O, shed no tear!*
> *The flower will bloom another year.*

There was a moment's pause.

'God bless you all.'

They heard the roll of drums, then the national anthem.

'You and Stan take care.' Jack stood up from the table. 'I'll be in touch when I can.'

'Where are you going?'

No point in staying. The black enveloped him totally. No point in anything any more.

'North.'

BOOK THREE

Occupation
September 1940 – May 1941

1

_____

SIX IN THE morning. In the cellar of the hotel opposite the railway station the four men waited to die.

In the streets of the city twenty miles away the night still hung on the wet of the cobbles and the heaps of stone and metal where the bomb damage had not been cleared. In the office on the third floor of the police station five blocks from the Victory Gate to what, until six weeks before, had been His Majesty's Dockyard, Portsmouth, the duty inspector glanced through the log of incidents that had occurred during the past twelve hours and shouted to the constable who knocked on the door with his mug of tea to enter.

Charles Holdaway had been a policeman since he was twenty-two and an inspector for the past three years. Two months before invasion he had celebrated his forty-fourth birthday. He was two inches over six feet tall, small by comparison with most of the men who policed a naval city like Portsmouth, yet held in the greatest respect by those he commanded, both for his personal integrity, his effectiveness as a policeman, and his loyalty to his men. On a hot and humid night the previous August three hundred sailors had rioted after a constable had tried to arrest one of them for slashing the face of a prostitute whom he claimed had overcharged him. When Holdaway arrived with one sergeant and three other men the lone constable had been pinned to a dock wall with a knife at his throat. The inspector had stood quietly at the man's side, told the sailor holding the knife to remove it, then called for the ringleader. The stoker who had stepped forward was nine inches taller than the inspector and five stones heavier. While the man was still laughing at him Holdaway had felled him with a single blow of the baton he always carried. By the time reinforcements arrived the crowd had drifted away.

Before the sky became light, Holdaway pulled on his greatcoat, informed the desk sergeant where he would be on the hour and half hour in case he was needed, and left the building. The streets were still quiet. He walked quickly, enjoying the morning, till he came to the dock. At the main entrance, where the naval guard had always manned the barrier, a *Gefreiter* stood on guard. Holdaway remembered the night the *Kelly* had brought the Duke of Windsor home and he had been the first to bring his men to attention, and stepped back into the shadows.

The place had been a favourite spot in the old days, the hourly point, the constable waiting for ten minutes in case he had to be contacted, then a quick mug of service tea, thick and sweet, in the guardhouse before moving on. Funny how he already thought of them as 'the old days'; how already the nation seemed to have accepted Occupation and was already making its compromises, sorting out how to live under it.

The constable stopped outside the barricade, ignoring the sentry, then moved on. The first light was in the sky. Holdaway stood looking at the docks for another ten minutes then made his way to the telephone kiosk opposite the café where the dockers took their breakfast. The constable waiting at the point had been in the guard of honour which had welcomed the Duke. Holdaway signed the man's notebook, returned to the station, called for a mug of tea and settled down to the nine files that had been drawn up overnight and which now required his attention.

Two were for drunkenness, one for prostitution, one for alleged rape involving an NCO from the infantry regiment stationed near the docks and which would require liaison with the *Feldgendarmerie*, the German military police, two for black market offences and three for larceny.

The first eight cases, with the exception of the rape incident, were straightforward. It was only when he came to the last of the larceny reports that Holdaway lifted the telephone and requested the sergeant who had signed the report of the constable dealing with it to report to him.

'This case of pilfering. The report states that the property involved was one can of corned beef.'

Davis had been promoted to sergeant at the same time that Holdaway had received his inspector's rank, and had been the sergeant who had accompanied him on the night of the August riot.

'Yes, sir.'

'Involving a boy of twelve.'

The sergeant knew what was going to happen.

'That's correct.'

'Why did he do it?'

'He said his family didn't have anything to eat.'

'Anybody talked to the boy's father?'

'The boy has no father. He was a docker, killed during the bombing.'

'Then why the hell are we taking this boy to court?'

A good talking to was all that was needed, they both knew, a few stern words and a kick in the pants.

'Chief Inspector Matthews insisted. The complainant was Walter Phillips.'

'Bloody hell.' Holdaway made no attempt to hide his contempt. The chief inspector looking after himself, the sergeant did not need to say it, playing his games with the magistrate who was a personal friend of the Chief Constable. Holdaway took his pen, wrote the words 'Verbal caution, no further action' across the bottom of the report, signed it and handed it to the sergeant.

'See the mother tonight.'

'What about Chief Inspector Matthews?'

Holdaway understood why the sergeant had asked. 'Wasn't there an allegation that Walter Phillips was mixed up with black market petrol coupons a few months ago?'

'Garage owner called Cairns. The case was put aside because of the invasion.'

'We must have had something on Cairns to have got him to co-operate though.'

They had always worked well together as a team. 'We did.'

'Still apply?'

'Should think so. I'll see him today, get a statement.'

'Good man.'

When he returned from breakfast in the canteen a second bundle of reports were on Holdaway's desk. The document was the third one down. At the top of the page, indicating that the information contained in it related to issues specified under what had recently been formulated as the Rules of Liaison, were the dual emblems of the Constabulary and the *Wehrmacht*. Across the top left corner of the page were stamped the words 'File copy. For information only.'

He read it then lifted the telephone. 'Sergeant Davis, immediately.' When the sergeant arrived Holdaway handed him the despatch. 'Ten constables, to leave immediately. You know who to choose.'

Davis skimmed through the report then handed it back. 'Shall I notify headquarters?'

Holdaway picked up his stick. 'I don't think that would be advisable.'

THE TOWN SQUARE was empty, as if the people who normally filled it were unsure what was about to happen or how they should react to it. Holdaway ordered the drivers to park on the hill facing the square and the clock which overlooked it and waited. A year ago, Davis thought, and he would not have believed what they were about to do.

In front of them the square began to fill. On the road to the right of the clock tower a *Wehrmacht* truck appeared and the troops jumped down and began to take their places. The square was almost full, the men, women and children waiting expectantly. At the top of the road the convoy drove into the square, a Mercedes in front, a lorry with the four prisoners following and a truck with the firing squad close behind. The crowd parted to let them through then closed together again. A lieutenant stepped from the car, and stood hands behind back while the four were taken from the trucks and led to the execution ground at the foot of the clock.

It was twelve o'clock.

'*Anschlagen*.' Prepare.

'*Ziel nehmen*.' Take aim.

Holdaway stepped from the car, slammed the door loudly so that the entire square could hear and pushed his way through the crowd until he stood in front of the officer in charge. Behind him Davis marched the men between the firing squad and the prisoners.

'And what, Lieutenant, do you think you're doing?'

The soldier wore the Iron Cross 1st Class on his left breast and the *Deutsches Kreuz* in gold on his right. 'These men were caught looting for the black market in London. They are to be executed.'

'An example, perhaps?'

The guns of the firing squad were pointing straight at the faces of Davis and his men.

'If you like. They are taking from your people more than from mine.'

The crowd waited.

'This firing squad is illegal, Lieutenant. Under the Rules of Liaison, the occupying forces are to liaise with the British Constabulary in terms of civil matters.' Holdaway quoted the precise wording of the agreement. 'Civil matters to include profiteering and looting. Under the terms of the Rules therefore, I am taking charge of these men.'

Over the inspector's shoulder the German saw the smile on the face of the looters' leader. Without warning Holdaway turned, strode behind the line of constables and faced the man.

'What's funny?'

We're together, the expression on the man's face was saying. You and me are the same, against the bloody Hun. But I'll be back, you stupid bloody peasant, I'll be back to make my profit out of you.

The movement was sudden and fierce, the hand rising in the air, fist clenching, then coming down, the entire power of Holdaway's arms and shoulders behind it, crashing into his face and felling the man.

'Pick him up.'

The two men on either side of the looter lifted him from the cobbles. Blood was pouring from his mouth and his jaw was broken. Bastard, they all saw the new look in the man's eyes. One day I'll get you. The second movement was as sudden and sharp as the first, the fist rising and falling, even the lieutenant aghast at the speed and force of the blow. Holdaway reached down and picked the man up by the front of his shirt. Don't think that, don't ever think that or next time I'll really sort you out. Almost as if he was playing with a rag doll he tossed the man to his companions. 'Go. Take him with you.'

He faced the lieutenant again. 'An example, I think we both agreed.' Before the man could react he turned and pushed his way back through the crowd to the cars.

By the time the Haslemere unit returned to Portsmouth it was mid-afternoon. Only when Davis had secured a statement from the garage owner named Cairns and prepared a preliminary file on the magistrate called Phillips did Holdaway allow the report on the theft of the tin of corned beef to be processed.

An hour later he was summoned to the chief inspector's office. The man was seated at his desk, the file open in front of him, and his face was already flushed.

'The prosecution will go ahead.' Just because I have political contacts, Holdaway could almost read it in the man's eyes, just because I will soon be superintendent and you will still be walking the cobblestones outside the bloody docks. 'I will inform Mr Phillips personally.'

Holdaway took the file containing the Cairns statement from under his arm and placed it on the desk. 'In that case, could you also arrange for him to come to the station and assist with enquiries about this.'

The chief inspector took the file and read it quickly, then snatched for his pen, scrawled his approval below Holdaway's recommendation and placed the other report in the drawer of his desk.

BY THE TIME Walter Schellenberg reached his office a cup of coffee was on his desk.

The promotion to *Gruppenführer* and the posting to London as overlord of Intelligence and Counterterrorism in Britain, had been neither undeserved nor unexpected. Schellenberg's role in the various SD successes of the past months, not only against the formal enemy but also the informal, the *Abwehr*, had been noted. It was also logical that *Obergruppenführer* Heydrich should wish not only to have an efficient operator in London, but one whom he could trust to report faithfully on the activities of the other groups vying for the attention of the Führer. In keeping with this, Walter Schellenberg had brought with him only those whom he knew he could trust from the Prinz-albrechtstrasse.

The sky outside was only just turning light. He settled at the desk, removed from his briefcase the documents he had worked on overnight in his apartment in Regent's Park, downed the coffee and called for another.

The first thing the *Sicherheitsdienst* had done after invasion was to commandeer the Grosvenor House Hotel in central London, and the first thing Schellenberg had done on his arrival in the building was to appropriate the best suite of rooms in the building, overlooking Hyde Park.

By eight-forty-five Schellenberg had cleared the administrative minutiae which seemed to clog his desk daily, at nine he asked his clerk to confirm the *Wehrwirtschaftsstad*, the Economics Ministry, meeting at eleven and the appointment with the general staff of the *Reichsstatthalter*, the Political Head of Occupation, at three. Then he requested Josef Straube to join him for their regular morning meeting.

The primary responsibility of *Sturmbannführer* Straube at that time was to identify for Schellenberg those individuals – politicians and civil servants, industrialists and trade unionists – who might be susceptible to collaboration, either on a public or private basis. It was also his function to recruit those members of the British police force deemed candidates for the organization which Schellenberg intended to create and for which he had already established two divisional headquarters, one in Birmingham to cover the Midlands and the North, and the other in the former prison in Maidstone in Kent, renamed The Citadel, for the South.

At first sight the plan seemed both illogical and unworkable: to create a political police, recruited from members of the traditional British police, to work within the *Sicherheitsdienst* itself. It was, however, no more than the way the Nazi Party had bent the police system to its own end in Germany, and in other parts of Europe the scheme was already operating successfully. In France, the organization was already as feared as the Gestapo itself and even enjoyed its own name, the Milice.

After the briefing, Schellenberg was driven to the headquarters of the *Wehrwirtschaftsstad*. Compared to Berlin London was grey and colourless, and he knew the meeting would be the same.

Under the original structure envisaged by Directive Sixteen, Britain was to be divided into five military/economic commands centred on London, Birmingham, Newcastle, Liverpool, Glasgow. Because of the failure to achieve total occupation the last had been removed until the new offensive in the spring, and probably for ever. In charge of each region was a *Kommissar*. The body in overall control of the economy of the occupied territories was the *Wehrwirtschaftsstad*, headed by a *Wirtschaftskommissar*. At the head of the entire organization was the *Reichsstatthalter*, beneath him sectional heads for police, army, navy and air force. The police chief, to whom Schellenberg was theoretically responsible, was a senior member of the SD.

The meeting opened with the *Kommissars* detailing the structure and scale of industry in their areas of authority, as well as estimates of how each could contribute both to the well-being of the Fatherland in general and the continuation of the war effort in particular. Written details were provided in reports distributed before each presentation. At the end of the first session the meeting was thrown open to a discussion, chaired by a civil servant from the *Wehrwirtschaftsstad*.

After lunch Schellenberg was collected by his staff car and driven to the meeting with the general staff of the *Reichsstatthalter*. The formal discussion that afternoon, recorded in the minutes which were sent to Berlin, dealt with the political and military situation in Britain, the plans to bring more troops in the spring to complete the process of Occupation, and the decision of the Führer to attend the coronation of King Wilhelm the following year. The informal discussions which took place in the coffee break mid-way through, and therefore not minuted, more accurately reflected the attitude and projections for the future of the German armed forces in Britain – their frustration and anger at not being permitted to press their attack and occupy the whole of the country. For this they blamed two factors: the strength of the British defensive positions in the Cheviots, and Hitler's stubborn and persistent refusal to commit more troops to overcome it when requested. From that sprang a hope that the anticipated spring offensive would receive in Berlin the political consideration that its military importance in Britain dictated, and the fear that this was not the case and that Hitler's real preoccupation lay with Russia to the east.

When Schellenberg returned to the Grosvenor House, Straube was waiting for him.

'One of the reports that came in this morning was of an incident at a place called Haslemere. The police broke up a firing squad, the *Wehrmacht* is demanding action. Might be interesting.'

'Why?' Schellenberg wondered why Straube had not waited till the morning.

'Just a feeling. The *Wehrmacht* is jumping up and down about it.

They want the man dealt with – loss of face and all that. If he's any good to us we'll have to move quickly.'

'Name?'

'Inspector Holdaway, stationed at Portsmouth.'

'Any other details?' Schellenberg shared Straube's instinct.

'Not yet. I've asked for his personal and service files to be sent overnight.'

'Good. Arrange an interview. Day after tomorrow.'

'London?'

'No. The Citadel.'

'You want me to handle it?'

'I will.'

THE LATE AFTERNOON was dark; it was the time of the year Holdaway used to enjoy the most, the smell of winter in the air and the fun and laughter of the Guy Fawkes bonfires. As he was going off duty he was informed that he was wanted on the telephone.

'They've asked for your personal file, it went this afternoon.'

The caller did not identify himself.

'Who?'

'SD.'

'Where?'

'London.'

'Thanks.'

At seven, when his shift ended, he left the station and began to walk the streets. By the time he returned to the house it was past eleven. The rooms were empty and quiet, he let himself in and went to bed. As he tried to sleep, he thought of the two people he treasured most in the world, the woman called Diana and the boy called Stuart, and the seemingly inevitable chain of events that his action at Haslemere appeared to have set in motion.

At eleven-thirty the following morning Holdaway was informed that the chief inspector wished to see him. Matthews was seated behind his desk, a typewritten sheet of paper on it.

'Haslemere.'

Since their last meeting there had been no mention of either the larceny case against the boy or the petrol coupons swindle involving the magistrate called Phillips.

'It's in my report.'

'It would seem that disciplinary charges are to be brought against you.' I've waited a long time and now you've given me my chance. 'You are to report tomorrow afternoon.' He leaned forward and affected to consult the typewritten order. 'The Citadel, Maidstone.' Not an internal charge, you bastard, not our own people. The bloody Germans. Not just the Germans, the heavy mob. '*Gruppenführer* Schellenberg, of the SD.'

That night, after he had made himself supper, Holdaway pressed his uniform and polished his boots, then sat in the kitchen and imagined the sound of his wife's laugh and his son's chatter. The next morning he had breakfast, made himself a flask of tea, looked at the photograph on the mantelpiece above the fireplace, and left for Maidstone.

Parts of the town were like the docks area of Portsmouth, the piles of rubble remaining from the September bombings and the remnants of the houses standing like relics, the people walking past them as if they had always been like that. On the outskirts he stopped to ask directions, found the railway station then drove through the back streets to The Citadel three hundred yards behind the town hall.

The entrance was through an arched gateway in the west wall, the doors themselves open in the daytime, one heavy metal barrier preventing access or exit and a second inside. There were guards both inside and outside the entrance and at the top and bottom of the road.

Holdaway stopped at the barrier and held up his warrant card for inspection.

'Meeting with *Gruppenführer* Schellenberg.'

In the office on the other side of the courtyard Schellenberg left the window and returned to his desk.

The guard indicated where he should park, the barrier was lifted and Holdaway drove through. Strange how easy it was, he thought, almost disconcerting.

The central area was filled with cars and lorries, the offices spread round the court. He parked the Austin then followed a corporal up two flights of stairs and along a corridor to an outer office where a clerk in the uniform of the SD sat behind a desk.

'Inspector Holdaway. Appointment with *Gruppenführer* Schellenberg.'

178

The clerk checked the clock on the wall and carried on working. Holdaway sat in the solid wood chair next to the door without being invited and waited. At two precisely the clerk rose and escorted him through to an office overlooking the courtyard below. Walter Schellenberg was seated at his desk, the windows behind him. He indicated a chair in front of the desk. 'Please sit down.' The first stage of the trap, he thought, just as there had been a first stage of the trap for Wilhelm Richter in Munich. He took the Haslemere dossier from the drawer in the desk and studied it.

Charles Holdaway, aged forty-four, the details were fixed in his mind: the inspector's police service, the date he had joined, the commendations he had received. 'The incident with the firing squad.' He turned the pages of the Haslemere report as if digesting them. 'The officer concerned wrote a report to his superior, who passed it to his, who passed it to me for a decision.'

It was not his decision at all, he would have to sort it out later.

'All slightly embarrassing really. What you did was totally in order.' Schellenberg had worked out precisely what he would say and how he would say it. There were three types of policemen, excluding the ones who would not co-operate at all: those who would assist merely by fulfilling the letter of the law, those who would edge a little farther, bordering on collaboration, and those who for whatever reason could be persuaded into collaborating fully.

'The buffoon was acting totally contrary to the Rules of Liaison.' He had worked through every detail of the meeting: assess the man, find the way in, then exploit it. 'But why did you do it? That's what puzzles me.' He sat back, his head and shoulders framed in the window. 'You must have known the trouble it would cause.'

Holdaway looked at him. 'Would you mind if I moved my chair, I can't see you against the window.'

'Of course, inspector, my apologies.' Straube had been right, and Schellenberg began to wonder only if his assessment had not gone far enough. 'Please sit wherever you want.'

Holdaway moved his chair to the left. 'As you said, the lieutenant was acting totally contrary to the Rules.'

'But why was it necessary to do what you did?'

'Because the man had to be punished.'

'Why?'

Two other details from Holdaway's personal file, Schellenberg remembered: that the previous spring he had been passed over for promotion to chief inspector in favour of a colleague named Matthews who was less qualified but who had better connections; and that two months later Holdaway's wife Diana had left him and returned to her home in Scotland, taking with her their only child, Stuart.

'Because he had broken the law.'

'But he was English?'

'Irrelevant.'

'Yet by letting the prisoners go you forfeited any chance of pursuing the case, of discovering their contacts, who they were working for.' He was looking at the report, as if quoting from it.

'I doubt they would have said much more after the lieutenant had shot them.' The delivery was careful, almost calculated. Schellenberg imagined how good Holdaway must be during an interrogation. 'In any case –' Holdaway was still looking at him – 'the lorry they were using was only just up the road. Two of my men followed them back to London.'

'You have the information you need?' Schellenberg slipped the faintest hint of professional admiration into his voice.

'Of course.'

'Excellent, Inspector, absolutely excellent.' Schellenberg laughed and snapped the file shut. 'I don't think I need waste your time any longer.' In one movement he rose and offered Holdaway his hand. 'Thank you for coming.'

The policeman's reaction was automatic. He rose, shook hands and turned to leave.

The meeting had lasted less than fifteen minutes. Schellenberg asked the clerk to show the inspector to his car then watched as Holdaway drove to the barrier. His man, he sensed; he waited for the last detail. The *Scharführer* on guard duty lifted the barrier and saluted as he had been instructed. For the second time that afternoon the inspector reacted automatically and saluted back.

THE WIND RATTLED the window, the room was cold and the fire in the grate had gone out. Holdaway tore a strip from a newspaper, folded it into a tight wad, jammed it between the panes and returned to the table. Then he poured himself a last whisky and read again the memorandum circulated to all police stations that day.

Under Section Twelve of the Police Decree, a special department was being set up to counter the increase in black marketeering and looting, which was expected to escalate the following year. The department would be divided into two units, one covering the Midlands and the North of England and based in Birmingham, the other dealing with the South and based at The Citadel in Maidstone.

Holdaway laid the memorandum neatly and carefully on the table, and picked up the typed orders he had received earlier that afternoon.

Effective from the following Monday, he was transferred to The Citadel, Maidstone, as head of the southern unit of the new department. He would cease normal duties immediately and liaise with London over the selection of personnel. The appointment, plus the authorization for him to operate across traditional county borders, was signed by the Commissioner of Police under the new joint structure and countersigned by his own Chief Constable.

He reached forward again, laid the orders beside the memorandum, and picked up the sheet of paper, also from his Chief Constable informing him of his promotion to chief inspector and offering his congratulations.

The photograph of his wife and son was on the mantelpiece above the fire. The last time you even think of them, he told himself. He pulled on his overcoat and left the house.

By ten he had crossed the city and was in the docks area. In the darkness a pimp negotiated a rate with two German sailors and the women climbed into the back of the truck parked round the corner. At eleven Holdaway stood in the shadows and watched the dockers and night workers drinking their mugs of tea in the café close to the walls of the naval yard. Funny how he knew the faces, how, even if he did not know an individual, he could tell his occupation. He pulled his coat collar higher and blew on his fingers to bring a semblance of warmth back into them.

The man came out of the dark and headed toward the café. Late thirties, Holdaway estimated, cap and scarf, his face was thin and he walked as if the cold had penetrated every part of his body. Not a docker. He wondered who he was and what he was doing there. The man turned into the café, stood at the counter, then took a mug of tea and a plate of stew to a table in the corner and sat down. When he had finished the stew he returned to the counter for a second tea, then went back to the table. Even through the condensation on the window Holdaway saw the way he held the mug, blowing on it to cool it enough to drink yet fingers wrapped round it to savour the last warmth. He turned away and went back to the house.

By six, even though there was no need, Holdaway was back at the station. At six-thirty, as was his custom, he informed the desk sergeant of the points he would make and left. The café was already open. He had been standing by the telephone kiosk opposite for ten minutes when he saw the figure. Same man as last night, the stubble on his face as if he had slept rough. The man went into the café and stood by the counter. Poor bugger, thought Holdaway, nobody to turn to and nobody to look out for him. For one moment he wondered who the man was. The constable was late for the point. Holdaway stepped towards the café. Not his business any more, he reminded himself, and went back to the station.

He cleared his desk and packed the books and the few items he had chosen to take with him in a cardboard box, then telephoned Davis and asked if the sergeant could come to his office. When he arrived Holdaway told him to shut the door and offered him a chair.

'You've heard?'

'Yes, sir. Congratulations.'

'It's better than a few pimps and prossies down the docks on a Saturday night. I'd like you to come with me.'

'Not so much action though.' Davis had guessed why he had been summoned.

'Oh, I wouldn't bank on getting away from the action.' He sensed that the sergeant appreciated being asked and tried to understand his reluctance. 'I know it means being away from the family for a while, but I'll arrange a good allowance and married quarters in Maidstone as soon as possible.'

'It's not that, sir, it's the nature of the job. It's the thought of working even closer with the Germans.'

'I understand, but it'll still be our people we'll be helping, dealing with criminals – looters and the black market.'

'As long as that's what it is, civil not political.'

'My feelings exactly.'

THE SKY ABOVE and behind him was dark grey, almost black, the wind whipping the tops of the waves across the loch. Jack Masters stood and watched the next roller building in front of him, the code names going through his head. The wave struck the granite of the rocks and broke into a thousand plumes, rising high above him then showering down upon him. Dearest Fran, he thought, I cannot tell you how much I miss you and Boy Jack. Only now am I beginning to understand what you yourself must have gone through. The next wave broke, the spray stung his eyes and the wet ran down his face.

The journey north had lasted three weeks, the damage decreasing the farther he went, until he had crossed what had become established as the border between the Free North and the Occupied South. It had taken two more weeks to make contact with Drake, during which time he had been arrested as a spy and threatened with execution. At the end of October he had been taken to Arisaig, on the west coast of Scotland where Drake had already established a training school for the Resistance of the future, spending only three days there before he had been spirited at night across the Sound of Sleat to the castle at Dunvegan, on the farthermost side of Skye, and agreed to Drake's proposal.

It was almost dark. He climbed off the rocks and began to walk back to the castle. And, you, my son, how I wish I had told you how proud I was of you, how I still see you and Ernie. How, now that you are gone, it is as if I myself am no more. The salt was staining his clothes and shoes. In front of him a log washed onto the beach, behind it he saw the shape of the castle, and the names began coursing through his head again.

> *Bryant, George. Wellington Street.* Swede.
> *Rogers, Harold. Castle Square.* Anvil.
> *Symons, Arthur. Bedford Place.* Sycamore.

Drake was waiting for him in the room overlooking the loch. The Scotch was on the mantelpiece above the fire and the logs were blazing in the cast-iron grate. Jack dried himself and joined him.

'How are the names?'

'Fine.'

They had been through it before, the impossibility of committing the details to paper and the danger to which Jack would be exposed if the occupying forces ever even suspected the truth.

'But no doubts?'

'No doubts at all.'

It was almost, Drake thought, a replica of his conversation with the agent called Prospero. 'Good.' There were three stages – he wished the process could have been quicker and safer – one: establish how much of the British Resistance still existed. Two: restructure and rebuild what remained. Three: rearm and re-equip it. Provided, of course, they still had Donovan's support and provided Donovan could continue to convince Roosevelt of their cause.

'You've thought about a code for yourself?'

Jack Masters laughed. 'Bit of a cricket man actually.' No matter what the subject, each conversation took him back to Ardley. 'Thought I might use Watchman.'

The night watchman, sent in to hold the innings when things were going wrong, to hang on until the next day when things might be better.

Two nights later, Jack Masters began his journey south. In his head he carried a complete list of the identities, addresses and code names of the unit leaders of what had once been the British Resistance.

TWO WEEKS LATER he made the first contact; another week passed before the natural order of the list took him to Portsmouth.

The address was in the middle of a small terrace on the edge of the Portsea area of the city, which had suffered so badly during the bombing of the docks during invasion. The houses were back to back, with small gardens at the rear and an alleyway between every eight houses. It would be difficult if he had to come out that way, Jack knew, almost impossible once he was inside. He parked the BSA in an adjoining street, removed the pluglead so that it could not be stolen, and began his wait.

John Disney, Auxiliary Unit code name Hammer. It was late afternoon, dark and cold. At least, he consoled himself, it was not raining. He pulled the cap firmly on his head and the scarf round his ears.

The woman returned to the house, a small bag of food in one hand and a child clinging to the other. It began to drizzle. By ten o'clock, when Jack assumed Disney would have been home, depending on where he worked and what shift he was on, no one else had entered the house. He waited another half-hour, trying to shelter beneath the overhang above a shop door at the top of the street, then left the area and made his way towards the docks.

In the dark in front of him he saw the lights of a café. On the pavement opposite was a telephone kiosk, a man in a dark overcoat standing beside it, his collar turned against the wind and the rain. The café was busy. He waited at the counter, his face and hands tight with cold, asked for a mug of tea and a plate of stew, and took them to a table in the corner. Most of the other men in the café were dockyard workers. He bought another mug of tea, blowing on it to cool it but wrapping his fingers round it in an attempt to warm them.

When he left the café the night seemed colder. He found a hole in the rubble of a bomb site close to the BSA and spent the next six hours trying to keep warm. At five-thirty he was back on the street in which the house was situated, in case the man called Disney worked an early shift. At seven, when he was confident no one would leave, he returned to the café for breakfast. The police inspector was standing by the telephone kiosk. Same man as last night, he realized. The policeman began to cross the road, then appeared to change his mind and walked away.

Once that day the woman left the house, returning an hour later. At five he checked the bike, made sure the engine would start first time in case he needed it, went to the house and knocked on the door. To his right a curtain moved as a neighbour looked to see who was visiting.

The woman who came to the door was younger than Fran, the child he had seen with her the afternoon before was in her arms and an older boy stood beside and slightly behind her.

'Mrs Disney?'

'Yes.' There was a look of suspicion on her face.

'I'm sorry to trouble you. I was wanting to speak to your husband.'

He saw the suspicion dissolve and the anguish that replaced it.

'He's dead. He went away the morning of the invasion and we haven't seen him since.'

THE REHEARSAL FOR the carol concert began at seven o'clock. The Reverend Brian Markham walked with his wife to the church then returned to the vicarage to prepare his sermon for the following Sunday. The carol service was always important, he was aware, but this year especially so. Already they had cancelled the Harvest Thanksgiving in October and the Guy Fawkes bonfire in November, already the divisions in the village were becoming apparent. He thought of the grocer and wondered what he could do.

Two hours later, he heard the group walking back along the road then the scraping as his wife opened the front door and came into the study.

'What's wrong?'

'I think there's somebody at Jack Masters' farm. I saw a light.'

It was only after he had gone that she realized he had taken the keys of the church.

The night was dark, there was no moon. There were no explosives left and little ammunition. He took a Smith & Wesson, twenty rounds and his knife, and left the crypt. On the other side of the river he waited for his eyes to adjust then moved up the hill until he could look down into the dip at the top in which the farmhouse was sheltered. From the kitchen came the soft light of a tilly lamp. For the next thirty minutes he checked that there were no vehicles hidden in the outbuildings and no traps concealed either in the fields around the farm or on the lane from the road. Only when he was certain did he move to the cover of the barn in front of the house where he could look into the kitchen.

The lamp was in the centre of the table, the women and children gathered round it. Fran and Boy Jack, Sarah and the boys, a third woman whom he did not know with one small child and two slightly older. All of them looked thin and dirty, their clothes ragged and torn. On each of their plates was a pile of potatoes, on the table next to the lamp a loaf of newly baked bread. Only after he had watched them for twenty minutes more did he slide back into the darkness, knowing he would spend the rest of the night deliberating what he would tell Fran when she asked him.

The dawn was still an hour off when Fran woke. She crept downstairs, hearing the children and the two other women breathing deeply, aware that Sarah and Helen had slept no more than she had. The kitchen was warming up; she filled the range, made herself a cup of tea and sat at the table until it was light enough to see what was left of the farm and stock, and how much had been stolen or destroyed. The first streaks of grey appeared in the sky. She put on a warm coat, socks and boots and went outside.

There was no sign of Jack in the house, no indication that he had returned after she had left. She had thought that when she returned Jack would be there as if nothing had happened. The hope was the only thing, other than the sheer animal will that she and her son should survive, which had kept her going.

The morning was lighter. Fran examined the barns and outbuildings, relieved that they were intact and that the hay and food that she and Jack had stored were still there, worried that there were no animals. There was a noise behind her and she spun round. Her son was standing against the sky looking at her. 'I've come to help.'

She tried to smile and walked with him across the fields.

In the bottom pasture by the river they found twenty ewes and three cows, all seemingly healthy and well cared for; in the top another thirty ewes and four cows, in the apple orchards and the fields where they had grown hay another straggle of animals. There were two ways of looking at it, she told herself as she returned to the house and pulled off her boots, that they had lost four-fifths of the stock which she and Jack had struggled to build up or that they had a good start for another beginning.

'That's good.' She went through to the kitchen. 'That's very good. Enough to keep us busy, plus more besides.'

After breakfast Sarah and the boys left to check the farm up the hill. Shortly after Fran heard the car coming up the track. Boy Jack ran outside and came back immediately. 'It's the vicar.'

The Reverend Brian Markham knocked on the door and came into the kitchen. He carried a basket of food. Helen ushered her children upstairs and suggested that Boy Jack come with them.

'Where's Jack?' asked Fran immediately. 'Is he alive?'

'I don't know.' He put the basket on the table. Even though he knew that Jack had survived the first onslaught, in his blacker moments he was convinced the man was dead, that he had given up his reasons for living. 'I saw him in the square on the morning you and Sarah left.' It was the last time the four members of the cell had been seen together, he knew Fran could check if she so wished. 'Ted was there as well.'

She sat at the table with him. 'What do you think happened to them?'

He wondered why he did not tell her the truth. 'I don't know.'

What will she think when she knows, he thought, what will she think of me and my religion?

'We thought the farm would have been looted,' she looked round the kitchen. 'You can't imagine what it was like getting back and finding nothing had been touched.' She looked at him, never stopped thinking of Jack. 'It was you, wasn't it? You looked after the farm for us, Sarah's place as well.'

'I had some help. We lost a lot of the animals, we couldn't stop them taking them away, but we did what we could.'

Fran was leaning on the arm of the chair. What happened, he almost asked, Jack found the pick-up on the road to Bearsted Green, spent days looking for you.

'We left when Jack and Ted told us. There were so many refugees from the battle. We picked up Helen and her children along the way, a lot of others as well.' He could see she was only thinking of Jack. 'The road was bad, we turned off it and tried the side roads. That's where they stole the pick-up from us.'

Jack found it, he almost said, shot up and destroyed; he went to your mother's.

'My mother was waiting for us, then the shelling started again. She went back in to get the food. That's when the house was hit and she was killed.'

Jack thought you were all inside, he wanted to explain. Even if you had survived the attack on the road he thought you had been killed in the house.

'After that we went to Maidstone.' She was shaking her head. 'It was terrible, people dying, the fighting all around us. We got to the town and thought we were safe. Four, five days, then the food ran out, there was nothing to eat so we moved on. The Germans were around London but they let us through, they were letting everybody through. In London it was just as bad but we couldn't walk any farther.'

She sat upright and tried to compose herself.

'In any case, the Germans wouldn't have let us out again. That was part of their plan, to fill London with refugees, starve us all out. We ended up in a camp in Hyde Park. As soon as we could we came home.'

The therapy was over. 'What about Ardley?' she asked, her voice stronger.

'The village escaped almost intact. The Germans came through, a couple of Home Guard on the barricade to the south were wounded, but they're all right now. Those manning the defences in the square realized what they were up against and surrendered. There was no option.'

He and Stan Bradley had merged easily back into the life of the village, had stood silently with the crowd looking at the German soldiers in the square, had shaken their heads with everyone else when people talked about Jack and Fran, and Ted and Sarah.

She nodded, not able to take it all in. 'Sarah's gone up to her place, get things started again. Helen and the children are staying here for a while until the time's right for them to go back to Dover.'

He listened while Fran explained who Helen was and how they had met, then took a five-pound note from his pocket. 'Things are difficult at the moment.' Not just with the Germans, he thought, with the village itself. 'You can pay me back when you can.'

When he had gone Fran tucked the money into her purse, put some water on the range to heat, washed and went across the fields to the village. A *Wehrmacht* truck was parked in the square, the soldiers stamping their feet against the cold as if they had always been there. She passed by them and went to the post office, then to the grocer's. The shop was well-stocked, despite the shortages; two of the younger members of the cricket club were lounging against the counter.

'Been away then, Mrs Masters.' The grocer began to add up the prices. 'Jack as well, I noticed.' He was reckoning quickly, as he always did. 'Anything else you fancy?' He looked at the other two men to make sure they knew what he meant.

When she returned to the farm Helen was cooking supper. She saw the look on Fran's face and took the children into the other room. Fran sat Jack by the fire and put her arm around him.

'There's something you have to know.'

'Is it about Dad?'

'Yes.'

'He's all right, isn't he? He *is* coming home?'

'No. I don't think Dad will be coming home.'

She saw her son's face and remembered so many moments together. 'I think Dad's dead. He was probably killed in the fighting.'

'But Dad wasn't in the Home Guard or the army.'

She did not know what to say.

'So what was he doing? Why was he fighting? He can't be dead. I don't believe it.'

She said nothing.

'Dad was a hero, wasn't he, Mum?'

'Yes,' she said at last.

The boy turned towards the door.

'Jack.' She did not know why she thought of it or why she should tell him. 'You must never talk to anyone about your father and the fighting. Ever.'

'All right, Mum.'

That evening, after the others had gone to bed, Fran sat in the kitchen, looking at the fire and listening to music on the wireless. The programme ended and the news began. Not the proper news, she thought, the propaganda put out by the Germans in London and the people who were already collaborating with them. She switched off the set and sat again at the table. No giving in, Fran, she told herself, it was what you accepted all along – what you and Jack agreed the first night he told you about the Resistance.

The following morning, after they had finished the animals, she walked with Boy Jack and the other children to school. Apart from the Germans outside the hall the village seemed normal, the people not even appearing to notice the soldiers. Fran arranged for Helen's children to join the class, then walked to the vicarage. The vicar was in. They talked about the farm and the village until Fran made herself come to the point.

'I'd like to borrow your car this afternoon.'

'Of course.'

'I want to see if I can find the pick-up. Just after it was stolen the Germans attacked the road, so it might still be there.'

'You're sure?'

'It belongs to me, it might be useful.'

He saw how brittle her strength was and did not question her. 'We'd better take a good towrope and some tools. Ned has one. I'll see him this morning.'

'I will,' said Fran.

The postman was in his kitchen. His wife made a pot of tea and the three of them sat in front of the range.

'Glad to see you back, dearie.'

'Thanks, Ned.' Her fingers were tight round the mug. 'Jack's gone,' she said at last. 'Ted as well.'

'I know.' There was a way he said it which gave her support.

'I'm going to look for the pick-up. The vicar is helping me. I wondered if I could borrow your towrope.'

'Course.' He smiled at her. 'I'll give you a hand.'

'Thanks, Ned,' she said again and tried to smile back.

The vicar came to fetch her from the farm at twelve-thirty. Stan Bradley was in the front with him and Ned in the back. A mile past the crossroads at Charing they saw the pick-up. It was half in the ditch on the left side of the road, its front wheels hanging over the dirty water, the ice already forming on the surface and the debris lining the road for as far as they could see in each direction. They left the car and stood looking at it. There were two rows of bullet holes along the planks which formed the floor and a third along the back of the cabin. The glass of the window which Jack and Ted had built into the rear of the cab was shattered, as was the windscreen. The passenger's door was jammed tight but the driver's was open. Fran stepped forward and looked inside the cab. Glass was everywhere and the seats where she and Sarah had sat were stained with red.

Two hundred yards in front of them a family were picking like scavenging birds at the remains of a car, behind them two men were rummaging through suitcases sodden with the winter.

'I'll get the rope.' It was the first time any of them had spoken since leaving the farm. Ned tied the towline to the axle beneath the rear of the pick-up while Brian Markham reversed his car into position, then Stan secured the other end to the car.

'Stand back.'

The vicar revved the engine, eased his foot off the clutch, and pulled forward. Slowly the pick-up edged out of the ditch and onto the road. Ned checked the brakes and steering while Stan examined the tyres and wheels and the vicar untied the rope from the back of the pick-up, then the four of them pushed it round so it was facing the correct way.

'Petrol been siphoned off.' Stan checked the tank. 'Engine's a bit knocked about as well.' He tied the towrope onto the front of the pick-up while Ned fetched a sack from the boot of the car and laid it across the driver's seat.

'I'll drive.' The postman got into the pick-up and shut the door before Fran could argue. 'You go with the others.'

By the time they reached the farm it was almost six. Boy Jack saw the headlights coming up the track from the road and called the others. As the vicar swung into the yard, the children stood in a line and watched. The men untied the rope and pushed the pick-up into the corner of the barn. It was almost like a funeral, Fran thought. She fetched a dust sheet from the house and laid it over the remains of the vehicle.

THE STREET WAS on the edge of the town. In the pub at the top he could hear the sound of glasses and conversation. Jack watched his breath forming clouds in the cold and waited. Christmas coming on, he thought. Funny how you could smell it, almost feel it, in the air. Almost near breaking point, he had been so close to it for so long that it no longer troubled him. But that was the danger point, that was when they would get him – when he was too tired to notice or too depressed to care.

The man came from the top of the street and entered the house. Jack waited another twenty minutes, checking that the man had not been followed, crossed the street and knocked on the door. At least the contact was still alive. Over two-thirds were missing, no more than fifty of those he had contacted still in place. A woman opened the door. He smelt the warmth of the house and heard the sound of the children.

'Hello, love. Is he in?' It was as natural as if he was a friend.

'Hang on, I'll get him.'

Just like home, he could not help thinking, just like the farm on the hill above the church.

The man came to the door. It was always the same – distrust in the eyes then relief that all was not lost.

'Hello, Jimmy. I've come about Hop.'

THE TRUCK WOUND its way down the pass and disappeared behind the trees. Drake stood in the porch of the lodge and watched it. Few had made it north, hardly any from Kent and Sussex. He consoled himself with the hope that some had stayed in place, melted back into their previous lives, and thought about The Watchman, about the agent called Prospero. Not many from the South, though. Sometimes, he questioned privately whether it had been worthwhile, or whether the sacrifice had been in vain.

The truck reappeared along the side of the loch then vanished again. There were fresh volunteers, of course, but not enough. They had already passed through the offices he had established in Glasgow and begun training in the crop of buildings at Arisaig. The truck came out of the woods. Not volunteers this time. He was always notified when a new batch was arriving, already knew who and what they were, had usually conducted the interviews himself. More survivors from the South, he thought, and felt his spirits rise. The truck stopped and the door on the passenger's side began to open. Only one this time – the depression set in again – not even enough to put in the back. He stepped forward to greet the man and thank him for what he had done, then saw who it was.

'Hello, Mary. Glad you made it.'

THE ROADBLOCK WAS perfectly positioned, sixty yards after the bend, the road behind covered by the car which was parked seemingly innocently thirty yards before the bend. There were two cars in front of him, the police bent over them, the water running off their capes. Not ordinary police – Jack saw the pistols and sub-machine-guns – the special team from The Citadel in Maidstone everyone had warned him about. He stopped behind the cars and a sergeant came towards him, two constables covering him.

'Where do you think you're going, then?'

There was the unmistakable hint in the way the question was asked which suggested they had been waiting specifically for him.

'Elliotts to look at some cattle.' It was not the first time he had used the cover story.

'Farmer are we?'

'Yes.'

Anti-looters, he remembered what he had been told about the squad, anti-black marketeers, but bastards anyway. Someone had said they had been brought from the rough area of the docks in Portsmouth. Already there was a name for them, an abbreviation of 'police'. The Lice.

'Got the papers for 'em?'

'Not yet. Only need the papers if I buy 'em.'

'Course.' Davis did not like being caught out. 'Let's see yours then.'

Jack undid the mack, aware of how the two men behind the sergeant followed every movement, and pulled out his identity card in the name of Chambers which had been issued to him in Arisaig. The sergeant glanced at them, then at him and back at the documents. Robert David Chambers, Jack had rehearsed the details, his address in Kent. He had even visited the place to make sure he knew the local details.

'Over 'ere, sergeant.'

'All right, Mr Chambers.' Davis stepped back and allowed him through, then followed the constable to the first of the other cars. Concealed beneath the rear seat were six bags of sugar, the driver standing by the side of the car already trembling. Routine, Davis knew, small stuff but the way they liked it, something to build on.

'Hills, is it?' He fingered the identity card contemptuously. 'Don't expect it's your real name. Soon find out, though.'

By the time the unit returned to The Citadel and he reported to Holdaway it was almost six. The chief inspector was seated at his desk reading a report. On a tray on the filing cabinet was a bottle of whisky and five glasses. Perks were already part of the job, especially with rationing biting, and whisky was one of them.

Holdaway motioned for the sergeant to sit down. 'How did it go today?'

'Not bad, we got three. Small stuff but you never know your luck.' Their network of informants, some recruited purely for financial reasons, others out of fear, was already growing.

'And how's the family?'

Davis wondered about the whisky. 'Fine, thank you, sir. The kids get a bit of a handful sometimes with my not being there, but the wife's coping.'

'How long have you been away now?'

'Seven weeks.'

Holdaway nodded as if he understood. 'I said when I asked you to come here that there would be married accommodation within two months. It'll be ready after Christmas. Only one problem, it's not for a sergeant.' He saw the disappointment which Davis tried to keep from his face. 'The department is being expanded. Schellenberg approved my recommendations for team leaders this afternoon.' He was unaware either of Schellenberg's motives for requesting the new plans from him or of his immediate acceptance of Holdaway's proposals for them.

'The other team leaders are coming up for a drink but I thought you'd like to hear the news first.' He left the desk, poured two glasses and handed one to Davis. 'Congratulations, Inspector, you deserve it.'

A smile broke across Davis' face. Holdaway had always been a good bloke, he thought, always led from the front, always looked after his men.

'Best Christmas present I could have, sir.' He raised his glass. A good move after all, he thought, especially as the boss had Schellenberg taped. 'Thank you very much.'

ARDLEY WAS TWELVE miles to the east.

It was four in the afternoon, cold but dry. In the stillness Jack could smell the wood smoke. Funny how Kent smelt different, especially his part of the county.

The road signs at the junction had been restored. He sat on the bike, feet resting on the ground, and looked at the names; Maidstone and Bearsted Green were fifteen miles to the right, Charing and the road to Canterbury then Ardley three miles to his left. Sometime he would have to go back. All the contacts had been made, all the cells accounted for except one. In one way, there was no reason to go back, he already knew the position of the Ardley cell; yet there was also every reason. Sometime he would have to face the truth, perhaps now was the time. He slipped the BSA into gear and turned right toward Charing and Canterbury.

The sides of the road were still cluttered with vehicles and carts. Jack passed a straggle of children, their faces pinched with cold, struggling under the weight of an armchair they had removed, then two men, their pickings stuffed into the suitcases they carried.

The place where the pick-up had been was empty. He stopped the bike and stood in the road. Looters – some bloody bastard had stolen the pick-up. He felt as empty and alone as the day he had admitted to himself that Fran and Boy Jack were dead, as if his last link with them had finally been removed.

He wiped his nose, turned the bike in the road, and headed north.

THE CHURCH WAS full, the decorations round the pulpit and the nativity below the altar just as Fran remembered them from last Christmas Day. The vicar was standing in the pulpit, singing loudly, the congregation joining in. She had not wanted to come, was glad now that they had. It wasn't just that the place was a church, as long as there was somewhere in the village for them to come together and find some support.

She smiled at Boy Jack and began to sing, thinking about the arrangements for the rest of the day. She had made sure the Christmas dinner was in the range by ten, they would have dinner at the farm and Christmas tea at Sarah's. The decision was deliberate; the fact that they maintained the tradition was important to all of them. The only change was the presents, one for each of the children but none for themselves, under the Christmas tree in Sarah's sitting-room to be opened together after tea.

The carol ended and the vicar began the sermon, talking of the babe in the manger and the first Christmas. Behind her Fran heard Harry Downton mutter about too much sherry too early, the younger men who seemed to be attracted to him in increasing numbers laughing. The choir began an anthem, the service ended and the vicar walked to the porch to bid his flock farewell. As Fran and the others left he asked them to stay. When the rest of the congregation had gone, Mabel Markham gave them a basket with presents for the children, Helen's included. That afternoon, as they laid them under the tree in the corner of Sarah's sitting-room, they would find there was also a present for each of the women.

Why, she wanted to ask; was grateful anyway. The vicar knew what she was thinking.

'Family,' he smiled. It was the same reply Stan Bradley had given when he had brought them a hamper of food and drink two evenings before, and Ned and his wife when they had brought the presents on Christmas Eve.

Ten days later, three days after the New Year, Helen announced that she and her children were returning to their home in Dover. It was a decision which Fran and Sarah understood. That evening they held a farewell party, then the following morning the three women and their families walked to the turning on the main road where they had first met. If only Helen had agreed to ask the vicar for a lift, Fran thought, if only she herself had possessed the courage to repair the pick-up. They kissed goodbye, then Helen picked up the case and took the bus to Dover.

THE CONVOY THAT left the field unit of the Seventh Panzer Division to return to headquarters consisted of two supply trucks, each carrying a driver and guard, with an armed motor-cycle escort at the front and rear. The journey had been routine, stationery and mail on the out journey, soldiers' letters home on the return.

The vehicles came down the hill, the woods thick on either side, and slowed for the bridge at the bottom.

'Look at the poor bastard.' The driver of the first truck laughed at the motor-cyclist. It was two weeks into the New Year, already they had forgotten Christmas. 'Bet he's freezing to death.' The man in the cab with him barely had time to agree before the explosives packed beneath the bridge detonated, killing them instantly, the guns of the ambush dealing with the second vehicle and its escorts.

At seven-thirty, when the convoy had not returned, the duty NCO contacted the unit and was informed it had left for the twenty-minute journey at five. At five minutes to eight an armoured patrol found the remains. In line with the instructions he had issued Walter Schellenberg was informed immediately.

In the two months after invasion there had been fifteen such incidents, and after each reprisals had been taken. In the period since Schellenberg had recruited Holdaway and placed him in The Citadel there had been another four. In each of the latter cases, although reprisals had been recommended by the local commander, Schellenberg had used the weight of the SD both in London and Berlin to veto such retaliation.

He left his desk and walked to the window. On one hand, he went through the arguments, it might still be too early to test Holdaway; on the other, if Holdaway was not the man then it was best to know now. There was also the problem of how many times he could stall the army, and a diminishing number of such incidents which he could turn to his advantage. He crossed back to his desk and lifted the telephone.

At six the following morning troops of the Seventh Division, supported by tanks and armed personnel carriers, sealed off the exit points from the nearest town to the scene of the explosion. At seven the mayor and his entire council were arrested in their homes. At eleven Schellenberg's London office contacted The Citadel and requested a meeting with Chief Inspector Holdaway that afternoon.

The meeting took place in the suite of rooms reserved for Schellenberg's use.

'We have a problem.' Schellenberg's words were as considered and his strategy as carefully planned as ever. He passed Holdaway the various reports, none of which indicated his role in the affair, and poured them each a coffee while the Englishman read them. Holdaway took the file and flicked through the pages. 'The general has ordered that the mayor and his colleagues be shot.'

'How does this concern me?' It was not his responsibility, Holdaway knew. The matter was political not civil.

'It concerns you because your unit is the only group with even the slightest chance of finding those responsible.' Give a professional a reason to do a job, Schellenberg had long understood, and he would do it. And when he had done it once, however abhorrent it might be, the chances were that he would do it again. Except that the next time he would not query it. 'Get those responsible and you save the lives of twenty innocent men and women.' Not get them, not even try to get them, the implication was clear, and you will be as responsible as those who pull the trigger.

Holdaway picked the reports off the desk and read them again. Anti-looting, Davis had insisted the day he had asked him to come to The Citadel, civil not political. He knew he had no choice. 'When?'

'The day after tomorrow.'

'It doesn't give us much time.'

'No.'

Holdaway leant across the desk, lifted the telephone and dialled the switchboard. 'Contact Inspector Davis wherever he is and tell him there's a meeting in my office as soon as he gets back.'

Davis' team returned to The Citadel at five and Davis went straight to the office on the third floor. Holdaway closed the door and poured them each a whisky. 'The incident this morning. We've landed it.'

'What do you mean?'

'Unless we get those who did the job last night the mayor and his people will be shot the day after tomorrow.'

'Shit!' Davis rarely swore.

Holdaway gave him the files. 'Do we have anybody in the area?'

There was no longer any time to consider what they were doing, only the method of doing it. Davis tried to remember the names on the list in his office. 'A man called Hills. We picked him up at a roadblock with a few bags of sugar he wasn't supposed to have. Long shot, but it's a start.'

'Good luck.'

Davis and the team he had chosen left The Citadel in early evening. When they arrived in the town centre the troops were no longer in the square and the tanks had been withdrawn from the surrounding roads. The lights in the baker's shop were still on and the man called Hills was tidying the shelves, the street quiet. They parked at the top of the road and settled down to wait.

'Check the back.' The car was unmarked and they were wearing civilian clothes. Four minutes later the constable returned. 'He's got to come out the front, there's no back door.'

After another quarter of an hour the baker pulled on his coat, switched off the lights, stepped outside and locked the door. Only as he put the key into his pocket did he become aware of the shadow beside him.

'Hello, Hills, got any spare sugar?'

The unit men on the gate saw the driver flashing his lights and raised the barrier. The car swept in to the yard and the doors opened before the vehicle stopped. Even as they pulled him from the back seat Hills could smell the fear he had brought with him. The entrance to the building was immediately by the car; without saying a word the two men on either side of him pulled him through the door and down some steps into a corridor, then down another set of steps and into a cell.

'Strip.'

He was already so frightened that he could barely undo his buttons. When he was naked a constable took his clothes and shut the door on him, and Davis reported to Holdaway.

'How is he?'

'Terrified.'

Holdaway sat back in his chair. 'Five minutes, then we'll have a little chat with him.'

The walls were stained and the cell smelt of urine. When they entered Hills had not moved from the position against the wall where he had been told to stand. 'Out,' Davis ordered the sergeant. 'Shut the door after you.' The sergeant had expected it and clanged the door noisily behind him.

'Hands on head.'

Hills moved his hands from in front of his genitals.

'Higher.'

He began to shake.

'Right up.'

They were already as high as he could manage.

'Why didn't you tell us?' Davis' voice was harsh, echoing.

The shaking was uncontrollable; Davis kicked the legs apart.

'I asked why you didn't tell us. You live in the area. You must have known about it.'

'Nobody knew.' It was not what the baker meant to say or how he meant to say it.

'What do you mean, nobody knew. Part of it, are we?'

'I didn't mean that.' He could feel the aching in his arms and the pounding in his neck.

'What did you mean then?' If Hills knew anything he would tell them now.

'Nothing, honestly. Only that they were formed before the invasion. That's all I know, just what I heard. Nothing more.'

'You could find out, though.' Holdaway spoke for the first time, friendlier than Davis.

'No, I couldn't.' Hills knew he had wet himself. Those responsible were Englishmen, he couldn't betray them. They would kill him if they found out it was him, they all knew he meant. He tried to stop but felt the excreta running down the inside of his legs.

'When are the other arrests?' It was almost an aside between Holdaway and Davis.

'Tomorrow morning.'

What other arrests? Hills' mind was racing.

'Who's in charge?' It was as if they had forgotten that Hills was with them.

'Seventh Panzer Division, same as the men blown up.'

'Oh, Christ!'

Davis grunted and turned his attention back to the man against the wall. 'Couple of kids, haven't you? What did you say they were called?'

You or them, Hills knew they were telling him; your family or the stupid buggers who blew up the lorry that morning.

200

'Nobody would ever know, we'd make sure of that.'

He knew the second man was on his side. You promise, he wanted to ask, could not believe the pain in his arms and his back. 'I'll try.'

Three-quarters of an hour later, after they had allowed him to shower and given him a large whisky, Davis left him in a side street two blocks from the square. At ten the following morning, in line with the instructions issued by Schellenberg, it was announced that the execution of those held as a reprisal would take place in the square of their town at three in the afternoon of the next day.

That evening, Davis left The Citadel and drove to the meeting with the baker.

At Hills' request the location was some distance from both his shop and his home. At five minutes to eight he slid from the dark and into the back seat of Davis' car. His eyes were frightened and the breath puffed in clouds from his mouth. The inspector turned in his seat and faced him. 'So what do you have for us?'

'Jimmy Bailey. Apparently he was part of a resistance during the invasion.' Hills was out of breath, panting. 'Didn't talk about it before, but does a bit now.'

Davis said nothing.

'There were a couple of others with him. There wasn't enough time to find their names.' He panicked that it was not enough. Davis turned away from him and looked out the front window. More than they could ever have hoped for, he thought. 'Address?'

It was as if the policemen knew what he was thinking. 'Pond Street, number thirty-five.'

'That all?'

Hills began to shake again. My wife and kids, he wanted to ask, they'll be all right, won't they? Nobody will know?

The constable to his right leaned across, opened the door and he got out. 'Hills.' The baker turned back to the car. Davis reached out the window and handed him a ten-pound note. The informant took it and hurried into the dark.

When Davis returned to The Citadel it did not surprise him that Schellenberg was waiting with Holdaway. He briefed them on what Hills had said and waited.

'I think the mayor and his people have a lot to thank you for.' The inflection in Schellenberg's voice was perfect. 'The question is, how do we handle it from here?' He had planned the moves from the first afternoon he had met Holdaway. 'Either we pick Bailey up and hand him over for execution, or we use him.'

'What about the mayor?'

'Don't worry, I'll sort it out.' The bargain, he let them understand; you kept your part, I'll keep mine. 'How to pick him up, though?' He turned to Davis. 'Where does he work?'

'Hills didn't know.'

'It'll have to be at his house, then.'

They all saw the problem. 'If we pick him up at home everyone will know.'

'Ten arrests, Bailey one of them.' Schellenberg glanced at Holdaway. 'Simultaneous. Keep them all for a few hours then release them. That way Bailey's covered.' He slid the last section into place. 'You want to handle it or shall I pass it over?' There was the faintest suggestion that the English units at The Citadel could not cope with the scale of the operation.

'We started it, we'll finish it.' Holdaway turned to Davis. 'Your people ready?'

'On stand-by.'

'Good. I'll get the others in. Briefing in three hours.'

THE MORNING WAS cold. Five o'clock exactly, Holdaway had ordered, the teams to move simultaneously. No questions once they were in the houses, not even to confirm identities, no interrogations until they had Bailey back at The Citadel. Two cars per house, eight men per subject. Two to cover the back, the rest to take the prisoner. Davis checked his watch and nodded to the driver.

The front door gave way easily. Kitchen in front, Davis flashed his torch round the small hall, sitting-room to right. He was already running up the stairs, two men checking the rooms below, another two moving to the bedroom on the left at the top, Davis himself going right, into the bedroom at the front of the house, the others close behind him. The man in the bed woke suddenly, the woman beside him beginning to scream. They bundled the man out, tying his hands behind his back. The children woke crying for their mother. Down the stairs, out the door and into the car, already Davis could hear the dogs barking and the other cars screaming away. It was thirty seconds past five.

THE SANDWICHES WERE stacked on plates on the table. Davis helped himself to two and poured a mug of tea.

'Said anything?'

'He's starting.' They waited while Davis took a bite. 'Bailey is a cell leader of what was the British Resistance.' He took another mouthful. 'Friend Hills was right: they were formed before invasion and have now gone underground. The attack on the convoy was an isolated one; they haven't any more explosives left.'

'What else has he said?' Our prisoner, Schellenberg saw Holdaway's eyes. No need to hand him over to anyone; we'll get whatever there is to get out of him.

'He's had a visitor.'

'What do you mean?'

'Came from the North, checking how much of the organization was left.'

'Who?'

Davis sipped his tea. 'Bailey doesn't know. The caller only gave a code name.'

'What?'

'The Watchman.'

2

THE MEETING AT the White House began at three, Roosevelt and Donovan sitting facing each other in front of the fireplace. Even in the past weeks the President had aged.

'I have asked you here, Bill, to discuss the continuing question of the British position. As you are aware, Mr Churchill has requested further arms and supplies. He has also pressed for greater American involvement in the conduct of the war.

'I have informed him that this country will stand by its commitment under Lease-Lend, as well as the commercial agreements made to date on the sale of various items.

'I have also informed him, however, that whilst this country remains opposed to the dictatorship which now prevails in Europe and is fully prepared to defend itself should the need arise, that is as far as this country can and will go in the present situation.'

For the next twenty minutes they discussed the global position: the German domination of Europe, the continuation of the Allied campaign in the Western Desert, with its implications for North Africa; the Non-Aggression Pact between Russia and Germany, agreeing that the pact was viewed by both sides as a mere temporary convenience and would one day be broken, the only disagreement coming over when and by whom; and the increasing tension between the United States and Japan.

'According to Ambassador Kennedy the coming year will be as crucial as the last.' Roosevelt returned them to the subject of the German occupation of the larger part of the British mainland. 'He anticipates that in the first weeks of this spring the Germans will launch an offensive against the remaining British position in the North. Given the relative strengths of the two sides, both he and his military advisors in London agree that the drive will be successful and that while pockets of resistance may remain in the Highlands, or on some remote islands, such resistance will be ineffectual and will eventually fade away.'

Donovan knew he was expected to reply. 'I probably agree with Ambassador Kennedy,' he conceded.

Roosevelt laid the report aside. 'Churchill has asked for a meeting to discuss the matter. The Ambassador will be there. I would like you to represent me.'

'Why represent you, Mr President?'

'Because the Prime Minister suggests that the meeting be held in what I believe is referred to in Britain as the Free North.'

DRAKE LEFT ARISAIG at six in the morning; the Sound of Sleat was almost lost in snow and the crossing took longer than he had anticipated. By the time he reached Dunvegan it was midday. After lunch he and Jack left the castle and walked on the pebbled beach.

'You move in three weeks. A radio operator goes with you. You re-establish contact with the cells and set up the drop zones. The first agents will come in two weeks after.'

'How many?'

'Three look like making it through the first course, two on the second. After that it looks a little better.'

'How will they come in?'

'Parachute to start with, probably Lysander later.'

To their left the surf was lost in the snow. They walked on, shoulders hunched against the cold and hands deep in pockets.

'What then?'

'When the organizers are in place we'll start bringing in supplies. By that stage there should be more radio operators available. Until then the one going with you will have to cover everyone.'

'Why?'

'Because everything takes so much time. Another three weeks is the minimum she'll need to become even reasonably proficient, and she's the best.'

'She?' Jack was surprised.

'The active service cells were only one part of the Resistance.' Drake's words were hardly audible; even now and even between the two of them, he was reluctant to talk of the subject. 'There was also a communications system, sometimes called Special Duties Section, which was manned by women. During invasion they operated from what were called zero stations. Their orders were that they should not leave the stations until the enemy was breaking down the door. Some of the stations had a back way out, each was also issued with a revolver.'

They turned toward the headland.

'Your operator was in a zero station with two other women; they continued transmitting even after the Germans located them and had discovered the entrance. When the Germans came in, two of the women managed to get into the escape tunnel at the back, the third lost her nerve and they had to leave her.'

Jack remembered the moment in the wood when Ted had looked at him.

'When they got out the other woman made a run for it and was shot. The one who will be your operator had hidden a bicycle at the back exit. There was a German roadblock forty yards up the road. She cycled straight at it. They fell for it and let her through.'

They reached the headland.

'There's an important meeting coming up. The Americans are attending. Churchill wants The Watchman to be there on the last day.'

It was strange how even Jack thought only of The Watchman, as if he were someone else.

'You no longer exist, Jack.' Drake read his mind. 'You died during invasion. We've brought you here, kept you separate from the others at Arisaig. Not even Churchill knows who you really are.' They began to walk back to the castle. 'Within six months we'll have agents in place to supervise the units, a whole new organization going. But someone's got to set it up, run it, take all the risks.' They had been through it before. 'Your decision, of course.'

When he went to bed at night, Jack thought, when he woke in the morning, even as he felt for the pistol under the pillow and waited for them to come for him, the one thing he carried with him were the faces of Fran and Boy Jack. No more.

'As you said, my decision.'

THE SKY WAS the colour of lead and the village seemed empty. Each day now the work seemed harder so that she felt exhausted before she had even started. In Harry Downton's shop the young men were standing just inside the door, smoking Woodbines and laughing at something the grocer had said as she went past the shop. Strange how things in the village were changing, how the order and authority that had previously seemed so natural were disintegrating. Fran knew what they were saying and hurried to the school to wait for Boy Jack.

'Cricket club annual meeting coming up,' the boy reminded her as they reached the farm. 'Can we go?'

She remembered how Jack used to take the boy, how he slipped him into the King's Arms for a drink after, Stan Bradley making a great show of pulling the boy his glass of weak shandy, and realized how much it meant to him, how much he was missing his father.

'I'll see if Stan or Mr Markham will take you.'

The annual general meeting of the cricket club began at seven-thirty. In good time Fran saw the lights of the vicar's car picking their way up the track and shouted to Boy Jack to put his boots on.

'Who's going to be captain?' she asked as he tied the scarf round his neck.

Last year it had been Ted, the year before Jack.

'Stan from the pub.' He sounded so much like his father, she thought, was growing more like him every day. 'Vice captain last year, got to be captain this.'

She saw how pleased he was that she had arranged for him to go and admitted for the first time how important it also was to her.

'You'll be all right by yourself, Mum?'

'Course I'll be all right by myself.'

She watched as the car disappeared down the track then returned to the kitchen, turned on the wireless and began some housework, planning already how she would try to get through the next day.

How tired she felt. Fran wondered how much longer she could manage. On the wireless she heard the news and was too weary to turn it off. When she heard the car return she opened the scullery door and the vicar and Boy Jack ran in from the snow.

'Long meeting.' It was what she always said when Jack and her son returned from the AGM.

'Had to have a quick one, didn't we, Vicar?'

The Reverend Markham glanced down at the boy, smiled at Fran, and left.

'Stan Bradley captain, then?' she asked as she made Boy Jack his cocoa.

'No.'

'But he was vice captain last year.'

'Outvoted.' There was a disgust in the boy's voice at what he had witnessed.

'Who?' She knew who.

'Harry Downton.'

When Boy Jack had gone to bed Fran went outside and stood looking at the stars. The night was cold and clear. Only six hours before she had to get up again, she thought, before she had to feed the bloody cows and make sure the sheep were all right. Her head throbbed and her back and shoulders ached with the tiredness. Perhaps she shouldn't carry on like this, perhaps she shouldn't make a point of turning off the wireless every time the so-called news came on. Perhaps she should just give in like everyone else. She was shivering with cold and realized how long she had been standing outside. Better check the animals, she thought, that's what Jack would do if he was standing here.

The following morning she went to the village, even though it was not normally the day she did her shopping. The grocer's was full — two Germans from the gun battery at the end of the village, a couple of wives trying to eke out their rations and the usual assortment of young men. She collected what she wanted then stood watching as the grocer wrote the prices on the back of a paper bag and added them up, talking to her and laughing as he did so, the pencil moving quickly.

'That'll be three and ninepence.'

The woman in the queue behind her knew what he was doing.

'You've overcharged me by tuppence, Harry Downton.' Everyone in the shop heard Fran's voice. 'Add it up again.'

She left the stores and went to the King's Arms. Stan Bradley was in the cellar. His wife shouted to him that he had a visitor and he came up.

'Hello, Fran, how's it going?'

Jack and Ted and you and the vicar, Fran was thinking, seeing it all, not sure how Ned fitted in but knew he fitted in somewhere. 'A friend of yours used to help Jack and Ted with the pick-up, didn't he, Stan?'

The publican wiped his hands and nodded.

'I wonder if he could give me a hand to check it over.'

'Of course he could. I'll get him to collect it this afternoon.'

'Thanks, Stan. Make it tomorrow morning.'

That afternoon, when she had finished the housework, she went to the barn, removed the dust sheet from the pick-up, swept the glass from the cabin, fetched a bucket of steaming hot water and cleaned the blood from the seats.

THE CABARET WAS good, not as good as Paris and the champagne was more expensive, but at least it was better than Moscow, and all the rumours amongst those with contacts in Berlin suggested that Russia was the Führer's main preoccupation for 1941. Walter Schellenberg allowed the waiter to pour him another glass, chatted inconsequentially to the woman who accompanied him and listened intently to the senior staff officers round the table.

The club, in London's West End, was busy, one of those which seemed to cater primarily for officers and their guests and where they therefore felt able to relax. There was a round of applause and a singer came on to the floor; her hair was blonde and she resembled Marlene Dietrich.

Jodl, Chief of Ops, had held a briefing on the *Atlas* train in Bad Reichenhall Station, near the retreat at Berchtesgaden, someone to his left was saying. Checked that all the doors and windows were shut then told them how the Führer expected them to be able to conduct war on both an eastern and a western front. The problem, someone else suggested, was that whilst this was possible, nothing could be done without the Führer's express and personal orders, and the Führer tended to become preoccupied with one issue at a time to the exclusion of most, if not all, others. It was for this reason that they had been sitting on their backsides awaiting the final order to push north and occupy the rest of Britain.

The woman began to sing, her voice low and husky; only when she had finished the song and begun another did they resume the conversation.

Russia in the late spring, it had been suggested, Leningrad by midsummer, Moscow before the autumn. That was why Hitler was reluctant to commit forces anywhere else no matter how small those numbers might be compared with those needed on an eastern front. And when he had secured Russia then he would have plenty of time to mop up minor territories like the remnants of England and Scotland. There was even a code name for the Russian operation: Barbarossa.

The next morning Schellenberg left his London office and was driven to Maidstone. The conference, in a meeting room at The Citadel, was of the team inspectors and their sergeants. Schellenberg sat in the corner and allowed Holdaway to conduct the meeting.

It was the last stage of his trap to ensnare the policeman and the most important of all: the day when he would offer the Englishman the fruits of collaboration and see if he would take them.

The purpose of the conference, Holdaway had already begun to explain, was to outline fundamental changes in the role of the department and the necessary expansion in size and organization. He moved quickly to the first point.

James Albert Bailey, known to his friends as Jimmy, aged thirty-three, married with two children, had been cell leader of an organization called the Auxiliary Units, trained at Coleshill, near Swindon, also at The Garth, in King's Wood off the Canterbury–Ashford road. The organization, or remnants of it, was still in place. Bailey had received a visitor from the North using the name The Watchman, as a preliminary stage of re-establishing the organization. Details and a description of The Watchman were in Appendix Two of the report which they would be given after the meeting. To protect his wife and family Bailey had agreed to work with them. Whilst Bailey could only lead them to his local cell, however, his visitor might give them the entire organization. The target was therefore The Watchman.

There was no discussion about the change in role and the switch to political work, Schellenberg noted.

Holdaway sat down and Davis continued the briefing.

The existence of the informer Bailey was obviously well known throughout the department. In future, however, for reasons both of security and co-ordination, the identities of such informers would be known only to the unit dealing with them, and to Chief Inspector Holdaway and himself. All details of informants would be passed to the two of them, Davis acting as collator, to avoid the obvious problem of one unit interfering with another's sources.

When the discussion ended Schellenberg rose.

'Gentlemen, if I could have your attention for one moment.' The transition of the unit into a political force had gone much more smoothly than he had even dared imagine. 'As Mr Holdaway has said, the department is being expanded and reorganized.' He saw how they appreciated his use of the term 'Mr'. 'Under the new system, the sections based at Birmingham and here in Maidstone will continue to operate separately, but there will be one man in overall charge.'

They all knew what he was going to say.

'Mr Holdaway will continue to run things here at The Citadel, but he will also assume overall responsibility for the operation as a whole.'

Someone began to clap, the others joining in. Schellenberg raised his hands for silence.

'There is one other matter connected with this, however, which Mr Holdaway does not know.' He let them wait again. 'Quite rightly, it is not in my power to promote or demote a member of the British police force. I think, however, that tomorrow morning Chief Inspector Holdaway might receive an official communication from his Chief Constable. When this meeting is over I would ask you to join me in a small celebration to toast Superintendent Holdaway.'

The party lasted two hours. When the others had left Schellenberg asked Holdaway to take a final drink with him in his office.

'There's something you should know.' The uncertainty in his voice was deliberate. 'The Führer, in his wisdom, has decided that England should not be without a king. George has fled, Windsor is enjoying himself in the sun.'

He poured two glasses, handed one to Holdaway and shook his head. You and I are just policemen – he knew Holdaway would understand the gesture – left to sort out the mess which the politicians create.

'Who is it going to be?'

'William, great-grandson of Queen Victoria. It will be announced tomorrow. I myself have only just heard but I felt it proper that you should know from me.'

'Thank you.' Holdaway drained his glass and Schellenberg handed him the bottle.

'The actual coronation will not be for some time, even the Führer had the decency to see that, but there is to be a banquet in London to celebrate the announcement at which William will be present.'

Holdaway refilled his glass and passed the bottle back to Schellenberg.

'I have been invited and have been asked if I would care to bring a guest. I would be honoured if you could agree to come.' He sensed Holdaway's hesitation and searched for the way round it. 'There will be a great many people, English and German. I appreciate the possible political connotation, but the invitation to you is purely personal, one policeman to another.' Suddenly, seemingly spontaneously, he began to laugh. 'Christ, we're doing all the work, why shouldn't we have some of the fun?'

Holdaway was staring into his glass. 'Great-grandson of Queen Victoria, you say?'

'Something like that.'

'Why not?' There was a change in the policeman's voice, the beginnings of a chuckle which grew into a laugh. 'Why not have some bloody fun.'

WILLIAM DONOVAN CROSSED the Atlantic by Pan Am clipper to Lisbon, then by train and boat via Paris and Dover to London. He was met at Victoria Station by an official Embassy car and driven to Claridges where his rooms had been reserved and the staff informed of his special status, the lawyer suffering no illusion that others were not equally interested. The restaurants and theatres were open and the hotel crowded, and although there was a preponderance of German uniforms, he could not fail to notice the numbers of well-off English who were continuing to enjoy themselves, not exclusively in the company of their own countrymen.

His first meeting with Ambassador Kennedy was for lunch the following day. The next morning they began their journey north, United States diplomats enjoying freedom of movement both within England and across the border into the Unoccupied Zone, the three men – Donovan, Kennedy and his defence attaché – travelling together with escorting vehicles in front and behind, stopping overnight and crossing the no man's land as dusk was falling the following evening.

The meetings with Churchill and his advisors took place in the family castle of Queen Elizabeth at Glamis on the east coast and were scheduled for two days, the agenda concentrating on the British requests for continuation of the arms supply across the Atlantic, the Prime Minister calling upon his service chiefs to present their various positions and Ambassador Kennedy introducing his own defence attaché, a colonel, to cross-examine on technical data. Even during the first morning, and especially when he considered himself centre stage, it seemed to Donovan that the attaché demonstrated both an attitude and an arrogance that reminded him of the First Secretary in the Berlin Embassy.

On the afternoon of the second day Churchill enquired of the Ambassador whether he had changed his view that Britain had not shown the commitment to justify continued American support, and Kennedy replied bluntly that he had not. When they broke for tea ninety minutes later Churchill asked whether the Ambassador would object to hearing the views of a man who, like himself and his defence attaché, was familiar with the position in the Occupied South, Kennedy agreeing and the defence attaché growing increasingly irritated at the entire process and deliberately not hiding that irritation.

When the two sides returned to the conference room Churchill introduced Drake and suggested he briefed them.

'The man you are about to meet is the head of the British Resistance in the occupied areas. The Resistance itself was created before invasion and fought through it, with seventy per cent losses in some areas. It is now being reformed.

'The man himself saw considerable action during invasion, escaped to the Free North after the government-in-exile was established and has since returned operationally to the South.'

The defence attaché snorted his impatience and checked his watch.

'Because of the position he occupies, his real identity cannot be given and I would ask you not to question him on this. His code name is The Watchman.'

'Bullshit.' The defence attaché drew a handkerchief from his pocket and blew his nose loudly and ostentatiously.

Drake left the table, walked to the door and asked the guard outside to collect the gentleman who was waiting in the adjoining study. One of their own, Kennedy sensed the British round the table were thinking, probably knew him, been at Eton and Oxbridge together. The man entered the room, hesitated for one moment by the door and then took his place in the single empty chair at the table.

The first reaction, among all the military hierarchy present and not just the defence attaché, was that he was not a soldier but a civilian. The second, again amongst the military élite, was that the man was not even officer class. The third, especially amongst those members of the English Establishment who monopolized the British representation, was how cheap the man's suit was and how badly it fitted. The last reaction was Kennedy's, the beginning of the uneasiness which he could neither identify nor shake off.

'Good afternoon.'

The man's accent was slow and country based, the impact more on the English present than the Americans, the disbelief showing on their faces.

The formal discussion was brief, even embarrassing, the English round the table patronizing and the American defence attaché abrasive, bordering on rude. After fifteen minutes, as the meeting seemed to be shuffling indecisively to a close, the colonel selected a cigar and began to light it, taking his time and making the meeting wait for him.

'Tell me about yourself.' There was a way he said it, a denigration of the man in front of him, which shocked even Kennedy. 'Tell me about your wife and family.' No personal details, they all remembered, nothing about the man himself. 'You have a wife and family, I assume.'

The attaché sat back in his chair and knew they all understood why he had asked: If I'm going to supply you, I want to know about your security, I want to know what the hell you're doing here. I want to know if you have a wife and family in the South who might be a danger to us all.

'I had a wife and family.' The voice was quiet and unemotional.

The colonel moved forward, his voice sharp, almost sneering. 'What do you mean?'

'They're dead.' Kennedy would never forget the eyes. 'They were killed during the invasion.'

'So what did you do about it?' It was almost as if the attaché had not heard the answer.

'What had to be done. My unit had used up its supplies, so the remaining members went underground again and I came north.'

It was not the answer any of them had expected, Kennedy was aware, not the answer to the colonel's question.

'What else did you do?'

'I don't understand you.'

The defence attaché glanced round the table. 'I mean, what did you do when you discovered your wife and family had been killed?'

I'm talking about commitment, he knew he did not have to say it, I'm talking about why I've wasted my time coming up to this Godforsaken place to listen to the likes of you snivelling away about your bloody little people in the wilds of the countryside.

'I'm sorry, I see what you mean.'

They had lost, the British chiefs of staff began to realize. Until thirty minutes ago they had stood a chance. Now Churchill had thrown it away.

Quit now, Kennedy urged the colonel, quit before this man with his ill-fitting suit and his funny country accent destroys you as you are seeking to destroy him.

'As I said, I came north.' The voice was still quiet and unemotional. 'To do otherwise would have been ineffective.'

The attaché relit the cigar, returned it to his mouth and closed for the kill. 'You mentioned the *remaining* members of your unit.' Kennedy knew that Donovan had hoped the attaché had not picked up the word. 'I assume, therefore, that you saw action.'

'Yes.'

'What sort?'

Jack was beginning to see the face again, Ted on the ground, Brian and Stan giving covering fire. 'Infiltration of enemy positions and sabotage of supplies and equipment, that sort of thing.'

'And you suffered casualties?'

Ted's face was white, his legs were bent at a grotesque angle underneath him and his insides were spilling out of his shirt. 'Yes.'

'How many?' The attaché twisted the cigar in his mouth and enjoyed the embarrassment of the British hierarchy around him.

'One.'

The laugh was contemptuous. 'Not many.'

'Out of four.'

'Dead or wounded?'

Jack hesitated. 'Wounded.'

'But you brought him out?'

'No.' They all noted the hesitation again.

'I'm sorry.' The attaché leaned forward for effect. 'I didn't quite hear that. You *didn't* bring him out?'

'No.'

'You left him behind.' He heard the gasp of astonishment from a brigadier on his right.

'Yes.'

'One of your own men is wounded, you leave him behind with all that implied for the security of your unit and yet you ask us to place faith in you as head of the Resistance?' The Ambassador was impressed, he knew, even Donovan, the English not knowing where to turn.

'He was badly wounded, we couldn't move him and we couldn't stay with him because we would all have died.'

Kennedy waited for the explanation and knew there would be one.

The man was my closest friend, Jack wanted to tell them. I grew up with him, he was best man at my wedding, I at his. We were godfathers to each other's first child, we shared Christmas together, opened the batting for the cricket team, took our families to the seaside together. We were like brothers, closer than brothers.

'So what the hell did you do?' The colonel was sneering, the cigar still moving in his mouth. Don't, Kennedy thought, or he will destroy you as clinically and mercilessly as if he walked round the table and strangled you with his bare hands. 'How in God's name did you leave him?'

Jack remembered what week it was, that last week they should have been attending the cricket club meeting, selecting the captain and taking Boy Jack and Ted's eldest to the King's Arms after, that this week they should have been enjoying the club's annual dinner, he and Ted stumbling up the fields to the farms after, their arms round each other and their singing waking Fran and Sarah.

Help me, Jack. Ted had barely been able to speak. *No comeback on Sarah and the boys.*

'I asked you a question.'

The light had gone from the day outside.

'We left him with what explosives we had left round his waist and with a trip wire running across his body, ten feet either side of him and concealed beneath his coat. Attached to the trip wire was a pull switch connected by a fuse and detonator to the explosives. When the enemy approached they would detonate the gelignite and make sure there was nothing left of him to trace him back to his family. There was also enough slack in the trip wire to ensure that they were close enough to him to take them with him.'

216

'He was badly injured and you trusted him to do all that to himself?' The defence attaché was incredulous.

Don't ask me, he pleaded for the last time. Don't make me remember. 'No.'

'Then who the hell *did* lay the trip wire and booby trap his body?'

Everything all right, Ted. No comeback on Sarah and the boys. Thanks, Jack.

'I did,' said Jack Masters.

THE DINNER WHICH would mark the end of the Glamis conference was scheduled to begin at eight. Before then, having bathed and dressed for the evening, William Donovan left his room and made his way to the suite which had been set aside for the Prime Minister. Menzies and Drake were already present. Churchill thanked him for coming, offered him a seat and poured him a whisky. No one else, Donovan realized, was even aware of the conference within the conference. He accepted the malt and wondered how many other cabals had been formed in such a way.

'The German advance north in the spring,' Churchill began. It was a subject that had been dealt with during the formal sessions in the preceding forty-eight hours, both sides agreeing that because of the uncertainties of the weather, the push would not begin until mid-April. 'It has become the practice to consider this in isolation. Suppose, however, we consider it as part of a whole.'

Menzies unrolled a map of Europe on the table between them and Churchill placed an ashtray at one end and a cigar box at the other to keep it in place, then selected a cigar and lit it.

'A month before the declaration of war, Herr Hitler signed his Non-Aggression Pact with Russia. Such an agreement, of course, was never more than a marriage of convenience, with both sides fully aware that some day one or the other would break it.' He allowed Menzies to pour him another malt. 'Suppose that the Führer decides it is in his interest to be the one.' He sat back, inviting Donovan to consider the implications.

'But he would have to do that no later than mid-May.' Donovan had seen the intelligence assessments in Washington, the suggestions that the *Wehrmacht* had been designed and equipped for blitzkrieg campaigns and not for extended or winter warfare, and that Hitler would therefore plan to defeat the Soviet army and seize its major cities, including Moscow and Leningrad, before the onset of the Russian winter.

'Precisely.'

'So what do you suggest?'

'That we assume that Herr Hitler plans to invade Russia this spring and that we do everything in our power to delay the start of that campaign.'

'How would that help you?'

Churchill allowed the smoke to rise to the ceiling. 'If Hitler does plan to attack Russia it might take his attention off us, particularly if we can make him worry about somewhere else as well.'

'How?'

The Prime Minister leant forward to the map and indicated the northern shore of the eastern Mediterranean. 'His underbelly. We attack him there before he moves against us or attacks the Russians. He cannot rely on Mussolini and the Italians to deal with the situation, and will therefore have to divert forces from elsewhere. That way we might prevent him advancing north against us and delay his march against Russia.'

'And if you delay his attack on Russia, he might become caught up in the Russian winter.'

The cigar was clenched firmly. 'Exactly.'

'What precisely did you have in mind?'

'Greece and Yugoslavia. We know that Germany has been working since September to bring these countries into the Axis. The indication is that they have failed in Greece. We therefore go into that country and make him retaliate. We know we will not be able to hold him for long, after that we withdraw to Crete and hold on there for as long as we can.'

Donovan indicated his agreement so far. 'And Yugoslavia?' He remembered the intelligence reports, the suggestions that because Prince Paul's wife was pro-German an alliance with Hitler was considered highly probable.

Churchill waited for Menzies. 'It is our understanding that the Commander of the Yugoslav Air Force, General Simovic, feels that a German invasion of Greece would constitute an intolerable danger to Yugoslavia, and that he would be justified in mounting a *coup d'état* in order to resist a similar move into Yugoslavia. Provided, of course, that he received certain assurances.'

'And you think I would be in a position to provide them?'

Menzies smiled. 'I think General Simovic would find them rather difficult to believe if they came from us.'

The American party left Glamis the following morning, Donovan and Kennedy travelling together and the defence attaché in the escort car. Shortly before noon they crossed the wilderness of no man's land and approached the border with the Occupied South.

'I was thinking,' said Kennedy, as their driver waved his diplomatic credentials and the stars and stripes fluttered from the wings of the car, 'as long as the British have the money to pay, I don't suppose there's any harm in selling them what they want.'

They passed through the checkpoint and headed south.

Amongst the several things the Ambassador did not know was that, included in his personal luggage in the boot, William Donovan had two small cases, each containing a morse set, one of which he would conceal in a wood near the village of Damerham, on the edge of the New Forest close to Salisbury, and the other at a secret location close to London.

THE FUTURE KING of England arrived at Croydon airport and was driven under SS escort to the suite which had been prepared for him at The Savoy overlooking the Thames. Present at Croydon, in addition to the official welcoming party, were photographers and journalists from the English newspapers which, like the BBC wireless service, were subject to strict control and censorship, as well as representatives of the German press. Walter Schellenberg left the Grosvenor House at one, was driven to The Savoy and escorted to the dining-room attached to the suite.

Wilhelm Richter was already talking to the *Reichsstatthalter*.

'Herr *Gruppenführer*,' Schellenberg addressed Richter by the honorary SS title which he had been afforded. 'How good it is to see you again.' It was a long time since the engineer had turned the corner and seen the black car of the SD outside his house.

'My dear Schellenberg.' Richter turned to greet him. 'You know *Reichsstatthalter* Scheimann, of course.'

Richter's eyes were even redder and smaller than Schellenberg had remembered, the jowls deeper round his jaws. His creation, he reminded himself. 'Of course.'

'The *Reichsstatthalter* was just saying that although Buckingham Palace is fine for the short term, I might also consider building something new, to mark the beginning of the millennium.'

So the *Reichsstatthalter* was feeling anxious, seeking to ingratiate himself. Schellenberg took the champagne which the waiter offered him and raised the glass. 'I think that's an excellent idea.'

HOLDAWAY LEFT THE Citadel at four, returned to his quarters, bathed, then changed into ceremonial uniform, the ribbons of his medals of service sewn neatly along the left breast of the tunic and the crown of rank on the shoulders. At six he was collected by an official car and driven to London. They crossed Tower Bridge and the driver joined the line of cars circling the historic building on the north side of the river. Precisely on time, the driver braked to a halt, a *Scharführer* opened the rear passenger door, and Superintendent Charles Holdaway stepped between the guard of honour and entered the White Tower.

The ground floor was already crowded, a flurry of waiters in starched white coats serving champagne. A large proportion of those present were military; yet although a majority of guests were German Holdaway was surprised at the number of English present, all of whom seemed perfectly at home and several of whom spoke fluent German.

He accepted a glass of champagne, saw Schellenberg talking to a group of officers in the far corner and made his way to him. The *Gruppenführer* was wearing the dress uniform of the SD, one of those to whom he was talking wore the same uniform and the insignia of *Obergruppenführer*.

'Gentlemen, may I introduce Superintendent Holdaway, who works at The Citadel.'

Reinhard Heydrich reached forward and shook Holdaway's hand. 'May I say what a pleasure it is to have you with us tonight.' He waved for more champagne and they moved upstairs to the banqueting hall.

At eight o'clock precisely there was a fanfare of trumpets and Wilhelm Richter entered, wearing the dress uniform of the SS. In front of him strode *Reichsführer-SS* Himmler and behind him Sir Oswald Mosley and members of the newly formed Government of National Unity. From the body of the hall came the first ripple of applause, gathering in strength and growing louder as it spread, those in front joining in.

Holdaway raised his hand and the waiter nearest him hurried to attend him. 'A carafe of water with ice and a glass.'

'Of course, sir.'

The seating arrangements had been specified beforehand. Of the eight guests at the table where Holdaway and Schellenberg sat six were men, five of the guests were German and three English. The conversation was light-hearted, those who spoke both languages interpreting for those who did not. The woman on Holdaway's right was English and in her sixties; her late husband, she said, had been a supporter of the Duke of Windsor and had met him after his return to Portsmouth in the autumn of 1939.

The waiter returned with the water. Holdaway allowed him to pour a glass and instructed him to leave the carafe on the table. Behind him the future King of England was holding court, his voice loud and overpowering. To his left he saw Schellenberg glance at the man, then at the other guests on the table of honour.

A number of those afforded places there were old and clearly influential, the younger guests tending to be positioned towards the ends. The only ones who attracted Schellenberg's attention were an English couple at the end closest to them. Both were in their twenties, the man slim, his chin slipping away from beneath his mouth, the woman listening politely to him and playing with the glass of wine in front of her, stroking the stem apparently absent-mindedly with her right hand, as if she was bored with the entire proceedings. Her dress was black, low-cut, and tight, the simple necklace she wore drawing attention to the point, just above the top of the cloth, where her breasts began to divide and fill out. She held her head slightly to one side, flicking her hair occasionally in the manner Schellenberg had come to associate with the English upper classes.

Already, he also noted, Wilhelm Richter was glancing at the woman, his eyes on her breasts. He turned his head and summoned a *Scharführer* from his department, neither the movement nor the presence of the man noticed by those around him. 'The guest list for the top table.' Five minutes later the man returned and handed Schellenberg a slip of paper. He glanced at the names: Fiona Egerton-Smith, Rupert Goodison.

At the centre of the top table Wilhelm Richter scrawled a note, the words unseen by those on either side of him, folded it in two and gave it to an attendant. To his right the woman called Egerton-Smith saw the way he looked at her and watched as the orderly made his way to the table below her. Schellenberg took the note and read it, wrote his reply, and handed it back. The attendant returned to the top table, waited till he had Richter's attention, gave him the paper and stepped back. Richter wiped his mouth with the napkin and opened the reply.

'I agree. Portland stone would be ideal for your new palace.'

He raised his glass to Schellenberg and smiled.

'Who's the officer who seems to know the King?' Fiona Egerton-Smith cut her husband in mid-sentence and addressed the lieutenant-general on her left. The man glanced at the table she indicated. 'Walter Schellenberg, *Sicherheitsdienst*.'

The *Scharführer* bent low so that only Schellenberg could hear. 'Rupert Goodison is her husband, he's a banker. Not too bright. The wife's father is the important one – that's why the invitation was in her maiden name – prominent in both national and international finance, excellent connections. Well thought of in Berlin before the war.'

'Address?'

The *Scharführer* gave him the street in Chelsea.

The woman in black was listening to her husband again, nodding her head as if she was hearing what he was saying to her, and stroking the glass, a glaze in her eyes. The guest on her right spoke to her and she turned, bringing her hand to her chin and seeing the way Schellenberg was looking at her. She tossed her hair again, listened attentively to what the banker was saying.

The tables were cleared and the champagne poured. Above them Heinrich Himmler rose from his seat. Holdaway filled the tumbler and replaced the carafe on the table in front of him.

'Gentlemen, I ask you to stand.' He looked around the room then turned to face William.

'The King.'

An illusion, the mere trappings of power; Schellenberg held the glass of champagne and knew that the general at his side was looking at Holdaway. The Englishman lifted his glass and held it high above the table.

'The King.'

Fifteen minutes before the banquet was due to finish, Schellenberg left the other guests and spoke briefly to an SD *Obersturmführer* assigned to the Economics Ministry. 'Rupert Goodison, third from the left on the top table. He likes gambling, make sure you take him with you tonight.' The man understood and grinned.

The celebrations ended, Schellenberg walked with Holdaway to the gate and waited while his car arrived, then returned to the hall. The woman in the black dress was waiting for him.

'My husband seems to have left me. I wonder how that could have happened.'

They left together. 'I think he's decided to go gambling.'

'So what am I going to do?'

Her eyes were teasing him. He remembered the way she had stroked the stem of the glass. 'Perhaps you would allow me to escort you home.'

'I'm not sure that would be entirely proper.'

Her lips glistened where she had drawn her tongue along them.

'I think it might be entirely improper.'

His car was waiting. He held the door for her, told the driver to go to Chelsea and wondered how she would react.

The driver pulled away from the Tower.

'Bloomsbury.' She gave him the address. Schellenberg looked at her and wondered what else the *Scharführer* had not found out. 'Bloomsbury,' he ordered the driver.

The street was quiet. A SSI sports tourer, white bodywork, red leather upholstery was parked outside the house. Schellenberg told his driver to collect him at seven, followed her across the pavement and waited as she unlocked the door. The lights were on. She allowed him to take her coat and went into the sitting-room on the left.

'My husband and I share the house in Chelsea.' She was looking at him as she had looked at him earlier. 'Sometimes, however, he is a little boring. Sometimes he also prefers the company of men.'

He was unsure which meaning she intended, became aware of the smell.

'The champagne is in the cabinet.' Her voice was almost cold. 'I'll be a moment.' She left the room and went upstairs. He crossed to the cabinet and opened it. Inside were six bottles of Bollinger, three on ice. He opened one, poured two glasses, and examined the paintings that covered the walls of the room. The subject matter of each was different, but the style and the theme identical: a stallion, a snake curling its way up a candle, an anatomical study of a young man, his muscles exaggerated, almost in the Teutonic mould.

He heard the rustle behind him and the woman came into the room. She had changed into a dressing-gown, the material thin and blue, hanging over her shoulders and tied loosely at the front. Her neck was longer, more slender than he had noticed before. Even in the half light he could see every line of her body.

He led her to the wall. 'Turn round.' She did as he told her. He lifted her hands above her head and placed them against the wall, so that she was leaning on them, and moved her feet apart. Her breasts were large, firm, the nipples already standing out. He slid his left hand beneath her arm and rubbed the thin material against her breasts, his right hand moving down her back and between her legs, drawing the material with him, then reaching through. She began to move along his lower arm, the movement becoming faster and her breath coming in short gasps. Her fingers grasped at the walls. Only when she was no longer in control of herself did he allow her to turn and begin to undress him, her hands moving quickly, sliding inside his trousers and holding him, her fingers wrapping around him.

The erection was hard and straight.

'*Heil Hitler*.'

She knew she had gone too far too quickly. His hand came down across her face and almost knocked her off her feet, the welts across her cheek and the tears of pain in her eyes. Suddenly, equally without warning, she struck back, her hand stinging him and the ring she wore cutting him.

'*Heil Hitler*,' he smiled.

The door to the bedroom on the first floor was open. She led him past it and up another flight, the stairs narrower and curving under the roof. The smell he had first detected in the sitting-room, but could not identify, was stronger. At the top was a small door. She opened it and stood back for him to go first. He stepped inside and understood what the smell was. In the centre of the floor was an artist's easel, a half-finished canvas on it and oil paints on a tray by the side. The walls were covered with sketches and part of the roof had been made into a window to allow in the light. In one half of the attic was a drinks cabinet and in the other a bed covered with fur.

'Lie down.'

He did as she told him. From a cupboard behind the easel she took a box of watercolours, mixed them, then selected a brush and walked to the bed.

3

THE FISHING BOAT was waiting at the quay. A car stopped on the granite rock above it and two figures hurried aboard. Ten minutes later, the sky drawing grey around it, the boat left the shelter of Lockinvay and slipped inconspicuously into the Firth of Clyde. The sea was choppy and the cabin smelt of oil. Mary went on deck and held onto the side, the coast to the east already lost in the night.

Training name Elizabeth, operational identity Martha Simms, secretary, domicile Southgate Street, Winchester. Both the address and the local registry office had been destroyed during invasion; there was no means, therefore, of a bureaucratic check if she was caught.

On the rail near the stern the other passenger was being sick. It was strange how she had been introduced to him, she thought. Not someone from the course, where they had been divided into organizers, saboteurs, radio operators and couriers, not someone she knew and trusted, but someone from outside. She walked to the stern and stood by him. 'You all right?' The moment she asked the question she realized its stupidity.

'Will be soon.' They had met the day before, in the house where they had received their final briefings. 'Only the second time in a boat.' He looked up and tried to smile. 'Thanks anyway.'

There would be up to four agents on each drop, he and Drake had decided, one network to organize the drop zone and the others standing by but knowing nothing of the arrangements. Once one group of organizers had been dropped and he had introduced them to their networks, Jack himself would move to the next area while the radio operator remained to pass on the messages they wished to send north, then join him for the next series.

To protect him no one, not even the radio operator, would know of his whereabouts, the only contact being at the daily rendezvous, the location of which would be known only to the two of them and changed regularly, safeguards built in if they suspected they were being followed or had been compromised.

To protect the radio operator no one except the leader or organizer of the network providing the safe houses and locations from which she would transmit would know either who or where she was.

The mate came back from the wheelhouse and told them there was tea and bacon sandwiches. The sea was slightly rougher. They turned and followed him into the wheelhouse. At half-past one they saw the flash of the morse signal to the south-west, and were transferred to the boat that would land them in England. At five, the night still dark and cold, they scrambled ashore and were taken immediately to a house two streets from the sea.

The beds were hard but warm, they lay on them fully clothed and tried to sleep. Now she was south again, Mary thought, she might be able to return to the hospital at Ramsgate, try to find out what had happened to Johnny. She had gone there after his escape from the zero station, been told that he was transferred to the burns unit at East Grinstead, but the doctors there had told her they did not know of him.

Now he was south again, Jack thought, he would have to visit Ardley, go to the farm, perhaps put up a cross to Fran and Boy Jack in the fields, even in the graveyard behind the church.

After they had eaten breakfast and when it was safe to be on the roads, especially so close to what the Germans had established as the prohibited zone along the border with the Free North, they were hidden in a furniture lorry and driven south before being passed to the next link.

Three days later they reached Birmingham. The city was busy and the streets crowded. Mary in particular was surprised both at the activity and the apparent normality with which the German troops mixed seemingly freely and easily. In a café near the bus station they sat at a table away from the window, but from there they could watch both the door and the rear exit, and ordered tea and cakes. It all seemed so normal, Jack knew she was thinking.

Her train was at four. At three-thirty she left and walked the four hundred yards to the station.

Nothing normal any more, she was suddenly aware, the enemy all round, the military police on the corner and the infantry farther down – not standing haphazardly and innocently, but strategically placed so that she could not get away if they spotted her. First time by herself, first time the identity card and papers she had been given would come under scrutiny.

Jack gave her two minutes then followed her to the station.

The ticket clerk was bright and cheerful. She made herself stop thinking of the zero station and Johnny, put her case down and reached into her purse. 'Second class single to Salisbury, please.'

'Straight through.' The clerk gave her the ticket. 'Ten-minute wait at Bristol, but don't get off the train.'

She thanked him and walked onto the concourse. There were police outside, *Wehrmacht* at the barriers to the platforms. Fifteen minutes to the train. Better to wait till the last moment and rush through, she thought, hope they wouldn't bother with her papers. No. Better to do it now, calmly and quietly as she would have to do it so many times in the future. The loudspeaker barked an announcement and she was back in the zero station, the sounds of the thumping on the door.

Don't stand still, Jack urged her. Don't draw attention to yourself.

The soldiers at the barriers turned and looked at her. She saw them and panicked again. Wait till the train is leaving, rush through.

No radio set in the case, Jack wanted to tell her, no reason for them to suspect you, every reason for them to look at you.

She pulled her shoulders back, and walked through.

FRAN FINISHED CHECKING the ewes and returned to the house, Boy Jack put the supper he had made in front of her and switched on the wireless.

So much to do, Jack, she thought. How did you manage? How do I organize it so that I can? Almost the beginning of lambing, the barn's ready and the bales of hay like you used to have them. Can't afford to lose any this year.

The music stopped and the news began. The propaganda from London, she knew, the collaborators who read it. She stood up to switch it off and heard the other voice, recognized it immediately: the voice of the BBC before invasion. She froze, trying to understand, trying to hear what he was saying, then the voice was lost and she heard again the news from London.

'Quiet, Jack.'

She concentrated on the set, moving the dial slightly and trying to hear the other voice again, found it for three seconds, too short a time to register what the man was saying. Then the wireless buzzed with static and she could only hear the broadcast from London.

The following morning, when she had finished the farm and house work, Fran went to the garage on the outskirts of the village where the pick-up was being repaired. The engine was running and the bullet holes in the back of the cab and the floor at the rear had been welded over. The woodwork had been repaired and the metalwork resprayed.

'How much?' She hardly dared ask.

Jack Masters' widow, the mechanic knew, remembered how Jack and Ted had coached him when he was a boy playing cricket for the first time, how the grocer and his cronies still encouraged the other boys to call the son a whitey.

'Lamb when they're ready will do nicely.'

'Thanks, Ken.'

That evening Fran and Boy Jack ate early, then went out into the fields. The ewes were clustered together by the bottom hedge. Fran and Boy Jack walked carefully between them, judging which were ready to lamb, then drove them into the barn. By dark the animals were in the pens made from the bales of straw and Fran returned to the kitchen, while Boy Jack checked the remainder of the stock. The kitchen was warm. She put the milk on the range and turned on the wireless in the corner.

It was almost nine o'clock. She heard the beginning of the broadcast from London and began to move the dial, slowly and carefully, unsure why she was doing it or what she expected or hoped to hear.

The set was crackling, the news from London fainter. She adjusted the dial fractionally and the voice of the collaborator strengthened. Behind her Boy Jack watched, not speaking. Fran turned the dial a fraction more and heard the other voice.

'In the campaign in the Western Desert the Allied Forces are expected to launch a major campaign against Rommel. In America

President Roosevelt has agreed to continue to supply arms and weapons to the war effort.'

The war's still going on, she felt the elation that they had not yet lost and the sadness that her husband was not with her to share the moment.

'Give me a pencil, Jack.'

Carefully, without moving the dial, she made two marks, one on the dial itself and the second opposite it on the set. Even after the bulletin ended she sat at the table, listening to the static, and thought about what she had heard.

The next morning she put the vehicle documents in her handbag, drove to Canterbury, went to the post office, and stood in line for petrol coupons. The queue was moving slowly, people arguing with the clerk about how many coupons they were allowed and refusing to move aside when he told them that they were not entitled to more. After fifty minutes she was three from the front. After another fifteen she stood in front of the clerk, gave him the documents, and asked for what she was due.

'Why do you need them?' The man was short with spectacles, his hair was parted down the middle and his voice was sharp and unfriendly.

'I'm a farmer. I need petrol to get my produce to market.'

'Farmer's wife,' he corrected her.

'Farmer.'

Someone behind her sniggered. The clerk looked at the log book then at her. 'Says here the owner is a Mr Jack Masters. Where's he?'

The people behind her were growing impatient and beginning to push.

'Dead.' There was nothing else to say. How, the man would ask. When? Show me some documentation to prove it.

'Wait here.' He turned away from the counter and disappeared into the office at the rear. Three minutes later he returned, pushed the log book across the counter at Fran and told her to complete it.

No point, she knew, did not know why she had even thought it was worth trying, and looked at the page. Across it were written the words 'Change of ownership', the amendment already certified and approved. Some people were already fighting back, she realized, already helping each other. She filled in her name, signed the page and returned it to him. He stamped it again and gave her the book of petrol ration coupons.

That evening, after she had shepherded the ewes who were due to lamb that night into the barn, Fran tuned the wireless and sat waiting at the table, looking at the set. It was almost nine o'clock. The interference stopped. She was suddenly aware that her hands were clenched and the palms were hot and damp.

It was nine o'clock exactly. There was a moment's quiet, then she heard the notes, played on a drum, the first three short and identical and the fourth long. G, G, G, E flat if they had been played on any other instrument, the slightest pause, then in the same rhythm, F, F, F, D. It was almost like the beginning of a great symphony, she thought, almost like a morse signal: dot, dot, dot, dash; dot, dot, dot, dash.

The notes were fixed in her mind, she knew she would never forget them or the words that followed.

'This is the voice of Britain talking to the people of Britain. Here is the news.'

Boy Jack was standing looking at her. 'What is it, Mum?'

She shook her head at him to be silent.

'His Majesty King George has held a special War Cabinet with the Prime Minister. Allied troops have landed in Greece. The Prime Minister has sent a message of support to the new government in Yugoslavia.'

At eight minutes past nine, according to the grandfather clock, the broadcast ended.

'The BBC,' she said at last. 'From the Free North.'

MARY LEFT THE safe house and turned left. At the top of the street a German staff car was parked against the pavement. She walked past it and into the city centre.

It was market day, the city crowded. Strange, she thought, how she had found it difficult to acclimatize to the sensation of being virtually a foreigner in her own country. She had not known what to expect, had almost expected the people to be talking a different language. Yet they carried on living, as if the Mercedes had always been in Fisherton Street, the roadblock on the Marlborough Road to the north-east and the swastika outside the Guildhall fronting the

Market Square which the Nazis had commandeered for their local headquarters.

She crossed into Silver Street. Time to check; three seconds, less, in which to do it. She turned, hands patting her pockets as if she had lost or forgotten something, and scanned behind her: woman with black hair, man with large ears. Just identify the features they could not change, they had taught her at Arisaig. Look for them next time. She walked on, into Market Square and turned right. Fifty yards along she stopped, appearing to look into a shop window, and checked behind her. Only when she was sure she was not being followed did she go to the house.

First check: both bedroom curtains either open or closed if anything wrong. She glanced up. Left curtain closed, right open.

The woman who answered the door was middle-aged, her hair was pulled back in a bun and an apron was tied round her waist.

'Yes?'

'I'm come about the advertisement.'

Second check: the advertisement genuine, confirmation that a job existed would signify that all was in order; the statement that the caller had the incorrect address was a warning that something was wrong.

'In that case you'd better come in.'

The radio set had been delivered that afternoon. The woman uncovered it and showed Mary into a small room at the rear, then left.

Mary opened the set, checked its contacts, the power supply in the room and the section of the roof where she could position the aerial, returned the set to its hiding place, and went downstairs.

That evening she left the safe house again and walked to the cathedral. The streets were quiet; she could hear the choir singing. She entered, knelt in front of the altar for a moment, then moved to the side wall on her right and read the inscriptions on the tombs there. Handbag in left hand all was well, right hand and she was either being followed or acting under duress.

The place was still. She heard the first unnerving note of the soloist's voice and remembered the season, the period before Easter, and knew what he was about to sing. Strange, she thought, the chemistry between war and peace, especially in such a place as this. Her bag was in her left hand.

'Everything all right?' Jack had watched her for the past ten minutes.

'Fine. With you?'

Already, he thought, her face and eyes were showing the strain, and knew he was looking at himself. 'No problems.'

He gave her the paper on which the message was written. 'Good luck.'

'You as well.'

He was gone again into the shadows, behind the altar the chorister began the 'Pie Jesu' from Fauré's *Requiem*.

The streets were almost empty. Even when Mary reached the house on St Edmund's Street she could still hear the boy's voice. The curtains were in the same position. She went upstairs, fetched the set from its hiding place, and took it into the attic room. It was thirty minutes before her schedule. She unwound the aerial, arranged it along the inside of the ceiling, placed the set on the bed, and began the encoding.

Twenty-five square grid, standard Playfair code. Five squares across and five down.

She began filling the squares with a line from her favourite Christmas carol which she would remember easily and had chosen as her personal key, counting the letters I and J as one, and omitting any letter already used. When the key was ended she completed the square using the remainder of the alphabet, again omitting any letter already used.

WHEN THE SNOW LAY ROUND ABOUT

W	H	E	N	T
S	O	L	A	Y
R	U	D	B	C
F	G	IJ	K	M
P	Q	V	X	Z

Only Mary and the decoder in the North knew her key, so that no one else could decipher the messages she sent. The man who had given her the message to transmit would have his own key, so that if he wanted to send a despatch but did not want her to know its contents he would encode it himself, and she would encode it a second time using her key but prefacing it by stating that the message was from whatever field name he instructed her to use.

When the square was complete she divided the message to be sent into bigrams, groups of two letters, and began to encode it by taking the two opposite corners of the rectangle each bigram formed in the word square. If both letters were on the same line she used the next letter to the right of each; if both were in the same column the next letter below.

WATCHMAN IN PLACE. FIRST CONTACT ESTABLISHED.
WA TC HM AN IN PL AC EF

NS YM TG BA KE VS YB WI

To reduce transmission time, and therefore the risk of being located by detector vans, words or instructions used regularly, for example *stand by* or *confirm message received*, were covered by single letters from the Q-and-Z code.

The other item she built into the message was her personal security code. Its presence would confirm that she was transmitting freely and its absence that she had been captured and was transmitting under duress.

When she had completed the initial coding she applied a second security measure, nicknamed the brandy code.

Along one line she wrote the letters of the alphabet, then above and below it two sets of numbers, each continuous but starting at a different point, no number being duplicated.

09	10	11	12	13	14	15	16	17	18	19	20	21	22	23	24	25	26	27	28	29
A	B	C	D	E	F	G	H	IJ	K	L	M	N	O	P	Q	R	S	T	U	V
46	47	48	49	50	51	52	53	54	55	56	57	58	59	60	61	62	63	64	65	66

30	31	32	33
W	X	Y	Z
67	68	69	70

Each week she would change the code by moving each line of numbers along one and bringing the last number to the front.

33	09	10	11	12
A	B	C	D	E
70	46	47	48	49

Then she applied the second system to the message, choosing numbers above or below the line at random.

WA	TC	HM	AN	IN
NS	YM	TG	BA	KE

[21/63] [69/20] [27/15] [47/09] [18/50]

Finally she formed the last code into blocks of five – 21/63/69/20/27 – for transmission. If any was received containing only four units the North would know the fault lay in that block rather than the message as a whole.

It was six minutes to her schedule. In the house in the North Drake left his office and made his way through the connecting passage to the signals room on the top floor of the adjoining building. It was twelve nights since Jack and Mary had left and four since they might have expected her to begin transmitting. He came to the top of the stairs and knocked on the door to be let in. In the future, when the agents and teams were in place and the other radio operators trained up and transmitting, there would be a row of signallers waiting to receive, at least one on constant stand-by for emergency transmissions. Tonight there was just one. He thought of the agent in the field and wondered if she was still alive.

Thirty seconds to go – her first real transmission since the zero station, she thought. 'For you, Johnny.'

At twenty minutes past nine exactly, she reached forward and tapped the key. In the room in the North the receiver heard the first signal.

THE FIRST BUDS were opening. Not the beginning of spring, Fran thought, just the end of winter. She left the farm and walked across the fields to the village. Three lambs had been born the night before. She had slept for only two hours, snatching whatever rest she could in the Windsor chair in the kitchen, and had finally crawled upstairs to bed at five. When he woke, Boy Jack fed the other animals, then brought her a cup of tea.

The *Wehrmacht* truck was parked outside the shop, a *Gefreiter* standing guard. She walked past and went inside. Some of the younger men who had voted for Harry Downton at the cricket club annual general meeting were lounged against the door.

'Morning, Mrs Masters.'

Another *Gefreiter* was paying for a packet of cigarettes. She knew the grocer had no option, as none of them had any option, but distrusted him even so. Even under Occupation, he seemed able to make a profit. Fran also felt uneasy about the young men who always seemed to be gathered at his shop and the stories she had heard in the post office of how, if a woman needed anything for her family or children that was either scarce or not available, all she had to do was to see Harry on the afternoon the shop was closed and his wife was in Canterbury.

When she finished shopping she climbed back up the hill to the farm. She could have driven the pick-up, she supposed, but had decided to use it only when necessary.

That afternoon she began the preparations for the lambs that would be born that night, Boy Jack helping her when he returned from school. Only when the work was done and the ewes comfortable in the barn did Fran stop to make their supper. At nine exactly she turned on the wireless and heard the sound of the drum beat again: dot, dot, dot, dash; dot, dot, dot, dash.

'Morse,' Boy Jack told her. 'Checked it this morning, V for Victor.'

'This is the voice of Britain talking to the people of Britain. Here is the news.'

Not quite Victor, she knew. One small letter on the end which made all the difference.

'In Greece the Allied forces are holding out against a German counterattack. In Yugoslavia the army and air force under General Dusan Simovic is in control of the country.'

There was the crackle of interference and she heard for a moment the news bulletin transmitted from London, the details of German successes in Greece and the continuing triumphs of the German army in Yugoslavia, then the voice of the BBC from the North again.

'That is the end of the news. Here are a few personal messages.

'The cat has had nine kittens. John is expecting a good crop of potatoes this year. Father's new armchair is very comfortable.'

She saw the bewilderment on Boy Jack's face. 'What's that, Mum?'

'No idea.'

'The new car is running well. Brian caught a large trout yesterday. The grass needs cutting.'

Messages to the Resistance, she suddenly knew. The organization was still in place – parts of it, at least. Her thoughts were mixed and confused: everyone numb from Occupation and winter, nobody doing anything, no one fighting back, even against the likes of Harry Downton; yet the whole world moving, the battles in Greece and Yugoslavia and the Western Desert, the messages to the Resistance in the Occupied South, even the post office clerk who had given her the petrol coupons.

The broadcast ended. Fran pulled on her boots and coat and went to check the ewes.

HOLDAWAY'S TELEPHONE RANG at ten minutes past nine. 'You heard?' Davis' voice was unmistakable.

'Yes.'

'You know what it means.'

'He's back.'

The next morning they met for breakfast in the canteen at The Citadel. Each evening for the past three weeks, at six and at nine, they had picked up the broadcasts from the North, weak at first then growing in strength. The previous evening's transmission at nine o'clock had been the first to include the personal messages.

It was, in a sense, what they had been waiting for.

'The first trip was intelligence gathering, to find out just how much of the organization was left and put it on stand-by. That much we know from Bailey.' Holdaway ate the bacon and eggs. 'So what's the second trip for?'

'Put the organization on an operational footing again.' Both men had spent the night thinking about it.

'And how does he do that?'

The canteen was filling up.

'He can't do everything himself, bad for security anyway, so he brings in other people.'

'Exactly.' Holdaway stabbed the knife in the air. 'He comes south again, puts the various networks on stand-by, brings in agents to organize them.' He counted the points off on the thumb and fingers of his left hand. 'The question is, how does he achieve all this?' He went to the counter and fetched them both another mug of tea.

'He can't bring the agents with him, so his immediate job is to set up the system for them to come in,' Davis cleared the plates to one side and continued the logic. 'He brings a radio operator with him for communication.' The two of them had worked so closely together for so long that they frequently thought and acted as one. 'The North starts transmitting to the organization, separate code for each network. Then he starts to bring in his agents.'

'How?'

'Probably parachute.'

Holdaway nodded. 'What about last night's codes?'

'Probably just setting up the system, he wouldn't risk anything on a first transmission.'

Holdaway nodded again. 'From tomorrow we monitor each of the broadcasts, verbatim transcripts of the news and messages, see what we can learn from them.' Somewhere, each man knew, there would be a pattern. 'We also bring in the radio detection vans. And we have a quiet word with friend Bailey.'

They rose to leave.

'What about Schellenberg?' asked Davis.

Holdaway laughed. 'I expect he's been on the phone already.'

THE MORSE SET was in the secret place where it had been concealed after collection from the location following delivery from the North. It had been difficult enough to retrieve it; too many days had been spent checking that it was not under surveillance and deciding when it could be approached. Yet the single overriding requirement of the place in which the set was now concealed, that the person concerned must be able to reach it without rousing even the slightest suspicion, had been infinitely more difficult to meet.

The aerial was laid in place and the set switched on. There had been a minor problem with it, due perhaps to a fault in a part or damage during transit south, but the fault had at last been repaired. The message, coded using the key assigned by Drake three months before invasion, lay on the table. When the transmission was complete the paper on which it was written would be burnt immediately.

Each message short and sharp, Drake had said. Give the detection

vans no chance to track you down, even to know you are on the air.
The agent called Prospero leant forward and began to transmit.

THE THEATRE WAS due to start at seven-thirty. The last item that
Schellenberg checked before he left his office in the Grosvenor House
was the list for that night. They had already picked up the big names
at the top; in a strange way no one seemed to have been surprised,
certainly none of the English with whom he dined and by whom he
was entertained had commented on it, though he suspected that this
was partly because old scores were being settled and partly because
the operation had been conducted so efficiently that few had really
noticed. Tonight, however, they were moving farther down the list
in terms of importance: not the well-known names but those whom
Straube referred to as *Würstchen*, smaller fry. The arrests, for logistical
reasons, would begin in London then take place across the country.

Fiona Egerton-Smith was waiting for him. The house was warm
and relaxing. She took his briefcase from him and guided him to the
bathroom. The water had already been run; as he sank into the foam
she brought him a whisky.

'Join me.'

She pulled a face at him and left the drink on the side.

The theatre was crowded and the performance excellent. When the
lights rose for the interval they left their seats and made their way to
the bar. The bottle of champagne and two glasses had been put aside
for them.

*The woman was in her mid-twenties, tall and slim; her hair was
long and her face, or so it seemed to the children she taught, always
seemed to smile. Across her left eyebrow was a small scar where she
had fallen as a child. She bent over the fireplace, lit the wood they
had collected from the bomb site at the end of the road, and began
to make supper. There wasn't much, of course, but more than most
people could afford. At least they both had good jobs, so that in a
way the Occupation had not affected them.*

*The soldiers were at the end of the road. She had noticed them as
she looked for her husband returning from work but had taken no
notice; there seemed to be German soldiers everywhere nowadays.
At half-past eight when she looked again there were more soldiers.*

The banging on the door was sudden and deafening, the sound echoing along the hall and into the kitchen. Even before they could rise from the table the door was forced open and the first men were inside, long coats and trilbies. Why us, she wanted to ask them, we have done nothing wrong; I am a teacher and my husband is a civil servant. The first two men seized her husband and dragged him towards the door. She was reaching for him, beginning to scream, when the next two pulled her after him.

The ends of the street were sealed off and two covered lorries were waiting outside. Her neighbours were standing, watching, numb with shock. Help us, she screamed, for God's sake somebody do something. No one moved. The engines of the lorries and the cars round them were running. To her left her husband was pushed into the first of the covered trucks and she was guided towards the second. For one moment, as he half-stood on the board across the back of the lorry, her husband was able to glance back at her and she saw the look on his face as he realized that she too was being taken away. Then a guard clubbed him with the butt of a rifle and he fell back, the shout to her still in his throat.

In the lead car Straube checked the next name and address on the arrest list and waved to the convoy to pull off.

After the performance finished, they went for oysters and champagne, then returned to the house in Bloomsbury. Before his driver collected him at eight the next morning Schellenberg had already spent ninety minutes studying the report from The Citadel on the return of The Watchman, as well as the details of the previous evening's arrests, which he had requested be delivered to the house during the night.

THE MEETING WAS at ten. Jack left the safe house, collected the BSA and took the back road from Salisbury toward the New Forest. The guide was waiting for him at the corner of the woods near Hale; he hid the motor-cycle in a thicket and climbed into the pick-up.

Gilbert was in his fifties. In his youth he had been in charge of a stallion and had walked the entire forest during the stud season so that there was not a track or byway he did not know.

'No trouble with petrol coupons then?'

'Not if you know where to get 'em.'

They turned off the road and onto the system of lanes which spread like a skein across the moorlands, then into the trees again and onto a complex of tracks and paths through the forest itself. In a rough flat pasture surrounded on all sides by woods, with hills sloping gently above and below it, Gilly stopped the engine. The nearest road was a mile away. Jack stood in the middle and looked round, imagining the night and trying to see the problems.

'How many farms in the area?'

'One.'

'With us or against us?' There was no longer a middle road.

'With us.'

On these first drops he would need to spirit the agents away from the DZ as quickly as possible.

'Looks good. Show me the map.'

At seven-thirty he made his way to the pub where he and Mary were to meet. The radio operator was already waiting, a glass on the table in front of her and her handbag to her left. In his left hand he himself carried a newspaper.

She moved over so he could sit beside her.

'Another drink?'

'Please, gin and tonic.'

The bar was busy, he had already checked the back ways out and knew that she had done the same.

'Everything all right?' she asked him.

'Fine.'

He slipped the message containing the map reference into her hand, finished his drink and left. A few minutes later Mary made her way to the house from which she would transmit that night. She encoded the message, feeling the adrenaline when she had read it and realized that the first drop was imminent. At nine-twenty she began to transmit.

Keep it short, she remembered, give the detection vans as little time as possible to obtain a direction on you.

She completed the transmission and waited for the acknowledgement. The set began tapping. Not acknowledgement, but the signal for stand by to receive. She felt her stomach jump and reached for the pencil.

When the message ended she confirmed receipt, packed the set, and began to decode. The first words were the only ones she could understand: the instruction to pass the remainder to The Watchman.

After that the message was further coded and she could not decipher it.

Something wrong, there was no other explanation. Nothing she could do until the meeting the following evening.

DRAKE LEFT THE signals room and walked back to the study. The room was dark. He switched on the standard lamp, pulled the curtains tight, as if to shut himself off from the world, and sat back in the chair.

Jack would be alone now, hidden away from the radio operator and planning what he would do the following day, who he would see. Probably making his arrangements for the drop.

Not many of those he had recruited were maintaining contact, Drake reflected. He tried to imagine the pressure they were under, poured himself a large malt and turned again to the despatch that had arrived that morning.

The message from the agent called Prospero.

More accurately, either because of technical interference or because either the sender or receiver had made a mistake, or even a fault in the set, only part of the message from Prospero. The agent assumed, however, that the message had been received in its entirety and that The Watchman was protected.

The section of message which had been received informed him of the existence of a traitor in the organization; that which had not been received gave the identity of that person.

His responsibility, Drake thought again, his fault for insisting that the paramount consideration was the security of the agent. No way they could contact Prospero. Only when the agent was in communication again could they check the identity of the traitor.

There were two options only: either run the risk and let Jack continue, or pull him out totally, start rebuilding the organization from the bottom up and ignore all that had gone before.

When Drake went to bed at three he still had not made a decision.

THE CITY WAS busy. Mary spent the day on the streets in the hope that she would see The Watchman. No problem, she tried to deceive herself, no reason to worry. A routine message, that was all. She returned to the safe house, washed, and made her way to the pub.

Jack came into the bar. Something wrong, he sensed immediately, bag to left, the signal that all was well, but something not quite right.

'Drink?' He greeted her as if everything was normal, as if it was a meeting of old friends. What the hell's happened, he wanted to know.

'Got one, thanks.' She was good, laughing back.

He bought himself a half of bitter and sat down, felt her slip the piece of paper into his pocket.

'Cathedral in half an hour.' He finished his drink and left.

The room at the top of the safe house was bare, only a bed and a chair on which he placed his clothes. He sat on the bed, laid the message on the pillow and decoded it, the bands tightening in his stomach as he read it.

Sixty-nine men and one of them had betrayed him, would tell the Germans the next time he called, have them waiting for him on his second visit. Abandon everything, he thought immediately, begin rebuilding from scratch, shut out all sixty-nine. Or run the risk, hope he could spot the traitor, pray to God he could withstand the interrogators if he didn't.

Not the network he had organized for the drop, he tried to argue. And not the other networks he had already contacted and who were in readiness to receive the agents who would come from the North. If it had been any with whom he had made contact on the second trip south he would already have been betrayed.

Why not one of the men he had already contacted? Why not one of the reception committee for the drop? No reason for the Germans to move while they still had the chance of getting everyone there. Every reason to delay, especially if they did not know that he was aware he had been betrayed.

Your decision, Jack. He could not get rid of the slightly sweet taste in his mouth. What you knew when you agreed. No reason for not going on, he remembered, no Fran and Boy Jack. That was why he had agreed in the first place. So that in the end, if he got it wrong and they came for him, he would not hesitate to put the Smith & Wesson in his mouth and end it all.

By the time he reached the cathedral Mary was waiting.

'There's a traitor in the organization, one of the men I've either contacted or am about to contact.'

Her face drained white.

'Who?'

'No idea. The North only received half the warning. Whoever sent it thinks we have the name.'

Oh Christ, she thought. 'So what do we do?'

'Tell them it's on. If it goes well then we know he isn't here. If he is, then at least they'll know that the other cells are secure.'

'What about later?'

'We'll sort that out after the drop.' He stood up to leave. 'Good luck. And watch yourself.'

FRAN AND BOY Jack finished bringing the ewes in and returned to the house. The evenings were lighter and warmer, in the sky above the outline of the moon was almost full. Fran turned on the wireless and Boy Jack began to peel the potatoes. Three more lambs last night, she thought, another eight ewes to go then it would be over. For the past two weeks she hardly seemed to have slept, the pain across her shoulders seemed to be permanent and even when she did eventually fall into bed she could not sleep because of the aching in her muscles.

It was one minute to six. She tuned the wireless and heard the notes on the drum, then the voice of the announcer and the details of the news, the bitter fighting in Greece and Yugoslavia. The news ended and the personal messages began.

'The fisherman has caught a cold. The weatherman says it will rain. The cider crop will be good this year.' Instinctively she turned the set down so that no one outside would know they were listening. 'Auntie Iris has a new kitten. The curtains are red. The plough is mended.' The supper was ready, she put it on the table and sat down. 'John has cleaned the carpet and is having sandwiches for tea. Grandmother has broken her best plate.' The broadcast ended, she turned off the wireless and moved the dial slightly so there would be no indication that they had been listening to the Free North.

In Salisbury Jack left the safe house and made his way to the pub on St John's Street. Mary was waiting. Jack bought a drink and sat down. 'You heard?' Inclusion of the code in the six o'clock messages and they were on stand-by; repetition at nine and the drop was confirmed for that night.

She nodded.

'If it's confirmed you know what to do?'

'Clear the safe house in case it's been compromised. Don't go back until we're both sure.' She understood what was in his mind and lifted her glass in the air. 'Big moment. Here's to it.'

He thought of the traitor in the organization and knew why Drake had said she was the best. 'Good luck.'

In his office in The Citadel Holdaway turned off the wireless, telephoned Davis and informed him that he was going home.

In the house in the North Drake stood by the window. The sun was sinking in a blaze of orange; even as he watched it slipped below the tangle of trees and disappeared, in the sky to the east the moon rose empty and pale.

It was not Jack's decision, he knew, but his decision and his alone. He turned back into the room and lifted the telephone.

'Duty Officer.' Radio contact for at least one-third of the trip, he thought. He could always issue a recall if anything went wrong.

'Speaking.'

'It's on.'

The first lamb was born at half-past eight. Only one more tonight, then at least she might be able to get some sleep. Fran made sure the other ewe was comfortable and walked back to the house. The moon seemed to hang above the farm primrose bright. She stood looking at it; the night would be so light that she would not have to use a lamp. She went into the kitchen and switched on the wireless.

It was nine o'clock. She heard the sound of the drum, then the voice of the announcer. In the barn thirty yards away, she knew instinctively, the ewe was in distress, grabbed her coat and ran, Boy Jack close behind her.

The news ended and the personal messages began. 'The cat had nine kittens. John is expecting a good crop of potatoes this year.'

'Breach delivery.' Only one foot was showing, the lamb bent the wrong way. Boy Jack passed her the soap and bucket of water, she took off her coat, rolled up her sleeve and washed and soaped her right arm up to the elbow, then knelt again by the ewe and felt inside. 'All right, my little lovely, soon have you out of there.'

'Father's new armchair is very comfortable. The new car is running well.'

The head was all wrong, back to front, upside down, she could not work it out. It was the rear foot sticking out, she decided – changed her mind, knew it had to be the front. The head was small in her hand. Careful, she told herself, soon have you, my beauty. The movement was sudden and natural, the head in the correct position and the lamb coming out almost before she was ready for it. It's not breathing, she thought, after all that it's bloody dead. She tied and cut the umbilical cord and swung the lamb in the air. Live, for God's sake *live*.

'The river is in full flood. Brian caught a large trout yesterday.'

There was still no movement, not even the slightest sign of breath. 'Come on, Jack.' She was running, the lamb in her arms, Boy Jack in front of her, opening the doors. She reached the kitchen, knelt down and put the lamb in the oven of the range. Come on, my little thing. You did it for Jack, now do it for me. She sat down at the table and realized the wireless was still on. In front of her the lamb raised itself and tumbled onto the floor.

'The blossom is pink. The weatherman says it will rain.'

Jack switched off the set and left the safe house.

'Just going out for a drink,' Mary told the people who had been allocated the responsibility of protecting her. 'Won't be too late.'

In the village on the western edge of the New Forest the pick-up slid out of the yard and disappeared into the night.

Holdaway's telephone rang three minutes later.

'Something's up.' Davis' voice was calm. 'The teams are already on their way in.'

When Holdaway reached The Citadel, Davis was already there. In the courtyard in the centre of the complex the car engines were running and the men were gathering in the briefing room.

'The duty clerk spotted something about tonight's messages.' The transcripts of the six and nine o'clock messages were laid side by side on Holdaway's desk. 'One message was repeated, first time it's happened.' He drew a red ring round the code reference to the weatherman.

'A drop tonight?'

'Looks like it.'

'What about Bailey? Nothing from him?'

'Nothing at all.'

'When did you last see him?'

'Three days ago.'

'I don't suppose he's making fools of us.'

'Two of the boys are picking him up now in case he is.'

The moon was above the cathedral, Jack left the city and rode south. Four of the sixty-nine cells with which he had made original contact, he thought, four cell leaders and one possible traitor. He pulled off the road and coasted the bike into the woods. The revolver was where he had buried it. It was too dangerous to carry a weapon in the daytime, too dangerous tonight not to. He left the hiding place and closed on the location, the countryside around bathed in moonlight.

Look after the way in, he had told Gilly, protect the way out.

First checkpoint. He flashed his headlight. From the right side of the road the lamp blinked in reply. The moon was higher, brighter. Second checkpoint. He flashed his light again and saw the reply on the left. Half a mile on he stopped the engine and listened for the sounds of the vehicles which might be following him. Nothing. He crossed Telegraph Hill and disappeared again into the trees, the bike bumping along the track. In front of him he saw the clearing. He parked the bike and walked forward, the men suddenly emerging from the trees, surrounding him.

'One hour,' he told them. 'Is everything ready?'

They had been in position since the afternoon, guarding the area and checking it was not under surveillance. 'Everything's ready.'

He walked with Gilly to check the beacons. 'Wind's changing every five minutes,' said the forester. 'We won't be able to position the markers until just before they're due.'

Already too many mistakes, Jack thought, and hoped they would have the time and opportunity to put them right. Should have duplicated messages in earlier broadcasts; tonight's stood out just like the bloody bonfires were going to stand out. Change the marking system for the drop zone, he was planning for next time. Bring in a torch system. Fires were too uncontrollable and left marks.

Fifteen minutes to go. He felt in his pocket for the Smith & Wesson. Ten minutes. No point worrying about the traitor any more, no point worrying about anything. No reason to worry. If they came for him he had the gun, knew what he would do if he could not get out. Five minutes.

'Wind's changing again.' He heard Gilly's voice and saw the men running, repositioning the marker fires, then heard the sound of the engine.

The wind was from the south, the markers in position. He took his position at the head of the square and waited, torch in hand.

The Whitley closed in on them. The traitor would not betray him yet, not till it was done.

'Light the fires.'

Jack switched on the torch and flashed the morse signal. One letter only, repeated constantly, the morse for that letter comprising dots and dashes, not a single dot or dash in case the pilot picked up an arbitrary flash of light and mistook it for the signal.

The fires were burning fiercely. The plane passed overhead, circled and came in again. Suddenly the shapes were coming out of the sky. They were jumping from four hundred feet; if they looked down they would see the colour of his eyes. In the stillness he heard the whoosh as the first silk opened and saw the ghostly mushrooms of the parachutes swinging in the moonlight, the Whitley already clearing the area.

The parachutists were rolling and stopping, winding in the cord and scooping the silk into a ball. It was all happening so fast. The traitor, he remembered, running forward, greeting the agents, shaking their hands, the men from the cells clustering round.

The first drop to the British Resistance – he knew they would expect him to say something historic, something they would tell their children and grandchildren. It was time to clear the DZ, time to get the agents away. If they had not been betrayed. If the Germans or the bloody Lice weren't waiting for them. They were looking at him, still waiting.

'Welcome home.'

MARY'S TRAIN WAS due at ten minutes past three. Jack parked the BSA and checked the streets and side streets. The area was clear, no waiting cars, no men or women looking for him. He went to the stall outside the platform and bought himself a cup of tea.

It was seven days since the drop in the New Forest. The following morning he had briefed the agents, then introduced each to the leader of the network he would be organizing, conscious at each meeting of the existence of the traitor and ensuring that there was no contact whatever between the various networks.

The following day he had moved to the next section he and Drake had agreed, Mary transmitting the code names of the networks he

247

would visit and the order in which he would visit them prior to his departure. She herself had remained in the Salisbury area to relay messages from the new organizers and their networks, and had finalized with Jack the arrangements for their rendezvous.

The afternoon was warm. Almost the beginning of spring, Jack thought, the first cricket practice. And only seven days to the next batch of organizers.

It was time for Mary's train.

Her bag in her left hand, all's well, he reminded himself; right hand, problems. Left hand and she would walk to the bus station, take the number 17 and get off at the third stop. Right hand and he would let her go, try to spot the problem and act accordingly.

He thought again of the traitor. Mary came through the ticket barrier and out of the station. Her eyes were glancing round, checking as he was checking, and the skin was slightly tighter round her cheeks. The case was in her left hand.

4

IT WAS THE first cricket match of the season, Fran had promised to make cakes for the tea. The ladies' committee had not insisted, some had even suggested that with so much to do she might prefer not to help out, but she had been adamant. The cricket club on Saturdays was like the church on Sundays, part of her link both to the past and to the future.

The date of the opening match had been decided the previous season when Jack had been on the committee. The boys were playing at the side of the pavilion, the ball thumping against the wood, no one minding. At the corner of the building the scorers sat at their table, the fielders already on the pitch and the two Ardley batsmen strapping on their pads. In the square a hundred yards away a German troop-carrier was parked, its crew relaxing in the sun.

'Good day for it.' There was a leer on Harry Downton's face; Fran was too tired to react and looked the other way. He tightened the strap on his pads and walked out with one of the men whom Fran had seen at the shop, the fielders clapping them. She saw the way the vicar and the publican watched them and remembered the way Jack and Ted strode out. At the side of the pavilion her son had stopped playing. For the first time, she thought, for the bloody first time since she had known about Jack, she was going to cry. She turned away so that no one would notice.

When the Ardley innings ended the Lydden fielders stood in two lines to clap the last two batsmen off the field. In the pavilion Harry

Downton had already settled at the head of the table and was shouting for his tea.

'Bit different from last year.' The man was in his fifties, slightly shorter than Ned but with the same complexion of a person who spent his life outdoors. Like Ned he was a postman and had played cricket for his village as long as either of them could remember.

'Just a little.'

They stood watching while the younger men helped themselves to the tea.

'Not playing today?'

'No, not today.'

'New openers this year, I notice.' There was already an edge in the conversation, as if they were part of the crowd but apart from it.

Ned nodded.

'Couple of our chaps missing as well.'

Fran watched the two men and wondered what they were talking about, remembered the final match of last season, the way Ted had asked the players if the ladies and families could join them for tea. In the pavilion Harry Downton was talking in a loud voice, at the side the boys knew there would be nothing left for them and began drifting away.

The other postman was looking across the pitch. There was something about the way he was staring, Fran noticed, as if, like her, he was remembering, as if he was undecided what to say. 'Pity about cricket.'

'Sorry?' Ned picked up the word and the sense in which it was delivered, but concealed the fact.

'I said it was a pity about cricket.'

Not cricket, Ned knew the other man meant, Cricket. The words were coming back to him, as they did every night, the voices of the women in the zero station. The radio he had clamped beneath the kitchen table was now wrapped in oil cloth and hidden in the woods. He glanced at Fran and the other women clearing the tea table. 'Good girls.' The words and the background against which they were spoken were deliberately ambiguous.

Harry Downton rose from the table and led the Ardley team onto the field. He was still chewing a sandwich and there were crumbs on his chin.

Why have you told me about Cricket, Ned wanted to know. Why

let me know you were part of the Intelligence network? Why ask if I was also part of it? Be careful, he warned himself, even if you have known the man for as long as you can remember.

'When did you first become a Cricket man, then?' The other man was as careful as Ned and his words equally ambiguous.

'About the same time as you, I should think.'

On the pitch Harry Downton opened the bowling as he had opened the batting.

'There's a problem.' The other man committed himself. 'There's some people from the village on the run, family with two kids. Gestapo came for them a week ago but they got out the back door. Couple of us have been hiding them since then.'

'Why were the Gestapo after them?' Even by responding he was involving himself.

'No idea. Apparently they're on some sort of list.'

If the man was not genuine and he agreed to help then he would have betrayed himself; yet if the man *was* genuine and he refused then he would have betrayed something else. 'So what do you want me to do?'

'Look after them. Just for a while, till they can get out of the area.'

'Why can't they stay in your village?'

'Too many people getting a bit inquisitive, one or two who wouldn't be averse to making a bob or two out of it if they could.'

The postman understood. 'When?'

'Soon as you can.'

Somewhere outside the village, the postman was already thinking, somewhere where they would be safe and Harry Downton wouldn't find out about them. There were not many people he could trust – not people he could *really* trust. Plenty who would agree but not many who could remain silent about it. Hardly any.

Only three in all the village when it came down to it. Stan Bradley was like him, too close to the village centre, no way anyone could leave or enter the pub without being seen. The vicar would do it, and he lived outside the village, but there was something about the vicar and Stan Bradley, as though they had always been up to something without telling anyone just as he had. Only one other place – he tried to avoid where his logic was taking him – only one other person.

'I'll see.'

The son was just like his father, he thought, same build, same shape of the face. You can't do it, Ned, he rebuked himself, not after she's lost her husband. What would you think of me, Jack Masters, what would you do if you had been asked? He crossed to the edge of the field and sat on the roller.

'Penny for them, Ned.' The postman suddenly looked old, Fran thought, a tinge of grey round his eyes and his shoulders not their usual squareness.

'Just thinking that it's not the same without Jack and Ted.'

'What else is it?'

'Nothing else,' he lied.

On the pitch Harry Downton was shouting at the fielders to get into position quicker. Fran sat on the roller and waited for Ned to tell her.

Not Fran, he thought, not Fran who'd lost Jack and who had the farm to run and the boy to look after. No alternative. He would explain to his wife, bring them in at night. A family with two children . . . it would be almost impossible.

'How can I help, Ned?'

'You can't, dearie.'

'Why not?'

He shook his head. Not just this family, he knew. They would just be the first. There were so many on the run.

'Tell me, Ned.'

'Someone's in a bit of trouble, they need somewhere to stay for a couple of days.' He wished that he had not even begun to tell her, or that he had told her the full truth to start with.

'That's all right, they can stay with us. We've got the room.'

'They can't.' The other man had brought no pressure on him, just asked if he could help.

'Why not?'

'Because they're on the run and the Gestapo's after them, that's why not.'

She felt the sickness in her throat.

'Who are they?'

'Don't know. Family with two kids.'

'Why are the Gestapo after them?'

He wanted to bury his head in his hands. 'They're on some sort of list, that's all I know.'

'Why did he ask you, Ned?'

Just like her husband, sharp as a fox, didn't miss a trick. 'I was up to a bit of no good last year, he was up to the same sort of thing.'

'Trust him?' The conversation was different. 'Sure he's not setting you up?' Not with the farm to run, she told herself, not with Boy Jack to look after. 'Times and people have changed, you know, Ned.' She'd already done enough, given them Jack, they had no right to ask her to do anything more. 'Lots of Harry Downtons around.' Lots even worse than Harry Downton.

'I don't know. How do you know who you can trust any more?'

He hadn't asked her, she was aware, it was she who had asked him how she could help. Around them the afternoon was like a dream – Boy Jack and the others playing again in the shaded area beside the pavilion, the oak tree on the side of the pitch fresh green, the men with their immaculate white flannels moving slowly, almost lazily, in the centre of the wicket. Just like last year, just like the year before and the year before that.

Jack dead, she brought herself up sharp, Sarah also a widow and the country occupied.

'How long?' Not a woman's job, she told herself, it was the men who did the fighting, the men who looked after this sort of thing. Just as it was the men who played the cricket and the ladies' committee that made their tea. She heard the voice again and saw the pictures. It was more than a year ago, the pictures of the women in Poland in the newspapers and on the Pathe Gazette when she and Jack went to the cinema in Canterbury, and the speech the Queen had made on the wireless.

War has at all times called for the fortitude of women. We, no less than men, have real and vital work to do.

She looked across to where Boy Jack was playing.

We all have a part to play, and I know that you will not fail in yours.

In the end she could either stand and be counted or give in like practically everyone else. No option, she thought. 'Just this once, two nights.' Work out your security – it was as if Jack was telling her – make sure you have a way out. 'No one is to know who I am or where I live. You bring them, not your contact. They come in the dark, so they don't know where they are, and they leave in the dark. They stay where I put them and they don't move from there.'

'When?'

No point hanging around. 'Tonight. Eleven o'clock.'

'You're sure?'

Ned who helped collect the pick-up from Charing, she thought, who brought the children presents at Christmas. 'As sure as you are.'

He stood up. 'I'll arrange it now.'

'Not now, Ned.'

'I thought you said tonight.'

'I did, but I'm the only one you've talked to since he asked you. Let him see you talking to Harry Downton and a few others before you tell him.'

THE DROP ZONE was prepared and the men in position. There were three torches under the new system: red torch at Point A downwind, white torch at Point B one hundred yards upwind and a second white torch at Point C, fifty yards to the right of Point B and at right angles to it, the three torches forming an inverted letter L, the position of the L and the red torch at the first point indicating wind direction and drop zone. The moon illuminated the sky. Jack sat and waited for the Whitley.

Three drops each moon period now, he and Drake had agreed, the period lasting from one week before full moon to one week after, with a flexibility at both ends to allow for events on the ground.

There had been four drops since the first in the New Forest, each, with the exception of the last, consisting of four organizers. Jack checked the Smith & Wesson and thought about the traitor. Each successful drop was a bonus, he smiled at the irony, each drop brought him closer to the Judas. Sometimes the calmness with which he considered his fate worried him.

In the sky to the north he heard the engine. On time, he thought, and ran to the first point. The Whitley was closing, a mile, he estimated, half. He began flicking the morse signal with the torch, the plane circled then came in again. 'Now,' he shouted to the men at the other points, checked that their torches came on. The Whitley was so low he felt he could reach it. The first shape hurled from the belly of the plane and the silk opened in the sky.

HALF-WAY TO THE full moon, Fran thought, the night fresh and clean. When Boy Jack was asleep she climbed the ladder to the hayloft above the barn and rearranged the bales so that they formed a room, two sides of which were the walls of the barn and two of bales, the entrance concealed behind another bale. If the Gestapo or the Lice came looking, she knew, they would have no trouble finding it, but at least it would protect her and Boy Jack from any casual visitors. When the hiding place was finished she brought spare bedding and blankets from the house, shook two bales of straw loose on the floor as a mattress and made up a large bed.

At fifteen minutes to eleven she unhooked Jack's shotgun from the wall in the kitchen, loaded it, stuffed the pockets of her coat with spare cartridges and went down the track to the road. The side road from the A2 to the village, she and Ned had agreed, five hundred yards from where the track to the farm cut off, before the bridge over the river which ran behind the church and the junction where she turned left for the village. That way the village would not know of the family, but, equally important, they would know nothing of the village.

It was eleven o'clock. She sat back in the hedge, the safety catch of the gun off, and waited to see if the man who had contacted Ned was a traitor. By midnight the moon was directly above her. Something wrong; perhaps Ned had already been arrested. She waited anyway.

At ten minutes to one she heard the noise and pulled deeper into the hedge. Not the sound of troops, but the sound of people walking and a child beginning to cry, a mother soothing him to stay silent. Sound carries at night, she reminded herself, and waited. It was almost fifteen minutes later that the figures came round the bend; five people, three adults, Ned one of them, and two children. There should be someone up the road, she thought, check they weren't being followed. Ned wouldn't let her down, Ned would have made sure before he brought them close to her. She slipped the safety catch on, broke the gun and stepped from the hedge.

'Bit late.' Ned was careful not to call her by her name, even to call her 'dearie'. 'Children got a bit tired.'

She thought of the pick-up in the barn and felt guilty. 'Almost there,' she told the mother. Ned shook their hands and faded into the darkness. 'This way.' Fran led them down the road, then through the hedge on the left and into the field. The children were exhausted, a girl about eight years old and a boy about four, their parents carrying them and the father also bearing the single suitcase they had brought with them. Four hundred yards on they crossed the track into the lower fields and approached the barn from below so that no detail of the farm was revealed.

The tilly lamp was inside. Fran closed the doors before she lit it, then put the ladder to the loft in place, the woman too tired to carry her son any farther and the man helping her. When they were in the hiding place she tucked the children into the makeshift beds while the parents settled down.

'Thank you.' The woman sat up and gripped her arm. It's nothing, Fran wanted to say, you'd do the same for me. 'There was no one else to help us, you see. We thought we were finished.' Her grip was like a vice.

Gently her husband prised her fingers from Fran's arm. 'Not many who would help, only Bill and a couple of others.' Fran saw the look of horror in his wife's eyes as he spoke the words. No names, they had been told, no clue to where they had been or who had protected them. 'Then he said there was someone who would help, make sure we were safe.'

'I'll get you something to eat.'

Five nights later Fran led them to the main A2 and pointed them north. The woman held up her son to kiss Fran goodbye. Not safe, she knew, same identities and papers as when the Gestapo came looking for them, nowhere to run and no one to look after them. Just once, she had told Ned, just for two nights. She kissed the boy and bent down to kiss the daughter. Somebody ought to organize it, set up a system; if one family was on the run there must be a hundred more like them. Full moon, she thought.

'Take care.'

The woman smiled at her for the last time then took her daughter's hand; Fran watched them as they disappeared towards Canterbury and wondered if Jack would have let them go like this.

THE INDUSTRIAL COMMITTEE of the Economics Ministry was scheduled for two. Schellenberg arrived early and was given the reports from the regions and the policy directions from Berlin on which it would focus. The *Kommissar* was ten minutes late. He brought the session to order, dealt with the minutes of the previous meeting and the regional reports and came to the third item: 'The decision by *Gruppenführer* Richter that a new palace be constructed and that such palace be built of Portland stone.'

The *Kommissar* indicated that an aide would deal with the matter. The official in question was known to Schellenberg, partly because of his regular attendance at such meetings and partly because of the file that was being compiled on his sexual proclivities and which Schellenberg considered might be used against him at an opportune moment. The man rose, coughed and opened the discussion, dealing first with the architectural plans, which he was at pains to point out the future King had personally overseen, and the range of engineering and technical requirements.

When questioned on the supply of materials he replied simply that the *Deutsche Erd und Steinwerke GmbH* had identified suitable facilities and made the necessary purchases and arrangements.

'What about labour?' Political prisoners, Schellenberg knew, those detained under the Gestapo arrest list, plus any others who had been rounded up and were fit enough to work. The details, even down to the most recent numbers, had been compiled with the bureaucratic efficiency which they had brought from Berlin and included in the sections of the appendices which few members of the committee ever consulted.

'Normal sources.'

There was a grunt of agreement around the table, a feeling that the discussion had gone far enough. Despite the acceptance of such a policy, Schellenberg had long noted, there was an occasional reluctance amongst those who were not required to dirty their hands to sweep the matter under the carpet.

'I assume that the DEST has done its usual calculation?' The question was unwelcome. Schellenberg sat back and enjoyed the prolongation of the discomfort.

'Yes.'

'And may I ask how long?' The question was based neither on an administrative need to know nor a moral decision to oppose, simply on the enjoyment he derived from seeing those he despised suffer, either physically or mentally.

'Between four and six months.'

'Thank you.'

They moved on to the fourth item, the latest instructions from Berlin on items it required to be produced in British factories for the continuation of the war effort, the *Kommissar* referring them to the appendices for details.

After the meeting, Schellenberg returned briefly to his own offices in the Grosvenor House. It had become his custom to dine with Fiona two evenings a week, when work permitted, usually spending the night with her, and to pass each weekend with her, usually in London, though on one occasion they had flown to Paris. That evening they had been invited to Claridges as guests of a group of staff officers accompanying General Strauss on a briefing visit to *Reichsstatthalter* Scheimann. The dinner, in a private suite, began at eight; in apparent deference to the English guests present, most of whom were women, there was no discussion of the reason for the general's visit.

The evening was amusing and the conversation light-hearted and animated, the visitors relaying anecdotes from Berlin and Paris, where two of them had recently been stationed. When someone mentioned an art collection he had been fortunate enough to view, without detailing how this had been possible, and Fiona expressed an interest in the subject, he asked whether she herself painted.

The party ended shortly after midnight. When they reached the house in Bloomsbury she led Schellenberg to the studio at the top of the house, undressed him and spreadeagled him on the bed.

'I was wondering.' Her voice was almost absent-minded. 'I've been invited to the country this weekend, old friend of the family. I used to spend a lot of time there when I was younger.' The brush was delicate across his flesh. 'Don't move, you're ruining the picture.' She laughed at him and drew the brush closer to the point where she knew he would no longer be able to endure what she was doing to him. 'I was wondering whether you would like to come with me.' She let the brush fall, drew her dress to her waist, and settled over him.

The following morning, in line with his new plan for the weekend, Schellenberg arranged a meeting with Holdaway at The Citadel for the Monday, then attended a committee meeting at the offices of *Reichsstatthalter* Scheimann, confirming with the staff officers from Berlin that he would join them at The Ritz that evening.

The dinner was for officers only, arrangements having already been made for the group to go later to a cabaret and a casino. It was only when the cigars were called for that the conversation turned to military matters, in particular the timetable for the anticipated advance into Russia and the repercussions of this on plans to complete the invasion of Britain.

The original D-Day for Barbarossa, the campaign against Russia, had been set for 14 May. The colonel who dominated the conversation was on the senior planning secretariat of the Combined Services High Command, and was therefore exceptionally well-informed. Because of the campaigns in Greece and Yugoslavia, the man from Berlin suggested, this date was even now being rescheduled. The overriding requirement of the campaign, however, would remain the same: the Red Army must be defeated, and the principal cities of European Russia, including Moscow and Leningrad, must be taken before the onset of winter.

Schellenberg allowed the cigar smoke to settle over the table, then snapped his fingers and called for more brandy. When the waiter brought it Schellenberg indicated that he should refill the glass of the speaker first.

The Yugoslav and Greek campaigns, the colonel raised his glass to Schellenberg and waited for the waiter to depart before continuing, had been unfortunate, powerful air and tank forces on their way east for Barbarossa had been diverted. Yugoslavia, however, had been dealt with by mid-April – 17 April to be precise, he took pleasure in adding – and he had it from reliable information that the Greek campaign would be over by the end of the month. Barbarossa, therefore, would only be delayed a matter of days.

Schellenberg checked his watch and wished that he had accompanied Fiona to the country that afternoon, rather than delaying his own departure until the following morning.

'But how will this affect plans to go north into Scotland?' The question came from one of the *Reichsstatthalter*'s staff.

'Just have to delay it a couple of months, I suppose.' The mood of the conversation had become more expansive as the evening had progressed. 'The Führer insists on giving everything his personal approval, and all his attention at the moment is on Barbarossa.'

The waiter returned with the decanter of brandy. Quietly, without seeming to attract attention, Schellenberg touched the man's arm.

'Make it a decent one this time, will you?'

It was the way he said it that drained the colour from the waiter's face. 'Of course, sir.' He left the room and returned with another bottle.

The colonel nodded his approval and drew on his cigar.

'But how did it come about that we became tangled up in the Balkans? I thought that the Foreign Ministry had assured the Führer that the situation there was under control?' Schellenberg's words rolled with alcohol but his mind was as sharp as ever.

'Exactly, old man.' Walter Schellenberg, he knew, close to Himmler and Heydrich. 'Ribbentrop and his fat cats at the Foreign Ministry really fouled it. Kept on saying they had Prince Paul in their pocket, through his wife, of course. Then the British land four divisions in Greece, Simovic throws Paul out and Peter II is installed in his place.' And troops and equipment on their way for Barbarossa are diverted to sort it out, he had no need to add. He snorted his contempt, threw back his brandy and reached for the decanter.

'But why the hell did Simovic have such power? He's only Commander of the Yugoslav air force.' Schellenberg showed he shared the frustration – the army let down again by the politicians. 'Who the hell set him up to it?' He wondered what Fiona was doing at this moment.

'Exactly.' The colonel waved his hand in agreement and almost spilt the brandy he was holding. 'Ribbentrop doesn't like people to know, of course, but it leaked out.' His voice was lower, conspiratorial.

'What exactly?' None of his business, Schellenberg knew, his concern was Britain. Everything his concern in the long run.

'According to Prince Paul's people, the consort had lunch with an emissary, call the bastard what you will, at which the suggestion was very strongly made that certain neutral nations would support Yugoslavia if that country opposed the Führer.' The colonel breathed deeply and enjoyed the attention Schellenberg was giving him. 'The consort rejects this approach and Ribbentrop thinks he's safe. After all, the Yugoslav premier and defence minister are already on their way to see the Führer at Berchtesgaden.' He leant forward and shook his head, the disbelief part mocking and part real. 'What happens? After lunch with Prince Paul the emissary crosses the Danube to Zemun and talks to Simovic, puts him up to it.'

'And what does Herr Ribbentrop say when he is informed of this?' His voice was a mimic of the German Foreign Minister's.

'Circumstances outside my control.' The colonel joined in the joke.

'And which neutral country did we have to tell the Foreign Minister was involved?' It was a natural extension of the ribaldry.

'America.' The first tears of alcohol and laughter appeared in the corners of his eyes.

'And who the hell took Ribbentrop for such a ride?'

'I'm not sure, he doesn't talk about him too much.' The colonel was laughing uncontrollably at the thought, the tears streaming down his face at the joke. 'Someone called Donovan, I seem to remember.' He felt for a handkerchief and wiped his eyes.

The party ended at two; before his driver collected him next morning, Schellenberg had not only bathed and breakfasted, he had also requested from the German Embassy in Washington and the relevant authorities in Berlin any information whatever on William Donovan, American politician and lawyer. It was unlikely that he would ever need the information, he was aware, but it was the sort of detail which, in his profession, it was useful to have anyway.

THE SOUTHERTON ESTATE covered four hundred acres in the country-side west of Maidstone and had been the family seat for three centuries. Schellenberg arrived at eleven, was shown to his room and informed that his hosts, as well as Lady Fiona, were out riding. He spent the next hour relaxing in the library, admiring the portraits which lined the walls and enjoying the air of natural and effortless superiority which hung in every part of the house.

The lunch was served in the dining-room overlooking the south terrace, his hosts friendly and discreet, accepting Fiona's relationship with him and never mentioning her husband or her marriage. They were also, according to the checks he had made, both reliable and well-connected. It was only when he and Fiona retired briefly to their rooms after lunch that he discovered that her bedroom was next to his and that there was a connecting door between them.

THE NIGHT WAS dark, the stars sparkling in the black of the sky. In the fields behind her Fran heard the rustle as an animal passed close. She held the shotgun and waited. Twelve o'clock, she had said, not the same location. If they were soldiers, she had thought, they would be well-trained, be able to remember the point where they left the A2 and the distance they walked before they turned off for the farm. For that reason the pick-up point was on the other side of the hill, so that she could bring them across more country. She had also told Ned to make sure they were completely lost before he brought them to the pick-up point.

Just once, she had said the first time. Just once more, she had said when he had asked her on the second occasion. There was no option for either of them. She did not blame him for coming to her again, did not tell him, however, that she had not dismantled the hiding place in the barn. It was almost as if, having done the job once, she had known she would do it again.

The men came out of the night, six of them, in the brown of the British army, Ned leading them. Without speaking they shook hands and she began to take them across the fields and through the woods, the path so dark that each held on to the man in front, the man behind her holding on to the belt of her coat. The gun was brushing against the bushes, she broke it and turned up the hill. By half-past one the men were concealed in the hiding place in the barn.

'When did you last eat?'

'Two days ago.'

'I'll get some bread and cheese.'

'I'll give you a hand, love.' One of the men moved towards her.

'Ground rules.' The gun came up and her voice was sharp. 'Nobody moves from here, even at night. I'll bring you a bucket. Nobody sees anything they shouldn't see.' She wondered why she had reacted so swiftly when the offer was probably innocent. 'If anybody tries anything on, I'll shoot him.'

'Understood, missus.' It was another man.

The next morning, after Boy Jack had gone to school, she brought them tea and more food. The soldiers had folded the blankets neatly on one side, cleared the floor, and were sitting round the walls.

'Sorry about keeping you cooped up.' She sat with them while they ate.

'It's all right, missus.' The man who had agreed with her the night before wore the stripes of a sergeant on his arm. 'You're in charge.' The light slatted through the chinks in the wall of the barn. Even now, he realized, he could not see enough details of her face to identify her later.

She left the barn, fetched more tea and bread, and sat with them, allowing them to relax and to tell their story in their own time and way.

The men had all been part of the British Expeditionary Force and had fought in Belgium and France until they had been evacuated from Dunkirk. During the bitter fighting on the morning of invasion and in the days that followed, they had been on the coast near Dover. Only when they ran out of ammunition had they been overrun and taken prisoner. As they talked, she noticed, they shook their heads in disbelief and rubbed their eyes. Some of them did not speak at all and most let the sergeant answer for them. Since October, he said, they had been held in a camp near the coast. Now some of them were being transported to Germany because of labour shortages in the country's factories.

'How many men are in the camp?'

The sergeant finished his tea. 'Four thousand, probably more.'

'And how many camps are there?'

'Three that chaps transferred to ours had been in – must be more that we haven't heard about.'

'And where are you going when you leave here?'

'Wales. It's too difficult to get north now, so we thought we'd try to make it there and hide up in the mountains.'

'For how long?'

'God knows.' There was no humour whatever in the laugh.

They should have organized themselves better, she thought, worked out a route for others to follow.

'Good luck.'

'Good luck to you, too.'

Three nights later she led them from the farm to the A2. The day before she had found them civilian coats and trousers and drawn maps for them. Bloody ridiculous, she thought as they faded into the night – no papers, no money, no back door out if they were caught. She remembered the family and wondered where they were.

SCHELLENBERG'S MEETING WITH Holdaway began at nine in the suite of offices reserved for his use at The Citadel. The Englishman had studied the latest arrest list sent to him from London and had dictated a memo pointing out that a number of names on previous lists had been inaccurate and that some addresses had not existed. At Holdaway's suggestion Inspector Davis joined them. Schellenberg ordered coffee and allowed the policeman to begin.

'It is our belief that The Watchman is back in the South, as we assumed he would be from our discussions with Bailey, and that he is now bringing in agents to revitalize the organization. It is also our belief that he is accompanied by a radio operator. The detection vans report a constant stream of intercepts.'

'But nothing you have been able to act on?'

The coffee was brought in, Holdaway allowed the clerk to pour it and leave the room before he answered.

'Not yet. The detection vans have always been too far away to give us anything accurate enough to work from.' He knew what Schellenberg would ask. 'Once they've established a cross bearing, of course, they're closing in for the next night, but the operator is smart, never transmits long enough for them to have a real chance of getting a fix.'

'How many intercepts so far?'

'That's what's interesting.' Holdaway indicated that Davis should take over.

The inspector unrolled a sheet of paper on which he had recorded the intercepts and grouped them into boxes. 'The teams have reported eighteen, sometimes they run on consecutive nights, sometimes there are breaks. Individually they are interesting, but considered as a whole they become a pattern.' He referred them to the diagram. 'Five groups, each based on the dates and general geographic area in which the intercepts in it were made.'

'Up to four intercepts in some, but down to two in others,' Schellenberg pointed out.

'It doesn't matter, the pattern is there.'

'Why?'

'The codes which the BBC transmits every night. There are more double messages, that is, codes transmitted both at six and nine. We have to assume that some of these are only included to confuse us but nevertheless they fit into the pattern of the intercepts.'

'How?' Schellenberg guessed how.

'A double message in the middle of the dates for each group.'

'The signal for a drop.'

'Exactly.'

'I assume you have also matched unidentified aircraft reports against your pattern.'

Holdaway allowed Davis his smile.

'During the period in question there were ten such reports. Assuming that twenty-five per cent are inaccurate that still leaves five or six planes which shouldn't have been in the air.'

'And?'

'They match. Bang in the middle of each grouping and always the same night as a double code from the North.'

'What about Bailey? Anything new from him?'

Holdaway sipped the coffee. 'Not yet, but it can only be a matter of time before The Watchman contacts him.'

'Why?'

'Because Bailey was a cell leader and it is the cell leaders whom The Watchman must now be contacting to arrange the incoming agents. It's just bad luck that Bailey isn't higher up the list.'

'But The Watchman is running out of time?'

'Yes.'

'And when the detection teams report radio intercepts closer to Bailey we know that The Watchman is probably about to make contact?'

'That is our assumption.'

'And when that happens?'

'Already arranged.'

THE ROOM WAS dark, the blanket was folded double and nailed over the window to keep out the light. Jack had been awake since five but then drifted back to sleep. Now he lay on the bed and looked at the shapes of the room. The bed, against the wall under the window, one chair. The bowl and jug of water on the floor and the mirror against the wall beside them. Nothing else. He rolled off the bed, dressed, then sat on the chair, his head in his hands, and tried to massage away the thudding inside his brain.

Three of the four contacts in the next group had already been made and the details given to the radio operator last night. The last contact was to be made today, then another meeting with the operator tonight. She had only come in two afternoons ago. He had been expecting her for three days and been surprised at how she looked, thinner than when he had last seen her and much tireder, her eyes almost like those of an animal on the run.

Four days to the beginning of the next moon period, just enough time to make the last contact and set up the drop zone, organize the security around it.

Saturday, Jack realized, fifth cricket match of the new season. Boy Jack would have been helping him with the farm work, Fran hurrying to help with the cricket tea if it was a home match. He was close to Ardley; not very close, but as close as he had been for a while – closer than he would be for some time to come.

He allowed his mind to wander. More than three-quarters of the contacts made, less than a quarter to go. The gun was under the pillow. It was strange that as the moment drew closer the physical side of what he had decided if he was taken concerned him less and less, that without Fran and Boy Jack it did not matter at all. As if, when the moment came, he would not hesitate to put the gun in his mouth and end it all.

At least, he thought, he would get a cup of tea this afternoon. He remembered the smell of the house, how it seemed warm and friendly, just like the kitchen in the farm, how Jimmy Bailey's wife had even offered him a piece of homemade cake.

MARY WOKE STILL weary. Each night now it was harder to fight off the shadows that seemed constantly to cross her mind. Each morning she woke with the same trepidation gnawing at her. Outside the birds were already singing; outside, she knew, the sky was blue and the air was warm. Soon it would be summer; soon, she tried to find refuge in the half-sleep in which her thoughts still drifted, she could lie on the beach and relax in the sun. She turned onto her side and tried to stop picking at her fingernails.

She was close to the hospital at Ramsgate, the knowledge had haunted her for the past three nights; not very near but as close as she would probably be for a long time. Nothing gained in risking everything and going to Ramsgate, she knew; she remembered the day she had last gone there, been told that Johnny had transferred to the burns unit at East Grinstead, only to be informed by the authorities there that they did not know who or where he was. Nothing lost either; at least she knew for certain that Johnny had been there.

She rose from the bed, poured a bowl of water and rinsed her face, looking at herself in the mirror. Almost there now, Mary, and The Watchman still safe. Christ, how awful he was looking nowadays, the colour gone from his face and his eyes never still, always looking behind him. Just a little lipstick, she thought, make herself look good. She reached in her handbag and took out the tube. Another meeting with The Watchman tonight, another set of messages. Sometime today the courier would deliver the radio to the safe house from where she would transmit.

She unscrewed the end of the lipstick, pursed her lips and drew the colour across them. You're doing fine, Mary, doing just fine. It doesn't matter about two nights ago, when your hands were trembling so much that you couldn't tap the keys and jumped at every noise outside the bloody window. Everything's all right. And soon it will be over. Soon they'll arrange for you and The Watchman to go north, take a break. She reached for the flannel and wiped her face where she had smudged the lipstick across it.

HOLDAWAY'S DAILY MEETING with Davis was at ten; on weekdays they held two such meetings, on Saturdays only one. This morning's was routine and brief: two arrests on the black market with which their unit occasionally concerned itself, mainly for the contacts it provided into the underworld which was beginning to flourish; and three possible radio intercepts, none considered positive enough to merit further action. When Davis left, Holdaway returned to the papers which seemed to flood his desk at the end of each week.

He lifted the telephone and spoke to the sergeant in charge of administration. 'The additions to the arrest list, when did they come in?' The seizure of people named on the Gestapo list was not strictly their concern. It did, however, provide another source of potential informants.

'This morning.' Three other arrests had already been scheduled for the duty team that weekend.

'Four males at a hospital?'

'Pilots.'

THE TOWN WAS busy and the market place crowded. Jack left the pub and walked to the street. It was strange how he could feel so alone when there were so many people around. The street was quiet, there were no signs of cars or men waiting for him. He remained in the area for twenty minutes, doubling back on himself twice, then went to the house and knocked on the door. The hall neat and well-decorated, he remembered, the kitchen at the end, sitting-room on the right and the stairs on the left. If he had called on Sunday, he felt, he would have smelt the beef roasting for dinner. The door opened and the woman stood in front of him.

'Hello. Is Jimmy in?'

She recognized him from the time before. 'Sorry, he's playing cricket.'

'Any idea what time he'll be back?'

She shook her head. 'Late, I should think. It's an away match.' A child crept up behind his mother and held on to her dress.

He smiled at the boy. 'I'll call again.'

'Shall I tell him when?'

'Tomorrow, if not tomorrow then Monday.'

THE CRICKET BEGAN at two; the other team had arrived two men short and Ned was fielding for them. As soon as he saw her and Boy Jack arrive Fran knew what he was going to ask her. At teatime she busied herself to avoid him. It was only when the Ardley team took the field and Fran could no longer find anything to do that Ned approached her.

'Hello, dearie, how's it going?'

'What is it, Ned?' She did not understand why she was so abrupt with him.

'Some RAF boys.'

On the pitch Harry Downton opened the bowling.

'Where?' It did not matter where.

'Ramsgate.'

'That's where the hospital is.' Don't be drawn into it, she told herself. Make up your own mind.

'They were wounded last autumn, left the hospital after invasion in case they were picked up, went back later.' He only knew the general details. 'Now they think they should leave again.'

'Why can't they go where they went last time?'

'I don't know.' Those that had sheltered them before were now too frightened, they both understood.

'What else is it, Ned?'

'One of them can't walk properly. You're the only one with any transport.'

She felt the anger and turned away. First the farm as a hiding place, she wanted to shout at him, now the pick-up. You've no right to ask me, you know I have Boy Jack to look after.

He put his arm round her shoulder as if she had spoken aloud. 'I know, dearie, but I didn't know what else to do.'

'Let me think about it.'

SINCE THE FIRST day Winston Churchill had moved north, the threat of kidnapping by specialist German parachute units dictated that his timetable and whereabouts were closely guarded secrets. He was accompanied wherever he went by bodyguards, and the premises and establishments he frequented were subject to special security arrangements. Because of this Drake arrived early. After his credentials and appointment were confirmed he was taken under escort to a sitting-room and asked to wait.

The room was panelled in oak and comfortably furnished. When Churchill entered he instructed those who accompanied him to wait outside, and settled in one of the high-backed armchairs. By the side of the chair was a low table on which had been placed two glasses and a decanter of brandy. Churchill poured them each a drink and enquired about the state of the Resistance in the Occupied South.

'Contact has been made with three-quarters of those cells that The Watchman confirmed still existed on his previous trip, and organizing agents have been dropped to them. By next month we will be in a position to start bringing in more radio operators and sabotage instructors, as well as additional couriers.' The Old Man was thinner, Drake thought.

Churchill nodded. 'When we first met you set out for me the functions of the British Resistance during invasion. Perhaps you could explain to me how you see its functions now and in the future.'

They had discussed the subject already, Drake wondered why he had been summoned. 'The Resistance can never be strong enough to expel the invader. Its function therefore is simple: to provide a structure and a foundation to prepare the ground for the armed forces at the point of liberation.'

Churchill lit himself a cigar. 'Greece and Yugoslavia have fallen, Crete can hold out for another two weeks. We should know after that time whether Hitler intends to invade Russia or whether he plans to complete the occupation of Britain.' He allowed the smoke to rise and changed the subject momentarily. 'How does The Watchman say our people in the South are standing up? Have there been any more dreadful reprisals?'

'No, there have been no more reprisals.' Drake did not answer the first part of the question.

The Prime Minister balanced his glass on the arm of the chair and came to the point of the meeting.

'There are in Europe a number of people who share the spirit of resistance but who, at the moment, can do less about it than can we. Should Hitler decide to invade Russia, and should he not try to occupy the rest of Britain, it seems to me imperative that we assist such people. If, in the next month, therefore, we have not been driven into the sea, I would like you to extend your organization to co-operate with those parts of Europe where the will to resist already exists, and to establish and organize it where it does not.'

ARDLEY WAS TWELVE miles to the east. Jack sat on the bike, feet resting on the ground, and looked at the sign that stood again at the junction, unsure what he was thinking. A car passed him, its head-lights almost blinding him. He slid the motor-cycle into gear and eased across the junction.

One day he would have to return to Ardley, he had always known; one day he would have to re-establish contact with Brian and Stan.

The memories were flooding back. It was summer, he was at the cricket pitch, Boy Jack playing at the side of the pavilion and Fran making the tea. Autumn, Boy Jack placing his box of fruit at the Harvest Thanksgiving. Winter, he could feel the heat of the Guy Fawkes bonfire and see the children wide-eyed and excited, their parents carrying the drinks and hot potatoes from the pub. Christmas, the tree in the square, he and Fran and Boy Jack laughing at each other as they sang the carols with the rest of the village on Christmas

Eve. It was spring again. The badger ran across the road in front of him and he braked, the shock jerking him back to reality.

The church was on his left, the hill rising behind it. He drove past and came to the vicarage. The line of light was just visible through the crack between the curtains of the sitting-room, another from one of the bedrooms. Mrs Markham always went to bed early, he remembered. He hid the motor-cycle behind the hedge, tapped on the downstairs window and went to the back, unsure that he was not still dreaming.

The kitchen door opened.

'Yes?' There were no lights in the room and no figure in the doorway, just the vicar's voice.

'Jack.'

'It's clear.'

He moved across the path and into the house, then waited in the dark as Brian Markham locked the door behind him, drew the kitchen curtains and switched on the light.

'Hello, Brian, thought it was time to pay you and Stan a visit.' He had not worked out what he would say, did not know what he expected Brian to reply.

'Fran and Boy Jack are alive. Sarah and the boys as well.'

He sat down. Not believing. Almost not hearing.

'They were held up by some people with guns, the pick-up was taken from them. They walked the rest of the way on the back roads. When Bearsted Green was shelled they made their way to Maidstone, then to London.'

He still had not comprehended a single word. 'What did you say?'

'Fran and Boy Jack are alive. They've been back at the farm almost six months.'

He felt the relief sweeping through him – that they were alive, that in the time he had thought they were dead he had not contacted the traitor. 'Tell me again.'

The vicar told him for the third time.

'What does she think happened to me?'

'She thinks you're dead.'

'I'll be back.'

The half-moon hung above the farm. Jack crossed the bridge behind the church and climbed the hill, then dropped into the hollow in which the house lay. Almost the moon period, the thought fluttered through his mind, in a few days he could stand here at midnight and see the farm as if it was morning.

You're supposed to be dead, Fran, he thought, you and Boy Jack. That was the only reason I did it, why I went north in the first place, then agreed to come south again. The fact that I no longer had you and Boy Jack was the only reason I took the risks, the only reason I was able to take the risks. Of course somebody had to do it but in the end I was the one who had nothing to lose.

He sat on the ground below a window and listened to the foxes in the wood behind the farm. The only reason I was prepared to go on after I knew there was a traitor in the organization and the Lice were waiting for me was that the two of you were dead. Now you're alive.

After half an hour he went to the sheds, talking quietly to the cows and noting how well Fran and Boy Jack were keeping the place, the implements stacked tidily and his tools cleaned on the shelf where he always kept them. In the barn, where he had always parked it, was the pick-up. It was two in the morning. He left the farm, walked through the orchard and the fields, the foxes still calling in Gorsley Woods, then crossed back over the river and through the churchyard.

For the next two hours he sat with the vicar and explained as much as his personal security and role in the organization would permit. At the end he had only one question.

'What am I going to do, Brian?'

'I have no idea.'

When the first streaks of light crossed the sky, Jack left the vicarage, taking with him food and drink, walked to the church and let himself into the secret base behind the pulpit.

For the next two hours he slept fitfully. At seven he ate, checked that the area was clear, left the church and made his way to the trees at the top of the hill from where he could see the farm. There was a light in the kitchen and he knew Fran was already up. The contact with the Hop network, he remembered, Sunday or Monday he had told the man's wife. He would stay until he had seen Boy Jack, he thought. Then he would make his decision.

HOLDAWAY RECEIVED THE call as he began breakfast and went immediately to The Citadel. Even though it was Sunday morning the cars were in the forecourt and he sensed an excitement about the place. Davis was waiting for him in his office, he was wearing casual clothes, old trousers and a sweater, as if he had also been taken by surprise.

'We might be on. Bailey telephoned half an hour ago, the duty officer transferred him to my home. I didn't want him to say anything on an open line, so I'm seeing him at eleven.' They both knew there was only one reason for Bailey to get in touch.

'Where are you meeting him?' Holdaway was already working it out – Sunday, bad day for surveillance, hardly anybody about to give them cover.

'Pub just outside the town. What about Schellenberg?'

'Leave him until you've seen Bailey. You'll go alone?'

'I thought I would.'

Holdaway understood the reasons. 'One man in the pub before you arrive, just in case he's playing silly buggers. Make sure it's someone Bailey doesn't know. I'll put someone near his house, make sure his wife doesn't do a bunk. How many teams are on stand-by?'

'Three. The duty team plus two others.'

Holdaway lifted the telephone and called the inspector in charge of the duty team. 'The arrest lists for the weekend. How many people have you picked up so far?'

'Two groups yesterday, we'd planned a third lot this morning and the airmen this afternoon.'

'You'd better hold back for a couple of hours till we know what's happening.'

FRAN FINISHED CLEANING the cowshed, went back to the kitchen and made herself a cup of tea.

'Church, Mum?' Boy Jack had been mending the fences at the bottom of the pasture near the river.

Ned would be at church; she would have to tell him. Most of the night she had worried about it, her duty to Boy Jack against her duty to people like the family on the run from the Gestapo and the sergeant and five men who'd broken out of the prison camp. Now there were more, and after them there would be still more.

'Not this morning, maybe this evening.' Perhaps by this evening she would have made a decision.

The sun was warm on his back. Jack watched from the trees as

Boy Jack crossed back over the fields to the hedge at the bottom. He would stay one more hour, he had decided when he had first seen Boy Jack that morning, then he would leave and contact the network leader called Bailey. The man would be waiting for him, worrying about him.

What do I do, Fran? What do I tell you? Do I tell you anything, even that I am alive? When I thought you were dead at least it was easy. But now I know you and Boy Jack are alive, what do I now tell you? Especially as the truth is so much more important now and the risk you would run so much greater.

Another hour, he thought. Then he could see what sort of job Boy Jack had done on the hedge, then he could make his decision.

DRAKE'S DRIVER COLLECTED him from the training school at Arisaig and drove him to Mallaig. The lunch, attended by some twenty guests, most of whom were military, was at the castle overlooking the sea which was being used as corps headquarters. Drake told his driver to collect him at three and joined the others in the lounge for drinks.

Sixty-nine men – the thought had never been far from him – one of them a traitor, the odds shortening every time The Watchman made a contact. Now just seventeen left, thirteen after the present group. So many additional things to think about after Churchill's instructions last night: recruitment, organization, liaison with the range of foreign nationals with whom he would now have to work. The Watchman above everything. A gong sounded and they went through for lunch.

DAVIS RETURNED TO The Citadel at half-past one. In the interim period Holdaway had summoned two more teams, with another two on call if necessary.

'It's The Watchman.' Davis had barely entered the room. 'Bailey was away yesterday playing cricket. He left just after twelve and returned home at eleven.' He stubbed out his cigarette and reached for another. 'Apparently it was an away match, which explains the delay.' Something for them to check, they both knew.

'How does Bailey know it was The Watchman?'

'His wife remembered him from the time before. Bailey says he

274

didn't contact us last night as it would have raised his wife's suspicions, which is probably correct. This morning he telephoned us as soon as he could.'

'So what have you arranged?'

The plans had existed since the first day Bailey had agreed to co-operate with them, the points and directions from which the cars would move in, the teams which would cover the back and the front, the empty house almost opposite from which they could keep watch.

'According to Bailey's wife, the visitor said he would call again today or tomorrow. Her exact words were "tomorrow or Monday". I've told Bailey to stay inside, so that The Watchman has to make contact at the house. I've agreed with him that they can go to a pub and that we'll pick up The Watchman after. That way nobody will know it was Bailey who fingered him.'

'But?' Holdaway knew exactly what Davis was planning.

'We'll take The Watchman as soon as he's in the house.'

Holdaway lifted the telephone. 'Get me Herr Schellenberg.' The *Gruppenführer*, he was informed, was neither at his offices or at his flat. The SD duty officer in London would request him to telephone Superintendent Holdaway as soon as he was contacted.

THE GENERAL ON the opposite side of the luncheon table was describing to the woman on his left his first experience of tiger hunting when he had been a subaltern in India. It was almost, Drake thought, as if there were parts of the British army which forgot that the world was now in the middle of the second world war in twenty-five years and that the country was two-thirds occupied. He would need to expand the communications section, his mind was still running through the implications of Churchill's directions. Air transport would have to be reorganized, probably a Special Duties Squadron from the RAF.

How does The Watchman say our people in the South are standing up? He could hear Churchill's voice and see his face. *Have there been any more dreadful reprisals?*

The orderly bent over him to serve the soup.

Christ!

By the time he reached the dining-room door he was running, the general looking at him in astonishment. The telephone was on a stand

275

in the hallway. He called the switchboard and asked for the number in Glasgow. The connection took ninety seconds and the captain in charge of the signals room another six to answer.

'Drake. There's an emergency. Try Orchid immediately.' He used Mary's operational code. 'Message reads: "Onpass urgentmost. No contact with anyone until further notice."' He wanted to say more but was conscious of being on an open line. 'Keep trying until I tell you to stop.' The officer began to ask why. 'Do it,' Drake told him. 'I'm coming back now.'

There were three cars outside, none of them his, a corporal sitting reading a newspaper in the nearest. 'Glasgow,' he told him. 'Now.' The man looked up at him in amazement. Not your car, Drake saw he was thinking, I'm not taking you anywhere. The keys were in the ignition. He opened the door and pulled the man out. Behind him someone was running, shouting. The driver was beginning to struggle. Drake hit him once and dropped him to the ground. Fool, bloody fool. The engine started first time. He slammed the car into gear and accelerated down the drive. See it, Jack. For God's sake see it.

The drive from Arisaig to Glasgow normally took three hours. Drake drove it that afternoon in under two. Only as he stopped outside the house did he notice the general's pennant fluttering from the flag stick.

A guard was on duty inside the main door. He showed his security papers, ran past the man and up the stairs to the signals room. All so bloody obvious, he cursed himself. He knocked on the door of the room and waited to be let in.

The operator was transmitting as he entered. 'Sorry,' the man shook his head. 'She'll only be waiting for us when it's her schedule.'

'I know.'

Drake sat at a desk, wrote out a message and instructed a clerk to take it for encoding. All so clear, he could not get the thought from his head. The attack on the German supply convoy just after Christmas, the arrest and threatened execution of the mayor and his councillors, then the sudden and inexplicable gesture of goodwill. The identities of the cell leaders still to be contacted and the towns in which they lived.

The signaller was still trying, still shaking his head. No point anyway, Drake knew, no way The Watchman would be in contact with his radio operator until it was too late. No way she would know where Jack was or how she could contact him. He remembered how the army would list its priorities and telephoned the duty officer.

'Slight problem with a car, I wonder if you could sort it out.'

THE FARM WAS quiet. At half-past six Jack watched as Fran and Boy Jack left, walked across the field, passing within thirty yards of the point where he was concealed, and dropped down the hill to the church and the village. Two decisions, the dilemmas hung over him like dark and looming clouds: whether and how much he should tell Fran, and whether he should continue to take the risks to which he had become accustomed now he knew she and Boy Jack were alive. No more risks, he decided, ignoring the first question. He would make the contact with Jimmy Bailey, arrange the next drops, then go north and work out a way of discovering the identity of the traitor without risking his life or anyone else's.

THE VILLAGE WAS not as empty as Fran had supposed it would be. Some of the men were sitting on the bench outside the King's Arms and a number of families were sitting and talking in the square, the children playing on the grass, the girls skipping with their ropes. Perhaps it was the fact that it was spring, she thought, perhaps simply that she seldom came to the village during the evening. Ned's wife answered the door and called to her husband.

'Boy Jack and I were having a stroll and thought we'd drop by.' Fran knew that some sort of explanation was necessary.

The postman and his wife fetched their coats and joined them.

'Tomorrow morning.' She and Ned had allowed Boy Jack and Ned's wife to draw ahead. 'You'd better give me the details.'

He nodded.

'The last time, Ned.'

'I understand.'

DAVIS RETURNED TO The Citadel at seven. Bailey had not left the house all day and there had been no sign of The Watchman. The surveillance was being maintained: two units were in position and two more would replace them at midnight.

'How many men do you need tomorrow?'

'Three teams maximum.'

'Good.' Holdaway telephoned the duty inspector. 'The arrest lists. Start on them again in the morning.'

Mary arrived at the contact point at seven-thirty. That afternoon she had sat in a field on the edge of a wood and tried to push from her mind the knowledge of how close she was to the hospital at Ramsgate. The pub was almost empty; it was always the same early on a Sunday evening, it would fill up later. She remembered the evenings with Johnny and Max and Sandy at the Black Swan, and the girls from the radar stations. She bought a gin and tonic and sat down to wait.

The Watchman was almost always on time, she knew. Only on two previous occasions had he failed to keep a meeting. At eight, when he had not appeared, she got up, aware of the suspicion a woman sitting by herself would cause after too long a time, walked in the area of the pub for another quarter-hour, then checked again and left.

Propped against the wall outside was a bicycle. It had been there earlier, she realized, except that she had not thought about it. The Black Swan was only fifteen miles away, the thought began to insinuate itself again, the hospital only ten miles beyond that. She could get to the pub tonight, see the old faces, go on to the hospital in the morning. No old faces – she had to confront the truth – everything too much of a security risk. No message for transmission tonight, the thought was persistent, no reason for her being there. Standard procedure, she heard the instructor, you always waiting on schedule in case they have a message. No contact with The Watchman therefore no message tonight; she could easily invent a story if they queried her next time, say she had waited for him. After her schedule – she postponed the decision – then she would make up her mind about stealing the bike and going to the hospital.

Mary made her way to the house in which the courier had placed the radio set, went upstairs, and checked the electricity supply and aerial. Her call sign came through immediately. She reached forward and tapped an acknowledgement.

The telephone rang only once before Drake picked it up. 'Contact with Orchid.'

'On my way.'

By the time he reached the signals room the operator had transmitted the message Drake had prepared.

'She's received.'

'Is The Watchman with her?' The Watchman would never be with her during transmission, Drake knew. 'Has he been in contact with her?'

'No idea yet.'

In the attic room of the house on the outskirts of the village in Kent Mary bent near the light of the window and decoded the message: ORCHID FOR WATCHMAN. URGENTMOST. IMPERATIVE AVOID CONTACT HOP NETWORK. REPEAT. WATCHMAN AVOID HOP. IMPORTANTMOST. CONFIRM.

The traitor, she knew. She wrote her reply, building in her security code, encoded it then tapped it out.

ORCHID. CONFIRM WARNING RECEIVED. REQUEST INSTRUCTIONS. HAS WATCHMAN BEEN IN CONTACT WITH YOU TODAY.

They waited again for her reply. It was as if she was in a foreign country, Drake could not help thinking, as if she was totally alone and a thousand miles away. In the attic room in Kent Mary decoded the incoming message and knew why The Watchman had not made the meeting that evening.

ORCHID. NEGATIVE. LAST CONTACT WITH WATCHMAN SATURDAY. NO WATCHMAN THIS EVENING CONTACT POINT.

CONFIRM YESTERDAY MESSAGE. HOP CONTACT SUNDAY OR MONDAY.

Already, Drake was aware, he was calculating the odds; knew that he was still not prepared to admit the inevitable and begin to plan for its repercussions.

ORCHID. CONFIRMED.

Still a chance, Drake tried to tell himself, still a possibility that for reasons of his own The Watchman had disappeared for a day, not yet made contact with the traitor. No point anyway, the desolation was growing in him, no way The Watchman would contact his radio operator before his next meeting with the traitor. The set began tapping again with the incoming message.

ORCHID. GIVE ME HOP CONTACT DETAILS.

Against all the rules, Drake knew, totally against logic.

5

THE HOUSE PARTY in Bedfordshire had been enjoyable; Schellenberg and Fiona Egerton-Smith had driven up on the Saturday morning, arriving before most of the other guests, and stayed until after lunch on the Sunday. The majority of those invited had been English, part of the circle into which Fiona had been born, though a few had been German. Not all those present had approved of him, Schellenberg had been aware, but most seemed happy to use him to cement their privilege just as he sought to extend his knowledge and control through them.

By the time he and Fiona reached Bloomsbury it was gone nine. Whilst she ran a bath he opened a bottle and settled in the sitting-room. The telephone rang at nine-fifteen. Schellenberg sat sipping the champagne and wondered how long it would take Fiona to come from the bathroom, or whether she would come at all. It was an agreement they had reached early in their relationship, that in her house in Bloomsbury only she would answer the telephone, just as only he would answer in the apartment in Regent's Park. He poured a second glass and waited. If it was for him, he thought, then it would be Straube, and if Straube was being so persistent, especially on a Sunday night, then it must be important.

Fiona came into the room and took the glass from him, sliding onto the side of the chair and ignoring the telephone. She was dripping wet and the towel was tucked round her.

The telephone was still ringing. 'You'd better answer.' He lifted the set from the receiver and gave it to her.

'For you.' She laughed as the cord tangled in the towel, pulling it loose as he took the telephone from her.

'Herr Schellenberg, I have been trying to contact you since this morning.' If it was business there was no need for Straube not to interrupt his weekend. 'Superintendent Holdaway asked that you telephone him as soon as you were contacted.'

'Where?' He motioned for Fiona to stop laughing.

'The Citadel.'

Fiona placed the glass on the table and slid off the arm of the chair and onto the floor between his legs. Schellenberg thanked him and dialled the number.

The switchboard answered immediately. 'Holdaway.' If the superintendent had gone home then it could not be that important, he told himself.

'Yes.' The answer was as immediate.

'Schellenberg.' The woman's fingers were teasing him.

'We might be on to something.'

There was no way Holdaway could tell him more on the telephone, Schellenberg was aware. He guessed anyway. The nails were scratching along his flesh. 'When?'

'Tonight or tomorrow.'

She saw the way his eyes changed. 'On my way.' He ended the conversation and telephoned Straube. 'Pick me up as soon as you can.' He replaced the receiver and felt the way her body was shaking. 'I'm sorry, I have to go.'

'Now?' Her voice was incredulous.

'Yes.'

'Is it that important?' She was beginning to shiver, he saw the disappointment in her eyes and lifted her from the floor. 'I'm afraid it is.'

'How long?' Her body sagged and she reached for the glass, pulling the towel round her.

'Tonight, possibly tomorrow.'

'Where?'

'Maidstone.'

IT WAS FOUR in the morning. Drake lay fully clothed on the camp bed in the corner of his office and tried to tell himself there was an outside chance that he was wrong, that there was no connection between the traitor and the execution that had been cancelled. In an hour it would begin to get light; in two hours, perhaps three, The Watchman would be waking, making his plans, getting ready to meet the man who would betray him. If the meeting had not already taken place. If the Lice were not already tearing Jack apart. He picked up the telephone as soon as it rang.

'Signals. Message for you to decode.'

The Watchman, via his radio operator. Drake felt the relief sweep through him. 'Send it down.'

'It's already on its way.'

There was no way The Watchman could have contacted Mary, he knew; no way Mary could have traced him at night, but he clung to the hope anyway.

The message was a single sheet from the message pad. Please God, he prayed. From the top drawer he took a fresh A4 pad, slipped a thin rectangle of metal under the top sheet so that his writing would not be indented on the sheets below, and decoded the message.

CONFIRM JIMMY BAILEY TRAITOR. TRAP IN PLACE. WATCHMAN EXPECTED TONIGHT OR TOMORROW. URGENTMOST WARN HIM.

Prospero, he thought, at four in the morning. What the hell's going on – Drake read the anger and confusion in the message: I risk everything, send you the warning, and you either fail to pass it on or The Watchman ignores it.

He placed the message in the file in the security cabinet, sat on the bed and waited.

HOLDAWAY WOKE, SHAVED and dressed, and made himself breakfast. He had not left The Citadel until almost two, after he and Davis had briefed Schellenberg. At seven he drove to the grim grey building dominating the town, aware that if anything had happened overnight he would have been informed at home. The men on duty at eight arrived, and the briefing began. The teams allocated to the Watchman surveillance were already familiar with their roles, which teams would block off the street entrances at the front and the rear, which men would enter by the front door and which would seal off the garden escape along the alleyway ten houses from Bailey's. At midnight the teams in the house opposite had changed, the men leaving their cars five streets away and entering and leaving through the garden at the rear, taking care not to leave their footprints in the soil where the neighbours had cleared the rubble to grow vegetables.

When the Watchman briefing was over Holdaway turned his attention to the duty squad. Four men could pick up the family on the arrest list, he suggested, the rest the airmen. The hospital at Ramsgate was ninety minutes' drive from The Citadel. The pick-up should be done by ten, ten-fifteen at the latest; the entire unit could therefore be back at base by midday.

Both Schellenberg and Davis understood his reasoning for having so many men immediately available: when The Watchman was arrested, and if they could break him quickly enough, it was vital that they should be able to seize as many of his contacts as possible before word spread that he had been taken.

At eight-thirty Holdaway and Davis watched as the cars left The Citadel.

'Everyone else on stand-by, all leave and rest days cancelled?'

Davis confirmed Holdaway's orders.

'Think he'll turn up?'

'No reason why he shouldn't.'

'And you're sure Bailey won't leave the house?'

'If he does I'll want to know why.'

FRAN WATCHED BOY Jack running down the hill for school, then reversed the pick-up out of the barn. The last time, she had told Ned. It was a thirty-minute drive to the hospital; ten minutes to make the contact and wait for them to come out, she thought, and she could be away from the danger point by ten. It was still too risky, she knew, even if it went well. She should never have agreed to both drive the pick-up *and* allow them to hide in the barn until they felt able to move on.

She knew she was delaying. She plastered the number plates with mud then went to the house and changed. No protection, she was aware, not even the shotgun she had held cocked as she had waited in the hedge. She left the farm, drove down the track, turned right at the bottom and up the hill towards the A2, then right towards the coast and Ramsgate.

THE MORNING WAS warm and sunny. Not the day for a betrayal, Mary thought, for such an act it should be bleak and cold. The station was close to the town centre. She asked a porter directions. At the gateway onto the street a *Wehrmacht* patrol was checking the identity cards of the passengers. Routine, no reason for anyone to be waiting for her, no reason for them to suspect anything. In front of her a young man who hesitated when asked his name and address was led to a truck for questioning and the line moved forward. No reason the Lice would tell anyone if they were waiting for The Watchman, the danger did not lie with the fresh-faced troops carrying out their cursory examination at the station. She smiled at the sergeant inspecting the documents, felt the middle-aged woman behind her stiffen in disgust, and passed through.

The square was busy with stalls, few people having enough money to buy much but the women pecking at the produce anyway, trying to find a bargain they could afford. Good day to lose herself in the crowd, bad day to spot those who might be waiting for her. She left the square and passed down the main shopping street that led away from it. At the bottom she turned right, then second left, stopping as if to look in a shop window and glancing behind her for the signs that she had already been identified and was being tailed. Nothing, so far. Five minutes later she came to the top of the street in which the man called Bailey lived. Number thirty-five, she checked the numbers at the top, probably half-way down on the right, the street sloping gently away to the line of houses crossing it at right angles at the bottom. A woman was scrubbing a doorstep on the left, two men talking on the right. Very quiet. Mary could hear every sound, see every movement.

Remember what they taught you at Arisaig, remember that you are almost as valuable to the bastards as The Watchman. Always a chance the people in the North were wrong, of course, that Bailey wasn't the traitor.

No cars, she thought, no men waiting. They would be tucked away somewhere, would not move until The Watchman committed himself and Bailey betrayed him.

'Morning, love.' She stopped to talk to the woman scrubbing the doorstep, make the watchers think she had a reason for being in the street, as if she belonged there, give them a reason to accept her when she checked the street again. The woman glanced up and returned her smile as if she knew Mary. They talked for two minutes then Mary moved on and the woman returned to her work.

Number thirty-five another ten houses on, alleyway on right leading to rear, gardens back to back with those in the next street. Almost to number thirty-five. The two men were still talking further down. Not Lice, too old, both in their sixties, one of them pointing with his walking stick. Number thirty-five, funny how the street looked nothing like she had imagined it would look. House opposite empty, the door boarded up and strips of wood crisscrossing the windows. Just enough space between the pieces of timber on the windows to look through, if they could get into the house without being seen, if there was a back entrance. Don't look, Mary, she knew they were looking at her. She passed the two men, smiling at them and wishing them good-day as if she knew them, and came to the bottom of the street.

Only when she had turned the corner and was out of sight was she aware of how frightened she felt.

FRAN PARKED THE pick-up in the town centre and walked to the hospital. A *Wehrmacht* patrol was positioned on the corner opposite and a troop carrier at the crossroads forty yards on. For one moment she thought they were waiting for her and panicked, then told herself that there was no way they could know of her.

Addington Street, four hundred yards down the hill, seemed full of pubs. She collected the pick-up, parked it on a bomb site next to the Queen Charlotte, and returned to the hospital. No one waiting for her, she was sure, no Lice or Gestapo watching from the corner of the street. The hall was cool and the floor smelt of polish and antiseptic. The only furniture, apart from the enquiry desk, was a large aspidistra on top of a stand and benches along either wall. The nurse at the desk looked up.

'Good morning, I've come to see Doctor Jennings.' It was the name Ned had told her to ask for.

'You must be Mrs Barrington. I'll tell him you're here.'

Fran sat down and glanced outside. Still nothing or no one. A door banged and she felt herself jump. Keep calm, don't let anyone see how terrified you are. The two men came into the hall from a corridor on the right and stood close to her. She looked up at them, her smile automatic. Not hers, she thought. The men she was collecting were service people. They would be wearing uniforms, not the suits these two wore. And there were four of them, not two.

'Mrs Barrington?'

'Beside the Queen Charlotte in Addington Street, ten minutes.' Her voice was calm, as if it was not her own. 'Where are the others?' There was no one else in the hall.

'On their way. We thought it best if we split up.'

'Well done.' There was a confidence in the words that steadied them, helped them more than she could have imagined. They turned and walked out, one helping the other. Two minutes later another man left the ward and stood in the hall. 'Beside the Queen Charlotte in Addington Street.' He nodded and went out. One more, she thought, heard the shuffle and looked up again.

The last man was in his mid-twenties. There was the faintest trace of a limp in his right leg, his suit was smart and the trilby he wore was set at a jaunty angle so that the brim partly covered the top right of his face.

'Beside the Queen Charlotte,' she began to tell him, then heard the engines outside and saw the black Wolseleys pull up.

No back way out, she saw he was thinking the same. That was the first thing they would have covered.

'Save yourself. They won't be looking for a woman.'

The Lice, she knew, the first almost at the door. She stood up, crossed to the man's right and slid her hand through his arm, cradling her head against his so that she helped cover his face. 'Lovely to see you so well, dear.' The Lice was close enough to see them, almost to understand what they were saying. They reached the door as the Lice opened it. Fran smiled at him as if she had only just seen him. Automatically he held the door for them. 'Thank you.'

There were more Lice coming towards them. No reason for them to be looking for you, she told herself, no reason for them to suspect a wife taking her sick husband for a walk.

They turned down the hill towards the town centre. In the front car the driver watched them then turned away in disinterest. Work it out, she told herself, work out what you can do and how you can get them out of here.

'It's all right,' the man at her side seemed to understand what she was thinking. 'According to the hospital records we left a week ago.'

286

She saw the disfiguration of his face and hands and understood why he was in hospital.

THE GARDEN BEHIND the derelict house opposite Jimmy Bailey's was well tended and could be approached by a small lane. Mary knew she had been correct and walked past, not stopping but not walking too slowly. At the top she turned back towards the town centre and the market square, and tried to work out how she could remain in the area without rousing suspicion, when and how The Watchman would approach the house, and how she could warn him.

THE OTHERS WERE waiting at the side of the pub. The Lice had passed the third man to leave fifty yards from the hospital, he had warned the first two but assumed that the fourth would have been caught and that Fran would have been lucky to have left by herself.

They began to clamber into the pick-up, the man who could not walk properly in the front and the others in the back. Four of them, Fran assumed it was they for whom the Lice had come, all sitting in what was obviously a farmer's pick-up with their suits and their white faces.

'You in the front with me.' She indicated the man she had escorted from the hospital. 'You in the back.' She helped the man with the bad leg out of the cab. 'Take off your jacket, collar and tie and roll up your sleeves. Make it look as if you belong.'

The remaining two were unsure. 'They're after four of you, so two groups of two will be safer. I'll take these first and come back for you.' Their eyes all suggested that though she might try there was no way she would be able to return. 'There's a pub on the Canterbury Road, I think it's called the Hare and Pheasant. I'll see you there.' They climbed down from the back. 'You have some money?' They wondered why she was asking and shook their heads. Fran opened her purse and gave them a half-crown piece. 'You can't sit in a pub without a drink.'

THE SQUARE WAS busy, the stalls lining the four sides and clustered into the middle. Not as busy as on a market day, Jack thought, but a good day to meet the contact: he could lose himself in the crowd and not stand out as a stranger as in so many small places. Bad day as well, more difficult to spot the watchers.

The Red Shoot was crowded. He sat in a corner and made the pint last. The final contact before he and the radio operator went north, he felt the relief sweeping over him, before he and Drake worked out a way of establishing the identity of the traitor. When he left the pub one remaining trader was packing his stall and the square and the town were quiet. It was still too early for Bailey to be at home, but nothing would be lost in trying anyway.

Jack left the square and headed for the street in which the leader of the Hop network lived. Already he could smell the cooking in the kitchen; Bailey's wife would tell the children to be quiet and offer him a cup of tea.

He turned the corner and saw Mary. In front of him, looking the other way. A policeman ten yards from her and the *Wehrmacht* patrol on the pavement opposite. He felt the panic, then the realization of what she had done. Two hundred yards from Bailey's house, his heart was beating and his whole body was turning to ice, less than ten minutes, probably only five, before he stood in the street outside and knocked on the door.

Mary was turning, seeing him, not able to speak to him, the policeman and the Germans still too close to her. Warning him anyway. The handbag was in her right hand.

He walked past, not looking at her. At the end of the street he turned right, away from the house, and back towards the town centre. Two minutes later she joined him.

'Thanks.' He did not know what else to say.

THE LAST TWO men were waiting at the Hare and Pheasant, the pints of beer on the bar in front of them, both of them standing where they could see the road in front and the houses to the rear. Fran turned the pick-up and waited. Two minutes later they left the pub and walked down the road, away from the town, as if they had no connection with her. She allowed them a minute's start then drove after them and stopped.

'Thanks.'

One climbed in the front and the other in the back.

'No problem.' She tried not to lose the confidence in her voice.

'Everything all right?'

'Everything's fine.' She glanced through the window in the back of the cab at the other man. He grinned and gave her a thumbs up sign. 'I'll drop you with the others. There's a wood where you can hide till dark. No one will see you there.'

They came to the junction at the edge of the town.

'I'll pick you up again at eleven tonight, take you to where you'll be safe for a few days.'

They turned the corner and saw the roadblock, a *Wehrmacht* truck half across the road and the troops covering the English policemen who were checking the documents.

'Don't worry,' Fran told the man beside her. 'Everything will be all right.'

The car in front pulled through the roadblock and she stopped level with one of the constables.

'Morning.' His dark blue tunic contrasted with the grey of the uniforms behind him. 'Number plate's a bit muddy, hardly make it out.' He walked round the pick-up, looking at the man in the back, and examined the rear plate, then returned to the front. 'Rear one as well.' He was looking right at her. 'Let's see your papers then.' The voice was hostile. She took her identity card from her handbag and showed it to the man.

'What about yours?' The constable switched his attention to the man sitting beside her and she felt him freeze. The pilot only had an RAF identity card, Fran realized, the same with the man in the back. Farmer's pick-up, she saw it in the policeman's face, farmer's wife, but the two men with her were nothing to do with farming, never had been. He knows, she thought. The last time, she had told Ned. Cursed herself.

Well done, lads, she suddenly realized he wanted to say, didn't make it, but thanks for trying. The policeman looked back at Fran. We haven't lost yet, he understood she was telling him. We'll still bloody well win.

'Thank you, ma'am.'

He stepped to the side and waved them through.

FRAN LISTENED TO the nine o'clock news and messages, adjusted the dial in case the Germans or the Lice came to the house, and switched off the wireless. After she had checked the animals and made sure that Boy Jack was asleep she moved the pick-up from the barn to the rear of the house, then walked the three miles to the wood where she had left the airmen that afternoon. The night was still not quite dark, the half-moon beginning to illuminate the hedgerows and fields, and the trees sharp against the sky. As she came to the point where they were waiting for her she whistled three times, heard the reply, then waited.

'I'll take you another two miles, then someone else will lead you to the place where you can stay.' She had arranged it that afternoon: she would take them to where she normally waited, as if she was simply part of the chain, then Ned would take them to the barn and show them the hiding place in the hayloft. That way they might not associate either her or the pick-up with the farm. And it would be Ned rather than herself who would bring them their food and who would tell them not to move from the hiding place, as if it was he who lived there rather than her.

They turned right from the woods and along the road, the night still. There would be no traffic at this hour; there had been no traffic the nights Ned had brought the other groups through. It was the best time to travel, yet totally the wrong time to travel. In the quiet she heard the first sound of the car engines. Only those who had a reason not to be seen or who had no documents to get them through the checkpoints travelled at night. The headlights blinked on the rise a half-mile in front of them, a second set behind then a third, then disappeared as the vehicles dropped into the dip towards them.

'Into the ditch. Routine convoy. No problems.' Her heart was thumping and her head was spinning; she slid into the ditch beside the men and waited. 'Heads down till I say otherwise.'

Lorries meant it might only be the *Wehrmacht*. The fear made her think with a clarity and calmness that she would only realize later, cars and there was a chance it would be the Lice. 'Heads right down.' Thank God it wasn't winter, thank God there was hardly any water in the ditch. The vehicles closed on them, the engines screaming and the cars moving fast. Lice, she thought, but not for them, for some other poor sod. She tucked her head against her body and waited. In front of her the man began to look up, she pushed him down and the cars swept past them. Only after another thirty seconds did she allow anyone to move.

'Thanks.'

'Next time do as I say.'

They climbed out of the ditch and began walking again. After half an hour, just before the turning to Ardley, she left the road and took them across the fields to the right. When they were half a mile past the turning she cut back across the road, through a copse, and onto the side road leading to Ardley. Ned was waiting. She shook hands with each of them and wished them luck.

'Will we see you again?' It was the man with the scarred face.

'Perhaps.'

'If we don't, thanks for this morning.'

'That's all right.'

Ned was impatient to move. Across the fields and through the woods to the north of the track, she had told him, as many detours as necessary to make sure they would not recognize again where they were being taken. In Gorsley, to the left, the foxes were calling. She walked down the road another fifty yards then skirted left and up the track to the farm. Half an hour later, the house in total darkness, she watched as the five shapes came from the blue-black of the orchard and into the barn, a single figure leaving ten minutes later.

The following morning, after Boy Jack had gone to school and she made a start on the farm work, Fran returned to the kitchen, put the kettle on the stove, and began to carve some bread and cheese. What am I doing, Jack? The thought had refused to leave her all night. What *should* I be doing? The kettle was singing. She made herself a pot of tea and sat at the table. The morning was warm and the room smelt clean and welcoming just like last spring – just as it always used to, as if things were getting back to normal. Except that there was no Jack or Ernie, except for the edge of nerves across her stomach.

She heard the noise outside and saw Ned leaning his red postman's bicycle against the fence.

'Morning.' He came into the kitchen and sat down. 'Everything well?'

He only called her *dearie* now when they were in the village, when there were other people around and they were not conspiring together.

'Everything's fine.'

She made a fresh pot of tea, poured four mugs and put them with the bread and cheese on a tray.

'Back in ten minutes.' Ned left the kitchen and carried the food to the barn.

Three or four days, she thought, then they would be gone like the others – gone without documentation or identity papers, with no idea where they were going or how they would get there. Gone without any hope of making it.

The postman came back across the yard.

If only you were here, Jack, if only you could help them, organize it all, give them at least a chance. She wanted to talk to them, ask them whether it was they she and Jack and Boy Jack and Ernie had stood and watched in the skies over Kent the previous summer, seemingly so many at first, then so few – none at all in the end. A bloody waste. Not then but now. A waste of the soldiers locked up in the prison camp and the pilots still alive but in hiding.

At three, though there was no need, Fran walked to the village and waited for Boy Jack to come out of school. It was the afternoon Mrs Downton and her cousin went to Canterbury. As Fran passed the shop she saw the young woman with the empty shopping bag knock at the back door. Half an hour later, as she and Boy Jack walked back through the village, the woman hurried past her with the bag half filled.

The following morning, after Ned had taken the airmen their food, Fran changed from her farming clothes, crossed the yard to the barn, and climbed the ladder to the hayloft. Bad security, she knew, but hoped there was no way they could make the connection. The bale that formed the door to the hiding place was in position, she began to pull it away then realized what the men inside must be thinking. 'It's all right.' She knew they would recognize her voice. 'It's me.' She saw the relief on their faces and pulled the bale behind her.

For the next two hours she listened as they talked of the battle in the skies the previous summer and autumn, of how the RAF had finally run out of pilots, of the hospital at East Grinstead where the brilliant New Zealander McIndoe had begun to repair the faces and bodies of those burned in the fighting.

'You went there?' she asked the man whose arm she had held as the Lice came for them.

'For a while.'

'So why did you go back to Ramsgate?'

'To convalesce.'

She knew there was another reason. 'Because if somebody was looking for me that's where they would come.'

That afternoon, as Boy Jack came across the fields from the village, Fran stood on the hill and wondered what Jack would have done in her place. In the churchyard on the other side of the river she saw the vicar and Stan Bradley go into the porch. That night, as she sat in the kitchen and listened to the broadcast and the messages from the Free North, she wondered what her husband had thought the day the stranger had come to him in the field.

The following morning, after Ned had taken the airmen their food, she made him toast and tea and sat with him at the kitchen table.

'What do you want, Fran?'

The farm was deserted and the door locked.

'You work in the post office, there must be some people you can trust in Canterbury.'

He had thought about it before, supposed that others had also thought about it. Except that no one had done anything. 'One or two.'

'They must have access to blank identification papers. No one would miss four sets.' Just this once, she had decided, give the boys a chance.

'I'll try.' He stirred his tea and waited for the question he knew would follow.

'At the cricket match, when you first asked me to help, you said you had been up to something.' They would need people they knew could be trusted, people who had already been tested.

'There was an organization.' Ned spoke slowly, each word weighed and considered. Resistance, she thought, but not the same part as Jack, otherwise she would have felt it, sensed it. 'There were probably several organizations.' The postman looked up from his tea. 'I was part of one of them.'

She did not interrupt.

'I was in Intelligence. Our job was to report on enemy troop positions and strengths.'

There were so many things she wanted to ask him, so many things she knew he should not tell her. 'Where?'

She was just like Jack, just like Boy Jack would be. 'Nobody knew where invasion would come, so it was all round the coast.'

'And the people manning it are still in place?'

'Most of them. The Germans found most of the zero stations. The girls in those would have been killed.' He told her what she had wanted to know. 'But most of the people doing the reporting are probably still alive.'

'All round the coast you said?'

'Yes.' It was something else he had considered, something they must have all thought about. Except that, again, no one had done anything about it.

'How far north?'

He wondered how she would organize it. 'All the way.'

Two mornings later, when he came to take the airmen their food, Ned brought with him four identity papers. False names, as well as personal details matching those of the pilots, had already been entered, and the cards carried the stamps both of the issuing authority and the German political office required to counterauthorize such documents. As soon as he left, Fran changed from her farming clothes and went to the hiding place in the hayloft. After four days the airmen's clothes were creased and dirty and their faces unshaven.

'You leave tonight.' The tone of her voice suggested that she was conveying instructions rather than instigating them. 'You will be taken to a hiding place just outside Canterbury. In the morning you will go to the station and take the train. In future you will not travel at night.'

They did not know what to say or think.

She checked the details and gave them each the relevant card. 'Memorize the names and addresses in case you're questioned. If you are it will just be routine. The papers are genuine, so you will have no trouble with them.' From her handbag she took two five-pound notes and gave them to the men. Almost the last of the money, Jack, but you'd understand. 'I'm taking your clothes. They will be washed and ironed and before you go tonight arrangements have been made for you to bath and shave.'

They began to thank her.

'I am only the messenger,' she said. Jack, why aren't you here? For three hours the night before, after she had listened to the Free North and known that her decision was irrevocable, she had sat at the kitchen table and worked out what she would say and how she would say it.

'Your orders are simple. You are to go north. When you get there, you are to contact the Resistance and arrange for a message to be passed south. The code is, "The rose will bloom in winter." It is to be transmitted at both six and nine o'clock. The day after the broadcast the North should arrange for someone to be by the tomb of Henry IV in Trinity Chapel in Canterbury Cathedral at three in the afternoon. In case of problems, the code should be transmitted and the contact maintained for one week after the first transmission.' She had pored over the details the night before, lain awake confirming them. If she was right and the codes after the news were to the Resistance, then there would already be people who could set up the escape routes, and when the system was established and the other people were running it she could go back to the farm and look after Boy Jack.

'A great deal depends on you. One of you must get through, no matter what the cost.' She remembered what they had said of the battle in the air, the numbers lost and the disfigurement of the man with whom she had walked from the hospital at Ramsgate, and felt a flush of shame.

'Don't worry, we'll make it.' Even with a plastic face, she thought, his eyes still smiled. The men stood up to undress. 'What name should we give?' The pilot pulled off his shirt and she saw how much of him had been burned. 'They'll need a name for the contact.'

It was the one thing she had not considered.

Take care, the first family had said as she kissed them goodbye and watched them turn north towards Canterbury. Only weeks ago, she thought, less than a month, but already a lifetime. Look after Boy Jack, she had always told herself; the one condition on which she had done the little she had, make sure you do nothing to endanger him.

'The Caretaker.'

THE CRICKET PRACTICE was on the Wednesday, the day after the first team's. Fran had forgotten about the junior match until Boy Jack had told her he had been selected. Ardley Boys versus Bridge. The age limit was fourteen and she knew he was only in the team to make up the numbers but was glad for him anyway. When they arrived at the pitch the vicar and Stan Bradley were already there, setting up the nets and stumps, the other boys beginning to arrive with their fathers, some of them unpacking their bats and pads and others making do with the equipment Stan had borrowed from the men's cast-offs.

At eight-thirty, when the practice ended, they said good-night and walked back along the road, through the churchyard and up the hill to the farm. One week past the full moon, two weeks since Ned had taken the airmen to the outskirts of Canterbury. She was just in time to catch the news.

'I'll make the cocoa, Mum.'

'Thanks.' She switched on the wireless and tuned it to the North.

'Did you see the bat that Danny had?' He put on the milk for the cocoa.

'Yes.' Her mind was half on the conversation, half on the wireless. She heard the familiar sound of the drum and the news began.

'And the pads that Sam and Mike had for Christmas.' He spooned the powder in the bottom of the mugs.

'Yes.' The news ended and the messages began. Quiet, Jack, she wanted to say, I missed the six o'clock broadcast, must listen now.

'The club bats and pads are all right, but I wish I had my own.' The milk was sizzling. He poured it into the mugs and brought them to the table. The broadcast ended and she switched off the wireless. It was too early, Fran told herself, they would still be on the road, would be being careful. Might be weeks before they even got through. She felt the disappointment anyway, sat down again and waited for Boy Jack to ask.

'Do you think Dad would mind if I used his bat and pads?'

Perhaps they wouldn't get through, perhaps they were already dead. 'I'm sure Dad would have wanted you to use them.'

THE END OF the moon period, Jack thought, almost the last of the first series of drops. Only one more set, then he and Mary would take a break, then the other radio operators would begin coming in and the pressure on Mary would be reduced.

The traitor Bailey had been isolated, no activity or drops in his area, though nothing had been done which might arouse his suspicions.

It was almost midnight. He checked through the details again, the protection at the drop zone, the courier who would carry Mary's radio between the houses from which she would transmit, the security of the networks concerned.

'Everything fine?'

The men nodded.

In the sky to the west he heard the sound of the Whitley.

THE DINNER IN the officer's mess of the *Oberkommando Grossbritan-nien*, the OKGB, at which Holdaway had been a guest had ended, and he had excused himself from the drinking which followed. When he returned to The Citadel, Davis was still in his office. On his desk was a whisky glass.

'Good evening?' It was half a question, half a greeting.

Holdaway took off his coat and glanced over the inspector's shoulder. 'Good enough. What are you doing here so late?'

'Checking on the reports from the detection vans.'

'Anything tonight?'

For each of the four preceding nights the teams had detected transmissions.

'Nothing.'

'What about the wireless messages?'

'Two codes transmitted at six and nine.'

Holdaway understood what Davis was thinking. 'So we wait and see if there are any unidentified aircraft this evening.'

On seven occasions a similar pattern had begun to establish itself; on four the series of radio intercepts, double codes and unidentified aircraft had been completed. The first time this had happened they had been confident of some form of success; now they merely waited to see where it would lead them.

'We'll know by ten tomorrow morning.'

'And nothing more from friend Bailey?'

Holdaway had maintained the full alert for seven days after the Sunday and Monday on which Bailey's wife had said the stranger would call. For a week after that he had continued the surveillance from the house opposite. Now, due to the increasing work load under which his department found itself, he had been forced to withdraw even this but had instructed that a daily contact be maintained with the informant.

'Nothing at all.'

There were several reasons which might explain why The Watch-man had not shown. They had discussed the matter endlessly, detailing and dissecting the various alternatives, setting them against

information from other sources and against the patterns of radio
intercepts which were updated daily.

Davis opened a drawer of his desk, took out a bottle of whisky
and a second glass, and poured them each a drink. 'The radio boys
have come up with something interesting.' Both men were tired, the
conversation jumping from subject to subject. 'They think it's the
same operator.' He passed Holdaway the drink.

'How?'

'Something about the way the morse is tapped out. They call it his
fist.'

'Interesting.' Holdaway downed the whisky and poured himself
another.

'There's something else that might interest you.' Davis' eyes were
red and his speech was slightly slurred.

'What's that?'

'Schellenberg has a woman.'

'How do you know?' It would surprise him, Holdaway thought, if
Schellenberg did not have several.

'One of the boys saw them and made a few enquiries.'

'Discreet, I hope.'

'Bloody right.'

'In London?'

'No, down here. Seems they were guests of Lord Southerton.
Second time this month apparently.'

Holdaway finished his drink and picked up his coat. 'Come on, it's
time you saw your wife.'

THE BUS ARRIVED in Ramsgate, Mary thanked the conductor, left the
town centre and walked to the hospital. It was almost done, she felt
the relief, no traitor to worry about and the system established and
working well. Personal security, she reminded herself, she was still
the one way into The Watchman. She pushed the warning to the back
of her mind and went inside.

The corridor was clean and empty, and smelt of polish and disinfectant. Just like last time, Mary thought. The nurse sitting at the desk
by the aspidistra looked up and smiled.

'Good morning. I've come about an airman who was here for a
while. I wonder if he still is.'

'What's his name?'

'Flight Lieutenant Watson.'

The nurse tried not to lose her smile. 'One moment.' She left the desk and went into the ward on her right.

Something wrong. Leave now before they close in on you. Something about Johnny, stay now you have the chance to know.

The nurse came back, the doctor following. Mary recognized him from the afternoon she had come to see Johnny the August before.

'You were enquiring about Flight Lieutenant Watson.' The doctor was professional and detached.

'Yes.'

'May I ask why?'

'I came to see him just after he came in. You let me stay with him and made me a cup of tea.'

'I remember.' The doctor nodded at the nurse and led Mary to the garden at the back. 'Your husband stayed here for three days, then was transferred to East Grinstead.'

'But they said they didn't know who or where he was.'

'They were probably protecting him. After invasion the Germans were rounding up every soldier, sailor and airman they could find, even those who were injured, and putting them into prison camps.'

'So what happened to Johnny?'

'After his treatment he came back here to convalesce. He's made a good recovery, not quite complete, but he's doing well.'

So why are you telling me in the garden, she wanted to ask, why haven't you taken me to him?

'Two weeks ago the Lice came for him.'

Her world collapsed around her. I should have come the night I waited for The Watchman; if I had, I could have saved him. But then I would have missed the message from the North, and The Watchman would have been captured.

'It's all right. He was taken away before the Lice arrived.'

'By whom?'

'By friends.'

She felt the warmth of the day again. 'And where is he now?'

'I honestly don't know.'

AT FOUR O'CLOCK the courier collected the radio set from the house from which Mary had transmitted the last schedule and took it to the one from which she would transmit that night. The set was contained in a battered brown leather suitcase and the man who carried it faded into the background as easily as the case itself.

At seven-thirty Mary collected the messages she would transmit that night from a second courier, and made her way to the address.

HOLDAWAY'S FIRST MEETING of the day with Davis was at nine. Half an hour before the inspector telephoned and requested that it be brought forward.

'I'll come down.'

'The pattern's there again. Radio intercepts, then a break; a code transmitted at six and nine, and an unidentified aircraft the same night. Now the transmissions have started again.'

'When?'

'Yesterday.'

'Where?'

'You're never going to believe this.'

'Where?' Holdaway asked again.

'Maidstone.'

The last place he should suspect, the place, therefore, which he himself would have chosen. 'What else? What did you say the other night about the operator?'

'That the radio boys think it's one man.'

'So what do you plan to do?'

'Bring in as many detection units as necessary and hope they can come up with an accurate fix fast enough.'

'It makes sense.'

Davis knew Holdaway was not referring to his plan. 'What makes sense?'

'Transmitting from a town. We've always assumed they would transmit from the countryside because they would feel safer there. Wrong, of course. If we got close enough, it would be relatively easy to pinpoint an isolated building, a farm or barn. In a town, on the other hand, we would be lucky to identify even two or three streets in the time available, and even then we wouldn't know which house.'

'So what do you suggest?'

300

'Tell me your plan again.'

Davis told him.

'The transmissions themselves. What assumptions?'

'Security essential. Different location each night.'

'But if the radio boys are correct and there's only one operator?'

'Then he's too valuable to risk carrying his own set.'

'And they'll have a courier to carry it for him.'

Davis lifted the telephone and spoke to the sergeant. 'Contact the inspectors for blue, red and yellow units and request them to attend a briefing in fifteen minutes, their units on stand-by.' They would have to be careful, he was aware, not make their presence so obvious that they would scare the quarry away.

'What about the courier?' he asked Holdaway. 'Any thoughts on him?'

'Not *him*.' Holdaway leaned back in the chair. 'That's what they'll expect us to assume. The courier will be a woman.'

THE UNITS ASSIGNED to the surveillance of Maidstone left The Citadel at ten-thirty. Of the forty men allocated to the operation sixteen were assigned to cars, two per car, and the remainder to foot duties, working individually to increase the area covered and to reduce the possibility of being observed. As always, they were in plain clothes. Each car and each man was assigned a specific area and three special lines were established with direct connections into Davis' office to avoid any delay at the switchboard. The units would remain on the streets until seven. After that two more units would take over, with the numbers of men involved reduced at a time when there would be fewer people on the streets, though those coming off would remain on stand-by at The Citadel.

The town was busy. By midday two possible targets had been identified, each woman for different reasons, and by mid-afternoon another one.

At four the courier left the café where he had been waiting and walked the half-mile to the house where he had delivered the set the afternoon before and from where Mary had transmitted the previous evening.

The man was in his early forties and had been a member of the Angel network for six weeks. During that time his age, his appearance and his disposition had suggested to those concerned that he rather than anyone else was ideally suited to the role: his age because it removed him, in part at least, from military service; his appearance because he seemed grey and colourless and possessed the ability never to stand out; and his disposition because he thought clearly and did not panic. On two occasions over that time he had been subjected to routine questioning while carrying the case in which the set was contained but had not been asked to open it.

He left the house with the case and made his way through the town centre, following the routine procedures which had been instilled in him and using every opportunity to check for a tail. He stopped, appearing to look in a shop window, and looked for the telltale signs which he could remember, then walked on. There were some Lice, he thought, had no trouble identifying them; more than usual perhaps. He crossed the street and saw the Wolseley.

Lice again. His instinct was to turn and walk away. There were two men in the car, one looking ahead and the second checking behind in the rear-view mirror fitted to the passenger's side of the windscreen. Enough people in the street to cover him, the courier calculated.

'Right size for it.' The man in the passenger seat saw the courier the moment he stepped off the pavement.

'What?'

'The case this bloke's carrying. Right size for a radio set.' The observer had been in the department a month and was both anxious to impress but cautious when teamed with a more experienced man.

The driver stared ahead, apparently not interested, waiting till the man the observer had seen passed the car before he looked at him. The courier neither slowed nor speeded up.

'No. The boss said it would be a woman.'

The courier continued up the road, passed two side streets and turned into the third.

MARY COLLECTED THE messages and the address where the set was waiting for her that evening. When she had transmitted, she packed the set and left the area.

The streets were quiet. At ten Davis reported to Holdaway that the detector teams had picked up a transmission from Maidstone and identified an area of the town, though the speed of the transmission had made it impossible to specify the street.

The following morning Holdaway stood at the back of the conference room while Davis debriefed the teams on the previous day. On the wall of the room the inspector had mounted a large-scale map of the town, the area from which the transmission had been made the previous evening outlined in red. For two hours Davis grilled each of the cars and men either assigned to that area or on the outskirts of it, then they were sent again onto the streets.

THE AFTERNOON WAS busy. The two policemen sat in the car and waited.

'Why the same place as yesterday?' The observer glanced in the rear-view mirror.

The driver offered the younger man a cigarette and lit one for himself.

'Your bloke, the one with the case. If he *is* the courier and the set was in his case, then odds are we saw him when he was delivering it.'

The area Davis had marked in red on his map began three streets away from them.

'So?'

'So if he was delivering it yesterday then he'll have to collect it today.' He saw that the younger man understood. 'If he's a regular, and he seems to be by how he acted yesterday, then he'll have his routine – probably collect at a favourite time, when he thinks he can move without being spotted, and deliver at a favourite time, when he thinks he'll see us if we're looking for him.'

It was three o'clock.

'So what do we do?'

The driver pulled on the cigarette. 'Wait and see. And keep our mouths shut if we're wrong.'

THE CAFÉ WAS crowded. The courier sat where he could see into the street and drank the tea slowly. For a moment the previous afternoon he had expected trouble. The Lice had been parked awfully close to the house where he had delivered the set; as he walked past the car he had felt the eyes examining him, expected them to take him. Even afterwards he had not been able to shake off the feeling. The door of the café opened and the network organizer came in, bought a tea and sat at the next table so that they were back to back.

'Problems?' He wondered why the courier had requested the meeting.

'I think I might have been spotted yesterday.' The conversation was lost in the general noise of the room.

'Tell me.'

'Two Lice in a car. I think they might have suspected something.'

'What did they do?'

The courier knew it sounded as if he could not tolerate the pressure. 'Nothing.'

The organizer rose, bought himself another tea and returned to his seat.

'I'll get someone else to do the pick-up.'

THE AFTERNOON WAS quiet again, the shops closing and the number of people on the streets thinning. The two men sat in the car and waited.

'A routine, you said.' The man in the passenger seat sat with his left arm out the window, his fingers drumming on the roof.

The driver grunted.

'Then he's late. He was here half an hour ago yesterday.'

'If it's him, he'll turn up. If it's not, then he won't.' He looked round the streets. 'Fancy a quick pint when we finish?'

'I fancy one now.' He swung in his seat and glanced up the road. 'That's it.'

'That's what?' The driver was suddenly alert.

'The suitcase.'

Seventy yards away a woman emerged from a turning on the left, crossed the street and began walking towards them.

'But it was a bloke.'

'It was yesterday, but it's the same bloody case.'

Forty yards away the woman disappeared into another side street.

'You're right.' The driver was already reaching for the radio. 'I think it's time you went for a walk.' The younger man slid out of the car and followed her.

FRAN AND BOY JACK walked to the village. When they reached the cricket field the Reverend Brian Markham was marking out the creases and the mothers were in the pavilion laying out the tables. Fran joined them, unpacking the cakes and helping to lay out the cups and saucers. She saw how proud the boys were. The two captains came out of the pavilion, shook hands and tossed, the opponents winning and opting to bat first. Danny Mates, the son of the blacksmith, led the Ardley team onto the pitch, then they stood and clapped out the Bridge opening batsmen.

'BUCKLAND HILL.' DAVIS looked at the faces in the briefing room. 'The suspect was tailed to the address carrying a brown leather suitcase which is thought to contain a radio set. She arrived at ten minutes to six and left five minutes later without the case. The radio transmissions have normally been made between nine and ten o'clock. We therefore expect the operator to appear at about eight-thirty. There will be no teams on the street at this time in case we scare him off. Only when the radio detection teams pick up a signal do we enter the premises.'

THE CRICKET WAS as tense as the first team matches. By six-thirty Bridge had scored twenty-three for four; by a quarter to seven another two wickets had fallen for fifteen more runs. When the innings closed the last batsman had brought the score to fifty-one.

'Reckon we'll just about make it, dearie.' The postman watched the teams come in and the boys sit down to the tea.

'Hope so, Ned, or I'll never hear the last of it.'

MARY LEFT THE safe house at six-thirty and spent the next half-hour walking beside the river which ran through the town. Almost there, Johnny, six transmissions, seven at most, then I'll be back north. See you there, Johnny. Know that's where you are. She left the river and went to the railway station. The courier was waiting for her, the conversation so brief and natural that no one noticed the woman slip the messages and address into her hand.

Children were playing in the street. Both window curtains fully drawn or both totally open and there was danger, Mary had forgotten how many times she had looked for the warning. No sign of the Lice, no indication the house was under surveillance. Christ, how she hated this moment, how she sometimes had to force herself to keep walking. First bedroom curtain totally open, second half closed, everything totally natural, nothing to indicate it was a signal. She knocked on the door and was let in.

THE TEA ENDED and the opening batsmen came out for Ardley. The Bridge bowler was fast and looked sixteen. The first Ardley wicket went for six and the second for eleven. Fran glanced round and saw that Boy Jack was gnawing his fingers with nerves. When six wickets had fallen for thirty-three runs he went into the changing room and strapped on his father's pads.

Seven for thirty-five. At the side of the pavilion Boy Jack practised his strokes. Eight for thirty-six.

'Still make it,' said the postman confidently.

Nine for thirty-eight, the last Ardley batsman. The crowd of mothers and fathers clapped him on. The pads almost reached Boy Jack's waist and the bat and gloves were too big. The postman saw the way Fran was looking and knew what she was thinking. 'Can't keep a good man down, dearie.'

'Thanks, Ned.' Just like his father, she could not shake away the thought, the way he held the bat, even the way he took guard at the wicket. Her hands were tight together and her fingernails dug into the palms of her hands.

The bowler came in. Four more balls this over, Jack, she thought. Just hold out and give Big Danny the strike.

The ball struck the ground in front of Jack. Fran heard the snick of the leather on the wood and saw them running for two. Three more balls, she thought, saw the way the vicar looked at her and smiled back. The bowler came in again. Jack picked up the lift of the ball and steered it down the offside, beginning to run then hearing the applause as it went for four. Two more balls this over, Jack. The ball came through low, beat the bat and hit the forward pad with a thump. *The bowler turned to the umpire and appealed for leg before* wicket. The umpire seemed to take for ever before he shook his head.

'Well done, Jack.' Fran could not help herself saying it aloud. 'Well left.'

The bowler turned and came in again. Just hold out for one more ball, Fran thought, then Big Danny can win the match for us. Go for it, Jack, she also urged him, no point hanging round now you've got him. One run to draw, two to win. The ball bounced head high, Boy Jack guided it past square leg, took one run then turned back for the second and raised his bat in triumph.

'Told you we'd make it.' Ned's face was flushed. 'Said you can't keep a good man down.'

'RED UNIT. WE have a contact.'

Too quick, thought Davis, too good to be true. 'Confirm area.'

The line was almost inaudible with static.

'Area confirmed.'

'Go.'

Mary finished the first message, was already half-way through the second. Soon she would be finished, be out of here. Concentrate on the keys, she disciplined herself, make sure the message is correct. She was going fast, the signaller in the North thought. He knew how she felt. In the street outside, cars began to converge. In the room on the first floor she began the third message. At least they were short, at least there weren't as many of them as usual, only one more. She began sending it. The first unit entered the building and began running up the stairs. Almost finished, the signaller in the North sensed, half-way through the last section. The signal stopped.

She heard the front door crash open and knew what it was, tried to disconnect the set, looked for where she could hide it. The feet were running up the stairs, the men splitting up, two to each room. She threw the set into the case and tried to push it under the bed. No way out through the house, Mary, only the window. Get across the roof. No point, they would have the place surrounded by now, would see her. She pushed the window open anyway. The men were in the room, pulling her back and pinning her hands down, throwing her to the floor. The panic seized her and fear shot through her body and into her throat. Back way out, she was still thinking, her mind confused and jumbled, fighting for clarity. The hands were hurting her, the fear worse than the pain so that she hardly noticed. Twenty-four hours, the thought began spinning somewhere inside her brain.

'Red Unit. Bringing her in now. Blue and green units dealing with house occupants.'

THINK STRAIGHT, MARY tried to tell herself, think what you're going to say, what you're not going to say. Twenty-four hours to hold out, she remembered the instructions, for the Resistance to realize that she had been taken and clear the area. Her mind was in turmoil with the fear of what they were going to do to her. Don't even think about what you mustn't tell them. Never think of it again. Her face was hurting from where they had hit her when they had burst into the room and her wrists were bleeding from the handcuffs. The car drove under the barrier and into The Citadel.

She knew where she was, had heard the stories of what they did here. The car stopped and she was dragged out as if there was nothing about her that mattered. They pulled her up the steps, one man on either side, her feet running to keep up. It was all deliberate, the training she had received at Arisaig struggled to tell her, give her no time to think, disorientate her. Only twenty-four hours before the network heard and went underground.

They turned into an office. Before it had been so dark, now the light was suddenly so bright.

'Where?' She heard the voice, could not see the face. Where what, she thought, where who? She knew what they wanted, that they were already trying to catch her out. Nothing, say nothing. 'Where?' Holdaway asked again.

'You know what we mean.' The other voice came from behind her. She had not expected it. Her mouth began to move, trying to frame an answer. Say nothing.

'Take her down and start on her.' A third voice, German accent.

No, she was silently pleading.

They picked her up and dragged her down the steps, her feet banging on the stone. More steps, another corridor, the smell different – even in her fear she could tell – into a cell. They tore off her clothes until she was standing, shivering, in her slip.

'Arms up, above your head.'

She did as she was told and the sergeant hit her.

'The animals can have her for ten minutes,' Schellenberg poured himself a coffee. 'Then you and Davis talk to her.' Holdaway sat at his desk, Davis in a chair in the corner. 'What do you imagine she's thinking at the moment?'

'Probably how long she has to hold out till her people know she's been taken.'

They finished the coffee and went to the cells. The woman's face and body were black and bruised. Already she could barely stand or keep her hands above her head. She was sobbing, partly with the pain of the position and partly with the anticipation of the next blow.

'I'm sorry.' Holdaway nodded and the team Schellenberg had referred to as the animals left. 'I don't want to see you going through this but there's nothing I can do about it.'

'Not our fault, you see.' It was Davis from her left, close to the door.

She began to relax, not much, just a little.

'When did he leave you?' Holdaway slipped the question in. 'This evening?'

No, she thought, The Watchman had already left, standard procedure. Good, thought Schellenberg from just outside, saw they had her. Something in her mind clanged the door shut again. Say nothing, show no reaction, nothing at all. Schellenberg opened the cell and let the animals back in.

It had been going on for so long, she thought, the beatings, the questions. There was no natural light in the room, only the electric light, no window to the outside so she could know what time it was. Twenty-four hours, she reminded herself, and wondered how many hours had passed, how much longer she had to hold out.

Eight in the morning, Holdaway thought. Not that she would know, not that she would know anything any more. He left the office and went to the cell.

'I want to show you something.' The inspector and sergeant knew where he was going to take her and dragged her between them.

The room was on another corridor. Holdaway opened the door and showed her what was inside. 'You think these two don't like you. These two are your friends. This is what the Gestapo do to you.' There was nothing left in her body to react, she felt the nausea retching up her throat anyway. Holdaway nodded to the two men and they dragged her back down the corridors.

Light. She saw it through the window at the end, knew it was the next day, that the terrible passage to the Gestapo room had told her what she wanted to know. Ten hours, she thought, the network would know by now, felt the fresh strength.

Mary had been in the room nineteen hours, almost twenty, had lost count of how many questions they had asked, how many times they had asked them – who had talked to her, bullied her, befriended her. Tried to trick her. In his office on the top floor Schellenberg poured Holdaway and Davis each a whisky, took a sheet of paper from his desk, wrote on it and gave it to Holdaway. 'Call the animals off, move her to an ordinary cell and read her this.'

She could not remember when the pain had stopped then started again, could barely remember when they ceased beating her, dragged her along the corridor, up some stairs and pushed her into another cell. The door opened and she heard a different voice.

'Stand up.'

She did not know how long it took her to do as she was told.

'I have here an order for your execution. It will take place in the morning.' Davis threw her clothes on to the bed.

'What time is it now?' They were the first words she had spoken.

'Nine o'clock.' He shut the door behind him.

The last of the evening light shone through the bars. The window was too high to reach, even if she had been able to stretch up. Kill me and put an end to it, she had pleaded so many times during the past hours, now she would rather go through anything than have her life taken from her. In the corner of the cell was a bucket of water. She crawled across the floor to it, cupped the water in her hands and tried to sip it but her lips were too swollen. The strength was almost gone from her. She pulled herself back onto the bed and lay down, her body shivering from the new fear. Outside a bird was singing; she looked at the light and hung on to it for as long as it lasted.

The night was cold. She lay on the bed and tried to sleep, tried to stay awake. There had been a night when she was a child when she had lain awake all night, thinking the day would never come and waiting for the charabanc ride to Margate. Now she lay awake and tried to stop thinking what the dawn would bring.

The night grew colder. She felt in the dark for a blanket and realized only now that her clothes had been returned to her. A trick, like the notice of execution, a technique to try and make her talk. More than twenty-four hours now. She struggled to find some consolation. They would know, would have cleared the area. All except The Watchman. The Watchman would not know for another week, almost ten days, when he would wait for her at the station at Colchester as they had arranged.

She touched the clothes again. It was not a trick, she realized, not if they had given her back her clothes. She felt the hot of the first tear on her cheek. All right in the dark, she rebuked herself, all right when nobody else could see. Never in the daytime, never when they would see that no matter what they did to you, you did not want to die.

The first light crept back into the cell: four o'clock, probably four-thirty. Two hours to live, three, four, if she was lucky. The light was filling the room. She rolled onto her side and tried to push herself up, her body and limbs tearing where they had beaten her. The clothes were in a heap at the foot of the bed. She stood up and began to go through them, straightening and folding them then laying them neatly on the dirty brown of the blanket. Three and a half hours, she calculated, probably only three now, before the footsteps would stop outside her cell.

Her underskirt was in ribbons. She tore off two strips, placed them on the bed and went to the corner. The bucket of water was heavy. She knew it would be easier to bend down, to kneel like a dog on the floor beside it, but instead she put her fingers round the handle, feeling the pain, and lifted the bucket onto the bed.

Outside she heard the first birdsong. No regrets, Mary, better to die on a morning like this than to have told them anything.

She took the first section of cloth, dipped it in the bucket, and began to wash the blood and dirt from her face and body, wringing out the cloth and ignoring the way the water tinged pink. When she had finished she took the second piece and dried herself.

The cell was warmer, the first stem of sun piercing through the window. Half-past five, probably almost six, the footsteps were not far off now. She put the bucket back in the corner and began to dress, hardly able to pull her skirt over her feet or to see through the swelling round her eyes. Two hours left, perhaps just one. She pulled on the last of her clothes and straightened her blouse, laughing at the irony of her thoughts.

She had read the books on the Suffragettes, had been taught by her mother of the fight for emancipation and known at first hand of the prejudice against women, how even in war they had not been allowed to join the Home Guard.

In the corridor outside the footsteps came towards her.

She walked to the centre of the cell, brushed the creases from her skirt, straightened her shoulders and prepared to die as an Englishman.

The footsteps went past.

A trick – she felt the resolve drain from her and the strength wither and die. The sun was still coming in the window, the bird outside still singing. You are an Englishman, she straightened again, you will never give in.

The sun filled the cell then passed from it, the day ending and another night beginning. Sometime, she was not sure when, they gave her food. Sometime, again she was not sure when or for how long, they asked her more questions. This time, however, they did not beat her, almost as if, the brutality having failed, the one thing left against her was herself.

That night, as the last light drained from the cell, Mary took off her skirt and blouse and folded them neatly at the foot of the bed, ignoring the pain which still occupied her whole body. The next morning she washed and dressed, and stood again in the centre of the cell waiting to die.

The night came and went again, the first light, the first trickle of sun, always at the same place on the same wall, then the darkness again. Six days, seven, eight, she had forgotten, could no longer count. The light filled the room and the sun shone on the wall. She pulled herself up from the bed, washed and dressed, and stood in the centre of the cell floor. The footsteps stopped and the door opened. This morning, she knew.

'Name?'

'Lieutenant Mary Atkinson, First Aid Nursing Yeomanry.'

He led her from the cell. There were three more guards outside. She followed them along the corridor, up the steps, and into the courtyard. Two more minutes to savour this beautiful life, she told herself, two more minutes not to break.

'Love you, Johnny.'

THE RENDEZVOUS WITH Mary was at three. Jack arrived early, confirmed that the area was not under surveillance, and waited. The last series of drops were coming up, as soon as Mary arrived and he sent the messages. At three-thirty, when she had not come, he left the café but remained in the area, checking that she did not arrive by a later bus. For the next two days he continued his wait, understanding that there were a multitude of reasons which might delay her. On the fourth day he notified the local network leaders that he was temporarily leaving the area, though he did not explain why, and returned to the zone adjacent to the one where he had left her. At eleven the following morning he was given the news.

THE TRUCK WAS in the corner of the yard, the tarpaulin stretched over the back. Mary felt the fear and knew what they were going to do to her before they killed her. A guard pulled back a corner of the canvas and pushed her up, other guards inside grabbing her shoulders and dropping her onto the floor. The engine started and the truck drove out of The Citadel, the movement throwing her over again as she tried to pull herself up.

The lorry left Maidstone and took the A20 towards London. Only after they had been driving for ten minutes did she find the strength to raise herself and look around. On the seats along each side of the truck the women were staring at her. Most of them were her age, some of them were well dressed, others wore prison uniforms. Without warning the truck lurched to the right and she was thrown against the metal stays of the seats. One of the women bent down, helped her up and made a space for her.

They had been travelling seven hours when the truck stopped and the canvas was pulled open. The guards jumped down and the women closest to the back began to climb out. The guards outside had changed, were no longer *Wehrmacht*, but the Death's Head units of the *Allgemeine SS*, the black band and skull on their caps. The women were moving slowly, afraid and confused. As Mary climbed down the woman at the front slipped, the guards screaming at her and almost beating her senseless with the butts of their rifles. Behind her, almost clambering over her, the other women hurried on, the guards pushing them and dogs snapping at them.

In front of them was a gate, the frame made of wood and laced with barbed wire. Mary had no time to see anything other than the perimeter fences, the watchtowers facing in at each corner and at the centre of each side, then they were marched into an administrative block in a long wooden hut to the left. The clerks were seated behind a row of desks facing the door, the first checking that any jewellery the newcomers possessed was removed from them. In front of her, a woman tried to conceal her wedding ring and it was torn from her finger. Thank God she had left Johnny's ring at Arisaig, Mary thought. She passed along the desks and gave her personal details, name, rank and date of birth, nothing more, then the column assembled outside again. The gate was opened, they were marched through, and the gate was closed behind them.

'*In eine Linie stehen. Aufrecht.*' No one understood. Long huts inside the fence, Mary noted, one at the far end with a tall chimney. The guards were hitting them again, shouting at them and pushing them into line. '*Ausziehen.*' They still did not understand. A *Scharführer* stepped to the woman closest to him and struck her across the face and body with his baton. '*Ausziehen.*' A look of horror spread across the woman's face as she understood. Slowly she pulled her dress over her head and dropped it to the ground, her shoulders cowed with fear.

'*Ausziehen.*' The *Scharführer* hooked the end of his baton under the strap of her bra and pulled at it. '*Ich sagte ausziehen.*' His stick was raining down upon her, whipping her. She half turned her body, trying to protect herself, and removed the bra, the blows still falling on her, then hooked her fingers inside her pants and stepped out of them.

'*Ausziehen.*' The *Scharführer* spun round and shouted at them all, the other guards joining in, hitting them, lashing at them, until all the group had copied the woman and stood naked against the wire. They're going to rape us, Mary thought. They're going to choose which ones they want and throw the rest of us to their friends.

'*Los March. Ihr Schweine. Los March.*' There was to be no rape, Mary began to understand, saw the way the guards were looking at them, treating them, not as if they were women, rather as if they were mere cattle. The line shuffled forward towards the hut closest to them, the first half dozen going in and the others waiting. Inside was a line of showers. The water was cold. They hurried through them and into the next room. It was only when she came to the doorway that Mary could see what was being done.

Seated on a wooden stool was a barber. In front of him was a lower stool and at his side a bucket of water. In his hand he brandished a cutthroat razor. As he finished with each prisoner he sharpened it on the leather strap at his side and beckoned to the next. Mary stepped onto the lower stool and waited. The barber brushed a handful of water against her pubic hair, lifted the razor, and began shaving her, the guards forcing her legs apart and the barber shaving between them, not caring whether or not he cut her. When he had done the front the guards spun Mary round, opened her legs and pushed her head forward, and the barber shaved her rear. When her pubic hair had been shaved the guards pushed her onto the stool and the barber shaved her head and beneath her armpits.

The blood was streaming from between her legs, from her head and under her arms. She rose from the stool and joined the line waiting against the wall. Without hair she could recognize no one, not even the woman beside whom she had sat in the truck.

When the last prisoner had been shaved a woman entered wearing the same uniform as the male guards and carrying a bucket and a large paint brush. Quickly she passed down the line, dipping the brush into the disinfectant and splashing it under their armpits and between their legs, the disinfectant already burning.

The queue moved forward to the next room. In the centre of the floor was a pile of clothes and shoes. A woman who seemed to be a prisoner picked a series of garments and a pair of wooden clogs at random from the pile and pushed them into her arms. Mary went to the side of the room and began to dress. Around her the women from the truck were doing the same, few of the clothes fitting. To her right a woman was laughing hysterically, at the size of the shirt she had been given; to her left a large woman was trying to pull a small pair of trousers up her thighs.

Please God, where have they sent me, she wondered. What are they going to do to me? She pulled on the underclothes, was relieved that they fitted, then the trousers, coat and clogs, and folded a cloth she had also been given into her pocket. The sleeves of the coat hung below her wrists, she rolled them up and shuffled to the next hut.

'Name.'

'Atkinson.'

The woman checked her name in the register, allocated her a number and handed her a strip of material on which was an inverted red triangle and the same number. Another checked a separate list then gave her more pieces of cloth of different shapes and colours and told her to sew them onto her uniform, together with her number.

Some of the clothes they all now wore were dyed with blue and white stripes, others were simply jackets and trousers with the colours painted on them. Red stripes ran down the outside of each of Mary's trouser legs. On the front of the coat she stitched the rectangle of cloth bearing the triangle and her number, on the back a large red X.

The triangles on the cloth bearing the prisoner's numbers were a variety of colours signifying, she would discover later, the prisoner's classification: red for political prisoners and Resistance, green for criminals, black for gypsies. In other camps, there would be another colour: an inverted red triangle on a yellow triangle for the Jews.

In addition, Mary's coat bore three other marks which singled her out. On the back, one either side of the large red X, were two capital Ns. Below the cross, and beneath the triangle and number on the front, was a large red spot, like a firing target, unmistakable against the off-white cloth.

It was already dusk, the sun sinking in a brilliant red. The column marched silently between the rows of huts to the area at the far end surrounded, even within the camp itself, by its own perimeter fences of barbed wire. The gate was opened and they were thrown into the quarantine barracks inside.

The disinfectant on her body still burnt like a fire. She sat on the bunk and hung her head in her hands, feeling the scalp beneath her fingers.

When she raised her head she recognized that the prisoner with whom she shared the bed space was the woman who had made the space for her in the truck.

'Annie,' said the woman.

Pray for me, Johnny. Never forget me. Still a trick, she knew, still part of the plan to make her reveal the details of The Watchman and his organization. She rolled the blanket round her, ignored the woman and tried to sleep.

BOOK FOUR

Resistance
June 1941 – April 1942

1

PRESIDENT ROOSEVELT READ again the letter that Albert Einstein had written eighteen months before to accompany the recommendations by the scientist Leo Szilard. In that time the Uranium Committee, which he had sanctioned after the first meeting shortly after war had been declared had seen its role and limited authority shifted to the National Defence Research Council, in its turn superseded by the Office of Scientific Research and Development. Yet the programme had remained on a back burner. Sometimes, Roosevelt pretended, this was because of the other issues that required his more immediate attention. Occasionally, he acknowledged, it was because of the nature of the project itself.

In a way, he supposed, the decision he would face that evening was among the most awesome he would ever confront.

The meeting lasted one and a half hours. Present were only two other men: Vice President Wallace and the director of the OSRD, Vannevar Bush, former president of the Carnegie Institution and head of the National Defence Research Council, who had created the OSRD and absorbed within it the NDRC. Bush himself led the discussion, summing up the scientific advances made over the past twelve months then dealing with the recommendations of the British scientists evacuated to the United States and whose papers were still referred to as coming from the MAUD Committee.

After forty minutes Roosevelt requested a precis of the position of other nations in the scientific area under discussion. Russia and Japan, Bush informed him, had now entered the race for a military application of the process; Germany, through its scientists at the Kaiser Wilhelm Institutes, was well advanced and enjoyed good access to raw materials, through its control of the heavy water plant at Vemork, in Norway, and uranium ore stock-piled in Belgium and the Belgian Congo.

It was the moment the programme became a reality. From that moment on America, though not yet committed to the final military application to which the scientific research pointed, was committed to examining whether that application was possible. From that evening, Roosevelt was not only thinking of the use of that application in the war to which the United States had not yet committed itself, but to its significance thereafter.

When Vannevar Bush left the White House that evening it was beginning to drizzle, though he hardly noticed. In his briefcase he carried presidential authorization for the programme which would become the Manhattan Project and which would result in gleaming canisters of destruction called the Little Boy and Fat Man.

THE TREES AND the house beyond shimmered in the sun, in the pasture below the King watched his daughters begin their morning ride. A beautiful country, Canada, he thought, but not as beautiful as his England. Item Six on the agenda, the subject had haunted him all night, was the reason he had risen at four and left the house without waking his family or those who protected them, walking alone through the trees and heading west so that when he returned he would see the sun dappling through the leaves. His shoes and the bottom of his trousers were wet with dew. Item Six, he thought again and remembered the other reports, the arrests of the Jews and the deportation of part of the workforce to the factories in Germany.

It was nine months since he and his family had been driven in the early morning to the docks in Liverpool, the men and women still shouting 'God save the King'. He remembered that morning as he remembered his wife's reply to William Donovan at Buckingham Palace: *My daughters will not leave me, I will not leave my husband and my husband will not leave his people.* Yet he had allowed the Cabinet to persuade him, accepted as real the possibility of an attempt to kidnap him by enemy paratroopers, agreed for the good of the country that he and family should come to Canada.

Item Six. The King still did not know what he would do. He left the woods and returned to the house.

The King, as usual, chaired the meeting, the Prime Minister sitting on his right and the three politicians who had accompanied Churchill across the Atlantic placed round the circular table at regular intervals. The meeting was the third of its kind, George having insisted that he be informed of, and play his part in, the key decisions of state.

Item One dealt with the situation in the Western Desert, the Eastern Mediterranean and the Far East; Item Two the position of American neutrality and payment for the continued supply of US war material to Britain; Item Three the secondment of British scientists to what would become the Manhattan Project and the participation of His Majesty's Government in any decisions relating to the use of the item under research should its use ever be considered.

At eleven, after coffee was served, they came to Item Four, the anticipated German advance into the Free North to complete the occupation of Britain.

'The advance, Your Majesty, has so far not materialized.'

'And there is no troop movement or fresh activity in the area of no man's land?'

'No, Your Majesty.'

'And what of The Watchman and the Resistance?' There had never been any doubt amongst those present that George VI was in anything other than total control of the Cabinet papers.

'I am informed that The Watchman has returned north, that a total of sixty-six new agents have been dropped into the South, and that the rearming of the Resistance will begin shortly.'

They passed to Item Five, the campaigns in Greece, Yugoslavia and Crete, and the related subject of the anticipated German advance into Russia.

'According to intelligence, Operation Barbarossa, the German invasion of Russia, was due to begin on May the fourteenth.' Churchill again led the discussion. 'Because of Hitler's need to divert key troops to the Balkans, Barbarossa is delayed. As you are aware, Greece and Yugoslavia have fallen, but our troops are still holding Crete.'

'For how much longer?'

Once Crete had fallen, they were all aware, the last obstacle to Barbarossa was removed.

'A matter of days, Your Majesty.'

'But their sacrifice will not have been in vain? We will have delayed Barbarossa enough?' The King wondered whether the Prime Minister would be honest even with himself.

'I hope so.'

'Item Six.' The King moved the agenda paper to one side and turned to Churchill. 'I have read the report, as well as the details provided. Perhaps you would care to support the recommendation.'

The Prime Minister took the cigar from his mouth. 'I am aware, Your Majesty, that this is one of the most terrible decisions any of us will ever be called upon to make.' The King nodded his understanding and Churchill continued. 'In one way it is inevitable that the enemy will seek to use our factories to maintain their position and assist their own economy. Within this there is a degree which we must tolerate. We have a responsibility, for example, to ensure that our people continue to be clothed and fed, that they have jobs and money to survive. There are some areas, however, which will never be acceptable.' He stubbed the cigar in the ashtray and selected another.

'We have received intelligence that certain factories are now being used to provide direct support to the Nazi war effort, specifically engines and parts for tanks and aircraft.'

'What is the source of this information?' There had been no indication, either on the intelligence sheet itself or the copy of the original report he had requested.

'The source is protected.'

'You mean that you will not tell me.'

'I mean, Your Majesty, that not even I know.'

Item Six – George had not stopped thinking about, agonizing over it, since he had first read the report and realized what the Prime Minister might be forced to suggest.

'And the recommendation?'

Even Churchill, who had privately conceded that there was nothing he would not do in order to repel the invader, could hardly bring himself to say it. 'The recommendation, Your Majesty, is that the Royal Air Force be instructed to bomb the factories concerned.'

'Where are they located?'

'In the cities.'

'Of the British mainland?'

'Yes, Your Majesty, of the British mainland.'

It seemed an eternity before the King spoke again. 'And how precise can the bombing be?'

Churchill had discussed the issue with the Head of Bomber Command, estimated the casualties, been informed of the possibility that RAF crews would refuse the mission. 'There can be no guarantee of precision.'

The King rose and went to the window. 'How important is it that we stop this supply?'

'Imperative.'

He remembered again the morning he and his family had been driven through the streets of Liverpool, the woman at the dock gate who had held her child in the air so that the boy could see his King.

'I am sorry, Mr Churchill. I cannot allow the RAF to bomb my people.'

'In all honesty and conscience, Your Majesty, I cannot see an alternative.'

The King turned back from the window. 'Have you considered The Watchman?'

THE ROAD TO Alexandria disappeared like a ribbon across the sands, from the window of his room in the Mena House William Donovan could see the military convoys lurching across the desert. For two months now, and especially after his involvement in the Balkans, his practice as a lawyer had been subordinated to his increasing preoccupation with military and political matters. Five days before he had arrived in Cairo, every day the vehicles of the Eighth Army poured in lines through the streets or wound their way towards the battle fronts in the deserts to the west, and each evening its officers, accompanied sometimes by their ladies, sat and drank in the bar on the ground floor of the hotel. Four days ago Donovan had spent three hours with General Auchinleck, Commander-in-Chief Middle East; three mornings before he had been collected and driven south to meet a young captain from the Scots Guards named David Stirling who had recently been authorized to raise a clandestine group known as L Detachment, Special Air Service Brigade; that evening he was due to dine with Robert Laycock, originator of the commando force which bore his name, Layforce. In the intervening period he had also been briefed by the local offices of SIS and the fledgling SOE.

Cairo, as usual, was racked by rumour: Crete had fallen or was about to fall and Rommel was on the advance, his forces closing so fast that Headquarters were already burning documents. When he returned to the hotel the reception clerk handed him his room key and a note requesting him to go at once to the American Embassy.

The telegram, forwarded by his New York office, was short and oblique and appeared at first sight to refer simply to a weekend's pleasure in the country: it was hoped that he had enjoyed his ride and would come again for the hunting. The secretary offered him coffee; he sat drinking it and reading again the telegram. Hunting, he began to see, the lodge at Adelboden and the German called Fuchs, the car ride to Dachau.

It would be difficult, he was fully aware; particularly after his visit to Yugoslavia. When he returned to his hotel after dinner he wrote a long letter to his wife, having arranged through the Embassy that it be sent in the diplomatic bag. The next morning, he confirmed his acceptance of the invitation, arranged the identity under which he would enter Germany and left Cairo. Three days later he reached Geneva, checked into a hotel, and the same evening took a sleeper to Munich. By the following afternoon he was in the hunting lodge at Adelboden.

Fuchs himself arrived at seven. Donovan's instant impression was that beneath the confidence which he still appeared to exude the man was tired. They greeted each other warmly. After Fuchs had bathed they met again for dinner in the dining-room where they had sat four months before.

'You said when you were last here that if there was anything you could do . . .' Fuchs was dressed casually. The family retreat, Donovan began to understand, was the only place the German could even begin to relax.

'I did.'

'I need six American passports.' There was no hesitation or thought that the American would not help him. 'As you will know, there is already in this country an opposition to Hitler, still weak but growing. Unfortunately, perhaps inevitably, it has already been penetrated. A number of key people are now sought by the Gestapo.'

'How urgent is it?'

'Extremely.'

'Give me the details.'

Fuchs took a sheet of paper from his inside pocket and placed it on the table. 'Two families, four passports for the husbands and wives, children to go on their mothers' passports, the other two passports for single men.'

'What about help getting them out?'

'Everything is arranged, all they need are the documents.'

Donovan folded the paper and placed it in his wallet. 'What about you, Konrad?' It was the first time he had addressed the man by his first name.

'What do you mean?'

'What about a passport for you?' If Fuchs knew of people in the opposition then he must be part of it.

Fuchs sat back from the table. 'I am a German, this is my country.' He tried to shrug away the implications. 'William or Bill?'

'Bill,' said Donovan.

They continued the meal.

'And how is Germany?'

There was a hardness in Fuchs' laugh. 'The country at the moment is happy, we have conquered Europe and are about to defeat Russia. If we lose then the Prinzalbrechtstrasse will be overflowing.'

'What about the DEST and its calculations?'

'Working well.' The irony was undisguised.

'The Jewish problem?'

'Soon it will no longer exist, either here or in Poland or Belgium or Holland or France.'

'England?'

'Why should England be an exception?'

'And Dachau?'

'There are now many Dachaus.'

The following morning William Donovan returned to Switzerland. Two days later, he was back in Munich, again using the identity he had arranged in Cairo. The restaurant that lunchtime was crowded and the food excellent. Half-way through the meal Donovan went to the cloakroom, thirty seconds later Konrad Fuchs joined him. His suit was immaculate and there was an assurance and arrogance in the way he hung up his coat and washed his hands that reminded Donovan why he had so detested him at their first meeting.

There was one other person in the cloakroom. The American waited until the man left, then took the envelope from his pocket and gave it to Fuchs. The German put on his coat and placed the envelope in his inside pocket.

'Thank you.'

'Wish them good luck.'

'You also.'

Donovan turned to leave. 'What do you really do, Konrad? What is so important that you cannot leave?'

Fuchs brushed his jacket straight and looked at him. For one moment, Donovan thought, his eyes and face were those of an old man. 'One day, perhaps, I will tell you.'

THE BREEZE CAME through the window from the sea, the curtains moving gently. In his mind he saw the waves glistening bright on the loch, then his subconscious pulled him back to the half-sleep of his guilts and fears. He was standing at the bus stop waiting for Mary, the waves changing, dazzling, Mary's face white, sinking beneath them; Fran and Boy Jack; Ted with the explosives tied round his body. Last check, Fran was saying to him, Boy Jack giving him covering fire as he attached the charges beneath the fuel lorries, Mary walking with him down the road outside Jimmy Bailey's house to open the Ardley innings. We can hold them for thirty seconds, Fran was saying. Your choice, Dad, Boy Jack was changing the magazine. Your decision. Jack woke, dressed and left the castle. When Drake arrived he was still sitting on the headland.

'No reason to feel guilty, Jack. It wasn't your fault.' Drake took off his jacket and sat beside him.

Drake was right, but if he had not continued with the contacts after Jimmy Bailey Mary would not have been transmitting, would not have been taken. 'Any news?'

They had discussed it the night after Jack had reached the North, before Drake had spirited him again to the castle at Dunvegan.

'None. A few people were picked up, but only because the family in the house talked and identified the courier. Mary must have held out, the network had time to hear the news and go underground.' He picked up a pebble and rolled it in his hand. 'Two more jobs we have to talk about if you feel up to it.' He tossed the pebble away and watched it roll down the cliff.

The last time, Jack had decided after he had seen Fran and Boy

Jack. He had done his job, now someone else could do theirs. Not quite: what he had decided was to stop the contacts after meeting Bailey, to allow him to identify the traitor. 'What jobs?'

Drake reached for another pebble. 'Jimmy Bailey has to be dealt with.'

'And the second?'

'A number of British factories are being used to produce material for the German war effort. Churchill considered bombing them but was overruled. We've been given the job of sorting it out.'

'How?'

'Recruit key people in the factories, men and women, persuade them to sabotage the process. You'll be briefed on the industrial side – I have some engineers who will talk to you – but most of the time you'll have to rely on the locals knowing what to do and agreeing to help.'

The gulls were circling above them. Drake threw the second pebble down the slope. The Watchman still stared at the sea. 'It's hard about Mary, but she knew the risks, just as you know them. A great many other people will suffer before we win.'

'It isn't Mary.'

They climbed off the headland and walked past the sawmill towards the castle.

'If it's not Mary then what or who is it?'

Jack stopped and breathed deeply. 'Fran and Boy Jack are still alive.'

'How do you know?'

His hands were thrust deep in his pockets. 'I saw them at the farm.'

'I'm glad for you, Jack, I really am.' Drake remembered the night they had walked on the beach in the snow. 'They know about you?'

'No.'

They entered the castle grounds and stood looking over the jetty, the water rising and falling. 'Who suggested it was The Watchman's responsibility to deal with the factories?'

'You shouldn't let that influence your decision, Jack.'

'Who?' he asked again.

'The King.'

'Which factories?'

'The Rolls-Royce factory in Derby, the Spitfire factory in Castle Bromwich, and the Elswick ordnance company on the Tyne. Then some more in the South near the Thames.'

'Why?'

'If Hitler really is about to invade Russia he'll need all the spares he can get.'

They had already discussed the relationship between the invasion of Russia and the future of Britain.

'Who sent the warning about Jimmy Bailey?'

'Code name Prospero, that's all you need to know.'

Same source as the factory details – the connection was obvious – highly placed or in a social position which gave access to confidential planning and policies. 'Still in place?' He thought of Fran and Boy Jack. No one else to do his job: he reached his decision even though he did not understand the feelings that lay behind it. All the more reason now to put the Smith & Wesson in his mouth and finish it if they caught up with him.

'Still in place,' confirmed Drake.

HARRY DOWNTON WAS looking at her, Harry Downton was always looking at her; his face was against the window of the shop and his eyes were following her. Don't go into the shop alone, she told herself, never go into the shop when it's just Harry Downton and his cronies there. From inside she thought she heard a sound; the grocer glanced behind him then looked back at her, the laugh in his eyes. The door opened and the woman came out, saw her, understood that Fran knew what she had allowed the grocer to do to her for the few extra items she carried in her shopping basket.

Not even the back door any more, Fran thought, Harry Downton did not even seek to reduce her humiliation by allowing her to use the door at the rear where no one would see her. As she walked away, she heard the sound of the grocer and another man laughing.

At six, when she tuned the wireless to the Free North, the jamming was so effective that she could not hear either the news or the messages which followed. At nine the code she had given the airmen was again missing.

DRAKE LEFT THE liaison meeting with SIS and the representatives of the various Free French organizations who had escaped from their country after its fall and before the invasion of England, and returned to his offices. Although basic areas of agreement had been established the factions were already obvious: the suspicion between SIS and SOE; the battle over who would control the French operations, the French themselves or the British; even the conflict within French ranks between the Communists and the Gaullists.

He closed the door, told the switchboard and outer office that he was not to be disturbed, and concentrated on the message that had been brought from the South. Code name Caretaker; request assistance to establish escape network through South to North; contact at Canterbury Cathedral to be indicated by inclusion of specified message in codes transmitted after six and nine o'clock news.

Someone was fighting back. The hope had been with him ever since the report had been passed to him; someone already organizing, asking for help. Plenty of people must have seen it; only one had done anything about it. The possibility of a trap, he was aware, the Germans or more probably the Lice trying to infiltrate the beginnings of the Resistance. He had read the debriefing reports from the two airmen who had made it north. Nothing known about The Caretaker, they had stated, even though the beginnings of his organization were already in place; they themselves had only met those in the hospital who had arranged their departure, then the man and woman who had acted as couriers.

For two days after the Intelligence people had finished with them he himself had interviewed the pilots, taking them through the details of their escape, and bleeding with them as they described how one had been shot by a *Wehrmacht* patrol as they approached no man's land and the other had died in a minefield less than a quarter of a mile from safety. Then he had taken them back to the beginning and gone again and again through their story and the details of the man who had sent the message north with them. Who was The Caretaker, he had asked them. Think back to even the smallest clue to his identity. What did it smell like, feel like?

A trap, he feared even now, yet already The Caretaker had proven himself, risked his men and women and given evidence that his organization existed. He had spirited the airmen out of the hospital in Ramsgate and supplied them with identity cards and money, given them their orders.

Perhaps, he thought, The Watchman might check. It was four o'clock; he left the office and began the drive to The Cottage.

JACK WAS COLLECTED from Dunvegan at eight in the morning and driven across the island to Armadale Bay. A motor torpedo boat was moored at the jetty, its engines rumbling in the morning. As soon as he was aboard the ropes were cast off and the vessel slipped into the Sound of Sleat, its decks shuddering with the sudden power and its bow lifting as the RNVR lieutenant ordered full ahead. Jack stood in the stern, hands in pockets and watched the island disappearing in the wake.

> *Speed, bonny boat, like a bird on the wing,*
> *Over the sea to Skye.*
> *Carry the lad that's born to be King*
> *Over the sea to Skye.*

He remembered the pipers in the hills, the strains of the music and the words of the lament, then he recalled the other words of the lament and began to smile, the smile breaking suddenly and unembarrassed into a laugh.

> *All that was good, all that fair,*
> *All that was me is gone.*

Not gone, Fran and Boy Jack were still alive. Everything to live for. No more thoughts of the pistol in his mouth when they came for him. I'm going to win, the thought would not go away. I'm going to bloody well win. He was still laughing when he left the stern rail and walked to the bridge.

'Good day for it.' Cloak and dagger stuff, the lieutenant had known from the moment he had seen the lone figure get out of the car and witnessed the way he had stood in the stern. Funny job really, he supposed, they were bound to crack up sometime.

Jack was still laughing. 'Bloody good day for it.'

THE AIRFIELD SEEMED bleak and empty yet the main gates were guarded and the perimeter was fenced by barbed wire. The Humber drove past, swung in a circle round the field for eight hundred yards then turned right, up an unmade lane pockmarked by muddy water and mounds of wet earth, into the wood that formed the northern edge of the field, and stopped beside a small gateway flanked by a tall hedge. The driver sounded his horn and the gate opened. The two RAF policemen who appeared were dressed in civilian clothes. Both were in their mid-thirties, one tall and slim and the other shorter and rather stout. Jack stepped out of the car and followed them through the gate and into the kitchen of a small house almost hidden beneath the trees on the other side.

'Cup of tea, sir?' The shorter of the two men put on a kettle while the other led him through a narrow hall and into a room on the left. The room was low-ceilinged and the window small. Round the sides were two armchairs and a sofa, all worn and battered, and in the centre two long trestle tables with chairs drawn up. From the few words he had heard as he had passed the room on the other side of the hallway Jack assumed it was the operations and crew room. The door opened and the second man brought him a mug of tea.

'The squadron leader will be with you in a moment, sir.'

Jack thanked the man, took the tea, and walked to the window. Only when he looked out did he see that the house formed part of the airfield. Ten minutes later the door opened and a pilot came into the room.

'Welcome to Special Duties Squadron. I'm taking you down to-night.' Despite his youth the man wore the ribbon of a DSO and the two and a half rings of a squadron leader. 'Glad you're early. Gives us time to run through the procedures.' He waited until Jack had finished his tea then led him across the airfield. 'Nice and quiet here. We can use the things we want, met. reports and radio, but nobody knows what we're up to or who's coming or going.'

The four Lysanders were camouflaged beneath the trees. One of the ground crew pulled back the nets then stood aside and allowed Jack time to admire the plane. The Lysander was thirty feet long with a wing span of fifty feet, propelled by a single 905 HP Bristol Mercury XVA engine, the front of the aircraft some fourteen feet from the ground. There were two cockpits – the front one for the pilot reached by a foothold on the casing covering the port wheel, and the rear for the passengers reached by a metal ladder secured to the side of the fuselage, also on the port side, both covered by slide-back canopies. Jack climbed the ladder and opened the cockpit. Inside and facing aft was a two-seater bench and a shelf large enough to take a suitcase.

'You look out for night fighters. There's an earphone in the headset and a mike in the oxygen mask.' The pilot climbed up beside him. 'Comfortable for two passengers, bit of a squeeze for three, manage four at a pinch.' They jumped down. 'Normal speed is about a hundred and seventy knots, more if we're not worried about saving fuel.' He indicated the extra tank strung like a torpedo between the legs. 'Nine hours' endurance, so there'll be no problems tonight.'

Jack felt the nerves winding in his stomach.

'The flare path is an inverted L of three white lamps: lamp A first, lamp B a hundred and fifty yards into wind and lamp C fifty yards to the right of B. Our circuit is like a race track: two straight lines parallel with the flare path A to B, joined by two semi-circles, the second losing height as we come into A. We land on the right of lamp A, the agent in charge and any passengers keeping to the left. We turn between B and C and again into wind at the right of A to change loads. I keep the engine running and do not leave the aircraft. You get out fast. As soon as I get the thumbs up, I go.'

'How long?'

'Two minutes if there are parcels going in and coming out, not much more than a minute tonight. We'll have a practice later.'

'What about parachutes?'

'I'll show you how to fit it and what to do before we go.'

'What about at a pick-up?' If the turn round was so fast, he meant, if the whole aim was to take off as soon after the landing as possible. Especially, he really meant, if the enemy knew of the landing or discovered it as it was happening.

'In that situation I would imagine that a parachute would be the last thing any of us would worry about.'

Drake was waiting at The Cottage. He spoke briefly to the squadron leader then joined Jack outside.

'Penny for them, Jack.'

'Just thinking how quiet it all is.'

'That's the idea.' Sometimes Drake spoke as if he was writing a memo. 'Keep everything under wraps, make Hitler think we're no longer a threat to him. Bring out everything again when he's committed himself on the Russian front.'

The afternoon was warm.

'You're a different man today, Jack. What's happened?'

THE AIRFIELD WAS quieter and the songs of the birds softer. Jack stood in the trees behind the aircraft and breathed the scent of the pines. Been a bit grim up to now, almost as if you had a death wish. Careful though, no relaxing.

He looked at the planes again and turned back to The Cottage.

The meal was served at six-thirty; Jack sat at the table with Drake, the squadron leader and two other pilots while one of the men who had welcomed him, and who doubled as squadron cook, brought in roast pheasant and the other poured the wine. Outside the light was beginning to fade from the sky. ETA zero one hundred hours, the squadron leader's mind was not on the meal, flight time three hours thirty-five minutes, flare path six minutes thirty seconds from last navigational checkpoint. The reception committee would already be in place, Jack thought of the men waiting for him, the guards already out to protect the landing field, warn of discovery or betrayal.

The night operation dinner would become a ritual at The Cottage, those who attended would never forget them, partly because of the knowledge that the man or woman to be carried into the dark that night might never be seen again. There would, however, be one other meal which they would remember even more: the night operation breakfasts for agents picked up from enemy territory and returned — albeit temporarily — to safety.

The service policeman came round the table and offered Jack a second glass of wine. Jack put his hand over his glass and shook his head. None of the pilots were drinking.

'You flying tonight as well?' He turned to the man on his left. Three pilots, he had thought, but only one passenger so far.

'Training. Can't see in the dark yet.'

'What did you fly before you came here?'

'Spitfires.'

'Where?'

The right side of the pilot's face was scarred and the skin on his face and hands glistened with an unreal, almost plastic, sheen. 'Hellfire Corner.' It was the name the pilots had given to the skies above Dover the previous summer.

Might have seen you, Jack thought. Fran and Boy Jack and Ernie and I used to watch from the farm, cheer when a German went down. No details, he knew.

Behind them the squadron leader returned with the meteorological report on which that night's operation would depend.

THE SKY WAS almost transparent behind the rising moon.

'Nice evening, Mum.' Sometimes, often, he thought about his father, wanted to talk about him, did not do so to protect his mother. Sometimes, too, he wondered about Ernie, where he was and what he was doing.

'Lovely evening.' Fran turned from the fields and walked back to the house, Boy Jack watching her. Each evening now he wondered why his mother insisted on listening to the wireless at six and nine o'clock, no matter what else she was doing. Every time she turned the set off he saw the look on her face and the way she tried to hide it from him.

THE CITADEL WAS quiet. At five minutes to nine the shorthand clerk switched on the wireless and tuned it to the broadcasts from the North. When they were finished he typed the transcript of the messages that had followed the news and passed it to the duty sergeant with a note that the code 'The orange is ripe', which had been included in the six o'clock transmission, had been repeated at nine.

THE NIGHT WAS all around him. Jack wished he could see where they were and what they were doing. The Lysander banked to port and he heard the voice of the squadron leader in his helmet.

'Last checkpoint, should spot the field in six and a half minutes.'

He tried to look, felt again the tightness in his stomach and the shaking in his hands. Two minutes, one.

'Got it.' The pilot reached to his right and flashed the reply from the lamp in the belly of the plane. 'Fly over once, check it out, then we go in.' The plane was descending slightly, Jack held onto the side and saw the ground as the pilot banked. 'Going in now.' The Lysander straightened, the flare path coming up fast. Jack felt the thud as the wheels touched, then the bumping as the plane slowed. Point B, he felt the pilot turn right. 'Open the canopy.' Point C, right again. 'Already done.' Point A, turning again and stopping, engine still running. 'Good luck, see you for breakfast sometime.' Jack pulled himself to the top of the ladder, clanged the canopy shut, climbed down and hurried towards the waiting men. The organizing agent signalled to the pilot and the Lysander moved away.

THE CONFIRMATION FOR which he had been waiting reached Drake at six. He made himself another coffee and returned to his desk. The drive from the airfield had taken two hours, he had been back by eleven and tried to sleep, fully aware that he would not. At three he had risen from the camp bed, removed the Caretaker file from the security cabinet and sat again at the desk with the report on the message which Johnny Watson had brought north in front of him. The first sun touched the window behind him. He had already delayed too long, he knew, spent too much time balancing the two sides. If it was a trap then he would sacrifice the courier he sent to the meeting place in order to establish the truth, but he could minimize the damage by having a second person observe the meeting and report on whether the courier was arrested or followed. And if it was not a trap then people might already have been lost because of his indecision. He felt the stubble on his chin and came to the last dilemma. Even if it was a trap the Lice would not close in now, would wait until they had achieved what they wanted and he had given them too much. He returned the file to the cabinet and made his decision.

HARRY DOWNTON WAS in the village square, his hands were stuck in his braces and he was surrounded by the men Fran thought of as his usual crew. Even in the post office she could hear his voice, knew that the woman standing beside her was one of those who visited the store when the grocer's wife was away. The post mistress looked at the clock on the wall and asked Fran to change the sign on the door. Gone half-past five, she realized, almost twenty-five to six, no time to finish the shopping, barely time to get back to the farm. 'Something in the oven.' She made her excuse, even though she knew there was little or no point, left the post office and hurried through the village. The Reverend Brian Markham was digging the flowerbed in the front garden of the vicarage; when he saw her he put down the spade. It was fifteen minutes to six. No point, she told herself again. 'Sorry,

Vicar, left something in the oven.' He smiled and went back to his work. By the time she crossed the river behind the church and climbed the field to the farm it was six o'clock. In the door of the barn Boy Jack was repairing the handle of the wheelbarrow. 'Hello, Jack. Can't stop.' She ran into the kitchen, turned on the wireless and tuned it to the North. The news was just ending.

'Here are a few personal messages.'

Just in time, she thought.

'The cockerel is crowing. The boats are bringing in the fish. The weather is warm for this time of year.'

Tonight, she knew, knew why she had almost run from the village, felt the excitement, almost the nausea, remembered the day she had given her orders to the airmen.

The messages ended and she knew they had not made it.

THE STREET WAS quiet. Lice in the house opposite, the man knew; they had been seen going in at midnight. Routine, just making the record look good; he left his position at the top of the street and was replaced by a second man. Don't make it obvious, they had told him, if you think you have been spotted, pull out.

The door of the house half-way down on the right opened and the woman came out. Two youngest children with her, the man noted, oldest boy at school, all the family accounted for. He lit a cigarette and followed her towards the market square.

The stalls were busy. She stopped at the vegetable stall, opened her purse and worked out how much she could afford. It was all a bit easier now, ever since Jimmy had been earning more. She selected a cabbage, paid for it, put it in her bag and began to walk away.

'Hello Mrs Bailey.' She smiled at the man and wondered how he knew who she was. A second man was the other side, a third taking the children. 'Everything's all right, love.' They were already away from the market, no one realizing that anything was wrong, turning into the side street where the car was waiting. 'Nothing to worry about.' The car pulled away and the second team closed on the place where Jimmy Bailey worked.

FRAN ENJOYED THIS time of year. There was work to do as always, but the lambing had gone well and there was the summer to look forward to. She turned on the wireless, tuned it to the North and finished making the scones. 'This is the voice of Britain talking to the people of Britain. Here is the news.' She had given Quizzie Lizzie in the post office a dozen eggs for the extra flour, knew that the woman had probably done some deal with Harry Downton to get it anyway. It was the way things were nowadays.

'The war in the Western Desert is continuing. Reports that Rommel is attacking Cairo have been denied.' In the yard outside Boy Jack nailed the handle of the wheelbarrow into place. 'In Washington President Roosevelt has promised continued aid for the Allied cause.' She opened the door of the range and put the scones in. A little treat, she had decided, she and Boy Jack had earned it. 'That is the end of the news. Here are a few personal messages.'

She cleared the table and dusted the surplus flour back into the bag so that she did not waste any. 'The spring is here. The sun is in the heavens. Zeus is on his mountain.' Sometimes, she thought, the messages were just to confuse the enemy. 'The sea is warm. The tea is in the pot.' Sometimes the people who made them up must try to make them funny. 'The basket is full.' Boy Jack came into the kitchen and went to wash his hands. 'The rose will bloom in winter.' She smiled at him, left the table and put the bag of flour in the pot. Realized what she had heard, felt the sudden thumping in her chest and the sickness in her throat. They made it! At least one of them is safe. Don't look at me, Boy Jack, don't see the look on my face or the expression in my eyes. She put the top on the pot and placed it in the cupboard. Only when she sat down again did she realize the enormity of what she had set in motion.

After they had finished supper, she asked Boy Jack if he wanted to walk with her to the village. In the cricket field a number of his friends were playing against the side of the pavilion; Boy Jack joined them and Fran went to the postman's. The moment he saw her Ned knew what she was going to say.

'Tell everyone we're on stand-by. I'll confirm with you in the morning.'

THE INSPECTION OF the department's office in Birmingham had gone well; when Holdaway returned to The Citadel, Davis was waiting.

'Bailey's disappeared.'

The baton which Holdaway kept on the desk crashed down, smashing the mug and typewriter and scattering the other items. 'How?' His voice was still calm. 'I thought we had him under tabs.' The clerk came running from the outer office. 'Out,' Holdaway ordered him. The man retreated and closed the door behind him. 'I thought you said he was secure, that we had him wrapped up.'

'According to the surveillance in the house opposite Bailey went to work as usual this morning. He didn't come back.'

'You'd better bring in his wife and kids.'

'They've gone as well. His eldest son went to school at eight-thirty, at eleven his wife and the two youngest children left the house. She was carrying a shopping bag. They haven't been seen since.'

'The others he named as being in the cell?' Holdaway began to fear the worst.

'The same. Families, wives and kids. Just disappeared.'

Holdaway was thinking ahead, trying to work out what he would tell Schellenberg. 'Hills, the original informant, you'd better bring him in.'

'He's downstairs.'

'Said anything?'

'Nothing at all.' The telephone rang. 'Busy,' Holdaway snapped, not asking who or what it was, then sat back in the chair, hands behind his head.

'What will you tell Schellenberg?'

'The truth,' said Holdaway. 'I have no option.'

FRAN LEFT THE farm, collected Ned and drove into Canterbury. In some areas of the city the debris from the bombing was still piled high; in others, where it had been cleared, the gaps in the lines of houses and shops where buildings had been destroyed seemed even more stark. She parked the pick-up, left Ned, and walked to the cathedral, entering the grounds by Christ Church Gate and the building itself by the south-west porch. Before invasion the nave had been piled with sand as a form of protection, now it had been cleared. She checked that the door off the north-east transept leading to

Dean's Steps was locked and sat in the nave beneath the military memorials on the right wall, in a position from which she could observe the two stairways leading to the meeting place. In the choir school in the grounds the choristers began their afternoon practice.

The courier to enter and exit by Christ Church Gate and the south-west porch, she went through the details for the last time, Ned covering the outside in case the man was followed in or picked up on the way out, she herself the inside. It was two minutes to three.

The courier walked past her and up the south steps. The man was thirty years old and from another village, known to Ned but not knowing her. Almost immediately a woman came through the Martyr's door and up the north steps.

The tomb of Henry IV and Joan of Navarre was on the left of Trinity Chapel, close to where the remains of Becket had once been enshrined.

'When will the rose bloom?'

'In winter.'

The sealed envelope was given to the woman, the courier came down the steps, passed in front of Fran and left. Three minutes later the woman who had made the contact also left. Fran waited another five minutes then went outside. As she passed Ned he winked that everything was in order.

THE CHEMIST SHOP was in the centre of the High Street. The organizer searched along the shelves and counters then asked for the chemist himself. The man in the white coat who appeared from the back room was tall and balding with gold-rimmed spectacles.

'I'm sorry to trouble you. I was looking for some lipstick but couldn't find any.'

The chemist shook his head. 'None in stock, I'm afraid. Goes as fast as we get it, that sort of thing.'

The door opened and the girl who had fetched the chemist left them to serve the new customer. The organizer took two one-pound notes from his pocket. 'It's my wife's birthday, I'm sure you understand.' The chemist hesitated; the man took a third note and folded it with the other two. The chemist nodded for him to join him behind the counter and opened a drawer. In it were a selection of cosmetics and perfumes. The lipstick the organizer chose was a brilliant, almost garish red.

THE BARN WAS at the rear of the farm, the cart had been pushed against the wall and bales of straw had been pulled from the sides to form a U-shape in the centre of the floor. Amongst the beams thirty feet above, and unseen by those below, was an owl's nest, its occupant the only independent witness of what was about to happen. The front doors of the barn faced the farmhouse and the rear led into a yard which was awash with mud and manure from the cowsheds and pigsties around it, a gate leading from it to the fields below. The farmer himself was the leader of the network next to the Hop group. Ever since Jimmy Bailey had been spirited into the buildings early the previous evening the entire area had been guarded discreetly but effectively by members of the network. That morning, when he had received his instructions from The Watchman and suggested to his wife that she should take the children to visit their grandmother twenty miles away, the woman had simply asked what time she should return and been told that it would be sensible to keep away until mid-evening.

The Watchman arrived at five. After he had briefed the network leaders and organizers present and confirmed the arrangements Jimmy Bailey was led in. Since his seizure the previous morning he had been tied and blindfolded and had been given neither food nor water. His body was shaking with fear and his hands and wrists were numb where the ropes tying him had cut off the circulation of his blood.

'Sit him down.'

Bailey recognized the voice immediately.

'Take off the blindfold.'

He saw the face of The Watchman opposite him and the expression of the men sitting to his left and right as if at an inquisition.

'Untie him.'

He had worked out what he would say and decided it was best to tell them nothing, he felt the first splinters of pain as the blood flooded back into his hands and knew it would not be the last he would endure that afternoon.

'You know you are to be executed, Jimmy. You know I have no option.' The Watchman's eyes did not move from him. No revenge, Jack had resolved: if he allowed his personal feelings to intrude then he would lose all that Bailey could tell him. 'All I ask of you is that you remember your country and tell me what happened.' The bastard, the Judas who sold him on the day he had found out that Fran and Boy Jack were alive.

'What about my family?' The sweat was pouring off Bailey's forehead and into his eyes.

'Your wife and children are innocent. They have already been moved from the area and will be well looked after.' Do to him what the Lice would have done to you. Wring the truth from him as they would have sought to wring it from you.

'You haven't eaten?'

The traitor shook his head. His head was on his chest and his shoulders were bowed.

'Bring him something.'

Holdaway, Bailey thought. Schellenberg, bloody Davis.

The Watchman crossed the floor and sat beside him as if he was a friend. 'Tell me from the beginning.'

The interrogation continued until seven. Only when he was sure that Bailey could tell him no more did The Watchman rise from the bale.

'Take him outside.' When he had talked with the traitor The Watchman's voice had been relaxed and persuasive; now it assumed again the authority of his position.

The firing squad was waiting. As he was led from the barn Bailey's legs folded beneath him and his body collapsed, falling into the manure and filth which covered the yard. His voice pleading for mercy. His escorts lifted him up, dragged him to the gate on the right, tied him against the post and jerked his head upright.

'Take aim.'

The rifles came up. The traitor's eyes were rolling wildly and he screamed for pity. The man in charge of the firing party waiting for the order. The Watchman looked once at Bailey, then nodded.

'Fire.'

The shots echoed between the buildings and the rooks rose in a clamour from the trees at the foot of the field. The farmer stepped forward, slit the rope holding the man and the body fell again onto the filth of the ground.

'Turn his face up.'

The Watchman crossed the yard and stood looking down at the corpse. The men who had formed the firing squad and those who observed the execution from the door of the barn saw him take something from his pocket, then crouch beside the body. The eyes were wide and staring and the mouth had fallen open. The Watchman removed the cap from the tube of lipstick and drew two lines across Bailey's face, the first vertical, from the nose down the mouth and chin to the throat, and the second horizontal, from ear to ear, the line again through the mouth and forming a cross with the other.

'Tonight, when it is dark, put him in the square where the mayor and his people were to have been shot. Make sure that nobody sees you, but make sure that everybody sees him in the morning before he is taken away.'

THE CARETAKER'S MESSAGE was transmitted to the North at fourteen minutes to ten, fifty-five minutes later it had been passed to Drake's department and decoded. At eleven Drake poured himself a large malt and concentrated on the summary he had made of the information and requests from the South.

One: an urgent need existed for the setting up of an escape network connecting the South to the North. Two: the network should be based on the Intelligence section of the pre-invasion Auxiliary Units, most of which was assumed to be secure. Three: for reasons of security and logistics the occupied zone should be divided into regions, each controlled by an organizer, with escapers being passed from one to another. Four: money, false identity documents and petrol coupons were needed to help set up the system. Five: the significance and potential of members of the British Armed Forces held in prison camps should not be ignored. The freeing and transport north of some of these, as well as the preparation for their roles when Liberation came, could be provided by the escape network.

The lights flickered and went out as the power supply was interrupted. Drake ignored the black and continued his analysis. The Caretaker was right, yet the implication of his suggestion, even though he had not specified it, was almost too much to risk: the names and identities of members of the Intelligence section in his area in order to build his escape network around it. The possibility of a trap was still central to Drake's considerations. Yet The Caretaker must himself have been a member of the section in order to know of it. The lights came back on, flickered again, then stayed on.

The decision had been inevitable from the beginning. Drake took a sheet of paper from the drawer on his right and turned his attention to the security which would need to surround it.

'BAILEY HAS TURNED up.'

Holdaway stopped what he was doing. 'Thank Christ for that.'

'He's dead. His body was dumped in the square last night, he had been shot. The body has been moved and photographs are on their way.'

'What else?'

'Whoever put him there drew a red cross in lipstick across his mouth.'

'How many people saw it?'

'Practically everybody.'

'Shut the door.'

Holdaway lifted the telephone and told his clerk to inform London that he might be late. Davis closed the door and sat down.

'Who?'

'The Watchman.'

'Of course the bloody Watchman.' Holdaway's face was black with rage and his eyes were small and red.

'But how did the bastard know?'

'The same way he knew not to turn up when we were waiting for him.' One of the telephones on his desk rang. Holdaway picked it up, snapped at the switchboard that he was not to be disturbed, and slammed down the handset so violently that it shattered.

'The obvious start should be the unit covering the area. The problem is that every unit knew about the Bailey case. You'll have to go through the records of every man in the department. Don't let anyone know what you're up to.'

God help the man when Holdaway caught up with him, Davis thought. Holdaway reached for the other telephone. 'Get me Herr Schellenberg. If he's not in his office find out where he is.'

THE OYSTERS WERE fresh and the champagne was chilled to perfection. Fiona Egerton-Smith laughed as the *maître d'hôtel* eased off the cork and filled their glasses. 'A special toast.' Walter Schellenberg raised his glass. 'It is exactly three months since we first met.'

That weekend they had again been invited to the country seat of Lord Southerton.

'On Saturday perhaps you can give me some more riding lessons.'

'Depends.' She played with the stem of the glass and laughed at him.

'On what?'

'On whether you promise not to bring all that bloody paperwork back with you.'

When the lunch was finished Schellenberg returned to his office at the Grosvenor House. Fiona instructed his driver to return for her at four and walked through Leicester Square towards Oxford Street. The afternoon was warm and the first buskers were already on the pavements outside the cinemas. On the corner opposite the Cambridge Theatre a young man was leaning on a crutch and playing an accordion. The left leg of his trousers was empty and pinned with military precision three inches from the top of his thigh, and a peaked cap was upside down on the pavement in front of him. On his uniform he wore the campaign ribbons of the British Expeditionary Force.

Fiona glanced behind her, folded a pound note tightly together and dropped it into his cap.

THE DESPATCH FROM Berlin was the first item requiring Walter Schellenberg's attention. He called for a coffee, read it once then sat back to consider its implications.

Two weeks ago the American William Donovan had broken a series of engagements in Cairo and left the city unexpectedly. Three days later he had checked into a hotel in Geneva. Bribes to the staff had revealed that he had disappeared for forty-eight hours, re-appeared for two days, and vanished again for a further thirty-six hours. On his return he had spent only six hours in the city before leaving for the Middle East.

Donovan in Berlin and Munich in January, then in the South of England and making a trip north with Ambassador Kennedy. Donovan in the Balkans and the Middle East, then going to ground in Geneva.

Schellenberg called his clerk, ordered the man to telegram Berlin for a list of all Americans entering and leaving the Fatherland via Switzerland during the dates when Donovan was ostensibly in

Geneva, then turned his attention to the matter of a possible leak at The Citadel which Holdaway had raised that morning.

THE ROSE CODE was transmitted at six that evening and repeated at nine. The following afternoon Fran and Ned went again to the cathedral; at three-fifteen, after the contact had been made, then the two of them met in the tea-room in the undamaged part of Burgate. The café was busy – even during Occupation the cathedral attracted visitors – and they waited five minutes for somewhere to sit.

'The courier is to go back at four.' Ned thanked the waitress who brought the pot of tea and slid the envelope under the table. 'He wasn't told why.'

Fran felt the renewed fear of a trap, went to the ladies' room, closed and locked the door, and opened the envelope. The sheet of paper inside was covered with squares of numbers, each five across and five down, none of them making any sense at all. She went back to the table and finished her tea, then she and Ned resumed their watch in the cathedral each changing position slightly. At five minutes to four the courier entered the nave and went to the meeting place, and Fran waited for the woman. Two minutes later a man passed her and went up the steps. For one moment she felt the panic that the trap she feared was being sprung then began to understand. Within three minutes the men had left the cathedral and its grounds, each by different exits; then Fran rendezvoused with Ned, left him on the outskirts of the village and returned to the farm.

That night, after Boy Jack had gone to bed and she had checked that he was asleep, Fran opened the envelopes and laid the sheets of paper they contained on the table in front of her. The curtains were drawn and the door locked and bolted. She lit the oil lamp, placed it on the table, then moved the first sheet aside and concentrated on the second, reading it three times until she understood it fully. Two messages for The Caretaker that afternoon, each sent through a different radio operator and delivered by a different courier. The first contained the coded message to The Caretaker; and the second the format of the two codes used and the personal key and numbers he would need. It was ironic she was aware how even *she* thought of The Caretaker as a man.

She took a writing pad and pencil from the drawer, sat down again and began to work out the two codes by which she could interpret the message.

The number code, once she grasped the technique, was easy and she felt a surge of satisfaction, almost of pleasure. Security, she suddenly realized, no imprints of codes or messages on the pad after she had finished. She pulled the next sheet from the pad, rested it on the table, and started again.

The Playfair code was more complicated; only after twenty minutes did she understand it, and once she began to apply it she knew she had made a mistake with the brandy code.

Her head was spinning, but she continued, working quickly and with confidence, the first letters of the message suddenly uncoded.

AL BE RT RE ES PO ET

ALBERT REES, POET

She tried to understand what it meant but could not; she moved the oil lamp closer and pressed on. After another ten minutes the task was complete.

On the fresh sheet in front of her were the names, addresses and code names, as well as the code names of the zero stations to which they had reported during invasion, of the twenty members of the Intelligence section of the British Resistance who had been allocated to The Caretaker's region of the escape circuit to the North.

Not me, the thought filled her head. I was only suggesting something. Someone else was supposed to do it, organize it all: Ned or the man who contacted him in the first place, somebody sent from the North. Not me. Someone specially selected and trained. No farm or Boy Jack to look after, no other responsibilities. Someone who had volunteered. *You* volunteered, Fran. More than that, you began it, invented the person called The Caretaker. Her cocoa was cold. She poured it back into the saucepan and put it back on the range.

Two mornings later, when Boy Jack went to school, Fran explained that she had to go to Maidstone and that she might be late home. The trip was to do with her mother; if she was not back when he had finished the animals he should go to Sarah's and Fran would collect him from there when she returned.

The street was on the edge of the town, falling slightly to the road crossing it at the bottom. It was early evening, the smell of cooking coming from the houses and the children playing on the pavement. The house was a third of the way down on the left. Fran knocked on the door and waited. She heard the scuffling in the hallway then a woman opened the door.

'Good evening, I was looking for Mr Rees.' She wondered how much the woman knew, if her husband had ever told her.

'Hang on, I'll get him.'

The man who came to the door was in his late forties. His sleeves were rolled up and his hands were dirty with soil but he had taken off his boots to come through the house after his wife had called him from the vegetable patch at the rear.

'Mr Rees?'

'Yes.' It would always be the same, she would learn.

'Albert Rees?'

'Yes.' The distrust and suspicion were in the eyes, then the realization and the relief that all was not lost.

'I've come about Poet.'

THE LIST OF Americans entering and leaving Germany via Switzerland which Walter Schellenberg had requested was telegrammed to the Grosvenor House at mid-afternoon. Of the twenty-seven names, only one matched the dates of what he assumed were William Donovan's excursions from Geneva. Before he left his office Schellenberg passed the details to the Embassy in Washington; forty-eight hours later he was notified that the journalist concerned did not appear to exist and that the identity was probably false.

2

THE FIRST LIGHT came through the window. Mary was not sure whether she welcomed the dawn because it meant she had survived another night or whether she feared it because it meant she had to face another day.

There were two hundred women in the block and eighty bunk beds. Most prisoners therefore slept two to a bunk; where there were three the one in the middle slept with her feet between the heads of the other two. Mary climbed down, put the coat and trousers which she had used as a pillow over the collarless shirt and long pants which she wore continually, wrapped the two triangles of cloth into Russian socks and put them on her feet, pulled on the clogs, picked up her bowl and spoon, and joined the line of prisoners pushing for a place in the food queue.

In front of her stood the woman who had helped her from the floor of the lorry and told her her name on the first evening in the place. It could still be a trap, Mary told herself; it could all still be a nightmare induced by the bastards at The Citadel to make her talk, reveal the secrets of The Watchman. She ignored the woman as she always ignored the woman and waited with her tin bowl in her hand.

Breakfast was always the same: a bowl of artificial coffee and three pieces of bread, the coffee black and tasting of oil and the bread grey and tasting of dough. She carried the breakfast to her bunk, drank the coffee, ate one piece of bread and tucked the others inside her clothes.

It was almost six-thirty. She tidied the bunk and went outside for

348

roll call, the prisoners standing in blocks, each five deep and five across, the senior block officials in front. The gates at the foot of the camp opened and the SS officers strode in. When the head count was over the block secretary allocated the prisoners to their work *Kommandos* and they stood in lines waiting for the order. It was the way each day except Sunday began. Two weeks since Mary had come here – two months, two years, she was no longer sure. The *Kapo* shouted the command and they shuffled forward.

The women's camp at Portland was one of two, the inmates of the men's used primarily for work in the quarry and of the women's for the roads and fields around. It was surrounded by two layers of electrified barbed wire, with watchtowers at each corner and in the centre of each perimeter, manned by SS guards with machine guns. More guards with dogs patrolled outside.

The barrack blocks ran in two neat lines up the compound itself; the first block on the right, nearest the gate, was the shower room through which each prisoner passed on her first day and the first block on the left the office in which they had been processed and which contained the camp records. Beyond the quarantine blocks at the far end of the camp was that used as the hospital and, opposite it, the crematorium, its chimney belching its grey pall into the sky whenever it was used. Because Portland was not an extermination camp, however, the crematorium was used primarily to dispose of the bodies of prisoners who died.

Just as the camp was a world within a world, so each block was an entity within the camp; although the overall command of the camp lay with the SS, with an SS *Block Führer* in charge of each barrack, the day-to-day running of the place lay with the prisoners. At the head of each barrack was a block chief, normally a prisoner with a criminal classification, often a murderer or a prostitute. If the chief so wished, she appointed two assistants, in charge of each of the two sections into which the barrack was divided. Each section chief in turn appointed an assistant, who in her turn selected those prisoners who would be responsible for such jobs as cleaning the block and bringing the food from the kitchen.

In addition the chief appointed the block secretary, normally a political prisoner, who was in charge of the block's administration and who in her turn could appoint an assistant secretary for each section of the block.

Membership of the system carried obvious privilege. No one in it was required to join the work *Kommandos*, and even the lowest member could bestow favours on those not a part of it. Such favours, like membership itself, were usually bought at a price, normally sexual. The appointees of the block chief were almost always younger girls and referred to as her 'little friends'. So important and all pervasive was the system that it had even been given its own name. The prisoners of the camp knew it simply as the Organization.

THE SIREN SOUNDED and Mary saw the men move back from the rock face. The quarry itself was next to the section of road to which Mary's *Kommando* had been allocated. The sun was hot on her back and the blood where her flesh and nails had torn against the rock was caked onto her hands. The sky above her began to swim, the sun going round and round, her body not yet healed from the beatings at The Citadel, not being given the chance to heal by the relentlessness of the work and the meagreness of the food.

She heard the explosion and felt the shock waves rebound through her head, the pain building up as if it had no way to escape, then someone was shouting at her, ordering her to work, the sun still circling in the sky, standing still, her body moving in circles around it. Never stop work, those round her knew, never stop work or you knew what they did to you. She wrapped the strips of rag round her hands and began again to make the road which would carry the lorries taking the Portland stone to the palace being built for the new King.

Along the track Mary saw the assistants coming with the containers of their midday meal. The other women were already queuing, the bowls in their hands. Mary picked up hers and joined the end, shuffling slowly forward, her head still swimming and the images in front of her still muddled and unclear.

The soup was water and rice, with an occasional piece of potato or swede and an even more occasional sliver of meat. Dig deep into the pan, she pleaded silently, put the spoon deep into the bottom so that I may get even a little of the goodness that lies there. The woman skimmed the wooden spoon along the surface and poured the thin unnourishing liquid at the top into her bowl. Mary shuffled back down the road and half squatted on the side, her eyes furtive and her glance like that of a fox. With her left hand she held the food close to her, the forearm around it so that no one could steal it and the hand holding it tight so that no one would even knock it as they passed. With her right hand she took the second piece of bread from her coat and began to eat, raising the bowl to her mouth and sipping from it, never relinquishing her iron hold on it, then scraping the bread round it when it was empty.

In the dust of the roadside opposite her the woman from the lorry held her bowl and ate her food in the same way. To survive in this place, Mary knew, even to die decently, she needed a friend. Yet even now she could not bring herself to trust the woman, could not shake off the terrible legacy beaten into her at The Citadel that in order to survive herself, even in return for such a small favour as a piece of meat in her soup, the woman might betray her.

The *Kapo* shouted, she wrapped the cloth round her hands and went back to work, the SS guards never far away and the dogs never ceasing to growl. The sun above her was even hotter, the hammer still pounding through her head and the aching consuming her limbs so that the afternoon, like all the afternoons, seemed to last for ever. She could not even remember when the *Kapo* shouted for them to line up by the roadside and they marched back into the camp, again in blocks of twenty-five, five by five, the SS guards counting them as they passed through the gates. All she could remember were the block assistants coming with the containers. She climbed off her bunk and went outside, bowl clasped in hand.

Supper was either a piece of sausage, never more than an inch long, a spoonful of artificial jam, which made your teeth black, or a cube of margarine for the last piece of bread. She stood in the line and wondered what it would be that evening. The trustee dropped the sausage into her bowl and she carried it back to the bunk.

Unless you have a friend, she told herself, you will not survive. Unless you have a friend you will become one of the blanket people, who roll themselves in the rough cloth and lie in the dirt and the filth till death comes for them. Unless you shake off the fear they beat into you at The Citadel and trust someone then you and the woman who helped you on the lorry will both die.

She walked across the floor and sat on the bunk.

'Mary,' she said.

'Annie,' the other woman said again.

3

THERE WAS NO reason for there to be a tail on him today; there was, on the other hand, every reason for there to be a tail on him every day – a team job probably, no single tail for more than two or three minutes, one picking him up then handing him over, picking him up again later. You're getting paranoid, Jack Masters, he laughed at himself. Better to be paranoid than dead. Only when he was certain that he was not being followed did he walk the half-mile to the café and go through to the back room. The network organizer was waiting for him.

'The manager is called Dunster. His office is on the third floor. His secretary sits outside, she leaves to collect his tea at ten-thirty and three-fifteen.'

'What do we know about him?'

The organizer gave him the man's family details.

'What times are the shifts?'

'There used to be one shift, eight to six. Now there are two, six to two and two to ten.'

At one the following afternoon Jack drove to the factory. He was wearing a blue boiler suit, stained with grease and oil, and a donkey jacket. The complex was built along the Thames, houses and other factories around it, and a variety of buildings inside the fence that surrounded it. The entrance was quiet, with only an occasional individual passing in or out, their identity cards and their works passes being checked by the guards on the gate. When he returned at ten minutes to two the gate was thronging with people, the afternoon shift arriving and the morning leaving.

Jack waited until the crowd was thickest then drove in, parked the BSA close to some other motor-cycles and followed the stream of men and women into the factory.

The shop floor was busy. He picked up a bag of tools and walked around with it, going from building to building. The machines in each of the work shops seemed to be working at full capacity and he understood why a two-shift system had been introduced.

'Excuse me.' He stopped by an older man repairing a fan belt which had broken. 'I'm new here. Where's the boss's office?'

'Two behind this one,' the mechanic hardly looked up. 'You can't miss it.'

'Cheers.'

It was ten minutes to three. He went to the toilets, locked himself in a cubicle and took off the boiler suit. Underneath he wore a collar and tie, and jacket and trousers. He made sure his shoes were clean, rolled the suit into a ball and stuffed it behind the cistern, then made his way to the third floor of the office block. The fourth room on the left was empty, he took a file from a desk, placed it under his arm and walked down the corridor. Exactly on time a middle-aged woman with grey hair came out of the main office and walked past him. He confirmed the name on the door and went in.

The woman sitting at the secretary's desk glanced up at him. There wasn't supposed to be a second secretary, only the one who'd gone for the tea. 'Production quotas. He wants them immediately.'

The woman began to get up. 'Thank you, I'll take them in to him.'

Jack was already past her. 'It's all right, I want to see him anyway.'

He knocked on the door of the inner office, the secretary trying to decide whether she would protest, heard the voice and went in.

The man called Dunster was seated behind a large desk in front of the window. He was in his fifties and wore a smart suit, the jacket of which hung on a hat stand to the right of the door. His sleeves were rolled up and he gave the immediate impression of a man who knew both the cost and the function of every bolt and screw in the entire place.

'Mr Dunster.'

'Yes.' There was an irritation which suggested a temper at being disturbed.

Jack closed the door. 'Your secretary has gone for your tea. When she brings it I suggest you ask her to fetch another cup for your guest.'

'Who the hell are you? What are you doing here?' Dunster reached for the telephone. The hand that came down on his wrist held it so that he could not move.

'I'm here, Mr Dunster, because of your factory. I'm here, Mr Dunster, because of what you are making.' Behind him the secretary knocked on the door and began to open it. He released his hold on the man's wrist and stepped back. The woman came into the room carrying a tray. 'A cup of tea would be very nice, thank you.'

The secretary glanced up for confirmation. Dunster felt the numbness in his wrist and made his decision. 'If you wouldn't mind, Mavis.'

Someone from the Economics Ministry, he thought, he tried to rub the circulation back into his hand, the fear setting in. Worse, one of the bastards from The Citadel or the outfit who had their headquarters at the Grosvenor House.

'Prior to 1939 this factory produced vehicle parts. At the outbreak of war a percentage of your production was switched to the war effort.' It was the third visit Jack had made, in each the response had varied and the pressure he had applied had therefore also differed.

The secretary brought a second cup and left.

'Three months ago, under orders from the Germans, you were again ordered to divert resources to war items.' The colour began to drain from Dunster's face. 'In the first month you produced three thousand units of Part Number 3001 and two thousand seven hundred and fifty of Part Number 5008.' How do you know this, Dunster wanted to ask. Who are you that you know it? 'In the second month output increased by twenty-three per cent.' There was no colour at all left in Dunster's face. 'Last month you produced six thousand units of Part Number 3001 and three thousand three hundred of Part Number 5008.'

'But they were only spares for lorries,' Dunster began to reply.

'We both know, of course, that they can also fit the Panzer I and Panzer II tanks, as well as other *Wehrmacht* vehicles being prepared for the invasion of Russia.' His voice changed slightly. 'I understand the pressures on you. I appreciate the number of people for whom you are responsible. I also know that if there was a way you could help but still look after your people then you would wish to do so.'

'Who are you?' Dunster asked at last.

'Resistance,' said The Watchman.

I want to believe you, the man was thinking, but what if you are not? What if you are trying to trap me?

'Give me a message, it will be broadcast tomorrow night.'

The slide into collaboration had been easy. At first Dunster had not even noticed it; he had a job to do and factory to run, and it had just seemed like carrying on as normal.

'I'm sorry?'

He had not even queried the change in quotas, his concern was for the overall running of the factory rather than the specifics of production. Only in the evenings, when he listened to the broadcasts from the Free North, or when his wife was fast asleep beside him, did he wonder what he should do and whether he had the courage to do anything.

'Give me a message and it will be broadcast tomorrow night.'

When he was young and driven by principles, he used to climb the tree in the back garden and throw the apples down for his wife and daughter. What would it be like to stand beneath the tree as an old man and know that the only time those principles had been tested he had lacked the courage to stand by them?

'There will be a good crop of apples this year.'

The Watchman stood to leave. 'One thing.' He was almost at the door. 'You understand what we do to collaborators and those who betray us?'

You paint a red cross over their mouths to explain why you've shot them, Dunster knew.

'I understand.'

THE EVENING WAS warm and his wife had opened the doors onto the garden at the rear of the house. Dunster poured himself a gin and tonic, turned on the wireless and stood in the doorway looking at the apple tree. The drum sounded and the broadcast from the North began.

'Shouldn't we turn it down a bit, dear? The neighbours might hear.'

He smiled at her as if his mind was somewhere else. If the words were broadcast he was a patriot, with all the honour and danger which that implied. If they were not then he was dead. Or worse.

The news ended, he heard the message, poured himself another drink and stood again in the doorway.

355

'Remember when you used to climb up and throw the apples down for Betty and me?' His wife switched off the wireless.

'I remember.'

AT TEN MINUTES to two the following afternoon Jack Masters again entered the factory. For forty minutes he checked the various ways out which might be open to him should Dunster prove to be a traitor, then made his way to the office on the third floor. Beneath his jacket he carried the Smith & Wesson.

'Good afternoon, Mr Johns,' the younger of the two secretaries greeted him. 'Mr Dunster is expecting you.' Jack wondered where they were waiting for him. She escorted him through to the inner office, asked if they wished to take tea early and closed the door behind her. The fire escape two offices along, Jack thought, the BSA parked by it.

'I heard the message. What do you want me to do?'

There was a knock on the door and the older of the secretaries entered with the tea. They waited until she had poured them each a cup and left the room.

'The main thing is what you *don't* do. You don't do anything which would alert the Germans that you are part of the Resistance.' The words, as the day before, were carefully chosen. 'What you *do* is simple. It's easy, for example, to slip a small amount of sand into an axle bearing, a truck will go hundreds of miles before it breaks down. On a more ambitious level, the aim would be to cut production. Not entirely – that would give the game away – but reduce or impede it so that the Germans are not getting as many parts as they need.'

'That shouldn't be a problem, the equipment is always breaking down. We can make sure it breaks down a little more, lose things, have the problems we always have but more often.'

'But it mustn't show.'

'Don't worry, I'll make sure of that.' If he had committed himself, he thought, then he should commit himself totally. 'There's another way I might be able to help. I obviously know when shipments are going from this factory but sometimes there are special shipments, not just from here but from other places as well.'

'How do they happen?'

'By train. We have a siding into the works. Then they're loaded onto a larger train with the other materials. I don't know where that would be.'

The networks on the railways would know. 'How frequent are these special cargoes?'

'Infrequent, but you're lucky. The next one is on Sunday.'

THE SITTING-ROOM of the house at the heart of the training school at Arisaig was panelled with wood and filled with large, comfortable furniture. The windows were tall and narrow and the logs were smouldering in the huge fireplace. The walls were covered with paintings – Highland watercolours and oils, and ancestral portraits of the family who owned the lodge, and above the fireplace hung a set of massive antlers. The bar was in the corner of the room to the right of the fireplace, the latest intake of recruits relaxing and talking to their instructors. Drake accepted a whisky and joined them.

Even in the past month the training centre had grown, matching the networks in the field. In addition to the training staff, there had been an expansion of technicians and scientists, as well as administration. The signals section had also been expanded, but because it was now also shared with other departments, including SOE, SIS and, less frequently, MI(R), it had been moved to its own premises and messages were brought by despatch rider to each department, and encoded and decoded by department rather than in the signals room as had originally been the case. In the granite building with the façade of innocence at the front and the secret entrance at the rear, Drake now had a personal assistant as well as a number of other officers who dealt with the collation of information from the field and recruitment.

The conversation in the lounge appeared light-hearted; under the veil of seeming relaxation, however, one of the women in the group had already referred to a boyfriend in Berkshire. The following morning she would be asked to report to the office on the second floor and told that she was being returned to her unit.

An orderly threaded his way across the room and handed Drake a sealed envelope. 'Just arrived by despatch rider, sir.' It was probably the general about his car, one of the instructors joked. Drake slit the envelope open and read the signal.

SPECIAL RAIL CONVOY FROM ALL REPEAT ALL SOURCES NEXT SUNDAY. RECOMMEND ATTACK. APPRECIATE IMPLICATIONS. IF AFFIRMATIVE SUGGEST OTHER RAIL ATTACKS AS COVER. AM PROCEEDING IN CASE AGREEMENT.

'Excuse me a moment.' Drake smiled at the recruits around him, nothing in his manner suggesting the significance of the message, and left the room. In his office he telephoned the code room at headquarters and dictated the reply, knowing the operator in the South would have been given a second schedule for it.

'Assume affirmative.' There was little time for either of them to make the arrangements. 'Decision tomorrow.'

Appreciate implications. There were two, each racked by contradictions. Drake poured himself a whisky from the cabinet at the side of the desk and considered what The Watchman had meant. The role of the Resistance was to equip and prepare for Liberation and their part in it, not necessarily to engage in acts of sabotage or aggression prior to it. Any such action might interrupt that preparation and bring notice to themselves, but the enemy knew of their existence anyway. An attack on the rail convoy might also indicate to the enemy that the Resistance had intelligence on the convoy, and might therefore jeopardize the security of the person supplying that information. The enemy, however, must already know of the existence of an agent because of the disappearance of the traitor Bailey, but, he hoped, not the level and type of information to which that agent had access.

Drake lifted the telephone again.

'Get me the Prime Minister.'

THE WEEKEND PARTY given by Lord Southerton included only eight guests. Walter Schellenberg and Fiona Egerton-Smith travelled separately on the Friday evening and spent most of the next day riding. As was his custom when guests were present, Southerton insisted that his staff be in full attendance all weekend and that those who did not live in report for duty early and stay until given permission to leave. On Saturday evening, therefore, even though there had been little for them to do and despite the fact that they would both begin at four the following morning, it was not until nine o'clock that the gamekeeper and his assistant took their normal places at The Fighting Cocks pub in the centre of the village where they lived.

For a Saturday evening, both men thought, the pub was a little quiet, one or two of the regulars missing. At half-past ten the gamekeeper's assistant went outside; at the rear of the pub was a small brick lean-to, but on a summer's evening he preferred to stand against the trees. As he was doing up his trousers the beam of headlights swept past him and he ducked, catching his head on a branch and swearing. The bus stopped, the girls got off and the bus pulled away.

'Lucky it was only your head you bumped, Tommy Smith.'

The assistant recognized the voice and knew they had seen him, were laughing at him. They were home early from the dance in Tonbridge, he thought, knew what they normally did and how they operated – one always assigned to finding someone with a van or car to give them a lift home. Bus, he laughed; somebody must have failed. The girls said good-night to each other and split up. Tommy fastened the rest of his trouser buttons and hurried after Rosie Clifford.

'Walk you home, Rosie?'

She pretended to ignore him but slowed down. He fell in beside her and they walked up the hill towards the terrace of houses where she lived.

'I'd better go in. Mum will be worried if I don't.'

'Why, where's your old man tonight?'

They reached the first of the houses.

'Out somewhere, he told Mum he'd be late.' The bedroom light was on. 'Looks like she's already gone to bed.' Rosie brushed deliberately against him as she pretended to leave.

Little bitch, he thought, hotter than hell.

'I'd better let Mum know I'm back, she'll go to sleep then.' She was still against him, teasing him.

'I'll wait.'

'Who said I was coming back?' She laughed and ran inside. Her handbag was still on the road beside him.

THE MOON WAS bright and round above them and the evening warm.

'All right, Charlie, George.' The organizer stopped by the two men assigned to the B torch.

'I was just thinking it was closing time. Wondered if they've missed us.'

'Shouldn't think so,' said the man crouched beside him. 'Not dominoes night, is it?' They had been together in the original Auxiliary Unit.

'Always blame Milly, I suppose.' The conversation helped pass the time.

'What, say you had to help her with the sewing?'

The organizer looked bemused.

'Charlie's wife does a bit of sewing on the side,' the man called George explained. 'Good at it, too. Did a shirt for me last week.'

The organizer began to reply then heard the noise. 'Here they are.' He ran to his position downwind and signalled on his torch. The Whitley circled once, the flare path bright and clear below it, then came in again. The three parachutes puffed into shape behind it and the plane disappeared into the night.

The containers on the chutes were heavy. The men disconnected them, one of the drivers reversed the pick-up into position and the others lifted them on. Charlie and George carried the chutes into the woods and buried them in the holes they had already dug.

'Nice bit of silk, this.' George shovelled the earth onto them. 'Be all right for your Rosie's wedding dress.'

'Not yet I bloody well hope.' Charlie packed the earth hard and pulled the bracken over the top.

By midnight the containers were hidden in a barn less than half a mile from the drop zone, and the Argos network had returned home. The following morning, having confirmed that the drop had been secure and the cache untouched, five of them returned to the barn. The organizer and another man were waiting.

The containers were six feet long and eighteen inches in diameter, and divided into three sections, each filled with a variety of items. Two sections of the third canister contained weapons and ammunition, and the third was packed with plastic explosive, detonators and pressure pads. That afternoon the explosives were hidden in a second location fifteen miles from the drop zone and, the men of the Argos network had no reason to know, a little under one and a half miles from the point at which The Watchman and the sabotage expert who had visited them that morning had decided was the optimum point to attack the special convoy should the action receive final confirmation. That evening The Watchman held his third meeting with the organizer who dealt with the Resistance network centred on the railway system.

SUNDAY BREAKFAST AT Lord Southerton's was served late. The meal was almost finished when Schellenberg was informed by a butler that there was a telephone call for him. He recognized Straube's voice immediately. When the *Sturmbannführer* informed him that the *Reichsstatthalter* had requested him to attend a special meeting at twelve-thirty Schellenberg knew what was to be announced.

He arrived at the headquarters of the *Reichsstatthalter* ten minutes early. The others in the meeting room were not those normally present at the regular committees but a range of high-ranking officers from the *Wehrmacht*, the *Abwehr*, and the Economics Ministry, mostly generals and including the *Kommissar* himself.

The room had been specially decorated, a large portrait of Hitler over the fireplace and swastikas hanging either side of it. The table which ran down the centre of the room was laden with food, and the champagne glasses were bright and sparkling in the lights of the chandelier above.

At twelve-thirty precisely the double doors at the top of the room opened and the *Reichsstatthalter* entered, rows of medals on his dress uniform and an aide on either side and he took his place at the head of the table.

'Gentlemen, I have requested the pleasure of your attendance today at the express wishes of the Führer.' The expectation ran round the table. 'He has asked me to pass the great news to you personally.' He cleared his throat. 'At seven this morning, the Führer ordered Operation Barbarossa. Even as I speak our tanks and infantry are crossing into Russia.' He clapped his hands, the door opened again and a line of orderlies marched in, each bearing a magnum of champagne, and filled the glasses on the table.

'*Heil Hitler.*'

They stood and toasted the Führer.

The conversation which followed was centred on which divisions were engaged at what points of the battle, the expectations from Berlin on the duration of the campaign and the confidence that it would be over by Christmas. Only after ten minutes did Schellenberg intervene.

'May I ask what this means for the plans to complete the conquest of Britain and remove the remaining opposition in the North?'

The *Reichsstatthalter* was in expansive mood. 'What it means, Herr *Gruppenführer*, is that the tiny problem of the North has been temporarily shelved whilst we deal with the Bolsheviks.' There was a ripple of agreement round the table. The only men who distanced themselves from it, Schellenberg noted, were the military. 'When we have won the rest of the war I don't think we'll have too much trouble with Churchill and his ragbag.'

FRAN SAT IN the kitchen, switched on the wireless and tuned it to the broadcast from the Free North. She heard the signal on the drum then the news began. Half-way through the jamming began to take effect and the voice was interrupted by the announcer from London.

'This morning the forces of the Reich began the invasion of Russia. It is confidently expected that they will be in Moscow within the month.'

Everything had been in vain, she felt depression sweeping over her: if Hitler can conquer Russia then what's the hope for us.

The jamming cleared and the messages began.

In the safe house forty miles away The Watchman switched off the set and left to confirm that the Argos network had heard the stand-by and was in position. In his office in the building overlooking the river in the Free North Drake waited for the telephone call which he knew would come. Barbarossa was six weeks late; perhaps the sacrifices in Greece, Yugoslavia and Crete had not been in vain, perhaps the gamble which they had discussed at the Glamis conference had paid off. The telephone rang, he picked it up and pressed the scrambler.

'You heard.'

'Yes, Prime Minister.'

'Both the Ambassador and the Security Exchange Commission have spoken to their contacts in Washington. The United States Government has received notification from their Embassies in Berlin and Moscow that Hitler's statement that he has invaded Russia is correct.'

There was a silence.

'I have been trying to imagine,' Churchill continued, 'what our people in the South must be feeling. How they must be reacting to the news.'

Drake understood what he meant – how morale, already low, might wither and die.

'The Watchman is ready?'

'The stand-by codes were transmitted at six.'

'In that case signal affirmative and wish him good hunting.'

'Thank you, Prime Minister.'

OF THE THIRTY personal messages transmitted at nine, ten were repeats of codes that had also been transmitted three hours before, and of those ten six were genuine. At ten minutes past nine Jack left the safe house and went to the meeting place. The Argos organizer and the explosives expert were waiting and the organizer from the railway networks came in close behind him.

'The convoy was assembled this afternoon. It will leave the depot at ten-thirty and will pass your location at eleven-fifteen. It will be eighteen carriages long, with locomotives at the front and rear. The crew is entirely German. No one else is allowed near it.'

'You're sure about the timings?'

'We control the signal boxes and junctions. Our people will make sure that the convoy sticks to the timings I've given you.'

'What about other trains?'

'One train is scheduled to pass at five minutes to eleven, give or take a couple of minutes. It is a German troop train, so we have not been able to stop it, but if it looks like arriving at your spot any later, we'll delay the special.'

The area outside was clear, they left the house and made their way towards the start point. Half a mile from it they left the track, cut across the edge of a field, and stopped. The organizer barked like a fox. From the thick of the hedge to their left came the reply. They moved forward again. The moon was almost full above them, the night so clear that it was almost unreal. A good night for a drop, Jack thought.

The men inside the barn were clustered round a tilly lamp checking their weapons, their vehicles concealed and guarded.

'The target tonight is a train.' Jack kept the briefing short. 'A specific train, not the line. We will therefore be using pressure pads.' All day the nerves had consumed him, now he felt cold and detached, the nerves disappeared totally yet the fear still in him, making him alert. 'The ambush point is on a bend, the ground rising above it and falling away below. Three of you cover the ground above, and two below. The last two stay to look after the way out and the cars.' He had already suggested that the organizer, George and Charlie should lead a group each. 'We have fifteen minutes to set the charges after the train before the one we want. As soon as they're in place we get out. We don't think the enemy is expecting us, but if there's a problem, you cover us until the job is done. Any questions?'

There were none.

They left the start point and crossed the fields, The Watchman and the saboteur carrying backpacks with the explosives they would use that night, plus their personal weapons, and the men who would cover them carrying sub-machine-guns. A thin layer of cloud cut across the moon like a knife then drifted away. They moved east, across a small stream and around the handful of farms between the start point and the target, then came to the beginning of the hill and climbed the sharp incline to the line itself. It was eighteen minutes to eleven. The men who would form the top lookouts moved past them and The Watchman and the saboteur searched along the rail to the point on the curve where they would place the first explosive.

'Here.'

The demolitions expert indicated the point where the two rails on the outer side of the curve joined. The Watchman held the torch in one hand and shielded its light with the other while the saboteur examined it and confirmed his decision. In the precious minutes between the two trains there would be no time to waste searching for the join between the two rails again. They built a small cairn of stones six inches high, moved back down the track and decided where they would place the other charges.

It was time for the other train, almost time for the convoy. The night was still calm, there was no sound of a train, no reverberation on the rails themselves. Already five to eleven. They went back to the cairn of stones and climbed the slope immediately above it. 'Come *on*,' Jack heard the saboteur whispering to himself. They took the rucksacks from their backs and opened them.

'Here she comes.'

She was late – only five minutes before the convoy was due. The train was suddenly level with them, they heard the noise and saw the flash of lights from the windows, then the hiss and smell of the steam and it was past.

'Come on.'

They picked up the rucksacks and ran down the slope. Thank Christ they had marked the spot, didn't have to waste time. The saboteur crouched over the point where the two rails joined and pulled the first charge from his bag, The Watchman again shading the torch.

Plastic explosive against the inside of the outer line by the fish-plate connecting the rails so that the charge would blow outwards and take the engine and first trucks or carriages with it. Pressure pad clipped over the top of the rail then crimped onto the fuse and the fuse onto the detonator, the detonator pressed onto the charge.

'Well done.' The Watchman kept his voice low and calm. Almost time to go, the blood was pounding in his ears, almost time to clear the area. 'Plenty of time.'

The saboteur placed the reserve charge in position and they moved back down the line. Twenty paces, no need to waste time being precise. The saboteur felt in his bag for the next explosives, behind him The Watchman unrolled the cordtex, cut a length, and pressed one end into the first charge and the other into the second. Once the first blew the rest would detonate automatically.

They moved back another thirty yards and repeated the process. 'Bit short of time?'

'Just a bit.' They were up and running again, setting the next charge.

'That's enough.' The Watchman whistled to the lookouts. 'Let's go.' The men appeared over the top and slithered down the slope. Jack glanced at his watch. The special was already five minutes late, the men on the railway had done a good job. 'Move out. Should be here any moment.' They were at the hedge at the bottom of the field, through it, across the next field and the stream, the next hedge. The Watchman stopped to check they were together and pulled the saboteur through, the thorns tearing his clothes and hands.

In the distance they heard the convoy.

THE TELEPHONE RANG. Drake picked it up and knew it would be the signals room.

'The Prime Minister,' the sergeant on the security desk informed him. 'Just arriving.'

'Thank you.' Just like Churchill, Drake thought, he should have known what The Old Man would do. He dialled the operations room and asked for the duty officer.

'Nothing yet.' The man mistook the reason Drake had contacted him.

'The Prime Minister has just arrived. He'll want to come up.'

'I'll lay on tea and sandwiches.'

There was a knock on the door and Winston Churchill entered, the four members of his bodyguard close behind him. On his head he wore a bowler hat and between his teeth was clenched a cigar.

'Bored waiting. Anything yet?'

'Not yet, sir. I'm going to operations now.'

Churchill nodded and followed him. As they entered the operations room the men and women manning the system stood to attention. Churchill waved at them to sit and shook hands with the duty officer. The Old Man was playing at what he was good at, Drake saw the impact on those in the room. An orderly arrived with a tray of mugs and corned beef sandwiches; Churchill helped himself and sat down.

The night was quiet. In the street outside they heard the roar of a motor-cycle and the screeching of brakes, then silence again.

'The Watchman?' Churchill queried.

'Not yet. He'll clear the area before he transmits, won't have his radio operator anywhere near the target.'

A security guard entered the room and gave the duty officer the envelope the despatch rider had delivered, the man slit it open and handed it to a clerk for decoding. Two minutes later she returned and gave it to the officer.

MUSHROOM SUCCESSFUL REPEAT MUSHROOM SUCCESSFUL.

'Important junction just outside London.' Drake took the decoded message and showed it to Churchill. 'Should stop all trains for days.'

'Acknowledge and out,' the duty officer wrote the message for transmission to the field and gave it to the clerk.

'One moment.' Churchill took the paper from the woman, sat

down again, rummaged in the inside pocket of his coat until he found a pen, then crossed out the words the duty officer had written and substituted his own. 'With your permission, of course.' He handed what he had written to Drake.

Drake read it and imagined what the woman in the field would think, alone and frightened, hoping to Christ the schedule would end before the traces fixed on her and praying to God she would see another day; the men as well, still high on the adrenaline of the operation, some of them still running for home. 'Thank you, Prime Minister. It is greatly appreciated.' He passed the message to the clerk for encoding.

CONGRATULATIONS ON SUCCESSFUL OPERATION. HIS MAJESTY KING GEORGE INFORMED. WINSTON CHURCHILL.

'The scrambler to Canada,' the Prime Minister requested the duty officer.

'Where would you like to take it, sir?'

'Here.'

The connection took forty minutes, during which time two more signals were received, each reporting successful attacks.

At twenty minutes to two the Prime Minister was connected with the King in Canada. He stood up from his chair and placed the cigar in the ashtray.

'Your Majesty, I am speaking to you from the operations room of the British Resistance. It is my honour to inform you that units of the Resistance tonight carried out the first organized attacks against the forces of occupation. The primary target was that which was the subject of our recent discussions in Canada. I have, in your name, sent a message of thanks to those involved in the operations.'

He waited while the King questioned him. 'No, Your Majesty, we have received no word as yet from The Watchman. Yes, Your Majesty, I will inform you immediately I hear.'

He replaced the receiver and looked around the room. 'The King asks me to pass to all concerned his personal gratitude. I would like, ladies and gentlemen, to add my own.' He turned to the duty officer. 'How about some more tea?'

By two-thirty confirmations of successful attacks had been received from four of the networks operating that night, an hour after that from all except the network with which The Watchman was working. At twenty minutes to four they heard for the last time that night the roar of a motor-cycle in the streets outside then the running of feet. Within ninety seconds the message was being decoded. They stood watching the cipher clerk, seeing the concentration on her face then the relief and the suggestion of a tear in her eye as she passed the message pad to the Prime Minister.

'Canada again,' Churchill asked the duty officer.

It was almost the longest day of the year. Outside it would soon be getting light. When the Prime Minister had spoken to the King he and Drake left the house and stood in the garden at the rear, the mist hanging over the river.

'I have been thinking this evening about the state of our people in the Occupied South.' Churchill showed no signs of tiredness. 'Morale is low, they still have not recovered from the shock of invasion and Occupation.' Drake knew what he was going to say. 'It seems to me that it is not only necessary for there to be a Resistance, but for people to *know* there is. I therefore intend to broadcast a message informing the people of tonight's actions.'

The first red seeped into the grey to the east.

'It also seems to me that it will not be sufficient simply to tell the people of the Resistance. They will need something more, something they can hold on to. Something which will fire their imaginations and raise their spirits.'

The Germans already knew, Drake told himself, the Lice knew, the only people who did not know were the British themselves. 'All I ask, Prime Minister, is that you say nothing which might endanger his personal security.'

'Of course not.' The voice was that which Churchill reserved for such moments. 'Why destroy the myth before we have even created it?' He stopped and looked up at the sky. 'I wonder which bloody general has lodged himself at Chartwell.'

WHEN FRAN WALKED to the village on Monday afternoon, in the square where the single truck of German soldiers was normally parked there were three personnel carriers, the soldiers in and around them alert and on edge. She went past the schoolhouse and into the post office.

'What's up with them?'

Even if she did not know the post mistress always had a good explanation. 'Something happened last night, hush-hush.' She tapped the side of her nose and turned to the door as another customer came in.

That evening as usual Fran turned on the wireless and tuned it to the Free North. At nine exactly she heard the morse code and the voice of the announcer.

'This is the voice of Britain talking to the people of Britain. The Prime Minister, the Right Honourable Winston Churchill.'

We've lost. She remembered the news of the German advance into Russia and felt the despair consume her. We've finally given in.

'I am speaking to you from the seat of government in the Free North.' The jammers were already trying to stop the broadcast, Fran tuned the dial slightly and picked up the message again. 'Last night I spoke to His Majesty the King. He asked me to pass to you the great pride he feels in the way you have all refused to bow to the foe.'

The voice was the growl she remembered from the days before invasion; she motioned for Boy Jack to listen. 'He has asked me to pass his most sincere thoughts to those who have worked so hard to maintain the spirit and well-being of the people of this land.'

He thanked those in local government and the public services, the hospitals and the factories, the doctors and the railwaymen, the firemen and the police force. He thanked the miners and the women in the work places and the homes. At no time did he even mention the advance into Russia.

There was a pause and Fran felt the tension begin to wind.

'I told you once that we would fight on the beaches and in the streets. I said that we would never surrender.' The power was again in the voice. 'My duty tonight is to inform you that this is still the case.'

She felt the shivering in her spine and wondered what he was going to say.

'Last night, in operations across the entire Occupied South, the forces of The Watchman struck the first blows toward Liberation. Last night The Watchman, his men and women armed and equipped from the Free North, carried out a series of actions which have severely damaged the position of the oppressor in our land.'

It did not matter if he were exaggerating, she thought, remembering the propaganda in the newspapers in the weeks between the sending of the British Expeditionary Force to Norway and the invasion of England. It did not matter that in all probability The Watchman did not exist.

'Last night His Majesty King George commanded that these words be sent to The Watchman and his people: "When the darkness is over and the dawn is near, we shall all remember how we have placed ourselves in your hands."

'Good luck and God bless you.'

4

THE SUN BURNT into her back and her spine ached with a pain which she thought would never go away. One more hour, Mary told herself, then the whistle will blow and the *Kapo* will tell us to stop work and march us back into the camp. At her side Annie was coughing, chipping at the stones, her hands bleeding. Thank God tomorrow is Sunday, Mary thought, thank God tomorrow is a day of rest. She tightened the rags around her hands.

What will it be like in winter? What will it be like when we're cold with snow and the water at our feet has turned to ice?

She heard the whistle and realized that Annie was too weak to stand. The others were already forming into blocks, five by five; she helped the woman up and into line, encouraging her and reminding her that the next day was a rest day. There must be a way out of this, there must be a way they could survive. They joined the third block from the end and shuffled the half-mile back to the camp, the SS guards counting them in.

The woman with whom they had shared the bunk for the past three weeks was already there, a blanket wrapped round her and her eyes staring. Mary went to the washroom and splashed the ice-cold water over herself, then she and Annie joined the food queue. The workers from the Organization carried the containers from the kitchen and spooned the single cubes of margarine into their bowls. As they went back into the block the chief came out. You're the bastard who sends us to the work *Kommando* each day. Mary felt her anger rising. You're the one who's killing us just as surely and ruthlessly as the SS. The woman was almost opposite her. No point in making trouble, Mary tried to control herself, every point in not making it worse for yourself or Annie. The Organization controlled everything, dictated who went on the work *Kommandos* and who stayed behind. She smiled at the woman and stepped to one side so that she could pass.

The woman with whom they shared a bunk shuffled past, not seeing Mary, almost knocking her over. The woman's eyes were fixed and the blanket was still clutched tight around her. Her feet moved automatically and the top of her body rocked with each step, as if she were in a trance. Stop her, Mary wanted to shout. You all know what she is going to do. For God's sake stop her. Do something yourself, don't simply tell them to do it. Nothing you can do, she knew, nothing anyone can do now. The woman stepped off the path and onto the forbidden stretch of grass inside the inner of the electrified perimeter fences. Shoot her, Mary silently urged the guards in the watchtower twenty yards away, don't let her suffer. The woman looked to her left and right and shuffled forward. She must have seen it before, Mary thought, must realize that the power in the electricity would not kill her immediately, that death would come slowly and painfully. The woman reached the edge of the grass and threw herself like a crucifix onto the wire.

Find a way to survive, Mary resolved. Find a way into the Organization for Annie and yourself before they take your life from you or you take it yourself. But find a way so that you can survive with dignity.

THE AFTERNOON WAS hot and the threat of thunder hung in the air. For days now it had been building up, the atmosphere growing increasingly humid and the sky clear yet colourless. In the village the mothers who waited for their children outside the schoolroom grew listless and apathetic; at the farm even the animals seemed burdened and slow. As Fran passed through the churchyard the leaves on the trees and the flowers on the plants were dull and lifeless. July, going into August. It was the mood and the weather they would normally expect two weeks later. Cricket practice this evening if the weather held off.

She passed the vicarage and entered the village. Harry Downton and two of the young men who clustered round him like moths were lounging in the door of the grocer's shop. Wednesday. Also the afternoon, she remembered, when Harry Downton's wife went to Canterbury. She ignored him and went past. Just time to see Ned before Boy Jack came out of school. The woman who smiled at her as she passed was pushing a pram, the child in it nine months and laughing at the cut-out shapes of coloured cardboard the mother had hung across the top. The woman was young, no more than twenty; her husband was serving overseas and had not seen his daughter. Fran smiled back, the woman crossed the road towards the grocer's shop, and Fran turned into the lane behind Ned's house. If anything the afternoon was becoming heavier and more humid. The headache hammered across her forehead and the back of her throat was sore and dry. What they needed was a good storm, Quizzie Lizzie in the post office would have told anyone who asked, something to clear the air, put them all back on course.

Ned was in the garden at the rear of the house weeding his vegetables. When he saw her he dug the fork in the ground and wiped his hands on the back of his trousers.

'Cup of tea?'

Ned was the crossroads to which those at the gathering points of the network funnelled the men and women on the run. Sometimes she wondered how much he understood of what had been created, of the organization that took over once he had passed the increasing numbers of escapers to her. In the past two weeks alone ten people had passed through the network and begun their journey north. Even allowing for the fact that some had been waiting, Fran had been surprised at the scale.

'Cup of tea would be great, Ned.' She followed him through the garden and into the house.

'It looks as though we're in business again.' The cool of the kitchen was a temporary relief from the humidity outside.

'Who?' If Ned was talking in the house about the escape route it meant that his wife was absent.

'Soldiers from the camp. I've arranged the documents.'

'I'll start getting them moved tomorrow.' The load was already becoming too much for her, already she was having to spend too much time away from the farm. She would have to reorganize things, recruit more people. 'They're in the normal place?'

'Yes.'

'Tell them ten o'clock.'

She left the postman's house and walked into the square, a hundred yards away the vicar was talking to one of the church wardens, the two men looking at the sky.

The moment Fran heard the baby's cry she knew where it was coming from and what was happening. Not this time, she thought, and began to run. Brian Markham saw her and ran as well.

The door of the grocer's shop was closed but not locked. Fran pushed it open and went in. The pram was just inside the door, the baby crying. In the half-dark at the end of the shop she saw the group of men and the red and white of the dress. The woman was stretched over the sacks of flour, her clothes pulled up to her waist, two of the men holding her down and a third stifling her screams. Harry Downton was over her, breathing on her, trying to pull her legs open.

'Come on, my lovely. You know you want it really.' He reached down and began to undo his trousers. The woman was still trying to scream. 'Me first, boys, then you can have your turn.' He heard the door slam and looked round, saw Fran, began to laugh, then saw the shape of the vicar behind her.

'Bugger.' He stood back and began to do up his trousers, knowing the boys would laugh at his joke. 'Just coming, Vicar.'

The woman was shaking, beginning to cry. Fran pushed the men out of the way and helped her up. 'It's all right now.' She smoothed her clothes and tried to comfort, her arm around her. 'It's all over now.' Thank God she had heard the baby; thank God the vicar had seen her run.

'Slip of the hand, Reverend.' Harry Downton winked at the vicar and challenged him to do something. 'Sure you understand.'

He walked back behind the counter. 'Now what can I get for you?'

It was unreal. They had just caught the bastard and his cronies trying to rape someone, the rest of the village standing outside, knowing what was going on but doing nothing about it, and now it was as if they were back to normal, as if Fran and the vicar were there simply because they wanted to buy something.

'Can of condensed milk, please.'

Is that all you can say, Fran wanted to shout. Why does everyone put up with him? What's happening to the village that nobody has done anything about him, allowed him to be like this? She began to help the woman push the pram out the door and the vicar turned to

374

help. If you don't sort him out, Vicar, then I will. The message in her eyes was clear and unmistakable. She did not know what she would do, could do, only knew that she would do something.

'Cricket practice tonight, Vicar?' The grocer reached for the milk and put it on the counter.

'Afraid not, meeting of the ladies' committee.' The vicar turned back to him and felt in his pocket for some change. 'On the other hand, why not?'

'Exactly, Reverend, why not?' The grocer made no attempt to hide the sarcasm in his voice.

The woman was sobbing, huge bitter sobs, her shoulders rising and falling. Fran stood by her and tried to decide what to do and where to take her and the child. The vicar came out of the shop. 'You all right?' It was a stupid thing for him to say, they all knew, understood there was nothing else he could say.

'I have something to arrange.' He produced the can of milk. 'I wonder if you would mind dropping this off, I'm sure Mrs Markham would be glad to make you both a cup of tea.' He put the milk in the pram and held the mother's hand. 'I know it must have been terrible for you, all I can do is promise that it will never happen again.'

In the doorway of the shop the four men were still laughing at them. How can you say that, the woman wanted to ask, frightened even to look at the shop. All the village knows what's going on, but everyone is afraid. Not just afraid. Numb. As if the Occupation has drained everything from them.

'Don't worry,' the vicar patted her arm. 'Everything will be taken care of.'

Not just Jack and Ted, Fran began to understand, there must have been more in the local Resistance than the two of them. Brian Markham the vicar and Stan Bradley the publican and poacher, too. That was why they had looked after the farm and taken such special care of her and Sarah and Helen when they had returned. Not the vicar, she rebuked herself, not the man of peace.

When Fran looked back he had disappeared into the King's Arms.

BY EIGHT O'CLOCK cricket practice was almost over and the men were talking about going to the pub. Storm tonight, they all agreed, the clouds were already gathering.

375

'Fancy a quick bowl before you go, Vicar?' It was Ned.

'Can we stay and watch, Mum?' Boy Jack asked.

Fran remembered what the vicar's wife had told her that afternoon, knew what was going to happen. 'Yes, you can stay and watch.'

Brian Markham shook his head. Too many sherries already, Harry Downton laughed, either that or not enough.

'Come on, Vicar,' Stan Bradley picked up a bat and began to walk to the nets. 'Just a quick over.'

The trap set, the poacher now baiting it. It was all so natural yet so organized. Just like the way The Caretaker conducted his affairs, Fran supposed.

The vicar seemed uncertain, as if he were anxious not to spoil the fun.

'Yes, come on, Vicar.' Harry Downton pushed Stan Bradley aside, winked to his supporters, anticipating the fun he was about to have, and went to the nets.

'Very well.'

The vicar trundled to the stump and the ball looped from his hand and struck the side netting, not even reaching the batsman. 'Oh, well bowled, Vicar.' The grocer walked forward and hit the ball back. The bowler trundled in again, the ball still too wide to hit. 'Try again, Vicar.' He came in again. Harry Downton struck the ball hard and shouted to one of the boys to retrieve it then glanced at his followers. 'Come on, Vicar, I'll give you a catch.'

In front of the pavilion the men stood and watched as the vicar bowled, Harry Downton hitting the ball hard and low straight back at him, the intention undisguised, the vicar stopping it and the leather stinging his hand. Brian Markham took off his sweater and draped it on the bowling stump. 'Mean business now, do we, Vicar?' Brian came in again, the ball still slow and easy to hit. The grocer stepped forward and struck the ball back even harder, face height.

'Take it easy, Harry.' There was genuine concern in the voice. Not the vicar, the boys watched. What are you doing to the vicar? Why doesn't somebody stop him?

'Had enough, Vicar?'

'Go on, Harry.' It was one of the men from the shop. 'Let him have one more over.'

'All right, one more.'

Something different, Boy Jack noticed, almost as if the vicar were pacing out his run-up. At the side of the nets Stan Bradley edged slightly to his left so that he was between the vicar and Harry Downton's allies.

Brian Markham came in, the run-up slow and relaxed, and bowled. The ball whipped under the bat and took out the middle stump. There was a burst of nervous applause. Careful, Vicar, they thought, don't rile him. Whatever you do, don't put his back up. He walked up to the wicket and put the stump back in its place. In the pavilion they saw he was saying something to the grocer but could not hear what.

'Exodus twenty, Harry. Verses one to seventeen.' The run-up was longer and the ball faster, hitting the stumps before the grocer had moved his feet. The vicar came forward to replace them and saw the puzzlement on the grocer's face. 'The Ten Commandments.'

The run-up was five paces; the ball flew off the grass and hit Harry Downton on the shoulder before he could move. The run-up was ten paces; the ball struck the ground short of the wicket and flew over the stumps. The run-up was fifteen paces; they could hardly follow the ball. The run-up was twenty paces; the ball bounced head high.

Brian had played a lot of cricket as a young man, Mabel Markham had said as she poured tea that afternoon, Cambridge blue, played in the varsity match against Oxford. Bowler actually, as fast as Larwood some said. *Harold Larwood, Boy Jack would have told her, MCC tour of Australia, the so-called Bodyline series. Couldn't bowl the great Don Bradman out so they went for his body.* Lined up to play for Surrey – Mabel had offered them scones and jam – then it happened: almost killed a man, fractured his skull, never bowled again. She had smiled and poured them another cup of tea. I think that was one of the things which decided him to enter the church.

The Reverend Brian Markham walked down the wicket and picked up the ball, came to the last commandment.

'Thou shalt not covet thy neighbour's house.' He was looking straight into Harry Downton's eyes. 'Nor thy neighbour's wife.'

The grocer's allies moved towards the nets, tried to step past Stan. He shook his head.

'Not your business.'

The run-up was twenty-five paces, the movement as if in slow motion. Not the Lord of Peace, Fran thought of the images on the stained-glass windows of the church, the God of War, the visitation of the Angel of Death. The Resistance, too: Jack and Ted and Stan and Brian. The movement still seemed in slow motion, every person present seeing every single moment, the ball coming off the pitch, rising, striking Downton between his legs and rupturing its way into his genitals.

The Reverend Markham took his sweater off the bowling stump and walked up to the nets.

'Slip of the hand, Harry. Sure you understand.'

In the sky above the coast they saw the first lightning and felt the first drop of rain.

THE MEETING WITH the six escapers from the prison camp was the following morning; one of the men was a major, two were captains, one a lieutenant, one a sergeant and the last a private. At that meeting Fran questioned them on the camp and the details of their escape, as well as their plans for going north, then informed them that the necessary paperwork was not yet available and that they would have to wait. The following day she cross-examined them again. Only on the third day, when she was as satisfied as she could be, did she make her selection. That evening she met them in the safe house where they had been hidden and gave the major and one of the captains their false identity papers.

'We're splitting you to make it easier. You two go tonight, the others tomorrow.'

The major began to protest that if they were divided it should be down the middle, and Fran knew she had been right.

'Orders,' she told him sharply. 'I obey them. You as well.'

The next afternoon she returned to the safe house with new identities and fresh sets of clothes for three of the four men remaining. As soon as she opened the door she felt the anticipation – that night they would begin their walk to freedom.

'You're not going north.'

She gave the captain his identity papers. 'You will follow the escape route to Wales. A base is already being established there for men who have escaped from the camps.'

'A secret army?'

Fran nodded. 'When the arms are available it will be supplied from the North and await its orders for Liberation. Your job is to recruit men from other camps who have escaped to there and give them their orders.'

There was no indication what those orders were. Fran turned to the sergeant and private and gave them their new papers. 'You two are now couriers in the escape circuit. Your job will be to escort escapers to Wales or the Free North as the case may be.'

She faced the lieutenant. 'How easy was it to escape from the camp?'

'Not too difficult.'

'Good.'

'Why?'

'Because you're going back.'

The man's look froze.

'There are nearly five thousand highly trained soldiers in the camp, few of them can get to Wales. Your job is to organize them inside and act as communication point for instructions from the North. Arms caches will be prepared outside, there will need to be diversion plans to cover a mass break-out when you receive the order. If any key people are included in the lists of those being sent as labour to Germany you will have to get them off them.'

The captain Fran was sending to Wales understood the function of the men he would select there.

'Your people will return to the camps they escaped from and do the same thing,' Fran confirmed.

That night the four men left, the captain to Wales, the two couriers to familiarize themselves with the escape networks, and the lieutenant to break back into the prison camp. Two nights later observers reported morse confirmation by torch that he was safely inside.

CHARLIE CLIFFORD WOKE at seven, even though it was a Sunday, dressed without waking his wife or his daughter in the other bedroom, went downstairs and boiled a kettle, partly for a cup of tea and partly for some hot water to shave. On the night of what the Argos network already referred to simply as 'the railway job' he had reached home at five. At breakfast that morning his wife had not asked him where he had been and he had not told her. That evening, when they listened to the Prime Minister on the wireless, he guessed that she suspected though she had not questioned him on the subject and he had no intention of telling her.

The house in which he and Milly had lived for the past twenty years was in a terrace on a hill on the edge of the village. At the rear was a cobbled yard onto which the houses backed, each house having an outbuilding on the far side of the yard and in which Charlie kept the rabbits he bred. Behind the outbuildings were a set of allotments.

When he had washed and drunk his tea he went to the outbuildings and killed, and skinned and dressed one of the rabbits for their dinner. By the time he returned to the house Milly and Rosie were clearing up from breakfast. He sat at the table while Milly went to what they called the front room and started the sewing machine, and Rosie made him tea and toast.

Sometimes, he thought, the factory work had changed her, made her grow up too quickly. Sometimes, he also worried, she might get up to a little too much at the dances she and her friends attended, either in the village or, just occasionally, near where she worked. In the moments when he did consider it, however, he told himself that it was the war, that everyone was changing and that it was unfair to expect that his daughter should not.

In the next room he could hear the machine whirling as Milly worked on the dress she had promised to deliver that morning. He went to his allotment; Milly brought him a mug of tea and told him she was delivering the dress. An hour later Charlie stopped work, washed and changed, and walked down the road to the pub on the corner.

George was already at their favourite table, playing dominoes with the gamekeeper and his assistant from the Southerton estate.

''Ello, Charlie. Saw your Rosie at the dance last night.' Tommy Smith studied the pieces in his hand.

'Enjoying herself, I expect.'

'Expect so.'

'How's m'lord then?'

'All right.' The assistant's reply was not what they expected. 'Makes sure of it, doesn't he?'

The keeper put his pieces face down on the table and went to the bar, as if he agreed with what his assistant was about to say but disagreed with the fact that he was about to say it.

'What's the trouble with old Bert?'

Tommy shrugged. 'Same as me, really, but he's been there too long to say anything about it.'

'About what?'

'Lady bleddy Fiona. Friend of the family, been coming down for years. Now she's got a boyfriend. She's married, of course, but no bugger seems to mind that. Brings her new bloke instead.'

'What's wrong with that?'

'Bleddy Jerry, that's what's wrong.' He sniffed. 'All right with m'lord, of course. Good contacts for him in London, bit of this, bit of that, know what I mean.'

He finished his drink. 'Your round, George, or is it time for dinner again?'

'Bugger off.' George picked up their glasses and went to the bar.

'Why, who is he?'

'The Jerry, you mean?'

Charlie nodded.

'Dunno properly. Nasty bit of work if you ask me.'

George came back with the drinks and they started another game. By the time the pub closed and Charlie returned home the rabbit he had killed that morning and the potatoes he had dug from the allotment were sizzling on the table.

That evening when he went to The Fighting Cocks for his Sunday evening drink, the gamekeeper's assistant was standing by the bar. 'Remembered that bloke's name.'

'What bloke?' Charlie bought himself a half and looked for George.

'The tart's Jerry boyfriend.' He glanced behind him to make sure he was not being overheard. 'Schellenberg, that's what he's called.'

THE MEETING BETWEEN Holdaway and Davis to discuss the investigation into the leak that had led to the execution of the contact called Bailey was inconclusive.

The enquiry had taken six weeks and had been conducted in secret, partly not to reduce morale in the units and partly not to alert whoever was responsible. At the end of that time, according to the conclusion on the final two pages of the report, Davis had not only been unable to find any indication whatever of the source of the leak, but the activities of all the units under suspicion had been so effective that any act of disloyalty from the men in them seemed totally inconceivable.

A clerk brought in two mugs of tea and left.

'I don't know where to go from here.' Davis waited until the door was closed. 'Perhaps there was no leak, perhaps we were wrong.'

Holdaway shook his head. 'If there wasn't a leak how would.The Watchman have known about Bailey?'

'God knows.'

Holdaway closed the meeting and left for London.

His first appointment was at the security subcommittee of the *Reichsstatthalter*'s main policy committee, and his second was at the Economics Ministry. Walter Schellenberg was present at each. When the latter ended, shortly after six-thirty, they stood together on the steps of the inner courtyard and waited for their cars.

'You're going straight back to Maidstone?' Schellenberg asked. His car stopped, Holdaway's immediately behind, and the driver opened the door for him.

'Another meeting with Davis at eight.'

'Doesn't he like his wife?' Schellenberg began to get into the Mercedes.

Holdaway laughed. 'Perhaps he's after promotion.'

'Why don't you phone him and put it back to tomorrow, then join me for dinner?'

Holdaway decided immediately. 'Thank you.'

The West End was busy, a number of buskers already playing to the well-dressed and affluent who were going either to dinner or to the theatre. At the head of one of the queues was a young man playing an accordion. As his driver slowed for the traffic Holdaway noticed that the man had only one leg and that on the threadbare jacket of his uniform he wore the campaign medals of the British Expeditionary Force.

The doorman of The Ritz was standing under the arches outside the hotel. In some ways it reminded Schellenberg of Paris. Holdaway instructed his driver to return for him at ten then used the courtesy telephone to contact The Citadel and joined Schellenberg at the bar in the foyer. The pianist in the corner was dressed in evening suit and the singer was tall and slim, her long blonde hair falling over her black dress. She sang in German.

'I hope you don't mind.'

'Not at all.'

Schellenberg lit a cigarette and ordered two large whiskies. The bar was crowded, as the song ended there was a round of applause. The woman moved away from the piano and looked at them. Even before they heard the first chords of the next tune the entire bar knew what she was going to sing.

'*Ich bin von Kopf bis Fuss auf.*' The voice was low and sensual yet still powerful. 'Falling in love again.'

'Not as good as Marlene, but not bad.' Holdaway accepted the cigarette Schellenberg offered him.

'You know Dietrich?'

'Of course. *The Blue Angel* is one of the great films.'

Schellenberg nodded. 'It was a pity she moved to America, but the Führer can't have everything.'

The singer's voice was lower, more haunting, nobody in the bar moved or spoke. When the song was finished Schellenberg ordered the waiter to take her a glass of champagne.

'How's Davis getting on with the leak?' The question was not hostile.

'Not well, he can't find a connection anywhere. That's what this evening's meeting was about.'

At the piano the singer raised her glass to them.

'How much do you think about The Watchman?'

'How long is a piece of string?'

'I'll be in Kent next weekend.' Schellenberg waved for a menu to be brought to them. 'Country do, Friday to Monday, guests of some people I know. They wondered whether you would care to join us for dinner on Saturday, stay overnight.'

Holdaway took the menu. 'Perhaps I should tell you that one of my men saw you near Lord Southerton's a few weeks ago.' He wondered what else he should or should not say and how the other man would react.

Schellenberg smiled and raised his glass. Holdaway and his department were sharp. 'In that case you will know who is responsible for inviting you.'

'Perhaps you could thank her for me.'

'Thank her yourself on Saturday.'

TRAINING TOOK PLACE in a farm four miles from the village. For three hours the members of the Argos network were instructed in the use of plastic explosive, weapons training having already taken place. When they began to leave Charlie Clifford stayed behind.

'Who's Schellenberg?' He waited until the farmer had gone to the barn to fetch some cider and he and the organizer were alone in the kitchen.

'Why?' The sharpness of the response took him by surprise. 'What do you know about him?'

'Just wondered if you fancied a crack at him, that's all.' He knew he was going to enjoy himself.

'You're joking; you couldn't get anywhere near him. Bastard's too well protected.'

'Can't catch him with his trousers down, you mean?'

'Why?'

'Because I know when and where he takes 'em down.'

The farmer came into the kitchen. 'Five minutes, Andrew,' the organizer said to him, then turned back to Charlie. 'What the hell are you talking about?'

Charlie told him what Tommy Smith had said.

'Speak to him again on the quiet. Find out when Schellenberg is down next.'

'Who is he?' Charlie asked for the second time.

'Walter Schellenberg is head of Amt IX, which deals with security in this country, including the Resistance. It was Schellenberg who recruited Holdaway and the Lice and set up The Citadel.'

'Bloody hell.'

DRAKE LEFT ARISAIG and returned to his office in Glasgow. Of the several messages from the South which needed his attention and decision, two also required his personal decoding. The first requested approval of the plan to infiltrate men back into the prison camps. The second was a summary of the key recommendations of the industrial subcommittee of the policy committee of the Economics Ministry and contained the most recent production details and future output targets at those factories in Britain being used to assist the German war effort, as well as a precis of the various ways of achieving those targets in view of what seemed to be falling production at the key factories due to unavoidable factors such as machine breakdown and equipment obsolescence.

The first message was from The Caretaker and the second was from Prospero.

WHEN CHARLIE CLIFFORD arrived at The Fighting Cocks that evening the gamekeeper was in his customary place against the bar. Half an hour later his assistant arrived. Charlie nodded at him, let him settle in the corner where he always sat, then went across. Sometimes, he thought, Tommy Smith reminded him of a ferret.

'That chap you mentioned the other day,' Charlie was careful.

'Schellenberg?'

'That's the one. Come down often does he?'

'Who wants to know?' There was a glint in Tommy Smith's eye.

'Friends of mine.'

'What friends?'

The assistant was either being very careful or too clever by half. 'Just friends.' The assistant keeper knew anyway, he began to think, had already worked it out.

'Not on the estate, Charlie, or anywhere near here.' They both understood the threat of reprisals and the danger to those who worked on the estate or who lived in the village.

'Don't worry, Tommy, I already thought of that.' The threat to Milly and Rosie above everything else.

'What do you want to know then?'

'Whatever you can tell us.' It wasn't just the shape of Tommy Smith's face, Milly had said once, it was the teeth as well.

'They normally come together, the tart and the Jerry. If they come for a weekend it's usually Friday night, occasionally Saturday morning.'

'Any details?'

'His car and driver. Mercedes of course. Black.' Just like a ferret, Charlie thought again. 'Schellenberg and Lady Fiona sit in the back, Schellenberg on the right.' He laughed. 'Same side in bed as well.'

'Which way do they come?'

'A20. Always come into the estate from the village.'

Charlie bought them another round.

'How much notice do you get that they're coming down?'

'Enough.'

The bugger was playing a game with him. 'If you could let us know when they're due to come again.'

'Thought you'd never ask. They're coming this weekend.'

'Why do you know so much about him?' Charlie asked.

The eyes glinted again. 'Like I said, he's a nasty bit of work. Somebody was bound to ask about him sometime.'

THE REPORT FROM the Economics Ministry dealt primarily with the increased reliance on British output for the war effort in the east. When Holdaway enquired he was informed that Inspector Davis was away from The Citadel with his unit and would be back later. He left a message that the inspector should report to him as soon as he returned and turned his attention to the appendices of the report. In the margin of the section dealing with a fall in production in key factories, Schellenberg had scrawled a note.

IS IT POSSIBLE THAT NOT ALL SUCH DECREASES CAN BE ATTRIBUTABLE TO BREAKDOWNS AND OLD EQUIPMENT? MIGHT SABOTAGE BE A FACTOR? PLEASE INVESTIGATE.

Davis returned at six. At Holdaway's suggestion they left The Citadel and drove to the pub outside the town. The bar was quiet, Davis bought two pints and joined Holdaway at the table farthest from the door.

'The Bailey leak.' Holdaway enjoyed the flavour of the hops. 'I think we might have been looking in the wrong place.' Davis waited for an explanation. 'One, all our men were hand-picked. Two, the lapse of time between our knowledge of Bailey and his disappearance. All our men knew immediately; if it had been one of our people he would have known the danger and told the terrorists on day one.' He downed his beer and bought another round.

'So whoever was the leak only knew about it recently.'

'That's not all. So far we've been concerned with one leak, but suppose that leak is only one of a pattern.' He took the Economics Ministry report from the inside pocket of his jacket and handed it to Davis. 'Page five, paragraphs eight to ten. They're marked.'

Davis read the paragraphs and passed the report back.

'Just suppose that the fall in production *isn't* an accident. Just suppose that it wasn't a coincidence that one of the trains the other night was carrying vital war supplies.'

'The same leak?'

Holdaway finished the pint and nodded.

'Who?'

'Who came on the scene just before the leaks started? Who's close to the man with access to all the information covered by the leaks?'

Davis did not see it.

'Suppose Schellenberg takes work home with him?'

Davis saw it. 'It makes sense, she's always with him, either down here or in London. And she's got all the right contacts for other stuff as well.'

'The trouble is, we can't prove it, and until we can, we can hardly suggest to Schellenberg that his woman is a spy.'

Davis began to chuckle. 'Do you think he's the only one she's got going?'

'God help her if Schellenberg finds out that he isn't.'

'So what can we do?'

'Put a team on her but for God's sake make sure they keep their mouths shut. Confirm that Schellenberg does take work home with him. Check her movements, when she would have a chance to pass anything on, how she passes it and to whom.'

'When do we start?'

'This weekend. She's down here with him again, ideal time and place to go through any papers he's carrying.'

'How do you know?'

'She's also invited me.'

THE POINT ON the A20 which the organizer had chosen for the ambush was at a point where the road bent and dipped slightly, the ground sloping up from it and the trees giving ample cover.

'Two lookouts.' They had already checked the positions. 'The first identifies Schellenberg's car and warns the second. He confirms the identification and alerts us. We operate in two sections in case the car gets through the first.'

They rehearsed the procedure one more time, the organizer driving the car he had borrowed and Charlie checking that it could be seen at each of the points they had decided, then drove back to the village.

'Looks good.' They had set the ambush to intercept Schellenberg on his way to the estate on the Friday evening. 'Any confirmation?' In twenty-four hours, Charlie would be waiting in the trees.

'Not yet.' The organizer had sent the signal informing the North of the proposed action and asking confirmation almost two days before.

'Bit close.' The nerves were already tightening in his stomach. Reprisals would be inevitable. The Germans were bound to round up everyone who worked on the estate plus half the village. Already he was worrying about Milly and Rosie.

'Probably hear tonight.' The organizer knew what had happened: Drake had gone to Arisaig and there had been a delay in getting the signal to him. 'No problem.'

When Charlie reached home Milly and Rosie had already eaten. His wife took the dinner from the stove and laid it on the table in front of him. He tried to eat, then went to the pub. Tommy Smith was waiting for him.

'You've got yourself a bonus.'

'What do you mean?'

'There's another guest this weekend, coming Saturday night for dinner and staying till Sunday.'

'Who?'

'Holdaway.'

THE MEETING WITH the organizer was at ten the following morning. Charlie made an excuse to leave work, saying that Milly was sick, and cycled to the rendezvous point. They could change the plans, he had thought about it all night. It was still dangerous, still too close to home, and the reprisals if they got Holdaway as well would be horrific. But it might work if they planned it properly, waited until the Sunday, got them all as they were leaving – the tart, Schellenberg, and the bastard who ran the Lice. He checked that he was not being followed and went into the house. Risky, he thought again, but worth it.

The organizer was already there. 'It's off. I heard from the North last night. They consider that the scale of reprisals is too great.'

THE BLANKET WAS rough around her and the image of the woman on the electrified wire refused to leave her. I am going to die, Mary thought. Tomorrow I will be too weak to work and they will kill me. She felt someone shaking her. Please God may I not be like the woman on the wire, please may I die better than that.

'Come on, Mary, they're bringing the food.' All morning since breakfast and roll call she had lain on the bunk and tried to find a strength within her body. Please God may I not die at all. Annie pulled the blanket from her and helped her down. 'Come on, now.'

They left the block and joined the queue, the sun hot above them and the lines shuffling forward slowly. Thank God today is a rest day. Please God, may I get more than just the thin water at the top, please may we both get some of the vegetables, even a single piece of meat, from the bottom.

In front of her Annie held out her bowl to the orderly. 'I'm an artist, I'd like to draw your portrait.' Mary could not understand what Annie was saying. The woman in charge of the soup looked at her, also unsure. 'I'm an artist,' Annie repeated. 'If you could get me a pencil and some paper I'd like to draw your portrait.'

What are you saying, Annie? Mary tried to understand. What are you doing?

'When?'

'This afternoon.'

'All right.' The orderly dug the spoon deep into the container and poured the contents into Annie's bowl.

'My friend as well.'

The woman scraped the spoon along the bottom and poured its contents into Mary's bowl. 'In an hour.'

They went back to the bunks and began to eat. There were so many vegetables, more than Mary had ever had before. She held her arm tight round the bowl so that nothing would happen to it and slipped the first piece of potato into her mouth. Only when she had finished and wiped the bowl clean with her bread did she ask Annie what she was doing.

'I trained at art college and would have become a designer if it had not been for the war.'

'But can you really do her portrait?'

'I can do a pencil sketch of her.'

'You know she is one of the chief's "little friends", you know what will happen to us if the chief finds out and thinks you're trying it on with one of her little girls?'

'I know, but we need the food.'

It would be Annie who would bear the punishment, she knew, Annie who would be singled out by the block leader. 'Thank you.'

When they went outside the orderly was waiting with four sheets of paper and a pencil. Annie told her to sit down and began to draw. 'The first is just practice, I haven't done a portrait for a long time.' She saw the suspicion that she had been duped in the woman's eyes, that the prisoner to whom she had given so much meat and vegetables would give her nothing in return. 'But don't worry, the second will be good.' She finished the first rough lines, screwed the paper into a ball and threw it away, then settled back against the wall of the block and began to draw, quickly and confidently, sometimes applying only the tip of the pencil in light strokes on the paper, at other times using it more heavily, shading the face and giving both a depth and definition.

'Smile.'

The subject had a square face and small eyes, yet in the sketch that was taking shape she seemed different. Mary looked over Annie's shoulder and saw what she was doing – making the face slimmer and the eyes larger, making the woman attractive.

The bottom of the soup container again tomorrow, Mary could taste the vegetables in her mouth already; a job in the block, no more work on the roads. Make it good, Annie, she whispered, but not too good.

Already a crowd was gathering, looking at the sketch and telling the orderly how good it was. Annie finished the portrait and handed it to the woman.

'It's absolutely beautiful.' She held it up so that everyone could see.

'Can I borrow it for a moment?' Mary asked her. The woman held the sketch close to her as if she was afraid to lose it. 'Come with me, then.' They went into the barracks. 'What did you say your name was?'

'Linda.'

The block chief was sitting in the corner. 'Good afternoon.' Mary was polite. 'A friend of mine just drew this sketch of Linda and I thought you might like to see it.'

The woman remembered her from the day she had stood back to let her pass. She took the sketch from Mary and looked at it, unsure whether to admire or envy it.

'If you wouldn't mind, my friend would like to do a portrait of you. If you could get some paper like this I'm sure you would like it.' Behind her Annie understood.

'When?' The chief was still suspicious.

'Tomorrow. The light would be better then and she could take her time. If it was possible to get some crayons, or paint, it would be good to do it in colour.'

The chief held the sketch of the orderly at arm's length and looked at it again. 'All right. Tell your friend to report to me tomorrow morning after roll call.'

'What about me?'

The woman knew why she had asked. 'You as well.'

'Thank you.'

The next morning at six-thirty Mary and Annie stood at attention for the SS inspection and body count. When the SS left the chief returned to the block and the block secretary began to call out the numbers of the prisoners assigned to the works *Kommandos*.

'Four-five-seven-nine.' She came to Annie's number. 'Special duty, assigned to block chief.'

'See you in a moment.' Annie left the group and returned to the block. The sun was already getting hot. Mary imagined what it would have been like on the road, how her back would have burned and her spine and body ached with the pain.

'Four-five-nine-three.' The secretary came to Mary's number. 'Road *Kommando*.'

She felt the shock in her body, the anger then the fear, did not hear the other numbers as the secretary read them. Not me, she wanted to say, I'm not supposed to be on the work *Kommando*, I'm supposed to be with Annie, the chief said so. The instructions were complete and the prisoners began to form into the *Kommandos*. The secretary turned and began to walk back into the block.

'Excuse me.' Mary broke rank and stepped towards the woman. 'I think there's been a mistake.' The bloody chief, she tried to control her panic, reneged on her promise. 'The chief said yesterday that I was assigned to the block today.' Behind her the *Kapos* in charge of the work *Kommandos* stirred uneasily. 'I arranged the portrait painter, that's why she said I would be assigned to the block.'

The woman looked at her. Like most block secretaries, she wore the red triangle of a political prisoner. 'Turn around.'

Mary did as the woman ordered.

The secretary looked at the two letters on either side of the cross on the back of her coat, and the unmistakable target of the red circle with the white inner circle beneath the cross, repeated on the front under her number and classification.

'You're NN?'

Not still a trap, Mary thought, not a last trick after so long. 'Yes.' The other work *Kommandos* were already being marched away.

'You say the chief assigned you to the block?' There was no mercy in the woman's eyes.

'Yes.'

'I hope you're right.' She turned and led Mary into the block.

The block chief was sitting on her bunk. Opposite her, Annie was sketching details of parts of the woman's face, the paper on a square piece of wood for support.

'This prisoner said you assigned her to the block today.'

The woman looked up.

'She's with me,' Annie intervened. 'She's the one who arranged the portrait.'

'Sorry, I forgot.'

Mary felt the relief.

'Come with me.'

It was still not over, she knew as she followed the woman into the other section. The block secretary ordered the cleaners to fetch them coffee and sat on her bunk.

'I know who you are and why you're here.'

'How?' It was neither a confirmation nor a denial.

'I speak German.'

The orderly returned with coffee and bread. 'Her as well.' The woman filled Mary's bowl and left again.

'The letters on your back. NN. *Nacht und Nebel.*'

Mary wiped the bread round the bowl and said nothing.

'A poem by Goethe, the hero condemned to journey for ever in *der Nacht und Nebel*, the night and the fog, and never to return. That's what's meant to happen to you, to disappear into the night and fog and never be seen again.'

Mary still said nothing.

'You're Resistance, more than just Resistance. There are plenty of them in the camp, or people the Germans thought were Resistance. But none of them are NN, none of them have the target on the back and front of their uniforms which means they can be shot on sight.' She was looking right at Mary. 'You must have come from the Free

392

North, you must be an agent.' It was not a question. 'You were caught and interrogated. That's why you were in such a condition when you arrived.'

Retain her support for you, Mary thought, but never confirm who or what you are or were. 'I am an officer in His Majesty's forces.' It was neither more nor less than what she had said on the morning she thought she was to be executed.

The secretary stared at the floor. 'My husband was on the Gestapo arrest list,' she said quietly. 'I have no idea why.' It was the first time the woman had told anyone, the first time she had shared her burden. 'We were arrested after invasion. I have not seen him since.'

'What about your children?'

'Mercifully we have none.'

Mary began to understand.

'I have been here from the beginning. I was given the job of secretary because I was a teacher.' The face was hard and without expression; behind it remained the structure of her previous good looks and sparkling eyes. Bisecting the left eyebrow was a small scar where she had fallen as a child. 'Sometimes I wish I was not, sometimes I wish I were dead.' She looked around and regained her strength. 'It is in my power to appoint an assistant for each section. I have one, the other is yours.' There was no need to add the words *if you want it.*

'Thank you.'

The woman shook her head. 'I will help and protect you as much as I can, but remember, you are NN. No matter what I or anyone else can do for you, in the end you will always disappear into the night and the fog.'

IT WAS THE last match of August. On the pitch Ardley were batting, at the side of the pavilion the boys were playing their own game. Fran helped finish preparing the tea and thought of the last match of August the previous year, the planes battling it out in the skies and the countryside tight with expectation. So much had happened since, she reflected, sometimes she wondered where she stood in it all. The escape routes had been firmly established, the communication between the camps and the outside was in place and the first hide-aways in Wales where those ordered to escape would rendezvous were already set up. The Caretaker, she had to laugh at herself, yet here she was still making the tea for the bloody men at the cricket club.

At half-past five, the match still under way, she climbed the hill to the farm and began to feed the animals. She was half finished when Boy Jack joined her.

'Match over?'

He shook his head. 'I thought you might need some help.'

'Thanks, Jack.'

She went back into the shed and he walked towards the house to change.

'Mum, Mum! Come quick.' When he had been a child she had known by instinct which cries were important – which meant he had hurt himself or was in trouble, and which did not matter. 'Mum! Mum!' He was still shouting, she heard him running from the farm-yard and down the track. Jack, she thought, alive, coming up the track just as if he were coming home from cricket. She dropped the bucket, the animal feed spilling everywhere, and ran.

The figure coming up the track was limping, the coat and trousers were in rags and the body in them was thin and weak. The hair did not look as if it had been cut for weeks and the shirt was torn and stained. The only baggage was a bundle wrapped in newspaper and tied together by string, and the frame of the spectacles was bent and twisted, the right lens missing.

Fran was running down the road, then holding him, hugging him as if she had never expected to see him again. Boy Jack took the bundle.

'Hello, Auntie Fran, Uncle Jack said to come back one day to milk the cows.'

She could hardly stop herself crying. 'Hello, Ernie.'

'Where's Uncle Jack?' He asked as if he knew the answer.

'Uncle Jack's dead, he was killed during the invasion.'

The boy nodded and the three of them turned and walked together up the track towards the farm.

That evening, after they had eaten and Ernie had washed in the tin bath in front of the range, they walked together round the farm. When it was too dark to be outside they sat in the kitchen and he told them as much of his story as he wanted or they felt able to ask: how he had been moved twice after invasion, how he had finally gone on the run, and how in the end he had come back to the farm.

It was only the next morning, when Ernie was outside looking at the cows, that Boy Jack told his mother the story Ernie had told him in bed: how he had returned to the East End of London and found that the house where his parents had lived had been bombed during the blitz and they themselves killed.

'We're the last place he's got now, Mum. We're not going to let him go away again, are we?'

The escape routes, Fran thought, the messages from the Free North, the organization of the men in the prison camps and the secret places in Wales. The bloody Caretaker — if it wasn't so serious she could laugh at it — the whole world seeming to move around him, relying on him, and now she no longer had one boy to look after but two.

'You'll tell him it's all right, won't you, Mum?'

'Of course I'll tell him.'

Ernie had finished the milking and was sitting by the hedge looking across the fields. Fran walked across the yard and sat down at his side.

'I'm sorry about Uncle Jack, I really am.'

'I know you are, Ernie. He would have been pleased that you came back.' She picked a blade of grass and split it down the middle, uncertain how to say what she meant. 'You know you don't have to go from here ever again, don't you Ernie? You know this is where you belong?'

He looked up at her and smiled. 'Thank you.'

5

THE LAKE HAD already acquired the first cold grey of winter. Donovan stood with his hands on the side rail of the ferry and watched the bow wave slide along the shore. It was almost the end of October, the first snows on the mountains above: a beautiful country Switzerland, he thought, yet also a country whose neutrality and central position in Europe allowed him and his kind to fight at least some of their battles. Three months ago William Donovan had been appointed founding head of the Office of Co-ordinator of Information, the organization on which America would build its intelligence gathering bodies.

The ferry berthed against the wooden jetty. The operation would be his last field job. In many ways he should not be undertaking it now; he was too important in his new role. He walked to the station and wondered why he was doing it: whether it was out of a professional responsibility or whether it was a misbegotten attempt to prove that there still remained in him a last flush of Irish youth. Or whether it was a sense of guilt. Eighteen hours later he stepped off the train onto the wooden platform that constituted the railway station at Adelboden and passed through the ticket collector's shed at the end. Konrad Fuchs was waiting for him.

In all tangible respects the hunting lodge was the same, yet Donovan sensed a difference. After dinner that evening, as on his previous visits, he and Fuchs sat on either side of the log fire that burned in the dining-room and drank schnapps.

'I have to leave Germany.' The conversation over the meal had been relaxed, now it was functional.

Fuchs would tell him the reason in his own time and his own way, Donovan understood. 'In what way can I help?' The same way as before, he assumed.

'American passports will no longer work, nor can we come out through Switzerland; if anyone in my position even approached the border of a neutral country he would be in trouble.'

'How then?'

'Next weekend my wife and children will come here for their traditional autumn holiday. I have invited myself on to a group going to Paris at the same time.' He smiled wryly. 'For some, Berlin is rather boring nowadays. My family will then join me in France. It is a reasonable drive from here and will not attract suspicion.'

'Why not?'

'Because the occupied part of France is considered safe, there is no country bordering it into which one can easily escape and Spain, which is theoretically neutral, is a bedfellow of the Reich.'

'And you wish me to arrange your departure from France?'

'Yes.'

British Intelligence would have to be involved. Donovan saw the problems already. The British would want something in return and Washington would therefore need to have a reason for asking. It was part of the new politics, the new battle into which he had been thrown.

Fuchs smiled again, a fuller smile this time. 'I know that you would help me anyway, but I also understand that you will be asked what the British and Americans will get in return.'

'Something like that.'

Fuchs poured them each another drink. 'The reason I am under surveillance is not because of my involvement in the opposition to the Führer, which has so far remained undetected, it is because of my position and the knowledge which it brings.'

'Why?'

Fuchs was staring at the fire.

'During the last war a German scientist named Fritz Haber was ordered to set up a special unit for gas warfare. The gases and their effects, as you are aware, were horrendous. Haber's wife was also a scientist, the first woman to win a doctorate in chemistry from the

University of Breslau. When she objected to what he was doing he replied that in times of peace a scientist belongs to the world but that in times of war he belongs to his country. The day he returned to the front, his wife committed suicide.' He turned to face William Donovan.

'It seems to me that the best way I can belong to my country at the present time is to pass to its enemies those secrets which Hitler will one day seek to use.'

'And what secret is it that would persuade my government to get you and your family out of France?'

The following morning Donovan returned to Munich, then to Bern. For the next thirty-six hours, using only lines and codes confirmed to be secure, he communicated with Washington, and with the Free North of Britain, the latter sometimes directly, though mainly through the Securities Exchange Commission which fronted for British Intelligence in the New World. During that time two considerations occupied the minds of those with whom he was dealing: the first concerned the details of the operation to spirit Fuchs and his family from France, which it was agreed would be dealt with by British Intelligence; and the second was the confirmation of Fuchs' identity and credentials.

Sixty hours after he had left the hunting lodge at Adelboden Donovan returned. It was three days before Fuchs was due to go to Paris and twelve hours before his wife and children were due at the lodge. That night Donovan stated that his government was prepared to assist, the following morning he returned to Switzerland.

LONDON WAS COLD and dismal, the rain was trickling down the window and even though it was not yet five in the afternoon it was almost dark. The following weekend, Schellenberg thought, he and Fiona might go to Paris. He pushed the rest of the paperwork to the side and turned his attention to the report which Straube had just given him. Five days ago the American William Donovan had appeared without warning in Bern, though there was confusion about his movements after. William Donovan, Schellenberg was aware, who three months before had been made his country's first secret intelligence supremo. He read the report a second time then called Munich and requested details of an American journalist Philip Carver, believed to have entered Germany from Switzerland in the last five days.

398

FOR THREE-QUARTERS OF Drake's journey from Arisaig, the road had been swathed in mist, and the drive had taken twice as long as normal. Amongst the paperwork that had accumulated in the twenty hours he had been away was a request from SIS for the use of an SOE radio operator to organize a Lysander pick-up near the French town of Beauvais, their own operator in the area having been moved south. It was the type of request, given the rivalry between the two organizations, which Drake knew SIS would be loath to make unless it was absolutely necessary. He dictated a confirmation and ordered that it be sent by despatch rider immediately.

THE AIR TRANSPORT form to the Special Duties Squadron was typed in mauve: SIS, the squadron leader knew; SOE typed theirs in black. It was the end of the moon period, there would be barely enough light to see the landing field and SIS had requested the operation for that night only, with no alternative dates. Somebody in trouble, it was written all over the details. He checked the crew sheet and decided to do the run himself.

THE CAR WHICH crossed from Germany into France shortly before midday attracted little attention, the guards accepting the woman's story that she was taking her children to visit their father who was stationed in Paris and allowing themselves to be impressed by her well-cut clothes and friendly but authoritative manner. Six hours later, at an *auberge* on the left side of the road three hundred yards past the N411 east of Nancy, the woman pulled onto the rough ground at the side of the inn and switched off the engine. The other cars were waiting. William Donovan confirmed the woman's identity then introduced her to the representative of the British Secret Intelligence Service who would drive her and her children to a safe house near the landing field and the Frenchman who would dispose of her car.

THE CABARET, AFTER Berlin, was loud and evocative and the dancers extremely attractive. Nor was there any doubt about the availability of the equally attractive women who were dispersed round the bars behind the dining area. At eight-thirty Konrad Fuchs pushed back his chair and asked the other members of the group to excuse him, there being no doubt in any of their minds why he was leaving. They watched as he made his way to the bar then turned back to the show; only when he was confident that they were no longer interested in him did Fuchs collect his overcoat and make his way to a café close to the hotel. William Donovan was sitting as arranged at a table near the door. After two minutes the American left and walked to the car and driver three streets away, Fuchs fifty yards behind him and unaware of the woman who checked that he was not being followed.

The safe house was a farm on the edge of a village – Donovan had no idea of the exact location – approached along a series of winding roads which he could barely see in the night and protected by a set of heavy gates which were closed behind them. They were led inside and Fuchs was reunited with his family, the children, a boy aged nine and a girl of five, exhausted and confused, while Donovan and the Englishman in charge of the operation sat at the table in the kitchen with the Frenchman who had organized the landing field. The room smelt of garlic mixed with the kerosene of the lamp and the wine which the farmer's wife brought.

'The pick-up was confirmed an hour ago.' The Englishman seemed nervous, fiddling with his glass. 'The plane is due between midnight and two o'clock.' Not the adrenaline which came naturally with such an operation, Donovan sensed, nerves born of an unfamiliarity with this type of work.

'Bit of a rushed job, actually.' It was not quite a complaint. 'Not the area we normally use. Few problems there and we've had to lie low.' The man spoke in short bursts. 'Had to come up from Paris myself.' It explained his nervousness.

'You've checked the field?' asked Donovan.

'Yes.'

'And everything is in order?'

The man was still playing with his glass. 'Yes.'

'Radio operator?'

'Clear of the immediate area but on stand-by.'

'Back-up if anything goes wrong?' It would be eight hours before Fuchs was missed or could not explain away his absence so there would still be time to get him back to Paris, yet there was no way Fuchs would wish to go back, Donovan knew, and no way he could allow him to, given the knowledge for which Washington was waiting. Twelve hours, he also calculated, before Fuchs' absence was relayed to Berlin and they threw the net out for him.

'The plane's on its way, nothing will go wrong.'

It was eleven-thirty. The farmer indicated that it was time to leave.

'How far is the landing field?'

'Twenty minutes.'

In the sky above the Channel the squadron leader dropped to four thousand feet, checked his dead reckoning against the shape of the coast below and turned for the thirty-minute flight to the last navigational point before the run-in to the field. No moon, but everything would be all right, he told himself.

THE DRIVER PULLED the car into the woods at the side of the track and they walked the last eight hundred yards to the field. Almost there, thought Donovan, in less than five hours Konrad Fuchs and his family would be safe in the Free North and he himself would be lying in the bath in his room in the George V in Paris. In front of them the farmer whistled and the men came out of the hedgerows.

The loop in the river stood out like a ribbon. The pilot changed to his new course and set his watch. Morse sign five and a half minutes. If they asked for a pick-up at such short notice it must be important. He concentrated on the ground ahead and wondered who his passengers might be.

Donovan felt himself shivering and knew it was not the cold. In the sky to the west he heard the first sound and saw the agent begin to flash his morse.

'Thank you, Bill.' Fuchs shook his hand. There would be no time for farewells once the plane was on the ground.

'See you in America.' For one moment he thought of the meeting between President Roosevelt and Alexander Sachs, the letter from Einstein and the succession of committees which had followed it, and the programme which the president had finally authorized. The lamps of the flare path came on and they hurried across the grass.

The field was a bit small, the pilot thought. There had been no time for the usual photographic sortie, the vertical overlapping pairs of photographs from which the interpreters could pick out the smallest detail of a field and declare whether or not it was safe. He banked over the B and C lamps. Bound to be okay though, otherwise the details would be on the air transport form.

'You checked the field?' Donovan did not know why he asked. Beside him the agent was concentrating on the morse signal.

'It was checked.' The answer was not quite the same as he had given in the farmhouse.

'And everything is in order?'

The squadron leader banked again, losing height, a hundred yards to lamp A.

'I assume so.'

The trees were not supposed to be on the run-in, nothing like that mentioned in the briefing document.

'You did check the field personally?'

Torches a bit wonky, everything all right though. Fifty yards, twenty-five. Touch down.

'Like I said, old man, bit of a rushed job. Couldn't do everything myself.'

The pilot saw the tree stump too late, knew there was nothing he could do. Power full on anyway, try to climb, get around or over it. No time. The right wheel of the undercarriage struck the stump and the plane jerked up and to the right, cartwheeling across the field. The entire structure turned tail over nose twice, the tail and the starboard wing tip tearing off, then came to rest upside down two hundred yards away from where the waiting group was standing.

They were running, Donovan, Fuchs, his wife, the agent in a daze behind them and the Frenchmen around them. The starboard wheel was bent at an angle against the sky, there was a smell of petrol in the air and the slide-back canopy of the front cockpit was smashed. Donovan grabbed a signal torch from the man nearest him and crawled as close as he could. The pilot was hanging upside down in his straps, there was blood trickling from his mouth and his neck appeared to be broken. Donovan backed out and stood up.

'You,' he turned to the farmer, 'get us out of here.' He turned to the other Frenchman in charge of the field. 'You get the pilot out. If he's not dead take him somewhere safe.' He knew what they would do to the plane. 'Wait till just before dawn to burn it, give us a chance to clear the area.' There was no point going to the original safe house, once the pick-up was discovered and known to have been aborted every place for miles would be searched. By the time the agent caught up with them they had reached the car.

'Where's the radio operator?'

'About eight miles.'

'Show the driver the way.' Bad security for one circuit to know the details of another, Donovan knew, especially when the first had been compromised, but there was no option.

'Bit against the rules, old man,' objected the Englishman.

'Do it anyway.' The voice allowed neither dissent nor discussion. There was no way Fuchs could go back to Paris now. Have to get to another safe house before the enemy were on to the first and the second.

The two cars pulled out of the trees and onto the track. They had been driving twenty minutes when they heard the explosion and saw the flames in the sky above the landing field.

THE TELEPHONE WOKE Drake at five.

'Breakfast with the Prime Minister at six. You'll be picked up at a quarter to.'

No need to check, he recognized the voice. 'I'll be waiting.' There was no point asking what it was about; if he was being summoned at such short notice it would be important, and if it was important the Prime Minister's office would not give him the details on the telephone. He shaved and dressed then telephoned the operations room of SOE and the signals unit it shared with SIS. The car was already waiting. He slipped into the back seat and wondered what was going on in France. Ten minutes later he was ushered into the house where Winston Churchill had resided for the past two months.

Since the German advance into Russia four months before the Prime Minister had led a less secretive life, though the security screen around him had been maintained. Now he sat at the table, the first cigar of the day smouldering in the ashtray to his right and the plate of scrambled eggs in front of him.

'Not as good as at Chartwell but help yourself.'

Drake took a helping from the hot plates on the side, poured himself a coffee and sat down.

'How much do you know?' Churchill reached for the cigar.

'Only that SIS borrowed one of my radio operators in France and that she came through outside her normal schedule at half-past four this morning.'

Churchill grunted. 'Two days ago Washington requested the help of SIS to pick up someone in France. A Lysander was sent last night but the landing field was inadequate and the plane crashed. The people are still there. I want you to liaise with SIS and sort it out, get those concerned out.'

'If it's my operation I'm in charge and I use only my people.' Drake was too experienced not to establish the ground rules. No committee meetings with SIS, Churchill understood he meant, no prevaricating while the two departments sorted out what each would get from the operation. 'Agreed. You're in sole charge.' He summoned an orderly and asked for more coffee and toast for his guest.

'May I ask what the position in France is at the moment?'

'Originally there were four passengers, there is now a fifth, the American who was in charge of them. At this moment they are in a safe house with your radio operator and a member of SIS. They anticipate that the area around the landing zone will soon be searched, but think they are far enough away to be safe from that. Their problems will begin when the enemy realizes that the man the American is bringing out is missing. It is expected that will be around breakfast time.'

Why was Washington involved, Drake was trying to work it out. Who the hell were they bringing out? Remove the SIS man from the scene, he decided, trust only his own people. After that he would have three options: fly another pick-up tonight, keep them in France until the next moon period, or get them into Britain, even to the Occupied South.

'Who will be dealing with it: Paris or Berlin; SD, *Abwehr* or Gestapo?'

'Everybody,' said Churchill.

There were two possibilities if he had to bring them out to England: The Watchman or The Caretaker. 'Who is the American in France?'

The orderly brought the fresh coffee and toast and left the room.

'William Donovan.'

It couldn't be Donovan, Drake knew, not in his new job with all it implied for the future; Donovan would never be allowed into the field again. 'And who is he bringing with him?' A politician, he guessed, someone from the Intelligence world, perhaps someone in the Red Orchestra, the German opposition.

'A man named Fuchs.'

'Why is he so important?' He should not have asked but Churchill told him anyway.

'You have heard of Niels Bohr?'

Drake knew then who the German Donovan was bringing out was; not *who* he was, *what* he was, what he knew.

'The Danish physicist, Nobel Prize winner in 1922.'

Churchill lifted the cup, not drinking. 'For some time Bohr and other scientists have concerned themselves with what I am told they call nuclear fission, the splitting of the nucleus.'

Drake had read in *The Times* of the developments around the Christmas of 1938, the breakthrough achieved by the Germans Hahn and Strassman in the Kaiser Wilhelm Institute for Chemistry in Dahlem, the development of the work by the Jewish exile Meitner and her nephew Frisch in Copenhagen and Stockholm, the burst of activity and progress in America and Britain immediately after.

'During this time a scientist named Leo Szilard has been talking of the possibility of not just one reaction, but a chain and the energy which would result from this.'

It was the Leo Szilard whose recommendations, supported by a letter from Albert Einstein, had been presented to Franklin Roosevelt the month war had been declared and which had inspired the American Uranium Council and the bodies which spawned from it, the National Defence Research Council and the Office of Scientific Research and Development.

'One use of that energy is a new weapon called the atomic bomb.'

It was the spectre which had haunted Franklin Roosevelt during the meeting with Vice President Wallace and OSRD director Vannevar Bush at which the embryo of the Top Policy Group had been conceived and from which the Manhattan Project and the bombs called Little Boy and Fat Man would follow.

'British scientists working along the same lines were evacuated to America the week before invasion, though their reports are still addressed to a body named the MAUD Committee.' Churchill sipped his coffee. 'They have stated that such a bomb is possible and their recommendations have, in part at least, decided President Roosevelt to press ahead as quickly as possible with such work.'

It seemed a long way from a Lysander accident on a landing field, Drake thought, a lifetime from the people hiding for their lives in a barn in France and wondering what was going to happen to them.

'How does Niels Bohr fit into this?'

'After Denmark was invaded Bohr was invited to the United States but decided to stay in his native country. Two weeks ago a number of German scientists, including a man named Heisenberg, attended a scientific meeting in Copenhagen. Bohr refused to attend, but afterwards he agreed to meet Heisenberg, whom he has known for many years. Heisenberg wanted to talk about the atomic bomb.'

The coffee was cold, Drake ignored it.

'Heisenberg told Bohr that the German programme was well advanced, indicating various aspects of the project there and enquiring whether America was also pursuing the idea of an atomic bomb and what avenue they were taking on certain key aspects where alternatives exist.'

'Why?'

'Either Heisenberg was trying to tell Bohr what was happening because he disapproved of it, or he was seeking information on the American and British positions, or he had been ordered to pass on misinformation in order to confuse the enemies of Germany.'

'And how does the man with William Donovan fit into this?'

'Because the man he is bringing out knows the truth about the German atomic bomb programme.'

DRAKE RETURNED TO his office at eight-thirty, ordered coffee and examined the remaining options, the importance of the German and the fact that the American escorting him was William Donovan having eliminated the possibility of hiding them in France until the next moon period. He telephoned the operations room, asked them to check whether any good landing fields were known in the Beauvais area of north-east France, then contacted The Cottage on the scrambler and asked the same question.

The pilot who answered was Johnny Watson. 'You're thinking of another shot tonight?'

'I know it's outside the moon period but it's a possibility. If it's on it will be a double.'

'I'll check, but I think it's the first time we've flown there.'

'Let me know.'

The operations room came through on an internal line and informed him that although three possible landing fields had been inspected in the region none had proved satisfactory. Ten minutes later Johnny Watson telephoned, also with a negative answer. Only The Watchman now, or The Caretaker. Perhaps both. Bring Donovan and Fuchs across the Channel, use The Watchman's organization to arrange and protect a landing field and the Caretaker network to conceal them and bring them north if a pick-up by Lysander proved impossible. Use the Anton *réseau* on the Normandy coast of France, with contacts in Boulogne on the Channel coast. In the safe house in Froissy Bill Donovan and his people would be wondering what was going on. Drake drafted a message informing Donovan that he was now in charge and setting out his provisional plans and timetable, and sent it to the cipher department for immediate encoding and transmission.

At eleven Johnny Watson was informed that he had been promoted squadron leader in charge of Special Duties Squadron. His first action was to place the squadron on stand-by and alert them of a double. If two planes were required because of the number of passengers involved he himself would fly the first Lysander in.

AT TWELVE WALTER Schellenberg received the latest report on the movement of William Donovan. The American, the report said, had checked into the George V Hotel in Paris two days before.

'Troubles in Berlin.' Straube was always in touch with the teams in other countries. 'Apparently some scientist has gone missing on a trip to France. His wife and kids left a place they've got in the country two days ago and haven't been seen either.'

It was the sort of disappearance, Schellenberg almost laughed at the irony, in which they themselves specialized. 'Who's dealing with it?' He really should arrange a weekend in Paris. It would be funny if he bumped into Donovan.

'Everybody. Seems he was working on something big.'

The V-rocket project at Peenemunde, Schellenberg assumed. 'Any idea what?'

'Nobody seems to know.' Straube began to leave the room.

'What did you say?' The question was unexpected and sharp.

Straube turned in surprise. 'What? About him working on something big?'

'No. Where he went missing.'

'Paris.'

Donovan on the move again, Schellenberg thought. Donovan in Paris, scientist goes missing from Paris. 'Check the details of the missing man.' Perhaps he was reading too much into it. 'Find out his name and the address of the place in the country where his wife went missing.'

THE BONFIRE HAD been built on the edge of Ardley green in front of the King's Arms. For more than two weeks the villagers had dumped their spare wood on it. The previous weekend the cricket team had scoured the woods around Ardley for fallen branches and logs. There were those who may have needed the wood and who in other years and in different times may have preferred to use it themselves but there were none that November who did not think it right that the village should have its bonfire.

When Boy Jack and Ernie came out of school Fran watched them pulling the wood that had been collected that day onto the pile. A strange double life she was leading, she thought. The boys finished and the three of them walked back to the farm. Even now she never stopped thinking of Jack. She watched as the boys went to feed the animals, made the tea, called to them, and switched on the wireless. There were two codes now, the original for the afternoon meeting and a second for a contact in the morning. As she put the boys' tea on the table, she heard the words, felt, as always, the surge of fear. *The rose will flower in spring.* At nine the code was repeated.

THE EARLY EVENING was cold and he could smell the season in the air: autumn nearly gone, winter coming. On Wednesday it would be 5 November, Bonfire Night. The last of the meetings in the Midlands was over. Perhaps he could get south, he thought, see if the village had a fire this year, make sure that Fran and Boy Jack were still all right. Perhaps, when he had known that they were alive last spring, he should have told Fran that he also was alive.

The safe house was on the edge of the town and he had stayed there before, the elderly steel worker and his wife believing that he was a courier. After he had shared their supper, he listened to the nine o'clock broadcast. The code for The Watchman to contact the North urgently, built into the system for the periods when he was out of normal contact with the networks, was included in the personal messages.

AN HOUR LATER Drake received confirmation that the Anton network could convey the Donovan party to the coast the following day and that a fishing boat had been arranged to take them across the Channel at night. At ten-fifteen he notified Donovan.

At ten-thirty Schellenberg was informed by Straube that the name of the missing scientist was Konrad Fuchs and that the country house from which his wife and children had vanished was near a village called Adelboden, thirty miles west of Munich. He was also informed that there was still no news of Fuchs, that William Donovan appeared to be missing from his hotel, though he had not checked out, and that the Paris office of the SD were uncertain whether there was a link between Fuchs and the crash of a British Lysander near Beauvais the night before. It was so obvious, Schellenberg thought. For one moment he considered informing Berlin of the connection, then decided to wait.

That night, in radio messages requiring their personal decoding, the two organizers whose Resistance networks covered the South of England were requested to reconnoitre possible coastal landing points.

THE FOLLOWING MORNING William Donovan and his group were collected from the safe house where they had hidden for the previous forty hours and taken in a furniture van to the outskirts of Boulogne. The inside of the van was dark and the Fuchs children frightened. For most of the journey, except when the vehicle stopped and they thought they might be at a roadblock, their mother told them stories. The journey lasted three hours. For every minute of that time those concealed in the van waited nervously for discovery and arrest. On one occasion the van stopped, they heard voices outside and the back began to open. Then it was shut again and the van continued.

At nine the courier from The Caretaker escape circuit made the prearranged contact with the Resistance. By ten Fran had received the message and deciphered it. The instruction was simple and startling. That night the French Resistance would bring a group of five people across the Channel by fishing boat. The group would land at a point still to be decided. They would be taken north either by Lysander pick-up or by the escape network if this was not possible. There would be close liaison between the Resistance groups of The Watchman and the escape networks of The Caretaker. The Watchman would arrange the landing field and the protection of the group; The Caretaker would meet the group and accompany them at all times in case the Lysander arrangement failed. A radio operator was at the immediate disposal of The Caretaker and The Caretaker should arrange a rendezvous point with The Watchman when other details were known. The message that The Watchman received and decoded an hour later provided the same information.

At ten Fran left Canterbury and began her arrangements. At eleven Jack left the Midlands and began the journey south. At eleven-thirty Special Duties Squadron was notified of a double pick-up in the South of England that night.

In France, Walter Schellenberg had already been informed, there had been no success in the hunt for the missing scientist.

EVEN AT TWO the light was beginning to fade from the sky and the air was becoming colder. At lunchtime Fran had gone to the school and told the boys that after they had fed the animals they were to go to Sarah's. As she left Boy Jack had wished her good luck. It was only as she drove into the courtyard behind the pub where she was to meet the Resistance organizer that she remembered it was what Boy Jack had said to his father on the day she had driven them from the farm to seek refuge with her mother in Bearsted Green.

The room reminded her of the King's Arms in Ardley, the same dark varnished wood and yellow paper and the hops hanging in bunches as decorations. There were more men there than she had anticipated. As she went in they turned to look at her, women not being usual customers, especially a woman they did not know and who was unaccompanied. The landlord finished serving the men at the end then turned to her.

'Cold outside.'

'Not as cold as this time last year.' The code had been passed from the North.

'Frank's upstairs, second door on the right.'

She left the bar and walked up the stairs. The beams were low and the steps swung sharply at the top. She knocked on the door and went in.

'Frank?'

The man was sitting at a card table in the corner, another chair opposite him. The only other furniture was a single bed and a washstand. His hands were below the table and she knew he held a gun.

'I'm expecting The Caretaker, not a courier.'

'And I'm expecting someone representing The Watchman.'

He stood up. 'I'm sorry, I wasn't expecting The Caretaker to be a woman.' He laid the Smith & Wesson on the table and shook her hand.

'Business,' she said and sat down.

'The suggested place for the boat to land is the beach east of the lighthouse at Dungeness. The area is isolated and there are plenty of escape roads across Romney Marsh.'

'How difficult will it be landing on the beach?'

'The entire area was heavily protected before invasion and there are still a lot of beach obstructions. The local fishermen have built a makeshift jetty through the old defences.'

'And the area around Dover is too well patrolled?'

'Exactly.'

'What about the landing field?'

'North of Sellindge, we've used it before.'

'Show me.'

He took a one-inch map from the inside pocket of his jacket and opened it on the table. Reasonable road out from the beach, she thought quickly but carefully, nearly fifteen miles to the landing field, good choice of roads across country between the two and an established safe house within two miles of the field where she could hide the group and meet The Watchman. The field far enough away from Ardley if anything went wrong.

'I'll need one of your men as a guide across the Marshes, don't want to get lost in the dark.'

'I'll arrange one.'

They turned their attention to the details. The boat would leave France at five-thirty and the crossing was expected to take three hours. The Caretaker plus two cars would wait at the beach from eight, Frank and the protection he would bring would join him there. They were both aware that they still referred to The Caretaker as 'him'. The signal from the beach would be the morse letter M and from the boat the letter P. The Resistance would guard the key road junctions to the safe house where they would rendezvous with The Watchman, the safe house itself, the landing field and all approach roads to the field. A radio operator would be on stand-by at the safe house from late afternoon, a schedule to receive any messages from the North every hour on the half-hour; outgoing messages, unless there was an emergency, would be restricted to acknowledgements to limit the possibility of detection. The Watchman himself would arrive in the area by mid-evening and would meet them at the safe house after checking the landing field.

When they left the pub the day was colder, by the time Fran had collected the couriers she had chosen for that night and the cars they would drive it was almost dark. They left one car at the safe house then drove with the Resistance guide to the beach near Dungeness. The line of shingle was bleak and cold, even though there was no wind; the beach itself was littered with the debris of invasion and the wooden jetty pushed forty feet behind what had once been the first of the shore defences. A hundred yards back the cluster of houses stood empty. By the time they returned to the safe house both it and the landing field were under guard and the radio operator was in position.

THE ROOM WAS damp. Even without going to the window they could smell the sea. At four, as the organizer left the house, William Donovan walked with him to the door and spoke to him outside the hearing of the others. It was getting dark. An old woman dressed in black entered the room, lit the lamp in the corner and laid plates and glasses on the table. From below they smelt the cooking. She returned carrying a large serving dish piled with fried fish, then another with potatoes and bread, and finally brought some wine. None of them had eaten properly since a small meal the night before. Now they sat round the table and ate ravenously.

They had almost finished the meal when the organizer returned.

'It's confirmed. The boat is ready and the reception party is waiting for you in England. The person in charge there is The Caretaker. He will meet you on the beach and take you to a safe house. From there you will be taken to a landing field and picked up by Lysander. By tomorrow morning you will be in the Free North.'

'When do we leave?'

'Now.'

The house seemed empty. Apart from the woman who had brought the food they had seen no one and no one had seen them. A Citroën van was parked at the back, its engine running, a man at the driving wheel. The organizer checked that the street was empty and nodded to them. As soon as they were all in he closed the back doors, jumped into the passenger seat and the driver pulled away. The van smelt of fish and the ride was bumpy. They had been in the vehicle only five minutes when the organizer turned to them.

'There won't be time at the quay, so I'll say goodbye now.' He leant back and shook each of their hands. 'Good luck.' They felt the van bump down a small slope, then the driver drove along the quay and stopped. The organizer jumped out, checked around him and opened the back door. The quay was dark and wet and the lights of the nearest houses were fifty yards away. The fishing boat, *Les Deux Frères*, was moored against a steel ladder in the side of the quay, rising and falling gently, the engine already running. Apart from the captain in the wheelhouse and the two crewmen on deck there was no one else in sight. Fuchs climbed down the ladder, his wife behind him, then Donovan handed him the children and climbed down himself. The organizer passed him something in a bag, untied the mooring ropes, threw them onto the deck, and the fishing boat pulled out of the harbour and into the dark of the English Channel.

THE WIRELESS WAS in the sitting-room. At five minutes to six Fran switched it on and waited. She could never use the house again – its secret was now known to too many people. Already it seemed like a fortress, the cars were concealed in the barn, mechanics checking them, and there seemed to be men with guns at every door and window. The morse of the drum sounded and they waited, hearing nothing except the single message which would dictate the events of that night.

'The sun is purple.'

Fran switched off the wireless and went into the kitchen. The members of her circuit whom she would use that night were sitting round the table studying the road maps. Fifteen minutes later the radio operator came down from the attic where she had rigged her aerial and handed her the sheet from the message pad. 'Just come through.' Fran read it then looked round. 'They left France half an hour ago.'

THE SCRAMBLE PHONE at The Cottage rang, the new squadron leader answered it then returned to the table. 'It's confirmed, ETA midnight. We take off in ninety minutes.'

WALTER SCHELLENBERG PLACED the call to the general commanding the Southern division of England at six-thirty. At two he had spoken again to Paris, at three to Berlin, on both occasions slipping an enquiry about the missing scientist into his conversation but giving no indication whatever that the enquiry was the reason for the call. That afternoon he had confirmed with the George V that William Donovan had still not returned. Just suppose, he could not shake off the thought. The call was connected and he made his suggestion, the general agreeing immediately. Nothing wrong with a few extra patrols along the coast that night, the soldier thought, particularly if the SD suggested it. More specifically if it was Walter Schellenberg who recommended it.

THE GERMAN MOTOR torpedo boat *Moëwe* left Dover's Western docks at seven; it was armed with two torpedo tubes, a light anti-aircraft gun and two 105-mm cannon, and had a maximum speed of thirty-six knots. The perfume patrol, the crew knew the locals called the shift, the occasional night patrol to dissuade the black marketeers who were supposed to be bringing cheap spirits and cosmetics into Britain to meet the flourishing demand. The coffin watch, they themselves called it, not because of any physical danger but because of the routine, which bored them to death.

414

THE FISHING BOAT *Les Deux Frères*, The Two Brothers, slipped out of the bank of fog, and rolled in the swells that ran up the Channel. Thank God the weather was good, Donovan thought; he left the deck and joined the skipper in the wheelhouse. In the cabin below Fuchs and his family sat nervously, not even the children sleeping.

'How much longer?'

'We're half-way there.' He switched off the engine and went outside, listening intently, then came back in.

'That's good, no one else about.'

THE TWO CARS left the safe house and drove to Dungeness. At each of the crossroads on Romney Marsh armed men watched as they passed. After thirty minutes, the lights of Folkestone and Hythe to the left, they pulled into the ramshackle sheds at the rear of the abandoned houses at the top of the beach, and men they had not seen closed the wooden doors after them.

BENEATH HIS FLYING boots Johnny Watson wore a civilian suit and his flying boots could be converted into ordinary shoes. The sectional map was tucked into the left boot and the Colt .32 was in the holster attached to the port cockpit coaming. ETA twenty-three fifty-five hours. Navigation by dead reckoning with checkpoints over rivers or coastal headlands, the water like silver against the grey of the land, the last checkpoint and bearing from it the most important. Six minutes thirty seconds from there and he would begin looking for the morse signal from the ground. Standard routine for a double, the second plane standing off until the first had made its pick-up and taken off again.

The field was probably not more than an hour's drive from Ramsgate, the last place he had seen Mary. He dismissed the thought and taxied to the runway.

THERE WAS NOT much moon for a Lysander landing, Jack thought, hardly any light at all. He powered the BSA down the A20 and skirted Ashford. The *Wehrmacht* patrol was parked in a layby. He passed them without slowing and picked up the Folkestone road. After another eight miles he turned off onto the skein of lanes that ran across the land to his right. A second *Wehrmacht* patrol passed him in the opposite direction. It was strange to see even one patrol in this area at this time of night. He slowed to a halt at the crossroads, keeping the engine running. The men who came out of the black were all armed. Watchword purple, he told them and moved on. Two miles later he passed through a second checkpoint then turned the bike right and up an unmade track between fields and orchards to the landing field. Every yard of his progress now, he was aware, was observed. At the top of the track he stopped the engine, pulled off his helmet and goggles, and greeted the organizer in charge of the field.

'Everything all right?'

'Everything's fine.'

'How's The Caretaker?' It was the first time his organization had worked with any other.

'Very efficient.'

He left the landing field and drove to the safe house.

THE BEACH WAS cold. Fran had been standing on the jetty for twenty minutes, her hands deep in her coat pockets.

'You go in, I'll wait.' The organizer stamped his feet and tried to bring the circulation back into them.

'They shouldn't be long now.' She ignored his offer. 'They're already late.'

'Listen.'

Against the murmur of the sea they heard the hum of an engine, the sound more distinct as the boat drew closer. 'Stand by,' she told the man on her left, then turned to look at the sea as he left the jetty and ran for the cars. On her right Frank began to signal, the beam of the torch shielded so that it could only be seen at sea. In the dark four hundred yards away a lamp flashed in reply. No *Wehrmacht* patrols, Fran glanced round her, no Lice. Behind the houses the cars were already pulling out of the sheds. Suddenly she saw the shape of the fishing boat, its high bow and its wide beam, then the figures on the deck, a crewman ready with a mooring rope.

In the wheelhouse William Donovan thanked the skipper and helped the Fuchs family up the ladder from the cabin. There was no time to lose, he knew, no time for the boat to stay moored. On the jetty ten yards away he saw the reception party, the cars already reversing into place. The boat bumped against the jetty and he jumped ashore, the bag in his hand and Fuchs behind him. The Caretaker and the courier stepped forward to greet him, he transferred the bag to his left hand and held out his right to the man.

'Welcome to England.' It was the woman who greeted him. 'We don't have much time.' He followed her to the cars. Four, he counted, first and last escorts, the Fuchses already being bundled into the third, all the men round them armed. At the end of the jetty the crewman cast off the mooring rope and the skipper pulled astern until he was clear of the beach, then spun the wheel and turned for France. It was less than a minute since they had landed, Donovan realized; he barely had time to wave his hand in farewell before the woman pushed him into his seat and the convoy raced away.

Four hours, the skipper calculated, depending on the tide, plenty of time to sneak home before anyone noticed that he had been away. He pulled the wheelhouse door open and glanced at the shore. The beach and jetty were already lost in the night. He turned back, reached for his tobacco tin and saw the shape of the E-boat cutting across his bow. The Frenchman barely had time to reach for the gun at the side of the wheel before the machine guns raked his boat.

'Jesus Christ!' Fran heard the exclamation of the man beside her and turned round. A mile offshore the fishing boat *Les Deux Frères* burst into flames.

The cars swept out of the black, through the yard and into the barns at the back of the farm. 'The Caretaker,' someone in the kitchen told Jack. He pulled on his coat and hurried outside.

The drivers switched off the engines and William Donovan stepped out of the car. 'The Watchman's arrived,' one of the guards told Fran. She helped the Fuchses out of the third car and led them towards the house.

He saw her, knew immediately. She saw him, also knew. The shock descended on both of them, the guilt that he had not been honest with her consuming him, the relief that he was alive spinning in her head. They shook hands, as if they were different people, and went inside.

'Take the passengers upstairs, make sure they are warm and dry and get them some food. The children will need a bed till we leave.'

They went into the kitchen and sat down, organizers and couriers around them. No chance to talk, no opportunity to ask about the other or what they were doing here.

'We have a problem. The fishing boat was blown up, I assume by a German patrol vessel.' *I thought you were dead, Jack. Why the hell didn't you tell me you were alive?*

'There are also more German patrols than usual out tonight.' *I thought you and Boy Jack were dead, checked the farm God knows how many times. I found the pick-up shot to pieces and saw how your mother's house in Bearsted Green had been destroyed.*

'But the landing field is secure?' *Why didn't you come back to look for us? Why didn't you tell me?*

'So far, but there might be trouble later.' *When I found out you were alive I was too committed. It was too late.*

'So what do we do?' *I'm your wife, Jack. I had a right to know.*

'Keep to the Lysander plan but be aware that we might have to use your circuit in a hurry.' *What the hell's going on, Fran? How the hell did you come to be here organizing all this?*

'Fine, I'll tell my people.' *Plenty of time to talk to Jack later. Probably no time at all.*

THE INCIDENT OFF the coast near Dungeness was reported to Walter Schellenberg immediately; when he telephoned The Citadel he was informed that Superintendent Holdaway and Inspector Davis were in Bristol and not expected back until the following morning. He therefore spoke to the duty inspector, briefed him on the situation, and suggested in a manner that was an order but did not sound so that all available units be sent to the coastal area because of the possibility of terrorist activity there that night.

THE CARS SWUNG out of the safe house, two for William Donovan and the Fuchses and two for the men guarding them. At each of the crossroads where the Resistance was positioned the lead driver flashed his lights and sped past. Twenty-five minutes before the Lysanders were expected they reached the landing field. From the east came the sound of small arms fire. After ten minutes the exchange stopped then broke out again, this time closer. From the north came the sound of more shooting.

'Don't worry.' Jack saw the way Fuchs was looking into the sky. 'We won't let you down.' The moon was so thin that no light came from it and the fighting now seemed less sporadic and closer. Madness, Jack knew. He wondered who the pilot was and what he would do, at what point he should suggest that The Caretaker take Donovan and his party out.

Last navigation check. Johnny Watson banked the Lysander, checked the compass bearing and began to time his run to the landing field.

The American, Fran noticed, was still carrying the bag she had seen at the jetty.

'Fighting's getting a bit closer, Jack.' It was the first time that night that she had called him by his name.

'How's Boy Jack?'

'Fine. Ernie's back as well.'

In the dark she thought she saw him smile then heard the sound. 'Come on, here he is.' They grabbed the passengers and ran with them to the safe ground to the left of the A lamp, the organizer already flashing the morse letter. Against the sky to the north they saw the blink of light as the pilot replied. Behind them the other lights of the flare path came on and the pilot turned and came in up wind.

To starboard Johnny Watson saw the flames as a truck exploded, to the left, and closer to the flare path, another fire. So bloody dark, he thought, can't see a bloody thing. The second Lysander circled behind him. Wonder who is so important that they're protecting the landing field, not pulling out. The flare path was three hundred yards in front of him, altitude dropping. So dark, the fighting so close. He pressed the transmit button.

'Two Three to One Five.'

'One Five receiving.' The second pilot understood why he was calling and wondered whether he would abort the landing.

'Two Three. Bit too much stick down there to ask you to hang around. Close in and follow me down.'

Bloody insane, the other man swore to himself. 'Roger, Two Three. Closing now.'

The first Lysander was dropping fast. Donovan remembered the horror of two nights ago and saw the burst of light from beneath the plane as the pilot flashed his undercarriage light again. What the hell's he doing, he heard the organizer mutter. No time for both planes to land, Donovan knew, the fighting around the field was already too close. Fuchs and his family must go. If necessary, he would trust his own luck with The Watchman and The Caretaker. The light flashed beneath the second Lysander. Christ, they're coming in together.

Bloody dark, Johnny Watson thought again, hope to Christ I get the height right. The A lamp was rushing up at him, he felt the wheels of the Lysander bump on the ground, slowed, then turned at the B and C lamps. As he approached the A lamp the second Lysander touched down. Not much time; he hoped the reception committee knew what they were doing. He turned the plane into the wind and stopped, engine still running, and pulled back the roof of the cockpit. The man was already climbing up and jerking open the canopy of the rear cockpit, then turning and helping the man and woman behind him, someone on the ground stretching and passing up a bundle then a second. Kids, he realized. The second Lysander pulled up behind him and to his right. Johnny glanced over and saw a woman running, a man behind her, then the man climbed the ladder, pulled open the roof and tumbled in. Behind him Johnny felt the roof shut, checked the all clear from the ground, and began to move down the flare path. Piece of cake really, he thought, wouldn't like to do it every night, though.

The planes pulled off the field and into the sky. On the field the men were already running for the cars, the sound of fighting now on the edge of the field itself. 'Frank will take care of you. I'll see you tomorrow night.'

Makes sense, she told herself. Try to get away separately and you double the chances of one of you making it. 'All right.'

THE PLATES AND mugs were spotlessly white and the cutlery was bright and gleaming, there had always been something special about the night operation breakfasts at The Cottage. The faces of the pilots were numb with fatigue and the two children who sat between their parents stared at the proceedings as if they still did not understand what was happening. On the opposite side of the table, next to William Donovan, sat Drake. The door opened and the cooks brought in serving dishes piled with fried bacon and eggs, then returned with toast and a large pot of tea.

'Ladies and gentlemen.' William Donovan stood up and waited for silence. 'In the years to come, we will all have reason to remember the last few hours. In the meantime I ask you to join me in my own personal thanks to you all.'

He reached to the bag on the floor and pulled out the two bottles of vintage champagne.

THE SINGING BEGAN at seven, the songs they always sang in Ardley on Bonfire Night. The ladies' committee of the cricket club were already putting the bread and cheese for the children on the collapsible tables the men had brought from the pavilion, others helping to bring the drinks from the pub. The baked potatoes would come later when the fire died down and the ashes were grey but still hot. Fran and Sarah helped while the boys played with their friends. At half-past seven the Reverend Brian Markham lit the fire, the children cheering and the sparks shooting into the night.

'Good isn't it, Mum.' Fran smiled at the boy and wondered whether Jack could see them, whether he was looking from the darkness. Without warning, the guy ignited, the straw stuffed inside the old clothes exploding with a burst and the bizarre figure toppled sideways into the flames, the children cheering and the adults joining in. Someone in the crowd, she was not sure who, put a finger under his nose, as if it was a moustache, his right hand held up mockingly in a Nazi salute, and they cheered again, a different cheer this time.

'Really good, isn't it, Auntie Fran?' She smiled again and wondered whether Jack had escaped from the landing field.

Only when the fire had died down and the potatoes had been placed in the ashes were the children allowed to queue for the food, returning to the fire and standing in a circle as the embers glowed and shone in the night. When the potatoes were ready Fran covered her face against the heat, picked them from the ashes then gave them to the children, wrapping them in newspaper so they would be able to hold them. On the other side of the fire someone began to sing again.

The celebrations ended and Fran, Boy Jack and Ernie climbed back up the hill to the farm. She kissed the boys good-night then tidied the kitchen, built up the fire in the range, made sure that the back door was unlocked, and went upstairs herself. The night outside was cold, she lay in bed listening for the noise of the door, her stomach tight with nerves. It was one o'clock. In the night outside she heard the screech of an owl hunting. Almost two. No chances, she thought, no risks. Always chances, always risks. She pulled on her dressing-gown, took the shotgun from the cupboard, loaded it, put a handful of cartridges in each of her pockets, and went downstairs. The kitchen was still warm, she sat in the shadows at the bottom of the stairs and waited. It was three in the morning. She heard no sound, only saw the door open and Jack standing there.

'Hello, love.'

She dropped the gun and crossed the floor, unsure what she was going to say or do. 'Bastard.' She hit him, hurt him, struck his face again, her anger coming out, the frustration of not knowing, of never knowing. 'Why didn't you tell me you were alive? Why did you let me think you were dead?' Why did you let me grieve over you, make me think that life would never be the same again? She was beating on his chest, her fists drumming against him, one anger subsiding and the other taking its place. She turned her face up to him and began to kiss him.

FIONA EGERTON-SMITH LEFT the Russian Tea Rooms in Harrington Road and returned to Bloomsbury to change, then her chauffeur drove her to the West End. The pavements round the theatres were crowded, the smell of chestnuts roasting on the stalls filled the streets and the first anticipation of Christmas hung in the air. The queue outside the Cambridge Theatre ran along the pavement and round the corner, the busker who was entertaining them played the accordion and supported himself on a crutch. She dropped a half-crown into his cap and walked to the restaurant off Leicester Square. A *Wehrmacht* major was waiting for her, and an hour later they were joined by Walter Schellenberg. After dinner, the three left the restaurant, the major going alone to a gaming session in Chelsea and the other two returning to the house in Bloomsbury.

'THE RUSSIAN TEA ROOMS are too obvious.' Holdaway adjusted the lamp on his desk and read the report of the team assigned to Fiona Egerton-Smith. 'Before 1939 they were run by a White Russian as the Right Club for anti-war agitators. It's precisely the place she would be seen if she felt she needed to convince anyone of her track record.' He tipped whisky into the coffee and handed the bottle to Davis. 'The busker might be interesting.'

'That's what the boys thought. When they saw him they split, one stayed with her and the other trailed him.'

'But still nothing definite on how or when she's passing anything or to whom?'

'Not yet.'

'Don't worry, it'll come.'

Davis nodded his appreciation.

'Who else has she seen?'

The inspector read Holdaway a list of names and ranks.

'And there's no suggestion she's sleeping with any of them?'

Davis shook his head. 'Most of them are either colleagues or friends of Schellenberg. She's quite open about it. He's there sometimes as well.'

Holdaway thought about the list. 'Good contacts, though, even if she only got a little out of each of them.' He closed the report and threw it onto the desk. 'What about Schellenberg? Did he take any work with him to the house?'

'He was carrying his briefcase.'

'Of course he was.' Holdaway reached across the desk, poured some more Scotch into his mug and passed the bottle back to Davis. 'Tell the boys they're doing a good job.'

THE WIND WAS cutting from the east. The women finished their coffee and bread and began to assemble outside for the roll call, stuffing whatever paper and rags they had found inside their coats and trying to pull their sleeves longer so that their hands disappeared inside. Each morning when she woke now Mary could feel the cold of winter, each evening when the work *Kommandos* struggled back into the camp she saw the pinched expression on their faces and the extra suffering in their eyes. The woman in the corner clutched her bowl to her side and walked stiffly towards the door. She could barely move, Mary thought, yet still she fought to survive.

The gates at the bottom of the camp opened and the SS guards marched in. When the inspection and head count was complete the block secretary stood in front and began the day's orders. Mary left her position, spoke quickly to the woman, and the secretary made two alterations to her list.

'Five-nine-four-three.' It was barely light. The woman from the bed in the corner turned automatically towards the field *Kommando*. 'Section two, cleaning.' The woman stopped. Not me, the expression on her face betrayed her. There must be a mistake, no such luck could fall on me. Go now, she decided, get inside before the secretary spots her mistake and sends her to the fields.

'Five-nine-six-seven.' The prisoner was young and relatively fit. Road *Kommando*, she knew, all day breaking her back and laying the stones in place. 'Section two, cleaning.' The astonishment poured over her face. She turned quickly and hurried after the other woman.

When Mary returned to her section of the block the regular members of the Organization had already settled into their jobs and the two women from the work *Kommandos* were waiting to be told what to do.

'Sweep the floors then clean the toilets.'

But someone is already sweeping the floors, she saw the confusion on their faces, the toilets are already being cleaned.

'The job isn't permanent,' she told the woman from the corner bed. 'But it will give you a chance to get fit again.'

The woman understood and thanked her. Mary turned to the younger prisoner. 'She's your friend and you're hers. From now on you look after her, help her when she needs it just as she will help you when you begin to weaken. That way you both stand a chance.' She saw the query in the younger woman's eyes. 'Why should you help her when you're young and fit and she's older and sick?' She voiced the woman's thoughts. 'How can she possibly ever help you?'

The woman lowered her eyes in embarrassment.

'Because you've done nothing for her and she's already done something for you.' The woman still did not understand. 'She's got you here, hasn't she? She's bought you two weeks off a work *Kommando*.'

The woman understood. 'Thank you.'

By THE TIME Charlie Clifford arrived home it was almost time for the early evening wireless broadcast.

'Dominoes tonight, love?' Wednesday was always dominoes night at The Fighting Cocks. Milly put his dinner in front of him and saw the way he was listening to the personal messages.

'The goose has laid three eggs. The kettle is on the stove. The farmer has a good crop.'

There was something about his body, the way he did not look at her, that betrayed him. She cleared his plate and made a pot of tea. 'Might have to go out for a while tonight, Milly love. Be a bit late. Don't bother to wait up.' He pulled on his work boots and heavy coat.

'Be careful, won't you?'

'Course I will.'

He kissed her and opened the door. As he left Rosie arrived back from the factory. When she had given their daughter supper and washed up, Milly went into the front room, took out the sewing machine and continued work on the dress for their niece's wedding in a fortnight's time.

The car was behind the pub and the other two were waiting. By the time they reached the drop zone it was gone seven. The men who had been on guard since late afternoon came out of the trees. 'We're on stand-by.' Charlie looked round and sniffed the air. 'Good night for it. No reason they should call it off now.'

At fifteen minutes to ten the organizer arrived, three other men with him and another van behind. 'It's on.'

The night was cold, made colder by the waiting.

'Don't half fancy a quick pint,' Charlie joked. 'Something in it.'

It was five minutes to midnight when they heard the plane. By five past the arms drop was complete, three of the chutes landing accurately on the drop zone but the fourth drifting into the trees to the south. When they found it the canister was hanging twenty feet from the ground.

'Bob and Chippy cut it down, the others carry on,' the organizer told them.

The other chutes were blowing gently in the wind; Charlie and George unhooked them from the containers and carried them into the woods.

'I'll finish here. You get the other one.'

There was no reason for anyone to know, Charlie thought, not if he was careful and Milly kept her mouth shut. He folded the cleanest of the chutes inside the others and pushed them into the hole. When George returned with the fourth he put it on top and pushed the soil and leaves over the hiding place.

The following morning, before he left home and whilst Milly was making the beds, he went to the front room and took the scissors from her sewing box. That afternoon he left work early and cycled to the drop zone, cut a large section from the cleanest chute, then put it in the bag he carried on the back of his bicycle, reburied the rest and cycled back to the village. Although he was confident that he had not been spotted it was only when he saw the lights of the first houses that he began to relax.

The roadblock was by The Fighting Cocks. He saw the grey uniforms of the *Wehrmacht* and the blue of the Constabulary and realized the stupidity of what he had done. Just routine, he tried to tell himself; they were not stopping everyone, perhaps they would not stop him. *Not* routine, he knew; they were searching cars and people after reports of last night's drop. A constable waved for him to stop.

'Name?'

'Charlie Clifford. I live just up the road.' He reached into his pocket and showed his identity papers.

'What's in the bag?'

'Tools. I'm a carpenter. Just going home from work.'

The policeman shone his torch at the bag, gave him back his papers and waved him on. Charlie cycled past the car and into the village.

Milly was waiting with his tea. He put the bicycle in the shed and locked the door. Only later, when Milly was working in the front room and Rosie had gone out, did he fetch the bag and take out the silk.

'Here, love, little present for you.'

She looked up from the sewing machine and ran her fingers through it. 'It's silk, Charlie, it's absolutely beautiful. Thank you.' The cloud crossed her face. 'Where did you get it? It must have cost a fortune.'

He bent down and kissed her.

'It's all right, isn't it?'

'Course it is. I wouldn't mention it to anyone, though.'

THE AFTERNOON WAS bright but chilly. Donovan sat hunched in his private box at the New York Polo Grounds and concentrated on the football: the Giants versus the Brooklyn Dodgers. Even though he was now nearly sixty he still remembered his quarterback days at Columbia, could still feel his body moving instinctively as he balanced for a throw. Shortly after two o'clock the Dodgers' Pug Manders broke through the Giants' centre for a gain of twenty-nine yards and a first down on the four-yard line. Above the roar of the crowd it was difficult to hear the loudspeaker announcement.

'Attention, please. Here is an urgent message. Will Colonel William J. Donovan call Operator Nineteen in Washington DC.'

Donovan paused only to see Manders crash over the Giants' goal line for his side's second touchdown, returned to his office, and telephoned Operator 19. Almost immediately his call was transferred to the President's son, James Roosevelt, who now worked for Donovan's Intelligence organization. Donovan listened calmly for two minutes without interruption, then informed Roosevelt that he was leaving for Washington immediately.

It was Sunday, 7 December 1941.

THE KING TOOK the telephone call from the Prime Minister in his study.

'Your Majesty, within the last half-hour I have received a communication from President Roosevelt in Washington.

'At seven-thirty this morning local time Hitler's ally Japan launched an air attack against the United States naval base at Pearl Harbor. The loss of men and ships is severe. As of thirty minutes ago the United States is at war with that country. I think it is reasonable to assume that it will only be a matter of days before she is also at war with Germany.'

6

THE WATER FROM the tap was freezing cold and the snow lay on the ground outside. Mary ate the last of the potato and meat from the bottom of the bowl and wiped the bread around it so that nothing was left.

In the room overlooking the loch at Dunvegan Jack thought of his wife. In the kitchen of the farmhouse Fran prepared the dinner and thought of her husband.

'Happy Christmas.'

Six days later, sixteen hours and twenty minutes before the New Year, the liner *Queen Elizabeth* prepared to cast off. On board were the first fifteen thousand American troops to enter the war. On the bridge, King George and President Roosevelt surveyed the activity and prepared to go ashore. Ten minutes later, the *Queen Elizabeth* cleared her berth, passed the Statue of Liberty and began her run for the North Atlantic and the U-boat packs that awaited her.

At ten, having declined the President's offer that he should stay for the New Year, King George returned to Canada in a Dakota of the United States Air Force. He lunched with his family then left the house to walk in the fields and woods that surrounded it. The afternoon was crisp and clear, and the snow on the slopes to the west sparkled in the sun. At first the King was accompanied by his equerry; after half an hour, however, he stated that he preferred to be alone and followed a route which took him in a circle through the woods and back to the house. As he neared the house he could hear a piano being played. He stamped the snow off his boots, took off his winter clothing, and went to the reading room. The door to the study was slightly ajar. He left it open so that he could hear his daughter playing and searched along the bookshelf until he came to a thin volume, bound in worn leather, the title inlaid in gold. Then he sat down, turned to the poem and began to read aloud, hearing not his own voice but that of his eldest daughter, the woman who one day would be Queen of England, as she had read it on the dark and terrible night when he had been most depressed, the night when all seemed lost and he had gone to the study and asked her to read the poem by Keats for him.

The voice was clear and still. She came again to the lines with which the work began and which the poet had repeated. His mind drifted back to the day he had quoted the lines to his people:

> Shed no tear – O, shed no tear!
> The flower will bloom another year.

The end of one year, he thought, the beginning of another. Suddenly he knew what he would do and how he would tell them.

OF THE SEVERAL functions to which Holdaway had been invited he had decided to celebrate New Year's Eve at one where Walter Schellenberg and Fiona Egerton-Smith would also be guests. The following evening he would attend a *Wehrmacht* banquet and spend the next two days at conferences in London and Birmingham before returning to Maidstone.

Jack Masters left the castle at Dunvegan and walked into the village. The Hogmanay celebrations were beginning. Even though they could understand little of his Kentish accent and he almost none of theirs, the locals had seen him before and made him welcome.

Charlie and Milly Clifford and their daughter Rosie left the house and walked to The Fighting Cocks. After they had bought her a drink, Rosie rose to leave, apparently for the dance in the village of Paddocks Wood, three miles away.

'Don't be late.' Her mother said it jokingly.

'No, Mum.'

'And don't do anything I wouldn't do.' It was what her father always said.

'No.'

He stood up and kissed her goodbye. 'Happy New Year, love.'

He wasn't that bad, she thought, a bit old-fashioned, and always going off at night, but quite good really. She kissed him back. 'Happy New Year, Dad.'

The other two girls were already at the bus stop; they waited five minutes then the bus came. 'Three singles to Tonbridge, please.'

The dance hall was already crowded, Rosie and her friends paid their entrance money and went inside. Some of the boys were local but most were German. They bought themselves a soft drink each and waited to be invited to dance, exchanging reasons for preferring the Germans and pretending not to look round them. When they were bought drinks Rosie asked for gin.

Between dances they met and discussed whether any of them had found anyone who had transport home for them.

'What about him? He's been looking at you all night.'

The corporal was two years older than them, tall and good-looking. On his uniform he wore the emblem of the 2nd *Luftlandedivision*.

'I suppose he's all right.'

When the next dance started and one of the local boys asked Rosie to dance she glanced at the soldier, saw that he was looking at her and refused. When someone else asked her, she again refused. 'I think he's finally plucked up enough courage,' one of the girls giggled. The corporal walked round the dance floor and stood in front of her. 'Would you like to dance?' His English was slow and he pronounced it with the faintest trace of a Kentish accent. Rosie held out her hand and he led her onto the floor. When the dance finished he asked her if she would like a drink. 'Gin and tonic, please.'

He bought the round and they sat together at a table in the corner.

'My name is Hans.'

'I'm Rosie.'

The band began to play again and they walked onto the floor. For the rest of the evening they danced together, Rosie not stopping him when he put his arm round her. After two more rounds of drinks they began to dance closer together.

'What's this?' Rosie ran her hands along his tunic and fingered the emblem.

'*Die Luftlandedivision.* The Airborne Division.'

'And what's this?' She was moving tight against him.

'My wings.'

'Why?' She giggled. 'Are you a bird?'

'A paratrooper.'

At midnight, when they had cheered and sung 'Auld Lang Syne', she let him kiss her, opening her lips and sucking his tongue into her mouth.

'Come outside.'

'I can't, I'll miss the last bus home.'

'It's all right, I've got the unit truck.'

'But it's cold.'

'It won't be, I've got my greatcoat.'

She told the others they had their lift and went with him to the ground behind the dance hall. Half an hour, they had agreed, then they would meet outside. The truck was in the corner, he led her to the back, pulled open the flap and helped her up, then let the cover fall back into place.

'It's dark, I won't be able to see what you're doing.'

She put her arms round his neck and kissed him, only pretending to object as he held her breasts then felt under her blouse and fumbled with the hook on her bra, helping him when he could not undo it and pressing hard against him. His hand moved down her back and inside her skirt.

She pulled in her stomach so that the skirt band was loose and he could slide his hand to the front.

'Lie down.' He laid his greatcoat on the floor.

'Why?' She lay back, ignoring the cold. He knelt over her and undid the buttons of his trousers.

'He's big.' She arched her back as he reached down and pulled her pants off. What she would tell the older women at work in the morning. She reached up, grasped his erection and guided him into her, moving up and down him then in circles around him. The paratrooper stretched out his hand, felt the texture of her pants between his fingers and knew that he had not been mistaken.

THE FIRST THING Rosie told the girls at work next morning was how good her new German boyfriend was and how he wanted to see her again so much that he had even insisted that she write her name and address for him.

An hour later Corporal Hans Gertan reported to his company commander that the night before he had met a local girl whose underclothes had been made of parachute silk. The captain's head was still throbbing from the excesses of the New Year celebrations and he seemed unable to understand the significance, other than that the corporal had struck lucky and was intent on telling everyone, until Gertan enquired, with all the subtlety of his rank and combat experience, how an eighteen-year-old girl in an occupied zone had access to parachutes. By ten he had written his report, by ten-thirty it had been typed in triplicate and the top copy filed. Then, partly because it made sense but mainly because he wished to enter the New Year with his record clean and his back protected, the captain ordered that rather than send the second and third copies to Corps Headquarters and Divisional Intelligence through the normal channels they should be taken by despatch rider. At Corps Headquarters the second copy was filed in the in-tray to be dealt with on the following Monday. At Divisional Intelligence, however, and following precisely the same reasoning as Hans Gertan's captain, the duty major ordered that additional copies be taken immediately to the Grosvenor House in London and The Citadel in Maidstone.

The Citadel itself was quiet. Holdaway was in London and Davis had telephoned to say that he was at home but would pass through in the late afternoon. The report, the duty inspector thought, was interesting, the sort of lead which sometimes paid huge dividends but which normally required a great deal of time and manipulation. He typed an accompanying memo, directed one copy to Davis for his information and sent a second to the unit covering the area for enquiries to begin the following week.

WHEN JACK MASTERS arrived at Arisaig, Drake was waiting for him. He closed the door, unlocked the security cabinet and handed Jack the report. The data concerned the German losses on the Eastern front with Russia and the projected depletion of the garrison in Britain to man the promised final push against Moscow when the snows thawed. It was based on material from Berlin and its source was the agent codenamed Prospero.

'It's turning, Jack. Hitler's bogged down and the Russian winter is devouring men and equipment faster than anyone could have imagined. The expectation is that he will begin to withdraw troops by the end of February or the beginning of March.' He poured them each a malt. 'Happy New Year.'

Jack wondered what Fran and Boy Jack were doing and how they had spent Christmas. 'Happy New Year.'

'No risks this time, Jack. It's just a recce, make sure that everyone knows what they're planning towards, confirm that local targets fit in with the overall strategy. Plus, a check that the arms dumps are in place, and that those men who have escaped from the camps are in position in Wales.'

'Any idea when?'

'April, I suspect.'

At three the first members of the Argos network took their positions near the landing field. Shortly after, Drake and The Watchman began the drive to The Cottage. At four Davis made his check visit to The Citadel. The address that the girl called Rosie had given to the corporal was in the village next to Lord Southerton's estate, the warning flashed the moment he picked up the duty inspector's memo and flicked through the report it accompanied. Schellenberg and the leak, he thought. Cover yourself, he told the inspector without giving a reason, put someone on to it tonight.

CHARLIE CLIFFORD CAME in from feeding his rabbits, washed his hands and sat down at the table. 'Where's Rosie?'

'Gone to some friends straight from work. I told her not to be late.' Milly put the plate in front of him. 'Smells good, love.' He leant across and switched on the wireless. 'Tastes good as well.' She heard the tones and the personal messages, and knew which affected him by the way he did not look at her. When the bulletin was over he switched off the set and adjusted the dial slightly. 'I might have to go out tonight for a couple of hours. You go to the pub as we arranged, I'll see you there later.' The evening of New Year's Day was traditionally an extension of the night before, one of the few occasions when the wives were as welcome as the men.

'Don't worry, I'll wait for you.' She tried to hide her nerves. 'You can pick me up when you come back.'

He left the table and pulled on his boots and working coat. 'You go. George's wife will be there, a few others as well. Can't have you sitting at home by yourself on New Year's Day, can we?' He was at the door.

'Take care, won't you?'

He looked back at her and winked. 'Don't worry, love, I always do.'

The night air was sharp and the half-moon concealed behind the clouds. Hope they're not late, Charlie thought, be a pity to miss good drinking time. He tightened the coat round him and walked down the road. The car was parked half-way between his house and the pub. The landing was not confirmed yet, of course. They still might get everything set up and then be told that the whole thing was off. He was ten yards from the car. Should be back in time for a few pints after, the pub would be open until well gone midnight. He stuck his hands in his pockets and began to whistle. Pity the poor buggers who'd been guarding the field since mid-afternoon; bet they were bloody freezing.

The car door opened and the two men bundled him in, a third shut the door and the car pulled away. What the hell's going on? Charlie tried to fight back, pull his hands from his pockets. Who the hell are you? Lice. He knew what was happening, tried to shout for help, to reach the door. The hand was over his mouth and his arms were pinned beneath him. The car skidded round the corner at the bottom and accelerated out of the village.

'We know all about it, Charlie.' The car turned into a wood, the driver switched off the engine and the man in the front passenger seat turned to face him. 'We know all about you.' Charlie Clifford watched as the man took a knife from his pocket and opened the blade. Someone had betrayed him. He was shivering with fear. The man took a box of matches from his pocket, opened it, selected a match and began to sharpen the end. Not George, he thought, it couldn't be George. He knew what the man was going to do and that it would hurt more than he could ever imagine.

'I don't know what you're going on about.'

'Of course you do, Charlie.' The man seized his right hand and locked it on the top of the seat, fingers outstretched. 'You know exactly what I'm going on about.' He took hold of the third finger. 'How's Milly by the way, still doing her bit of sewing?' He placed the sharp end of the matchstick between the soft flesh of the finger and the nail. 'Not that they'd be interested in Milly, of course. Rosie

434

now, that would be a different matter.' It was a pity they didn't have a photo of the girl and the corporal the sergeant thought, that would have really thrown the bugger. 'You don't know what the Germans are like with a woman, do you Charlie? Never seen 'em at it.' He sniffed as if it did not concern him. 'Especially when they've seen a couple of their mates shot by the terrorists.' He exerted the slightest pressure on the match. 'Take it in turns. Bloody animals.'

They're lying, Charlie tried to tell himself, braced himself for the pain. Not my Rosie. The other fear began to take over.

'Saw them at it once, made me sick. Good-looking girl she was, just like your Rosie.'

If they knew about him, the illogic of fear flooded through him, they knew about everything: the network, the plan to assassinate Schellenberg and his whore and the bastard called Holdaway.

'Promise you'll see Milly and Rosie are all right.' They must know everything otherwise why would they pick him up? And if they picked him tonight they knew about the landing.

'I'll make sure they're okay.'

He believed the man, convinced himself he had no option.

'So what is it?' The question was neutral, the sergeant too experienced to make it otherwise.

'Lysander. If it was an arms drop we'd have the barns ready to hide the stuff in.' I'm doing right, aren't I, Milly? I have to protect you and Rosie.

'So you're standing by till nine?' The interrogator used his limited knowledge to suggest that he knew everything.

Charlie's head had fallen forward. He nodded.

'What's the code?' The interrogator controlled his excitement.

'The daffodils are in bloom.' Sorry, Rosie love. He had forgotten who or what he was betraying.

'Same field?' He hoped he had the jargon and intonation right.

The man in the back seat nodded again. 'Vennards, like before.'

'What time are you due there?'

'Half seven.' He laughed grimly. 'Lookout. Make sure it was clear.'

'And the pub after?' It was delivered in a friendly tone.

'Yeah.' There was total resignation in the voice. 'Milly was going to wait for me there.'

No time to waste, the sergeant was thinking, they could get the rest from him later. 'Your place is empty then?'

Charlie grunted.

The house was dark. From The Fighting Cocks came the sound of singing. Charlie, the sergeant and two of the men went inside while the fourth parked the car out of sight at the top of the street. At nine o'clock they listened to the radio and heard the confirmation.

'Is that it?'

There was something in the voice that alerted Charlie; for the first time the suspicion began to come upon him that the Lice had not known about the drop that evening; for the first time the realization came upon him of what he had done.

'Have I got time for a pee?'

'Where is it?'

'The outhouse at the back.'

The sergeant turned to the first of the two men who accompanied him and the constable nodded that he had checked.

'Go with him. But don't let anyone see you.'

EVEN WITH THE singing the pub felt empty without Charlie. At half-past eleven Milly made her excuses and went back to the house. A nice hot drink in bed, she thought, perhaps a biscuit as well. She lit the light and put the kettle on the range, then turned back across the kitchen for the tin of cocoa. The room was cold, she went to draw the curtains and saw that the door to the outhouse was slightly ajar. Not like Charlie to leave it open, she thought. Better shut it before something gets at his rabbits. She picked up the torch, went across the yard, pushed the door open and looked inside. The chair was on the floor where Charlie Clifford had kicked it away, his belt was round the beam across the ceiling and his feet dangled six inches above the floor.

THE CONDITIONS WERE bad, a twenty-knot wind from the east blowing them off course and freezing cold. The only salvation was the rum Johnny Watson had put in his flask of coffee and the sandwiches the policemen at The Cottage had made up for him.

'Last checkpoint.'

At least the network manning the field was experienced. At least Jack had worked with them before.

'Four minutes.'

There was no return cargo, just a quick exit from the field, the car or van waiting, then he would hide up until it was safe to move.

'Got it.' Johnny Watson circled the field once then came in. The wheels struck the frozen ground and the Lysander bounced in the air then settled. He taxied back to the A lamp, the Colt in his hand as always, and waited to take off. Jack clambered out of the passenger cockpit, shut the roof and climbed down the ladder. The agent in charge of the field gave the pilot the thumbs up sign and the Lysander trundled down the field, gathered speed and took off.

'Everything all right?'

'Fine.'

They hurried across the field to the two cars and van hidden in the woods. There were two routes out – one to the west and the other east then splitting north and south a mile and a half from the field. Too many people, Jack noted, all right for a weapons drop but too many vehicles for just one person coming in. The cars bumped out of the woods, Jack and the agent in the rear seat of the lead car, the driver and another man in front, and turned east, the van following them and the other car turning west. His hands and feet were frozen, the organizer offered him a brandy flask and he drank from it, coughing as the liquid burned down his throat. 'Safe house in Marden.' The organizer took a drink himself and handed the flask to the men in front. 'Not much around, you should be able to move off as soon as you want.'

'Any problems?'

They were almost at the junction.

'None at all.'

A car slewed across the road in front of them and their driver braked instinctively.

'Accelerate.' Jack reacted automatically and glanced over his shoulder, saw that the van behind them was too close, that there was no room to reverse. A lorry came out of the field twenty yards back and sealed them in. Lice. 'Accelerate,' he shouted again at the driver. 'Get us out of here.' He reached for the gun in his coat, his fingers stiff with the cold. The driver pushed the car into gear and stalled the engine. On his right the organizer opened the door and began to get out, the first burst from the sub-machine-gun hitting him.

'He's The Watchman.' Jack knew the man was dead and hoped

437

the men in front would understand. Edward Marshall – already he was rehearsing his cover story. The figures were coming out of the ditches on either side of the road and surrounding them. Born 1907, family killed in the invasion. The guns were pointing at them, covering them. Bloody Lice, he knew for certain. 'He's The Watchman,' he told the men in the front again.

Everything in your head, Drake had warned him, you're still the one they're after. Edward Marshall, he slammed the details into his subconscious, new agent, details of training in Arisaig, names of a couple of instructors. Nothing that would help them; something, anything, that might help him. In front of him the driver put his hands on his head.

Decision time: end it now, take one or two with you, or hope that the men in the front have understood and that the Lice will believe your story after they've knocked the shit out of you. He held his hands above his head and waited to be ordered out of the car.

THEY HAD TOASTED the Führer and the port was being passed round when an orderly approached the banquet table at which Holdaway and the general who had invited him were seated and informed him that he was wanted on the telephone. Holdaway excused himself and went to the foyer.

'Davis. We've just intercepted a landing, picked up a cell plus the person brought in.'

'Why wasn't I told earlier?'

'We only knew ourselves an hour before it happened.'

'I'm leaving now.'

He returned to the hall, offered his apologies to the general and hurried to the car. 'Maidstone. Yesterday.' The drive took eighty-five minutes. When Holdaway's driver pulled up at the barrier at The Citadel the brakes smelt of burning rubber. Davis began briefing him as they crossed the courtyard.

'Corporal in the Airborne Division went to a dance in Tonbridge last night, got lucky. Smart operator, noticed that the girl was wearing pants made of parachute silk.' They went into the building. 'Didn't say anything but made sure he had her name and address. By the time it was passed to us it was gone five.'

He covered for the other inspector. 'We put a watch on the house and picked up the father on his way to the pub.' They went down the first flight of stairs to the cell block. 'The boys did a good job on him; he let slip about the drop tonight and we staked out the area. One man made a run for it, he's dead. We have five prisoners.'

Holdaway was still wearing his dinner jacket. 'Schellenberg?'

'On his way. The butler knew where he was.'

They stopped at the top of the cell block. 'So what do we have?'

'Two in the front seat of the car, one in the back; the other one in the back was the one who was shot. Two others in the van. We're still looking for a possible third vehicle.'

'Let's have a look.'

They walked along the corridor and looked through the door holes at the interrogations already being conducted. 'Anybody said anything?'

'Not yet.'

'Right, let's start with the car driver.'

The beatings had already lasted almost two hours. The man's face was a mass of blood and he could hardly stand.

'Out,' Holdaway told the two men questioning him. Davis closed the door behind them. They would have him in thirty seconds, he thought, or not at all.

'Name.' Holdaway was standing on the man's right, Davis on his left. Get him to say something, they both knew, get him talking and he might not think what he was saying.

There was no response.

'I asked your name.'

Nothing.

'Right cockup you lot made tonight.'

Still nothing.

'Couldn't organize a piss-up in a brewery.'

'Sod off.' The man almost spat the words.

Davis not only knew what Holdaway was going to say next but how he was going to say it.

'Right bloody shambles. Only lucky it wasn't The Watchman we shot.' The sentence was open, ambiguous, not even a question.

'Yeah.' There were so many things in the response: an arrogance that the prisoner could not control, his contempt of them, an admission that he not only knew who The Watchman was but had met

439

him, worked with him. Worse, the worst thing of all, a confirmation of the question.

'The Watchman was there tonight, wasn't he?' Holdaway was glaring at him, Davis watching his eyes for the slightest clue. 'But he wasn't the one we shot, was he? He was the other man in the back.' They both saw the quiver in the right eyelid, a fraction of a second, milli-fraction, before the man against the cell wall managed to control himself. Davis could not believe their luck, saw the look on the prisoner's face as they began to smile and he realized what and whom he had been tricked into revealing.

'Stupid bastard.' Holdaway turned away and banged on the door to be let out.

They walked along the corridor to the cell where The Watchman was being beaten and looked through the peep hole. 'So that's him.' Holdaway moved away so that Davis could see. A guard came down the stairs behind them. 'Schellenberg's just arriving.' Holdaway looked again at the man in the cell then returned upstairs.

Schellenberg was wearing the dress uniform of the SD. He was pulling off his gloves and hanging up his coat when they knocked on the door and entered his office. 'A good night's work, I understand.' He made no reference to where he had been or how Davis had traced him.

'Better than you think.'

'What do you mean?'

Holdaway turned to Davis. 'You picked him up, you tell him.'

'It looks as if we've got The Watchman.'

'Explain.' Schellenberg sat down and laid his gloves in his cap.

Davis summarized the events as he had relayed them to Holdaway and escorted Schellenberg to the cells so that he could see for himself, then returned to the office.

'We've done enough.' Schellenberg sat back in his chair and considered what he should do. 'I think the Gestapo should take it from here.'

'Why?'

'Politics.' He sensed the mix of surprise and hostility in them both and waited until they understood what he was saying. We've caught The Watchman. If we keep him to ourselves and he talks, then all well and good, but if we keep him to ourselves and he doesn't or if we kill him in the process then we have problems. If the Gestapo make him talk then we share in the glory, but if they don't or if *they* kill him in the process, then we still get the credit for the capture.

'What time could they be here?' asked Holdaway.

Schellenberg shrugged. 'If they got a move on, sometime in the morning.' He picked up the telephone, requested a number in London and spoke in German.

'It's settled,' he told them when he had finished. 'Unfortunately the people who wish to be present are celebrating and will have to be contacted. They should be here by nine, ten at the latest.'

It was two-thirty.

'One word with the bastard,' said Holdaway.

'Only one?' queried Schellenberg.

Edward Marshall, born 1907. They hit him again. Recruited into British Resistance and trained at Arisaig. The blood was running into his eyes and his ribs were broken where they had kicked him. Firearms instructor Bill Ferguson, self-defence Ian Gilroy. Think it, Eddie, think of nothing else. He did not know how long he had been in the cell or where they were going to hit him next. Believe it so they'll believe you when you tell them. Holdaway looked through the peep hole. Edward Marshall, Jack began thinking the words again. The door smashed open and a man in a dinner jacket came in.

'You stupid bastard.' The anger in Holdaway's eyes was more frightening and terrifying than all the beatings. 'You think you can fool us.' Holdaway was close to him, jabbing his finger against his nose where they had broken it. 'You think you can fool me.' The movement was sudden, Holdaway's left hand seizing the front of Jack's shirt and lifting him off the ground, his right reaching down, Davis, even Schellenberg, taken aback by its animal force. 'You know who I am, but I also know who you are.' The right hand was like a vice round his testicles. 'No more names. No getting out of it this time.' The shock of the pain was taking his breath away.

'A little lesson, my stupid bloody friend. Something for you to think about tonight.' The grip tightened and the needles shot through him. He felt the first panic, still not able to breathe. 'Well, this is nothing.' The pain was crucifying him. Anything to stop it, a voice in him pleaded. Holdaway's face was inches from his own, the eyes boring into him.

'Just wait till the Gestapo start on you, because that's who's coming in the morning.'

441

He passed out and Holdaway dropped him onto the floor of the cell. 'Leave him till morning. He should be ready to talk by then.' He left the cell, the others behind him, and nodded to the warder to lock the door.

THE FIRST INDICATION that something was amiss reached the North at ten the following morning. At that time, and eight hours in advance of her normal schedule, the radio operator covering the Argos network reported rumours that members of the network had been arrested the night before. The message was passed immediately to Drake. That evening the operator came through again: an unknown number of the network had been arrested by the Lice after the landing the previous night, together with the passenger they were escorting. Two members of the network who had taken a different exit route from the field were in hiding. She herself had cut all contacts with the group. Drake was informed immediately and ordered the following message to be sent to each network, each despatch to be in the personal code of the network organizer.

PROBABLE THAT WATCHMAN CAPTURED. ENTIRE ORGANIZATION AT RISK. TAKE WHATEVER ACTION NECESSARY TILL FURTHER NOTICE.

Then he informed the Prime Minister.

THE CELL WAS dark around him, the colours swimming in front of him and the pain still contorting him. Jack rolled onto his side and tried to pull himself up. Edward Marshall, he told himself, knew it was no good. The pain was all over him, his face, his ribs, his entire body. Marshall, he tried to say it again, the red and black clearing slightly, Edward Marshall. Stand up, he told himself, see what happens.

He pushed himself to his hands and knees, the effort seeming to take an eternity, and looked around, at the window in the wall and the blood on the floor. The pain was not as bad as before, not nearly as bad as when Holdaway had him against the wall. He straightened his body and tried to ignore the pain.

Total silence, no beatings or screaming. He remembered who was coming in the morning and understood why they had stopped tonight.

The window was too high up to see through. He looked round the cell again, at the stone floor where they had kicked him, and at the bed in the corner. Don't think that Mary was here, he told himself, don't think of Fran and Boy Jack, don't think of anyone except Eddie Marshall.

It was as if he were outside the cell and looking in on himself: the window high in the wall at the head, the moonlight playing on his blood on the walls and the floor, the door to the corridor in the wall opposite the window.

Sorry, Fran, but at least you know the truth. A pity it came so near the end when we both thought we had made it. Proud of you, old thing, can't tell you how proud I am of what you did. The anger began to seep in, at the unit which had arranged the drop, at himself for lacking the courage to end it when he had the chance. No anger, he admonished himself. If you feel anger they will sense it and use it against you.

The moonlight was mixing with the red on the floor. This is nothing, he remembered what Holdaway had said about the Gestapo in the morning. Edward Marshall, he tried to imprint the identity on his mind, to establish an image that he could hold on to as they tore the body and soul out of him. He looked round the cell again: the window in the wall above the bed, the moonlight playing on the wall, the red of his blood on the grey of the floor and the door in the wall opposite the window.

He saw it and knew he must be mistaken – the cell door leading to the corridor outside. The door was open. He knew it was a trick and shuffled forward anyway, knew that Holdaway was waiting for him. He stepped into the corridor. Nothing, nobody. The lights in the ceiling were dim, but there was just enough light to see by. Another door was at the end of the corridor. A trick, he still thought. The pain was now lost in his alertness. He moved along the corridor, the other cells still locked, nothing he could do for them. The door was open. He went through it and up the stairs.

The pain surged back into his testicles. He slid his right hand inside his trousers and supported them, nothing he could do about the pain in the rest of his body. All a trick, he knew. Two doors at the top of the stairs, one closed the other open. Edward Marshall, he was still telling himself, born 1907, wife and daughter killed during invasion.

443

He went through the door and felt the cold on his face, saw that he was in the courtyard, the glare of the lights in the main parking area to his left but the corner where he now stood lost in shadows. He looked round him and saw the door in the outer wall. No trick, yet he knew it must still be, that they were waiting for him outside. He crossed the five yards to the door, pushed it open and stepped into the street.

Not much of the night left. He struggled to make his mind function, to work out what he had to do and where he had to go. Twenty miles, he began to calculate, move at night, hide up during the day.

Prospero. He left the cover of the wall and shuffled down the road, away from the main gates, began to laugh. Bloody Prospero.

Thirty miles, he calculated again, nearer forty, almost fifty, the night so cold. He began to climb the hill out of the town, unaware how slowly he was moving or how badly he was limping, aware only that he must not stop. Two nights, he told himself, no more than three, four at the most, then he would be home. Then Fran could take care of him.

HOLDAWAY WORKED THE lather into the stubble on his face and smelt the hot of the water. It had been a good night, he dipped the razor into the bowl and began to shave. The clean uniform was on the hanger and the bacon was sizzling in the frying pan.

He had returned home at four-thirty and made do with the hour's sleep, felt fresh anyway. By the time he was back at The Citadel it was still not half-past six. The reports from the unit that had made the arrest near Marden had been written up overnight and were on his desk. He flicked through them, noted that Davis had not countersigned them and should do so before he passed them to Schellenberg with his own commendations, then went through to the office of the inspector in charge of the unit. The man was asleep in his chair.

Holdaway shook him awake. 'Good job last night. Well done.'

The inspector looked at his watch. 'Christ, what time are they due?'

'Couple of hours, but I expect they'll be late.'

'Better tidy up and get one of the lads to brew a pot of tea.'

In the yard below Schellenberg's car drove under the barrier. There was the sound of running in the corridor outside and the unit sergeant burst in. 'He's gone.'

'Who?' The inspector was still half asleep.

'The Watchman.' The sergeant was out of breath.

'Piss off.' There was the slightest edge of irritability in the inspector's voice.

'His door's open, all the doors to the outside are open.'

'Oh, Christ!' They ran down the corridors and the stairs, to the block below. The door of The Watchman's cell was open and the floor was still red with his blood.

Schellenberg came up behind them.

'Who was in charge last night?' Holdaway turned on the inspector. 'When was he last checked? Who checked him?'

Clear up the mess first, work out who and how later. 'Inspector Davis,' he told the sergeant. 'Right away.'

Holdaway looked at Schellenberg and waited for the blast. The *Gruppenführer* shook his head. 'The driver, the man who put the finger on The Watchman. He's the one they're coming for.' He looked around at them. 'You understand what I'm saying?'

They nodded.

'What condition is he in?'

'Like the others, not bad, not good.'

'He'll do. By the time he's admitted it they'll have finished him off anyway.' He turned to the inspector. 'Tell your people now, have them rewrite their reports.'

The man left them and hurried up the corridor.

'Thank you.' Holdaway tried to understand why the *Gruppenführer* had protected them.

'My balls as well as yours,' said Schellenberg simply.

Holdaway had been at his desk less than ten minutes when the sergeant knocked on his door and came in.

'I thought you went to fetch Inspector Davis.'

'I did, sir.'

'Well?' He remembered the morning in Portsmouth when he had invited Davis to join him in Maidstone, outlined the job to him. Davis' reaction.

'I'm sorry, sir.'

As long as it was civil, Davis had said, not political.

'Inspector Davis wasn't at his home.'

445

Davis always so thorough, always so dedicated to the job, the sergeant knew Holdaway was thinking, the first to arrive and the last to leave.

'What about his wife and family?'

'They're not there either.'

Davis the collator, the man with all the reports, who spent whole bloody nights at The Citadel when no one else was there.

'You're sure?'

Davis whom he had recruited, helped, trusted.

'Yes, sir.'

Not Schellenberg's woman, Davis all along, right from the beginning. He crashed the baton on the table and sent its contents hurtling across the floor.

THE ICE WAS layered on the windows of the kitchen. Outside it was still dark. Fran made up the range and put the kettle on. They had enjoyed Christmas and the New Year, but already both seemed so far away. She made herself toast, ate it quickly with a mug of tea, put on her warmest work coat and boots and went outside.

Overnight there had been a fresh fall of snow. She went to the barn, her footprints across the yard, fetched the hay for the animals and went to check those in the fields. When she returned to the house twenty minutes later the footprints had disappeared.

The shotgun was in the kitchen. Fran loaded it, thumbed back the hammers and walked carefully to the door of the barn. It was as if her footprints had been brushed away. The single drop of blood on the snow was so small that she almost did not see it. She opened the door, went inside and saw the second spot of red. Then a hand came over her mouth and she heard his voice.

'It's all right, Fran. It's me.' He began to release his hold on her. 'Don't worry, old thing, bit of a mess, that's all.'

She turned and looked at him, felt a scream coming then stopped it. 'Oh my God, Jack, what have they done to you?'

He flopped back onto a bale. She took off her coat and wrapped it round him, knew she must take him into the house.

'Not while the boys are there. They mustn't know.'

What's happened, she wanted to ask, who's done this to you? She half carried and half dragged him to the back of the barn and loosened

446

some hay for him to lie on. 'I'll be back.' She began to run, to get some blankets, to make him something hot.

'Leave the gun.'

She laid it on the bale beside him, brought some thick blankets from the house, wrapped them round him, and went back to the house again. Boy Jack and Ernie were just waking. She warmed a saucepan of milk, poured it into a mug, stirred in some sugar and went back to the barn. As she opened the door she sensed the gun come up and smelt the fear.

'Me,' she whispered. The gun was lowered and she went to the corner. Jack's hands and limbs were frozen, and the last of the colour had drained from his face days before. As she sat him up to feed him she realized he was wearing hardly any clothes. 'It's all right now, love.' She held his head and raised the mug to his lips so that he could sip. 'Just a little at a time.' The spasm shook him. 'All right, love,' she stroked his hair and held him close. 'Everything's all right now.' He tried to smile his thanks and moved his head for more of the liquid.

By the time Fran returned to the kitchen Boy Jack had begun to make breakfast. She took some of the red coals from the range and made up the fire in the bedroom, built up the range again and put water on to boil. The moment the boys had gone she poured three hot-water bottles, laid them in her bed, and went back to the barn. Jack could barely move. She checked that they were alone then half dragged half carried him across the yard into the kitchen, and laid him in the soft chair by the fire. Then she fetched the shotgun from the barn, brushing away the marks across the yard, locked all the doors, pulled the curtains, and laid the gun within arm's reach on the kitchen table.

Jack was shivering, his hands gripping the chair and his face still tight with cold and pain. Slowly and carefully she took off his coat and unbuttoned his shirt, fetched the scissors from the drawer and cut the rest of his clothes from him, aware that she was hurting him every time she touched him. His body was black and blue and caked with dried blood and she could see where his ribs were broken. His testicles were tight and shrivelled, and his penis was so shrunk with cold that it had almost disappeared inside him. She poured some water into a bowl, soaked a cloth in it, and began to clean him, stopping when she saw she was hurting him. When she had dried

447

him she went upstairs, fetched a long thick winter nightdress, cut it down the front and slipped it on him. Then she helped him up the stairs, laid him in the bed and sat with him as he fell asleep.

When he woke two hours later Fran propped the pillows behind him, sat him up, and fed him with soup.

'What time is it?'

'Eleven o'clock.'

'When Boy Jack and Ernie come back I'll hide in the barn.'

'You'll do no such thing.' She fed him another spoonful of soup. 'I've made a bed for you in the cupboard. You sleep there when they're about and come out during the daytime and at night.' He tried to object and she stopped him. On the chest at the side of the bed he saw the shotgun.

'Do you want some more soup?'

He shook his head.

'Do you want to sleep again?'

'I want to talk to you.'

She made sure he was comfortable then sat on the bed with him. 'What happened?'

He could taste again the fear in the car and feel the pain as Holdaway held his testicles. 'I came in by plane from the North. The Lice were waiting for me. I don't think they even knew it was me who was coming in, they just knew about the landing.'

'How did they know?'

He told her from the beginning, from the minute the car pulled across the road to the moment he had passed through the last door at The Citadel and stepped into the street. Who helped you, she wanted to ask. Why did they do it? If he did not tell her there would be a reason. The agent called Prospero, he would have told her if he could, inside The Citadel itself. He was beginning to shiver again. Fran helped him lie down and pulled the blankets around him. 'Is there anything you want me to do?'

Too many secrets in his head, he thought, too many in hers. 'Get the vicar and Stan Bradley.'

'I'll be half an hour.'

The vicar's car was parked by the house. Fran knocked on the front door and waited. When Mabel Markham answered she asked if the vicar was in and was told he was with someone.

'It will only take ten seconds.'

Mabel tapped on the door of the study, apologized for interrupting, and told him that Mrs Masters needed to see him. The vicar came into the hall. There was a smile on his face. 'Come in.' He guided her into the sitting-room and shut the door behind them. 'What's wrong?' The smile had disappeared.

'Jack's at the farm. He's in a bad way. He wants you and Stan.'

'What's happened?'

'He can tell you.'

The two men arrived separately to avoid rousing suspicion. While Jack spoke to them Fran remained in the room. He told them of his capture and detention though giving them even fewer details of his escape than he had Fran.

'Protection.' Stan dealt with the point quickly and easily. 'You can't move from here, but you can't stay here unguarded. Brian and I will both cover you at night, take it in turns during the daytime.'

'I'll need a gun.' Jack made himself forget his body and concentrate on the problems that faced them. 'What is there?'

'Smith & Wessons, sub-machine-guns, grenades.'

'Thompson, plenty of ammunition.'

'I'll bring one up tonight.'

'Two,' said Fran.

At four that afternoon she shifted Jack to the hiding place in the cupboard and removed any trace of him from the house and barn, making sure not even the smallest drop of blood remained on the snow. That evening, when Boy Jack and Ernie were asleep, she moved Jack back into her bed and held him close to her. At midnight, when the house was quiet, she sat at the kitchen table and wrote and encoded the message to the North.

THE CUT GLASS of the decanter sparkled like ice, a waiter poured them each a port and another offered them cigars. Schellenberg selected one, allowed the man to cut it for him, and sat back in his chair. 'No news?'

'None at all.' Holdaway was succinct.

'I'm sorry it was Davis. He seemed a good man.'

The matter had been dealt with quickly and efficiently, the reports rewritten as Schellenberg had instructed and the escape concealed. The Gestapo, in their turn, had been equally quick and efficient, the suspect having died of a heart attack two hours after his interrogation began and the report which followed suggesting that before his death the prisoner had admitted that the agent shot whilst trying to escape had been The Watchman. The other men had been removed from The Citadel immediately and sent to labour camps in different parts of the country, the balance of two bodies and two reports providing the bureaucratic equilibrium which was necessary for no further questions to be asked.

'The leaks,' Schellenberg watched the smoke curl from the cigar. 'I assume that at certain stages it was considered that someone else might have been responsible.'

Holdaway was uncertain why the man had seen fit to bring the woman into the conversation or how he should respond. 'Yes.'

Walter Schellenberg leant forward and balanced the cigar carefully on the side of the ashtray. 'Don't worry, it was something I also considered.'

THE DINNER WAS in the country house which served as the officers' mess of the general headquarters staff. Even during the past four weeks the build-up of men and equipment in the valleys and woods of the Free North had accelerated. Present that evening, therefore, were not only officers of the Dominions, but also from America and France. The conversation was sometimes professional and sometimes light-hearted. Near the top of the table a piper stood to attention and waited to be requested to play. Towards the end of dinner an orderly informed Drake that he was wanted on the telephone. Drake excused himself and followed the man through to the study.

'Yes.' He never identified himself unless he knew who was trying to contact him.

'Operations.' He recognized the voice. 'We've just received a despatch which needs your decoding.'

'Who from?' He hoped against reason.

'The Caretaker.' Drake felt his body sag and knew it was over. 'Send it over.'

'The despatch rider is already on his way.'

Twenty minutes later Drake was again called from the dinner. The message was in a sealed envelope. Drake asked the orderly to bring him a large malt then sat at the desk in the study, slit open the envelope, took out the message sheet inside and laid it in front of him. The orderly knocked on the door, brought him his drink then left, closing the door behind him. Almost reluctantly Drake began to decode the message.

AR GO SN ET WO RK TO TA LL YC OM PR OM

ARGOS NETWORK TOTALLY COMPROMISED.

From the dining-room came the sound of the piper. Drake left the desk and walked to the fire in the centre of the main wall, staring at the flames and occasionally sipping the whisky, considering not only the consequence to the Resistance but to the individual who had built it up. Only after five minutes did he return to the desk and continue the decoding.

ARGOS NETWORK TOTALLY COMPROMISED. WATCHMAN SAFE. BEST THANKS TO PROSPERO AND SINCEREST HOPES THAT HE IS WELL. HAPPY NEW YEAR.

Something The Watchman had not told him – why should The Caretaker know? He pushed the chair back from the desk and began to laugh. Then he picked up the paper he had used that evening, including the wad on which he had rested the sheet as well as the blotting paper, and placed it in the fire, watching it burn and still laughing. Only when the paper had turned to ashes and he had crumpled the ashes to dust did he return to the dining-room.

At twelve o'clock that night the first fifty tanks of the Tenth Panzer Division left the port of Harwich, on the east coast of England, bound for the Russian Front. Two hours later the first three infantry battalions also departed. At each sailing for the next four days the exodus continued, to be repeated again a week later.

7

THE RAIN RAN in streams down the windows and the glass glinted in the spotlights on the perimeter fence, the black of the night beyond. To the right, from the tier of bunks on the other side of the hut, Mary heard the rustling as someone rose from her bed and made her way towards the toilets at the end of the room, the blanket pulled over her head and shoulders, the shoulders themselves bent and curled and the eyes looking only at the floor. After ten minutes, when the prisoner had not come back, Mary went to check. The woman was dead on the floor.

At ten that morning, Annie went to the administration block to sketch the portrait of a guard who wished to send it to a relative in Germany as a present. It was one of the ways Annie not only survived but helped them all survive, the way she contributed extra food and items which those whose portraits she drew paid her. When she returned two hours later she took Mary aside and sat on the bunk.

'One of the clerks told me, the SS have asked for the names of all NN prisoners. There's a story that two men were taken from the male camp a week ago.'

I will help you and protect you as much as I can, the block secretary had told her, but always remember that you are NN, that in the end you will always disappear into the night and the fog.

'Why did she tell you?'

The portrait artist was known round the camp. 'I did a sketch of her once. She knows I'm a friend of yours.'

It would happen one day, Mary had always supposed. She had

made her plans against it but had always shunned putting them into practice because of what it involved. That lunchtime, however, after they had eaten their soup and bread, she told Annie and the secretary what she intended to do. That evening the secretary told her it had been arranged and she began to cough, holding a rag to her mouth. The next morning, after they had stood for the SS roll call, the secretary read her number and ordered her to report to the camp hospital.

The queue was fifty patients long. The two doctors attending them, one a prisoner and one from the SS, sat at a table at the end of the ward closest to the door. Mary stood near the back of the queue and shuffled forward with it. To the left, and at an angle to the main ward, was the section where those patients suffering from tuberculosis were sent. At the end of each bunk were spittoons into which the prisoners coughed and spat the contents of their diseased lungs.

After eight minutes the queue had been cut to ten patients, the two doctors allowing mere seconds for each person to explain her symptoms and why she should be admitted, and rejecting most and returning them to the work *Kommandos*. In the case of those patients coughing like Mary, a bowl was provided into which they spat their saliva. The patient then returned to her block and was recalled only if tests on the saliva proved positive.

You have only one chance, Mary told herself and tried to calculate how long it would be before she stood at the front of the queue, how long before she had to do it. The woman in front of her could barely stand. As the queue shuffled forward she lost her balance and fell against the spittoon, the contents running in a thick green slime across the floor. Mary turned away so that she did not have to look at the liquid. Either this, or the night and the fog. Now, or they will see you. She moved quickly to her left, took a spittoon, drank the contents into her mouth and stepped back in line. Whatever you do don't swallow. Don't think of what you've done or you'll vomit the whole lot up.

She turned back and saw that the hospital secretary had seen what she had done. 'You,' the woman called to her. It was all arranged, the secretary in her own block had told her; she had done the woman's portrait, Annie had said. 'You next.' Mary picked up the bowl, spat the liquid into it, and gave her camp number. The secretary wrote her number down and Mary returned to the block.

453

At the roll call three mornings later her number was called so that all would hear and she returned to the sick bay. The hospital secretary checked the number against her list and allocated her a bunk.

'You know why I'm here?' The question was deliberately ambiguous.

The woman glanced at the doctors to her right. 'Yes.'

'Will you help me?' It was still ambiguous.

'When you've done it.'

There were a hundred and thirty women in the room, the system the same as in the block she had left. Some of the women shuffled like the half-dead across the floors and between the beds, the rest lying motionless on their bunks and staring aimlessly at the ceiling. Mary clipped the paper with her details to the board at the foot of the bunk and waited.

At midday the hospital orderlies came with the soup, at six with the artificial jam. When the hospital had settled for the night, Mary rose from her bed and made her first inspection. The light from the watchtowers slanted through the bars of the windows. Some of the women were coughing, others crying. In the corner at the far end one was groaning, the rattle of death in her throat. Not that one, Mary prayed, may the one I choose not preface her departure from this hell in such a way. *Any* one of them, she told herself, any age or shape as long as it gave her the chance to survive. At ten o'clock she made her second patrol, an hour later her third. She allowed herself no sleep until it was done. At midnight, or a time she judged close to midnight, she made her fourth tour. The woman in the corner who had been groaning had stopped. Mary delayed going to her until she was sure there was no other, when she did so the woman was breathing peacefully. At five, when the block began to wake, no one had died.

The following evening Mary began her vigil once more. The woman was groaning again and her eyes were the eyes of the prisoner who had thrown herself onto the electrified wire. Mary bent down and read the details at the foot of the bed then returned to her own bed and listened to the voice, hearing it weaken, the coughs growing fainter and the patter of rain on the roof growing louder. She left the bed and stood by the window, watching the woman's life running down the glass. Not the woman's life, Mary told himself, *her* life.

The coughing stopped. Mary crossed to the bed and looked at the face; the head was tilted back and the mouth was hanging open.

The woman was heavier than she had imagined, or perhaps it was that she herself was so weak. She unbuttoned the jacket, turned the woman on her left side, pulled the shoulder across the woman's back and slipped it down her arm. The left hand was lying limp. Quickly, she told herself, while the body is still supple, before rigor mortis begins to set in. She tugged the sleeve off and turned the body onto its right side, half sitting the corpse on the bed and wedging her own body against it so that it did not topple over, and slid off the other sleeve. Then she took off her own jacket, put it on the other woman; buttoned it up, and dragged the corpse off the bed, along the floor and onto her own.

Someone must see, someone must ask what I am doing. Nobody cares, the response struck back, in this place nobody sees or cares about anything any more.

She heard the breathing, rasping and struggling, and thought that someone else was dying, then realized it was herself gasping with the exertion. The jacket was on the floor where it had dropped. Mary put it on and lay on the woman's bed, trying to control the shaking which suddenly engulfed her. The rain was still running down the windows. Not the woman's bed, she told herself, her bed. She was Freda Mitchell. Mary Atkinson was dead.

At five, even before the glare of the lights outside gave way to the dawn, the doors were unlocked and the two trustees came in, the metal stretcher clanging on the floor and the women glancing at the beds for their load. The woman whose identity Mary had taken was the only person who had died in the room that night. The trustees stopped, felt the pulse and flicked up the eyelids, then placed the stretcher by the bed and pulled the woman onto it, the body half stiff, the left arm flopping over the side, and carried it from the room.

Mary left her bed and walked to the window. It was still raining, the water spreading in puddles across the ground. The trustees left the sickbay and hurried across the open space to the long low building with the tall chimney less than thirty yards from where Mary was watching, the left arm still hanging from the stretcher and dragging in the wet. It was too early for the rest of the day's work, she knew, at this time of day they used the furnace only for the bodies from the sickbay. The single gust of flame rose from the top of the chimney and she turned back to the bunk.

455

When the orderly had brought the bread and coffee, and before the day's work began, Mary went to the hospital secretary. The woman was expecting her. 'I'll get you out this morning, send you to a different block where they won't know you. The secretary there is a friend of mine. I'll arrange it. You'll need to cut your hair again so that nobody will recognize you.'

THE SNOW WAS beginning to melt and the first of the spring sun was warming the pasture. The King walked slowly with his equerry, his bodyguard close behind, though he talked to neither. As they left the woods the two men with him noticed that he was walking faster. When they returned to the house he cloistered himself in his study and read again the reports from Scotland. That evening, having spoken on the scrambler to the Prime Minister, King George asked his family to join him and broke the news to his two daughters that the following morning he was leaving Canada to return to the Free North. He spoke of duty and loyalty and of the dangers of war, pointing out that he himself was no less mortal than any other man and saying that if he did not return he was confident that his daughter Elizabeth would rule with the wisdom and humanity he knew she possessed and that her younger sister Margaret would give her the support and understanding she would undoubtedly need. The night before he had told his wife the truth.

THE MESSAGE WAS too long and the person sending it too inexperienced, the operator in the signals room knew, and felt for the person as the morse was tapped deliberately and slowly, tried to imagine what he or she was going through. It was two in the morning. She concentrated hard, grimacing with sympathy and writing the letters down, five by five blocks, the mistakes in transmission obvious. Not one of the regular operators, she knew, not someone from SOE or SIS who were fast and good, but one of those who only came through occasionally, the lack of expertise obvious; one of those who was alone. To her left a clerk offered her tea, she waved the person aside and motioned with her left hand that she should not be interrupted. The morse stopped. No completion of letter. She felt the shock as she knew what had happened. The clerk shook her shoulder and asked if she wanted the tea now. She shook her head and slumped across the set. It must be bad enough for the regular operators, she had always thought, could not begin to imagine how it must be for those who came through only occasionally, with all which that implied. She stood up and stretched her arms, then heard the morse again and grabbed the pencil. SORRY, the incoming words were not in code, SOMEONE OUTSIDE. She wanted to tell the sender it would be all right. The code began again. When the message was finished she reached for her own keys to tap the standard acknowledgement and knew what she would do. Against the rules, she thought, but what the hell. GOOD LUCK. In the shell of the house in the South the agent called Prospero thanked her for it, slid the set into its hiding place and disappeared into the night.

THE MORNING WAS warmer, even in the North, the first smell of spring in the air and the sense of urgency all-pervasive. On the roads round Arisaig there seemed to be men and equipment everywhere. At ten Drake and The Watchman drove to the airfields where the men and equipment were still being landed.

'When?' Jack asked.

'Five days. Midnight Monday the twentieth.'

During the past two days they had both been locked in planning sessions confirming the liaison between the forces that would drive south and the Resistance networks that would liaise with them: the details of the bridges, railheads and roads which the Resistance would destroy in order to impede the enemy, and those they would keep open; the fighter and bomber fields they would attack in an attempt to reduce the enemy's strength in the air and the timings of the break-outs from the prison camps.

A number of those whom The Watchman had met at these sessions were present at the conference that afternoon. For many it was neither the first nor the last session of the day; it was, however, the most important. The Prime Minister himself opened the meeting then left for the next of his many engagements.

'The purpose of this meeting is to integrate any developments in tactics for L-day. I suggest we don't waste time.' The brigadier who had taken Churchill's place sat down and Drake rose.

'The information you are about to be shown has the highest security classification, for reasons you will understand when you receive it. You will be shown the full details in this room, but you will only take away with you those details which affect you.'

Amongst those present who had not met Drake or The Watchman there was the faintest hint of professional boredom. The brigadier nodded and an aide passed round copies of the report which was the subject of the meeting. The atmosphere in the room changed abruptly. On the nine sheets of paper comprising the report was the entire strength and battle order of German units and equipment remaining in England, together with details of their positions and the precise location of the GHQ line they would establish in the case of withdrawal.

'How old is this information?'

'It is valid as of yesterday.'

The meeting ended. As they left, Drake paused at the top of the steps and allowed Jack to ask: 'What was the source?'

'The same as ever.'

They began to cross to the car.

'Prospero is still in place?'

Prospero must have come out after his escape, Jack had understood. Not to have done so would have been suicide.

'Why should you think otherwise?'

At five they drove to The Cottage. Even though, over the past months, the airfield had become operational for other squadrons and was now packed with planes and men, the function of the Special Duties Squadron remained unquestioned, even unnoticed. At six the last night operation dinner for flights into the British mainland was held. Then the Lysander carrying The Watchman trundled onto the runway and took off into the purple of the sky.

The estimated flight time was three hours and forty-six minutes. They had been in the air for ten minutes short of an hour and were barely within the limits of radio contact when Johnny Watson heard the voice of the controller over his headset.

'Foxtrot to Shakespeare Two One. Repeat Foxtrot to Shakespeare Two One.'

'Shakespeare Two One receiving.'

'Foxtrot to Shakespeare Two One. Return to base. Repeat return to base.'

'Roger, Foxtrot.' He informed his passenger, banked the aircraft to starboard and turned north.

BOOK FIVE

Liberation
April 1942

1

THE EXPECTATION HUNG over the fields like mist over the river in autumn. Fran could not shake off the feeling, except that it was not autumn and there was no mist. It was two nights since she had heard the plane: she had left the barn and was walking back to the farmhouse, one, two in the morning, the second lamb just born, when she had heard it and had known immediately what it was. 'Only six more ewes to lamb.' Boy Jack came in from the fields, Ernie close behind him, and saw the tiredness in her face. 'Couple of days and it'll be done.' At five minutes to nine she locked the door and tuned the wireless to the BBC; at the table Boy Jack and Ernie were cleaning Jack's cricket pads, his bat already oiled. She heard the drum then the voice.

'This is the voice of Britain speaking to the people of Britain. His Majesty King George.'

Tonight, she felt the excitement. Everything was beyond her control now. She had done her job, now it was up to others. She wondered where Jack was and prayed that he was safe.

'On Christmas Day 1939, when I spoke to you all, I said that a new year was at hand, but that I could not tell what it would bring, and I read you a passage. "*I said to the man who stood at the Gate of the Year, 'Give me a light that I may tread safely into the unknown.' And he replied, 'Go out into the darkness, and put your hand into the Hand of God.'*"'

'It is because of those who went into that darkness that the dawn has now come.'

461

In the corner of the room Boy Jack was looking at her. What will he think when I tell him the truth, she thought. Please God, may his father live.

'When I left so many terrible months ago, I read you another poem, and said that I hoped that you would find in it the strength and comfort which I did. I wish tonight to read that same poem.' It was the code, she understood, the words they were all waiting for.

Two hours before the first column of commandoes had crossed no man's land and begun their drive south. Twenty-one hours before, under the cover of darkness, men of the Small Scale Raiding Force had penetrated as far as Harrogate and linked with the Resistance. Forty-five hours before, jeeps of L Detachment Special Air Service Brigade had slipped unseen into England and were already in position south of Birmingham.

The King began the poem. At their start points the tanks and armoured columns shuddered as their engines were started, in the prison camps the diversions which would cover the mass break-outs were prepared, the arms dumps close outside the wires. On the airfields the paratroopers waited in lines to climb into the Dakotas, in the secret places in Wales the men who had already escaped from the camps prepared to move off. In the South the Resistance waited. The King hesitated, then he came again to the lines with which the poet had begun the poem, and which he repeated.

> *Shed no tear – O, shed no tear!*
> *The flower will bloom another year.*

It was three minutes past nine on Monday, 20 April 1942.

'God bless you all.'

There was a roll of drums and the national anthem began.

'What is it?' asked Ernie.

'Liberation,' said Boy Jack.

IN THE VAULT of the church The Watchman turned to Brian Markham. 'Pick us up as planned at nine in the morning. We change the number plates when we're away from the village. Should be in Canterbury by ten.' He had argued against it, knew that Drake had argued against it.

462

'Do you think they will be expecting us?'

Not *if* Holdaway and the Lice would be expecting them, The Watchman knew, only *when*. 'Probably. Not tomorrow, possibly the day after, certainly the day after that.'

THE CATHEDRAL STOOD against the blue of the morning sky. Jack crossed the remains of Watling Street and remembered the night he and Fran and Boy Jack had seen the sky above Canterbury brilliant orange with the burning. The city was busy. At the corner of the Long Market a police sergeant was talking to a constable, a patrol of German paratroopers opposite and a second positioned by the Post Office. Jack turned into St Margaret's Street and remembered the day after the bombing, the way the King and Queen had visited the city, unexpectedly and without warning, and talked to its people. The grocer's shop was on the corner, the name on the sign above the battered door. He glanced through the window, saw that the woman was behind the counter, then checked the lane at the rear and turned back up the street.

The car was parked close to the station.

'Mrs Best.'

'Of course.'

It was madness, Jack thought again. He checked that no one could see him, took the Thompson from the boot and hid it under his mack, then crossed back into The Parade. A third German patrol was now positioned by Lefevre's drapers and a fourth near the Christ Church Gate. He turned into St Margaret's Street and went into the shop.

'Can I help you?' There was something about the man in the doorway, the woman behind the counter thought. A mack on a nice day, something under it. He raised the first finger of his left hand to his lips then pointed to the room behind and the door from it. Empty, she mouthed, nobody else here – did not know why she did it or why she trusted him.

Jack moved past her, checked the room and the lane onto which the door opened, then went to the front door again. As he did so a woman with a small child in her arms came in.

'Morning, Iris. Come for some sugar?' The shopkeeper was confused and frightened, watching as the man nodded to someone in the street. A second man came through the door, another close behind him and a fourth remaining outside. A lookout, she knew, wondered if she should call the police, tried to remember why she knew the third man. Mack like the others, she was thinking, mind half on whether she had any sugar and the woman enough coupons, cap pulled down over his eyes. He took the cap off and she saw the face.

'Your Majesty.'

She did not know what to do or say, could not believe it.

'Hello, Mrs Best.' George smiled at her. 'Glad to see you're still open.'

He had come back as he had said he would; he even remembered her name. She bowed, curtsied, still did not know what to say or think, what to do.

'It's been a long time, Mrs Best, but it's almost over.' So many men guarding him last time, the shopkeeper thought, now just three. The King smiled and turned to the woman with the child. 'Boy or girl?'

The woman was blushing, not knowing what was happening. 'Boy, Your Majesty.'

'And what's his name?'

'Michael, Your Majesty.'

The King touched the child on the cheek. 'Well, young Michael, I doubt if you'll remember my first visit to Canterbury, but you might my second.'

The crowd was gathering outside, looking in, seeing the man in the shop, remembering. The news was already spreading. The shopkeeper still did not understand.

'You were listening last night, I hope, Mrs Best.'

'I always listen, Your Majesty, to the nine o'clock news, and the funny messages after.'

He smiled again. 'I've often wondered what they meant as well.'

The crowd outside was getting larger. Two minutes, Jack was thinking, almost three, time to be off. The shopkeeper remembered the words of the poem, could hear his voice reading them now, understood what they meant: that the King was back with his people. Not in Canada or the Free North where he was safe but in the Occupied South.

'The first of our troops came south last night,' he told her. 'It won't be long now.' He smiled again at the child and went outside, left hand in coat pocket and right hand waving. The crowd were beginning to realize, unsure what to do, recognizing him and remembering the last time he had come, what he had said to them then. They began to cheer. Much too long, Jack Masters was thinking. The police sergeant he had seen pushed his way through to find out what was happening, the constable close behind him. 'Your Majesty.' The sergeant snapped to attention and saluted. Time to go, Jack was thinking. To his left Stan was looking anxious; to his right Brian was indicating with his eyes: the German patrol by Lefevre's were coming to find out what the trouble was about, the one by the Post Office also closing in.

Time to leave, Jack tried to tell the King, George not hearing, listening and talking to his people. He took the King's arm and began to pull him. The sergeant stepped forward, not knowing who he was, and tried to stop him, the constable looking back and seeing the patrol, telling the sergeant.

'Watchman?' the sergeant asked.

Jack nodded. 'Cover me.' He moved the King into the shop and through the back door into the lane behind, the crowd surging round the patrols and the two policemen organizing them. By the time the soldiers had extricated themselves the King was half a mile from the city.

THE REPORT REACHED The Citadel at one. Holdaway confirmed its contents with the area commander in Canterbury and telephoned Schellenberg immediately. The *Gruppenführer* was in conference with the *Reichsstatthalter* and returned his call at three, by which time Holdaway had already despatched a team to Canterbury.

The conversation was short and to the point, both agreeing that given the King's broadcast the previous evening and the advance from the North which had begun immediately after, the sighting should not be ignored no matter how unlikely the possibility that the King should expose himself in such a manner. Holdaway should therefore launch an immediate investigation and Schellenberg would attend a briefing at The Citadel that evening.

WHEN BOY JACK and Ernie returned to the farm they could barely contain their excitement.

'Have you heard the news?'

'What news?'

'The King was in Canterbury this morning.' Boy Jack was almost out of breath.

'The Germans tried to arrest him but the people stopped them and he got away,' Ernie added for him.

'Come and have tea.' Fran pushed them good naturedly into the kitchen. At six she locked the door and tuned the wireless to the BBC, then they sat at the table and waited for the news.

'At midnight last night, the Allied army crossed no man's land and re-entered the Occupied South. The most advanced units have reached Kendal and the German opposition is crumbling. The British Resistance, under the leadership of His Majesty King George, is liaising with the Allied advance. His Majesty was in Canterbury this morning.'

The news reader began to go into more detail. Fran looked across the table and saw the way Boy Jack was grinning at her.

'Quizzie Lizzie was right for once.'

THE ROOM WAS barely six feet high at the centre and sloping to where the roof met the eaves, a small window almost hidden between the slates. If he reached up Jack could see the garden at the rear of the house and the lane behind it along which they had brought the King two hours before. The trap door from below was in the centre of the floor and the straw mattresses on either side. The only other way out was through the concealed entrance into the cavity where the ceiling reached the wall and which ran the entire length of the terrace in which the safe house was situated. The back door out had been the first thing Jack had checked when he had hidden in the roof space nine months before.

The King was asleep on the mattress in the corner. His face showed the first tinge of grey and the lines were already drawn round his eyes. In the silence Jack heard the mice scratching and wondered how long the man would last before the physical and mental strain took their toll of him, how long it would be before Holdaway saw the pattern.

On the stairs below he heard steps, then the signal on the pipe at the corner of the landing that all was well. Thirty seconds later there was a knock on the trap door and Stan appeared. Jack leant across and shook the shoulder of the figure in the corner. The King woke, fear and bewilderment on his face at the darkness and the unfamiliar smells around him, only relaxing when he recognized the men around him and then only marginally.

'Supper,' said Jack. It was their first food since five-thirty that morning.

'THE FIRST APPROACH was made to the shop at ten-twenty-three.' The inspector's team had just returned from Canterbury. 'One man was involved initially, he then left and returned ten minutes later. When he had checked the premises and the lane at the rear he signalled and the others came in, one other escort, then the King. It is thought that one other person remained outside on watch.'

The shopkeeper had been thoroughly interrogated then released.

'Descriptions?' asked Holdaway.

'The only reliable one was of the King.'

'But no doubt that it was the King?' Schellenberg understood what his superiors in London were clamouring to tell Berlin.

The inspector was careful. 'Everyone says it was the King.'

'But is that because everyone wanted it to be?' Holdaway wondered how the inspector would answer.

'In a way it doesn't matter whether it's the King or someone dressed up as the King.' Schellenberg had witnessed both the implementation and the effect of *massenpsychologie*, the psychology of mass influence and persuasion, been present at the rallies staged with almost scientific precision at Nuremberg. 'The important thing is that everyone *thinks* it was the King.'

He turned to Holdaway. 'So what do we do?'

'Wait for a pattern.'

It was interesting, the superintendent thought, how they both not only assumed there would be a pattern but that they would recognize it.

The meeting ended and Schellenberg and Holdaway returned to the *Gruppenführer*'s office on the third floor.

'Why?' asked Holdaway.

'God knows. No need for it.'

'You believe it really was the King?'

'Don't you?'

'If it is, you know who's with him.'
'Of course.'

THE DOME OF St Paul's glistened in the sun to their left, the river in front of them. In the back seat, almost lost beside Stan Bradley, the King sat hunched and quiet. After today, thought Jack, they would see what he was doing. Tomorrow they would either be waiting for him or working out where he would run afterwards. He left the car and walked across the bridge.

The streets were full of people. He could sense the atmosphere in the air, the talk of the reports from the North and the news that the day before the King had been seen in Canterbury. Ernie came from near here, he suddenly thought.

On the corner of what had once been Settles Street and Commercial Road a group of dockers began to cluster. Jack stood close to them, seeing the several ways in and the single way out, deciding where he would leave the car and who he would leave with it. A group of women joined the men, their accents even sharper and faster, remembering the day after the bombing when George and Bet had come to the East End.

Jack left the corner and went back to the car.

THE REPORT REACHED The Citadel at twelve-thirty; within five minutes both Holdaway and Schellenberg had been informed and one of the teams on stand-by despatched to the Whitechapel area of the East End of London north of Tower Bridge. Holdaway walked to the window overlooking the courtyard and looked down at the convoys of vehicles arriving and leaving. Many of them were covered, he wondered whether their loads and destinations were concerned with the effort against the rapidly accelerating advance from the North or with the individual and collective acquisition which accompanied even an army in retreat. Enough for a pattern, he knew. He wondered who else would make the connection and what else they would see.

Present at the briefing that evening were Schellenberg, Holdaway and the officers in charge of the units on stand-by. The team sent to London that day were still in the East End but the inspector in charge had returned for the meeting. The report he presented was divided into three sections: the timing of the appearance of the King, the location, and a description of one of those who had accompanied him. When he had finished, the men round the table discussed each in turn, beginning with the timing, which they discarded as inconsequential, and moving on to the location, which seemed insignificant but which the inspector signalled he considered important.

'Yesterday we were unsure whether the man was the King. Today there is no longer any doubt.'

Schellenberg asked why. The inspector took a newspaper from his file and laid it on the table for them all to see. The paper was the *Daily Mirror* of Thursday, 5 September 1940, the day after the first bombing of the East End. The picture on the front page showed the King, dressed in naval uniform with the Queen beside him, standing on top of a pile of bomb rubble and talking to a group of men and women from the area.

'The man in the photograph is the man who was in the East End this morning, of that there is no doubt. The photograph itself was taken on the corner of Settles Street and Commercial Road, which is where the sighting took place this morning.'

'So what are you saying?' Schellenberg was seated to the inspector's right.

'The pattern,' Holdaway told him. 'Canterbury yesterday, the East End today.'

'And where tomorrow?'

'Maidstone.'

'Why?'

'The bombing raids in the week before invasion,' the inspector explained. 'The first was on Canterbury, the second was on the East End, the third was on Maidstone.'

Schellenberg understood. 'So what do we do?'

'We find out exactly where the King will appear in Maidstone tomorrow and saturate the place.'

'But won't he know that we know? Won't he work out that we can work it out?'

'Almost certainly,' Holdaway agreed.

An aide entered the room and informed Schellenberg that he was wanted on the telephone. When he returned three minutes later he gave no indication of the nature of the call. 'So why will he come?' he continued the conversation.

'Because he's the King. Because he said he would never leave his people but allowed the politicians to persuade him that he and his family should go to Canada. Because for the past two years he has felt nothing but remorse and guilt.'

'And where will he go after Maidstone?'

'Nowhere, Maidstone will be the end. He only visited those three.'

'So where will he go after Maidstone?' Schellenberg asked again.

'Two days before the first sighting an unidentified aircraft was reported in the early hours of the morning south-west of Canterbury.' It was the man who had replaced Davis as collator at The Citadel who spoke. 'There were no other sightings in the seven preceding days.'

'A drop or a landing?' Parachute jumps were always dangerous, night jumps even more so. A parachute drop and it would not have been the King.

'The unit that reported it can't be positive but they think it was a landing.'

'Canterbury, north to London, then south again to Maidstone.' Schellenberg crossed to the map on the wall, his excitement infectious. 'So what do we do?'

Holdaway waited for the collator. 'A series of roadblocks round the town. We don't know where he is tonight, whether he's already in Maidstone, but that way we have three chances of getting him; when he's going in, when he's inside, or when he's trying to get out.'

'But if he sees we're waiting for him and manages to break out?'

'Then at least we'll know in which direction he's going, whether he's heading back to the Canterbury area.' He anticipated Schellenberg's next question and took a sheet of paper from a folder. 'These are the villages within a three-mile radius of the presumed location of the unidentified aircraft.'

Schellenberg studied it. 'The *Wehrmacht* will be in place to surround each of these by nine in the morning. They will begin searching as soon as they hear from you.'

'My people are more familiar with the area than theirs.' It was Holdaway's first intervention for several minutes. 'It might be an idea to co-ordinate tactics tonight.'

'I agree.'

At ten-thirty Holdaway returned to his office, summoned the collator and began to plan the following morning's operations. At ten-forty-five Schellenberg closed the door of his inner office and placed a telephone call to the house in Bloomsbury.

'I heard an hour ago. The advance is much faster than anyone anticipated. The defences are like an empty egg, crack the shell and there's nothing inside.' Bloody Hitler, he was thinking, all the troop withdrawals to support the campaign on the Eastern Front. 'There's almost nothing left. They'll be in London in two, three days, the advance columns will probably reach the coast in five.'

He began to calculate the impact which the capture of the King would have on the campaign in Britain, how they could hold Churchill to ransom for whatever they wanted.

'What do you suggest?'

But even if they lost, even if they were forced back across the Channel, imagine the rewards in Berlin for the man who delivered King George of England to the Führer.

'That you leave London now.'

Five hours later, shortly before four in the morning and accompanied by an escort which Schellenberg had arranged for her, Fiona Egerton-Smith arrived at the house in the country where they had spent so many weekends.

THE LAST LAMB of the season was born at four-thirty. Fifty minutes earlier Holdaway completed the details of the operation within and around Maidstone and turned his attention to the villages that would be surrounded and searched that morning. At eight minutes past seven he came to Ardley.

'The village is situated on a road running parallel to the A2 and about two miles from it. I suggest you place one roadblock at the junction to the south and a second to the north, just past the church, where a minor road leads back to the A2.'

The major in charge of the local operation noted the positions.

'A river runs along the village to the east. There are only two bridges across it, both at the points where the roadblocks are situated. The river itself is too deep to wade across and I doubt whether the King will be in any fit state to swim, so you'll have him covered whether he's moving by car or on foot.'

The major saluted and left.

THE MORNING WAS colder than the day before, the clouds building from the east, grey and threatening. It began to drizzle. At nine, when Jack Masters looked across the roof of the safe house the slates were glistening with water. Canterbury, the East End, then Maidstone, he could not stop thinking; Mrs Best's corner shop, the junction of Settles Street and Commercial Road, and the Queen Victoria Monument. He knew they must have seen it.

'Have a look around, Stan, see what you think.'

The poacher moved towards the door. 'Back within the hour.'

'One other thing.' The King was beginning to wake. Jack told Brian what to do.

THE STREET CHART of the town occupied two-thirds of the wall on the right of the office and the road plan of the county filled the wall to the left.

'Market day,' Schellenberg said. 'Easy to lose our people in the crowd.'

'Easy for him to lose us.'

At eight-thirty the first teams had gone onto the streets. As the town became busier, the second wave and then a third would join them.

The Queen Victoria Monument, Holdaway thought, the streets leading off it and the side streets off them, the shops and houses with or without back doors or yards, the back yards with exits and no exits. The places where The Watchman could leave the car in which they presumed he was travelling and the locations where the teams from The Citadel could pick the King up without the crowd coming to his rescue. All of them covered.

Brian stopped by the Feathers pub and watched as Stan Bradley disappeared up the road then bought himself a newspaper and waited for him to return. In the control at The Citadel the first roadblock team reported that they were standing by and waiting orders to move into place. 'Not until he's had time to slip into the net,' Holdaway told the sergeant. In the concealed room overlooking the garden at the rear of the safe house the King finished the bread and tea which served as breakfast and asked when they would move.

'When Stan's checked it out.'

'Where's Brian?'

472

'Keeping a watch on Stan, see if he's followed when he comes back.'

The second roadblock team reported in, then the third.

'What if Stan thinks it's unsafe?'

'Then we don't go.'

'But we must.'

Jack looked at the King. 'That's probably what the enemy thinks.'

All the roadblock teams standing by, the collator informed Holdaway.

Stan Bradley finished his pint and wiped his mouth. Market day he thought, just like any other, the farmers coming in and the streets crowded. One Lice by the window, he noted, two more outside, one on the corner and another at the bottom where Jack would have parked the car. He left the pub and walked to the Monument.

'Twenty minutes,' Holdaway told the sergeant, 'then order them in place.'

The King sat on the mattress and pulled on his shoes. 'I appreciate the risks, but it's imperative that I be seen in Maidstone.' He was looking tired, Jack thought, as if he had not slept that night. 'We'll see.'

Brian watched as Stan returned, neither man showing any hint of recognition, and waited for the tail. Double check, Jack had told them, the first in the town, the second near the safe house itself.

'Something happening,' the sergeant in charge of communications alerted Holdaway. 'People gathering off Gable's Hill.' Wrong place, thought Holdaway. He knew he was right but glanced across at the street map anyway. 'Green and yellow units are covering it.' He saw the way Schellenberg was looking at him. 'They're good.'

Brian came down the road towards the safe house, Stan fifty yards behind him. When he was opposite the entrance Brian slowed and Stan walked past. No tails, Jack checked from the window, knew there would not be, that the two men were good. The King stood and straightened his suit. There was a tap on the pipes and Stan came into the room.

'Lice, the place is crawling with them.'

Jack saw the look in the King's eyes.

'Where's Brian?' The King knew what Brian was doing, what the three of them were thinking.

'Getting the car.'

'Where are we going?'

Jack wondered if Holdaway had worked out where he would run and knew there was no alternative. 'Home.'

The sergeant hurried back into Holdaway's room. 'False alarm. Couple of women selling black market ice-cream.'

The A20 was clear, the farming traffic still coming in. The Watchman skirted north then swung in a circle towards Canterbury and the villages beyond.

'Roadblocks in now,' Holdaway ordered the sergeant.

The farm was quiet. Fran checked the lambs that had been born during the night, fed the cattle and began the housework. In the schoolroom in the village Boy Jack and Ernie tried to concentrate on the arithmetic lesson.

The rain was harder, running down the windscreen, the wiper blade flicking the water away. Almost there – Jack felt the nervousness in his stomach, not just out from the trap the Lice had set for him in Maidstone – almost out of the war itself. Not long now, not long before the army from the North would reach London and Kent and he would be back on the farm.

'What do we do when we get there?' the vicar asked.

'Leave us at the church.' Brian was beside Jack in the front, Stan and the King in the back. 'You and Stan go home, check everything out, keep in touch with us when possible.'

'Jack.'

'Yes, Your Majesty.' Sometimes he addressed the King formally yet on other occasions there was not even time to call him 'sir'. They drove out of one bend and towards another.

'You made the correct decision in Maidstone. Thank you.'

'*Christ!*'

The three of them saw it at the same time, the Wolseley pulled into the side of the road on their right. No time to stop or turn round; that would warn them, tell the bastards what they wanted to know.

'Gate on right.'

The King was asking what was happening, not understanding. They passed the car, not slowing, not giving any indication they had been warned and went into the bend. They were twenty yards past the car, Stan and Brian checking their weapons, thirty yards, almost out of sight, forty, the car gone. Jack disengaged gear and slowed, the heel of his right foot on the brake and the toe still on the

474

accelerator, keeping the engine noise up, Stan and Brian hanging from the doors.

They were opposite the gate.

'Now.'

The two men rolled from the car. Jack reached across and pulled the front door shut; behind him the King closed the rear.

'Roadblock,' Jack explained. 'Just out of the bend. They always put a car before to catch you if you turn back.' He felt for the Thompson gun on the floor and the Smith & Wesson tucked into his right sock. 'Get down.'

He eased his left foot up and re-engaged the engine, maintaining pressure on the accelerator so that the men in front could hear him coming but moving slowly, giving Stan and Brian the time they needed. They came out of the bend and into the straight. The roadblock was thirty yards in front of him, two cars and one lorry, a machine gun mounted on its back. Lice with the cars – he summed up the position automatically – army on the machine gun.

He stopped the car, pulled on the handbrake and waited for them to come to him. Four Lice, two for each car, civilian clothes, sub-machine-gun on their arms. One soldier on the machine gun, a second talking to the Lice and a third in the driver's seat of the lorry. It was fifteen seconds since Stan and Brian had slid out of the car. The bloody machine gun, Jack thought, it would cut them down before they could even move. He released the handbrake, keeping his left foot hard on the foot brake, opened the door and stepped out, searching for any sign that Stan and Brian were in position.

Twenty-five seconds, almost thirty. The Lice left the cars and came towards him. In the dead ground behind the lorry he saw the movement. Thirty-five seconds, nearer forty. He lifted his foot off the brake and the car began to roll back.

'Bloody hell!' He reached inside as if he had made a mistake and pulled on the handbrake, hearing them laughing at him, grinning at each other and not looking where they should have been looking. He picked up the Thompson.

Now, Stan.

On the back of the lorry the left hand gripped the front of the *Gefreiter*'s helmet and jerked it back, the lip at the rear of the helmet breaking the man's neck and the knife in the right hand cutting his throat.

Now, Brian. Jack began to straighten, knew the vicar was waiting for the first shots, kept the door between the Thompson and the Lice.

The Lice saw the movement, turned, recognized the danger as the machine gun on the top of the lorry swung from the car onto them. Down, Jack urged the King, moved away from the car, drew the Lice's attention from it. The Lice were reacting, too late. The lorry driver looked up, Jack swung, dealt with him, heard the crash of the machine gun and the sharper sounds as the vicar fired on the team on the other side of the bend, then switched his attention back to the Lice, seeing that there was no need, that Stan Bradley had done his job.

The King raised himself gingerly and looked through the windscreen, then ducked as another burst from behind them broke the quiet. No prisoners, they all understood, no wounded behind them when they were not looking.

Stan began to pull the bodies clear for Jack to edge through the roadblock. The cars were equipped with radios, it would only be ten minutes, fifteen at most, before The Citadel checked, before they realized what had happened. Ten minutes, he reversed his thinking, five, even less, if there was another patrol in the area and they had heard the shooting. Brian ran round the corner and they pulled away.

'RADIO CHECK WITH the roadblocks,' Holdaway lifted the telephone and spoke to the communications room. Schellenberg paced in front of the window overlooking the yard. Everything quiet, the sergeant in charge of radio contact with the vehicles manning the blocks told him, but the unit at the intersection known locally as Bicktons had failed to reply.

'Nearest unit to them check immediately.'

Six minutes later the sergeant telephoned back. Even before Holdaway put the phone down Schellenberg knew what he had just been informed. Not only was every person manning the roadblock dead, but the bodies and car had been moved to allow something through, tyre marks in the blood confirmed this.

'Where's he taking him?'

'Home,' said Holdaway.

Schellenberg walked to the desk and lifted the telephone. 'The villages. Now.'

In the kitchen of the farm Fran peeled the potatoes and worked out what else she had to do that day. In the schoolroom in the square the teacher instructed his class to put away their arithmetic and begin their history. In the lay-by one and a half miles to the north of Ardley the major received the instruction and the convoys moved off.

The rain had stopped. To their left the tower of Canterbury cathedral rose into the sky. The King began to shiver with delayed shock. The roadblock, Jack thought, the Lice waiting for them in Maidstone, his assumption that Holdaway would not only work out where they would be on the third day but where they would run after. He tried to work out why he expected Holdaway to know where he would be heading. The Lysander must have given the clue the night the plane had brought the King in. It had always been too close to the village, to the place where they would conceal the King, but there had been no option. He continued the logic – unidentified aircraft, a three-mile radius around the estimated landing point including nine villages, perhaps ten. Cordon round each, then a search – Ardley and the church right in the middle.

'We leave the car in Denge Wood, and go the rest of the way on foot.' Thank God it was spring and there was a semblance of foliage under which they could hide the car.

The other two understood his reasoning. 'What about him? Do you think he'll make it?'

Four miles by road, Jack calculated, three across country but the going more difficult. 'Yes,' said the King, 'he'll make it.'

Jack swung off the road, drove as far as he could into the woods, and lurched the car into a thicket. 'You cover the tracks,' he told Stan. 'The rest of us will conceal the car.'

In the control room at The Citadel the reports began to come in that the cordons were in position round the villages and the first troops were moving in. In the schoolroom in Ardley Boy Jack looked at the clock and counted the minutes before they stopped for dinner.

Denge Wood was half a mile behind them. They kept close to the hedge so they could not be seen against the grey of the skyline, Jack and Brian with the King, Stan a hundred yards in front. Two and a half miles, Jack thought, Petham on their right, then across the old Roman road and up the hill. Less than two miles after Lower Hardres, a mile and a half. In front of them Stan sank into the hedge and motioned him to come forward. Below them, on the road into Lower

Hardres, he saw a roadblock and a circle of troops closing on the village. There was no way they could stick to the original route, no way they could go back, nowhere to go back to. Like a poor bloody fox when the hunt was up and after him and the smell of blood was in their nostrils, Stan thought. Only one other way to the sanctuary of the church, they both knew.

'You're sure?' Stan asked him.

'No option.'

The door of the schoolroom crashed open and the soldiers burst in. At the roadblocks to the north and south of Ardley the other units stopped the first vehicles, more spreading across the fields and sealing off the village; in the King's Arms the first troops poured through the kitchen and ran up the stairs, searching every room and smashing the ceilings and walls for the secret compartment they knew existed somewhere.

Jack brought the King closer to the front and allowed him thirty seconds to regain his breath. One mile now, less, only half a mile. In front of them the ground rose to the farm at the top. You're sure you want to go this way, Stan had asked him. No other way then, he had known, no other way now.

The stormtroopers left the schoolroom and ran towards the houses at the side.

The four men climbed the hill towards the farm.

'Red team keep half your men on the roadblock.' The major consulted the map on the bonnet of his staff car and radioed the unit at the junction to the north of the village. 'Other half check farms and outbuildings.' They had gone through it at The Citadel the night before: over the bridge and up the hill, track to the right, two farms at the top. 'Blue team report on progress.'

In the school the teacher and his pupils surveyed the shattered remains of desks and cupboards.

Almost to the top, Jack told the King, then it's just down the other side.

In the classroom the teacher told the children to collect their bags and go home. At the roadblock to the north the trucks accelerated over the bridge, up the road and onto the track to the farms.

Through the path between the trees, Jack told the King, then along the hedgerow and down the fold of the field to the river. They came to the top, the church below, the village to the left, the roadblocks

478

in position and the dark shapes of the personnel carriers in the square. Roadblocks by the bridges across the river, Jack thought. The stupid bastards were in the wrong places, guarding the obvious points but missing the footbridge behind the church.

'Stan in front, Brian with the King, I'll cover the rear.'

To his right he heard the sound of the vehicles coming up the track to the farm. In the schoolroom Boy Jack and Ernie pulled on their coats and walked into the square. In the kitchen Fran heard the noise and knew what it was, ran outside, the soldiers already jumping out and pushing her aside, racing into the house. They know about Jack, she thought, heard the crackling on the radio as a second truck hurtled past, up the track towards Sarah's. Not Jack, she prayed. Another armoured car pulled up, the troops jumping down and running towards the barn where she had found Jack.

Mum — Boy Jack hurried along the road to the church and the short cut. *Have to get home for Auntie Fran* — Ernie was already falling behind slightly and shouting to Boy Jack to go on without him.

Nearly there, Brian told the King, saw the man was almost finished. They left the cover of the hedgerow and stumbled down the fold, the King gasping, white-faced, trying to keep up with him. They reached the bottom and crouched in the last of the cover.

The exposed ground just before the bridge, Fran thought, the fifteen feet across the bridge itself. The assault teams were running out of the barn towards the top of the field. She knew what they would see, who they would see. The glance was deliberate, away from the fields on her right to the rest of the outbuildings on the left, the movement fast enough to suggest she did not want it to be seen but slow enough for them to see it.

'Over here,' the *Scharführer* tasted the glory.

'The church,' the major in the centre of the square checked the map. 'Remember the church.'

Twenty yards to the bridge — they heard the shouts from the farm and the sounds from the village — twenty yards in which they could be seen. No options any more, no more options at all.

'Now,' ordered The Watchman.

Boy Jack's head was pounding and his lungs were bursting, Ernie two hundred yards behind. He heard the lorries leaving the village and the sounds from the farm on the hill. Mum, he thought, pushed the gate at the side of the churchyard open and ran through, have to look after Mum. His school bag was banging against his back, he dropped it and came to the triangle of ground between the door at the back of the church and the bridge across the river.

The man came from between the trees, the strain showing on his face and the sweat and rain dripping from him, seeing him, looking past him, hearing the sounds of the vehicles on the road. The boy stopped, startled, recognized him. He saw the gun hanging from Stan Bradley's hands, saw the vicar close behind, also with a gun, the older man with the grey hair and the ashen face exhausted beside him. The sound of the lorries on the road was closer. The vicar saw him and stopped, Stan in front crouching, checking. The man the vicar was helping suddenly older and more frightened than Boy Jack had ever seen anyone or any thing.

The shouts from the top of the hill were louder, the lorries even closer. Now, Stan ordered. The vicar moved on, pulling the man with him. The vicar – the vicar with an old man and carrying a gun. The last figure came across the bridge and through the trees.

'Dad.'

The entire world stopped.

Absolute silence.

So many things Jack was suddenly thinking, so many things he wanted to say.

'Don't tell anybody anything.'

He heard the screaming of the tyres as the trucks stopped in front of the church. If the door to the church had been in front, Boy Jack suddenly thought, they would have already seen Stan and the vicar and the man the vicar was carrying.

'All right, Dad.'

The others were already inside, Jack running after them. I've left it too late, the thought pounded through his head, I should have kissed him goodbye.

The stormtroopers jumped from the truck and ran round the sides of the church. In front of him Stan was opening the concealed door behind the pulpit. The running was closer and the shouting nearer. Jack shut the church door behind him and the vicar pushed the King through the hole. No time left, they were all thinking, the first stormtroopers in the porch, no time at all. He reached the pulpit and dropped into the space, the porch door opening. Another fifteen seconds, even ten, and they would have made it, another five seconds and they would have been safe.

'What are you doing?' They all heard the voice. 'Why are you breaking into the church?'

The soldiers stopped and turned.

Almost there. Jack began to pull the secret door behind him.

'Who are you?' The troops looked at the boy standing alone beneath the trees. 'What are you doing here?'

'Going home. I live up the hill.'

'Where's your father?'

In the space beneath the pulpit they froze.

'Dead. You killed him two years ago.'

The panelling slid into place and the porch door crashed open.

The black descended on him, enveloping him. My dad was alive, he thought. My dad was alive after all and now they're going to kill him.

The vault was black. They tried to breathe gently so that they would not be discovered, heard the crashing as the church was searched, then the silence and the noise of the engine as the truck pulled away.

The yard of the farm was empty and the doors of the outbuildings were hanging open. As Boy Jack and Ernie reached the top of the field the trucks raced past and headed down the track. They crossed the yard and went into the kitchen. Fran was sitting at the table crying, the furniture was destroyed and the cupboards and fitments had been torn from the walls.

'They were looking for Dad?'

She nodded and tried to dry her eyes.

'It's all right, Mum, they didn't get him.'

They sat beside her, one on either side of her, and put their arms around her.

'There must be a secret hiding place in the church. Dad's there with the vicar and Stan Bradley and another man.'

THE LAMP FLICKERED in the corner of the vault.

'The boy in the churchyard,' the King said, 'he saved us, didn't he? If he hadn't stopped them they would have entered the church before we had time to conceal ourselves.' He was cold and shivering.

'Yes,' said Brian Markham. 'He saved us.'

That night Stan and Brian left the vault. They returned with hot food and warm, dry clothes, and the news that the village was clear.

'What about Fran?'

'All right.'

'She knows?'

'Yes.'

At one o'clock Brian and Stan left and Jack remained with his charge.

'The boy in the churchyard.' The spectre of the boy standing beneath the trees haunted the King, refused to leave him. 'You knew him?'

'Yes.'

'What's his name?'

It seemed an eternity before The Watchman replied.

'Boy Jack.'

The King began to understand. 'He's your son?'

Jack was crossing the bridge again, coming through the trees, remembering the look on the boy's face. 'Yes, he's my son.'

'Then why did he say that you had been killed two years ago?' Immediately he had asked the question he realized the answer and wished he had not.

'Because that was what he thought.'

TWICE A DAY for the next three days Stan Bradley and the vicar visited the vault beneath the pulpit, bringing food and details of the progress of the Allied army in its drive south. On the afternoon of the fourth day, five hours earlier than normal, they opened the secret door for the last time.

'Time to come out, Jack.'

The Watchman helped the King up the steps and followed him out of the hole. The vicar and Stan Bradley were standing by the pulpit, Drake behind them. At the end of the church, close to the porch, stood a number of men in battledress, the insignia of the Coldstream Guards on their shoulders.

Drake bowed and stepped forward. 'Your Majesty, London was liberated last night. Your wife and family are on their way from Scotland. I thought you would wish to rejoin them at the palace.'

The men from the Coats Mission stepped forward and escorted the King from the church. Drake watched as Jack's eyes followed them out and knew what he was thinking: we look after him, save his life, then at the last moment the bloody Guards arrive and escort him back in triumph.

Drake took The Watchman's arm and led him to the side of the church. 'On the coast near Portland we've found a concentration camp. It's still behind the lines and the possibility exists that the enemy will murder the prisoners there. A special force goes in tomorrow morning.'

Why me, Jack thought, how does that affect me?

'Mary might be there. I don't know whether she's dead or alive, but that was where she was sent after she left The Citadel.'

You've seen Prospero, Jack would have asked if Stan and the vicar had not been present.

Yes, Drake would have replied, I have seen Prospero.

THE NIGHT WAS dark. At two the L Detachment jeeps split, one column taking the men's camp to the east and the second the women's to the west. An hour later the advance patrols returned and they were briefed. The dawn began to break and they waited for the order.

'Go.'

The jeeps gunned out of the woods and along the road; the camp was suddenly in front of them, the gates closed and locked, exploding as they approached, the lead vehicles slowing fractionally to pick up the men in the ditches who had set the charges, then accelerating through. The next six divided – three screaming up the outside of the perimeter fence to the right, and three to the left. Those going into the camp also divided, the first racing up the avenue through the centre, another four up the inside of the fence to the right and the last going to the left. The sound was deafening, the twin Vickers mounted on the jeeps crashing, tearing the watchtowers to pieces, destroying them and anything or anyone in them, ripping apart the machine gun posts before they could open fire either on the attacking force or the camp itself.

It was less than forty seconds since they had appeared from the woods. The lead jeeps reached the top, spun round and hurtled down the enclosure again, the Vickers still firing, then swung in a circle by the gate and waited, the men with their fingers still on the triggers and the Vickers reloaded.

In the dawn the birds began to sing again and the first of the women came out of the barracks.

'Oh, God.' It was the gunner next to Jack. 'Oh, Jesus Christ!'

The figures were barely recognizable as women, their heads were shaven and their bodies were like skeletons. Some wore uniforms striped like pyjamas, others coats and trousers, yet more just blankets pulled over their shoulders. Their heads were like skulls and their eyes were black and sunken.

Not Mary, Jack thought, not in a place like this.

The women were creeping forward, slowly, like the beginning of a tide, seeing the men and the guns, still frightened, unsure who the men were or what was happening. The first woman saw the Union Jacks on the radio aerials of the jeeps and realized, pointed to them, told the woman next to her, the sound beginning, swelling, growing in strength, the cheering and crying. Yet more women poured from the huts and the tide became a flood. Hundreds, thousands, Jack thought, the numbers unending, horrifying.

Mary. I must find Mary.

The flood reached the jeeps, the hands stretching up, touching them, thanking them. On the right a group was dragging a fellow prisoner from beneath a hut, tearing the clothes from her and beginning to beat her, the women by the jeeps turning.

'*Kapo*,' one of the skeletons explained.

The change of mood was sudden and terrible, sweeping through the women, some of them turning, running between and into the barracks. To his left Jack saw three SS guards leave a hut and try to escape. The women also saw them, caught them and tore them to pieces. He reached down and held the arm of one of the women. 'I'm looking for someone. How can I find her?'

The woman stared at him as if she did not understand. Hopeless, he knew, in such a place it would be impossible.

'Come with me.' Another woman grabbed him and led him through the milling crowd to an office near the gate, two men of L Detachment close behind him, guarding him. 'They keep everything on record. At least you'll know which block she's in.'

He thanked the woman and began to go in. One of the troopers pushed him aside, kicked the door open and prepared to throw in a grenade. Jack stopped him.

'I need some papers.'

The man nodded and went in fast, the second covering him, sweeping the rooms and checking they were safe.

'The Colonel said you're The Watchman. He said we were to take care of you.'

The desks were neat and tidy, the filing cabinets along the wall opposite the window and the labels on the front of the drawers listed alphabetically. Jack opened the first of the drawers marked A-D. So many names, he thought, so organized, then began to panic as he could not find Mary's. He checked a second drawer, then a third. Another file, there must be another list. He pulled open the other cabinets, hearing the clamour outside and trying to concentrate on the words on each of the drawers, tried to fight off the foreboding which was growing in him.

A–H. Not the same as the other files, fewer names but still so many. He found the card.

Atkinson. Lieutenant Mary. First Aid Nursing Yeomanry. Entered camp 28.5.41. Diagnosed tuberculosis and transferred to sickbay 28.3.42. Died and cremated 30.3.42.

Jack sat on the edge of the desk and stared at the words.

'You all right?' the L Detachment gunner asked.

'My radio operator.' Three bloody weeks, he thought. Why didn't you wait, Mary, why the hell didn't I get here before? He tore the card from the file, put it in his pocket and walked outside.

The camp was full, women running, cheering, crying, the majority simply trying to believe that their hell was ended. He let the gun slip to his side and began to walk through the crowd of women and between the barracks, up the avenue and along the perimeter fence then back into the main body of the camp.

Not after all this, dear God, not after all she did, all she must have gone through.

At the bottom the jeep crews were handing out what food they had, to the right another group of women had caught an SS guard and were beginning to tear her clothes from her. Kill her, part of him was thinking, break her limbs and drag the life out of her for what she did to you, what she did to Mary. Don't do it, another part cried. Don't allow yourselves to become what she once was.

In another part of the camp Jack heard the beginning of singing. At the gate a jeep from the other column stopped and the driver announced that the men's camp had been liberated. Jack turned, noise all round him, hopelessness overcoming him. Against the wire to the right two women had stepped forward and were dragging the SS guard away from the other prisoners, telling them it was wrong and calling to the troops to take the woman away.

He walked past the jeeps to the gate, not hearing anything. The woods outside the camp were green. He took one last look inside and began to walk towards them, the feeling of emptiness in him total and overwhelming. The image of the two women flashed through his mind, coming forward, trying to save the SS guard. He saw the face of one of them. Turned. Ran. Through the gate and past the jeeps. Too late, he thought, she will already have gone. Knew it was not her anyway, could not have been her. Knew she was dead.

The woman was staring at him. Her hair was cropped short and her eyes had sunk beyond recognition; her cheekbones stood out from her face and the coat she wore hung on her as if she was a scarecrow. He began to laugh, began to cry, saw the tears in her eyes and felt them in his own.

THE ORDER FOR Special Duty Squadron to move south came in the afternoon: commencing the following day they would fly operations into Europe from Tempsford in Bedfordshire and Tangmere in Sussex. As the Lysanders taxied to take off, Johnny Watson was told that he had been re-routed to collect a special package from the airfield at Ibsley, in Hampshire. It was bloody typical, he thought, last minute change of orders and no explanation. He would be hard pressed to make the night's celebrations in London.

The last medical check was shortly before lunch. There would be just time to make it to London then the connecting train to Suffolk, Mary thought; her parents had been informed that she was alive and would meet her at the station.

Drake and The Watchman were waiting for her. The staff car left the hospital grounds and turned towards Southampton. Just enough time to catch the train, to make it home tonight. The car pulled off the main road and into the airfield. There was a special package coming in, Drake explained, Mary would still make her train.

Bloody typical, she thought. Nothing had changed. No warning and hardly any explanation.

In the sky above a single aircraft banked on its run in, landed smoothly and came to a halt. At least it was a nice day, she thought, at least it was spring.

Staff car coming up, Johnny Watson noticed. Big one, none of the normal rubbish. Must be someone important.

Lysander, Mary Atkinson recognized it, probably from the Special Duties Squadron they had told her about. The car stopped and the three of them stepped out.

Drake and The Watchman, someone between them. FANY uniform but small and thin, short hair almost like a boy's. He switched off the engine and pulled back the canopy.

Wonder what Drake's special package is? she thought.

Johnny looked again at the figure in the middle and realized.

Mary saw the pilot's face and began to run.

2

THE EVENING WAS warm and the sun was still high in the sky. In the orchards behind the farm the trees were in bloom, the first flowers in the garden in front of the house. In the bedroom upstairs they could hear Jack singing as he adjusted his tie and brushed the coat of his suit. It was three days since the King's speech, two since they had stood round the victory bonfire in the centre of the village square and sung until midnight. At half-past seven the Bentley stopped in the lane outside and Drake came up the path. Boy Jack rose from the table and opened the door for him.

'Hello, Jack. Animals done?'

He followed him into the kitchen and shook hands with Fran and Ernie. 'Is he ready yet?'

A celebration dinner, Jack had told Fran when Drake had issued the invitation, he and a few like him.

'Almost.'

Drake was staring across the yard to the trees and fields beyond. 'A beautiful place this, you must be very fond of it.' It was as if he neither expected nor wanted an answer. 'I used to think of this place, of where Jack lived, and the first day I came here.' Again, she sensed, he did not expect a reply. From his pocket he took two slim flat packages wrapped in brown paper and gave one to each of the boys. 'Not from me. I was merely asked to deliver them to you.'

'Thank you anyway.'

Drake smiled, reached again into his pocket and handed Fran a small velvet bag, tied at the top. 'The day after tomorrow I have been instructed to escort you and Jack to London. Boy Jack and Ernie are to accompany you. Tomorrow you are to buy Jack a morning suit and new clothes for you and the boys. I hope this will cover any extra expenses.'

Fran loosened the string of the bag and turned the contents into her hand. Inside were fifty gold sovereigns.

'Operational funds,' Drake saw the way she was looking at the money. 'If there's anything left I'm sure you will know someone in need of it.'

She wanted to ask why they were going to London and who wanted to see them, but understood that there was something else which her husband should know first.

Jack came down the stairs and the two men left. Fran watched as they walked to the car. The sun was still shining on the countryside. Like it had been before, she thought, like it had always been. Almost as if nothing had happened.

'A nice man.' Boy Jack came to the door and stood by her. 'A funny thing the man who gave me the present said, though.' He gave her the book and she turned it in her hand. The volume was bound in leather, the lettering inlaid in gold. She ran her fingers across it and saw the title: *The Selected Verse of John Keats*.

'What do you mean?'

Boy Jack opened the page for her. 'The writing inside.' She took the book again and read the first lines of the dedication.

> *To Boy Jack,*
> *Who stood at the Gate.*

At the bottom of the path the two men paused as the sun dipped. She looked at them, then at the other words, and knew who had summoned them to London and why.

> *And for his father,*
> *Sir Jack Masters.*

It was signed simply *George*.

THE TOWER OF the cathedral was to their left. They passed through Adisham and Wingham, the sun sinking behind them, then through Monkton. At Minster they drove through the village then turned into the drive, the gates reminding Jack of the manor at Coleshill, pillars on either side, a lion astride one and a stag the other. There was no one else in sight. Drake parked the car at the bottom of the steps to the house and walked inside.

The hallway was almost like a mausoleum, the floor and the columns which rose to the painted ceiling as well as the stairs which swept up on either side all made of marble. Their footsteps echoed as they crossed it. A sergeant from L Detachment saluted and escorted them to a room on the second floor, then closed the doors behind them. The room was spacious and well furnished, a log fire burning in the hearth.

'Before we go through for dinner there is something you will wish to know.'

Drake crossed the floor, opened the concealed door in the bookcase which covered the end wall, and stepped back to allow Jack to go through, then locked it behind them.

Whereas the room outside was comfortable, this, though smaller, bore the stamp of being both more personal and yet on which no expense had been spared. Covering one entire wall was a bookcase which Jack correctly assumed contained another door, family portraits looked down at them from the remaining walls and from above the fireplace, a Constable to the left and a Turner near it, and the furniture spread round the floor was both functional yet beautiful. Logs crackled in the fireplace and the windows opposite were leaded and exquisitely cast. In the centre of the room stood a rosewood table with three chairs placed round it, one at the head and the others on either side.

The person at the table sat facing the windows, back to the door. Drake escorted Jack to the table and indicated that he should take the chair facing the other guest.

Prospero? Jack was confused, unsure what was happening.

Drake walked to a cabinet against the wall, returned to the table, and placed on it a bottle of malt whisky.

Prospero – who had given the first warning of the traitor in the Resistance and who had engineered his escape from The Citadel; who had supplied the details of the German positions for the army of Liberation and who had told them where Mary had been sent.

490

Drake broke the seal of the bottle. The last time he had drunk malt with Drake, Jack thought, had been in the castle at Dunvegan.

The Lice – even now he could not cast the fear aside – the bastards who had been so powerful and the man who had almost crucified him with pain on the night of his capture, who had drunk the toast to the Nazi King of England in the Tower of London.

Dunvegan, the thought refused to go away, the Isle of Skye, the eyes looking at him, beginning to taunt him.

Drake walked again to the cabinet, returned to the table, placed upon it three glasses, and filled each to the brim.

Yet the Lice had not always been efficient, Jack remembered, there had been crucial mistakes at crucial times. The morning after the night Mary had been taken, the way they had dragged her to the Gestapo cell and allowed her to see the morning light which had told her how long she had endured and how much longer she had to sustain herself before the Resistance knew of her arrest. His own capture, the way they had told him that the Gestapo would deal with him in the morning then allowed Prospero to spirit him out of The Citadel. Even on the run for home with the King, the roadblocks on the bridges at either end of the village yet the oversight which had missed the bridge behind the church and which had given him the chance he needed.

Skye, he thought again, the Western Isles, the eyes still mocking him, challenging him.

Schellenberg and the whore who slept with him, Holdaway, who had held him against the wall and squeezed his testicles so hard that he had passed into unconsciousness. The same stupid bastard who had saved him from further beatings and given the inspector called Davis the opportunity to return and open the doors for him.

The mist began to lift, gently and without warning, as it had lifted off the water beneath the castle at Dunvegan, the sound of the pipers drifting across the Sound of Sleat the morning he had stood in the stern of the motor torpedo boat and told himself that Fran and Boy Jack were alive, that now he had something to fight for.

Speed, bonny boat, like a bird on the wing,
Over the sea to Skye.

The mist cleared a little more. The Western Isles, he thought again, why had Drake always spirited him like a ghost to the castle there?

Carry the lad that's born to be King
Over the sea to Skye.

The Lice had made so many mistakes, too many. Yet what if there had been fewer than he had supposed? The mist had almost cleared. What if there had never been any mistakes?

Drake walked for the last time to the cabinet, returned to the table, and placed upon it a carafe of water.

'I ask you to join me in toasting the King.'

The other detail from the interrogation reports, Jack remembered, the other item about the banquet at the Tower. He looked at the table between them: the glasses, the whisky and the carafe of water.

The Toast.

The last of the mist had gone.

The Jacobite Toast.

Charles Edward Stuart, Bonny Prince Charlie, the uprising of 1745 and the defeat at Culloden; the flight to the Isles and the last refuge before the exile to France. The toast with which the Jacobites continued to pay homage to him even in the midst of their enemies.

The King across the water.

They stood, no room in the glasses for the water on the table.

'The King,' Drake lifted his glass and raised it above the carafe.

Jack was back in the field at the bottom of the hill the day Drake had first approached him and told him of the British Resistance. You're asking a lot, he had said. I've asked a lot more of others, Drake had replied.

'The King.'

He was looking at the person opposite him, seeing it as Drake had seen it from the beginning, from the evening the *Kelly* had carried the Duke of Windsor into Portsmouth and the police inspector had been the first to bring his men to attention.

'The King,' toasted the guest opposite him.

All the King's men, Jack thought. Each one of them. Right from the beginning.

'You,' he said. 'All that time you were Prospero.'

Not Schellenberg's woman, not Davis – the removal of the inspector and his family had merely been a cover.

'Yes,' said Holdaway, 'all that time I was Prospero.'

EPILOGUE

THE SQUARE WAS quiet and the afternoon warm, the gnats hung in the air and the men moved as if they were ghosts, the white of their shirts and flannels against the green of the grass. I stood on the edge of the field and watched the cricket, the batsmen at the wicket and the fielders clustered around them, the boys playing at the side of the pavilion and the ladies' committee preparing the tea. It was the beginning of September, ten months since I had stood beneath the trees at the edge of the churchyard on that cold and bitter November afternoon, since I had started the enquiries which had become a homage.

The innings ended and the batsmen came off, the fielders clapping them in then joining them at the tables. The cloth was brilliant white and covered with sparkling plates and shining silver. I left the edge of the field and moved closer, no one noticing me as no one had noticed me almost a year ago. Beside the open doors of the pavilion the home captain stood and asked for silence.

'Gentlemen, as is the custom in this village on this day, I would ask your permission to invite the ladies and families to join us.'

September 1990 – fifty years to the day. In the distance I heard the sound of the battle and saw the last Spitfires and Hurricanes clawing into the sky. The ladies sat down and the families took their places beside them. I left the pitch and walked through the village, past the school and the square, the King's Arms and the grocer's shop, then along the road and past the vicarage.

The churchyard was quiet, the ground against the river calm and peaceful and the white marble of the headstones tranquil and serene. I knelt and looked on the inscriptions on the family graves: Jack Jenkyn Masters and Frances Joyce Masters; John Robert Watson and Mary Jane Watson, née Atkinson. Dragonflies hovered above the river. I straightened and moved to the first of the single graves, Edward Michael Roberts, then to the second.

On the gravel behind I heard the faintest sound of a step and looked round. The priest was old and white-haired, his face gaunt and his body bent with years. It was as if he had been waiting for me to return. I smiled at him, then looked again at the graves.

Sir Jack Jenkyn Masters, code name The Watchman, Knight Commander of the Most Honourable Order of the Bath; Dame Frances Joyce Masters, code name The Caretaker, Companion of the Most Honourable Order of the Bath, the highest honours the country could bestow. Squadron Leader John Robert Watson, Distinguished Service Order, Distinguished Flying Cross; Lieutenant Mary Jane Atkinson, George Cross, the first recipient of the award instigated by George VI.

Why was no one ever told? Why are the details on the headstones so simple, so devoid of fact? I remembered the file at the Public Record Office at Kew and the letter from the Prime Minister, one of only three small references I could find: *In view of the fact that your lives depended on secrecy, that secrecy will be maintained.*

Perhaps the government had considered that the threat of invasion remained, I could only suppose; perhaps it feared for another.

The river behind the trees was flowing gently, the field rising from it to the farm at the top of the hill. I looked across it then back again at the fourth gravestone and the simple words on it, the priest silent at my side.

Charles Edward Stuart Holdaway.

We had been so close, so proud of each other, yet even so he had not been able to tell me of what he had done during the war or the years which followed it. It was sad that I had been overseas for so long, especially for his last days, for his funeral. Yet after all these years I could still remember the day my mother and I left Portsmouth, the house bare and the single photograph of us he kept on the mantelpiece above the fireplace – could remember even more the day we came home, the day we were driven to Buckingham Palace and I stood with the other boys and watched the two men kneel together before the King.

Sir Charles Edward Stuart Holdaway, code name Prospero, Knight Commander of the Most Honourable Order of the Bath, the same honour as The Watchman.

'You knew him?' the Reverend Brian Markham asked.

'My father.'